Jo Watson is an award-winning writer whose romantic comedies were originally published on Wattpad. Her first novel *Burning Moon* won a 2014 Watty Award for being one of the site's most downloaded titles and has now had over 6 million reads. Jo is an Adidas addict and a Depeche Mode devotee. She lives in South Africa with her family.

Follow her on Twitter @JoWatsonWrites and find her on Facebook at www.facebook.com/jowatsonwrites.

Praise for Jo Watson's hilarious romantic comedies:

'Witty, enjoyable and unique' *Harlequin Junkie*

'Found myself frequently laughing out loud and grinning like a fool!' *BFF Book Blog*

'Heart-warming, funny, sweet, romantic and just leaves you feeling good inside' *Bridger Bitches Book Blog*

'Full of pure-joy romance, laugh-out-loud moments and tear-jerkers' *Romantic Times*

By Jo Watson

Burning Moon
Almost A Bride
Finding You

Almost A Bride

Jo Watson

HEADLINE
ETERNAL

Published by arrangement with Forever,
an imprint of Grand Central Publishing.

First published in Great Britain in 2017
by HEADLINE ETERNAL
An imprint of HEADLINE PUBLISHING GROUP

1

Cataloguing in Publication Data is available from the British Library

ISBN 978 1 4722 3796 5

Offset in 11.22/16.35 pt Granjon LT Std by Jouve (UK)

Printed in Great Britain by Clays Ltd, St Ives plc

Headline's policy is to use papers that are natural, renewable and recyclable
products and made from wood grown in well-managed forests and other
controlled sources. The logging and manufacturing processes are expected
to conform to the environmental regulations of the country of origin.

HEADLINE PUBLISHING GROUP
An Hachette UK Company
Carmelite House
50 Victoria Embankment
London EC4Y 0DZ

www.headlineeternal.com
www.headline.co.uk
www.hachette.co.uk

To all my Wattpad fans who helped me write this book, all the women out there who've ever wanted to get sweet revenge, and to Depeche Mode. (When I sell 100 million books and become rich and famous, I hope you'll play at my birthday party.)

Almost A Bride

PROLOGUE

⌐

D-day—A year ago

I knew something was wrong the second I walked up to my front door.

Call it intuition. Call it a sixth sense. But I just knew.

I blame the shoes. The shoes were undoubtedly the cause of all the problems that day. It was the shoes' fault that I came home early, and the shoes' fault I was fired.

I suppose I can't blame the shoes for making me late, though— that was the alarm clock's fault for rudely deciding *not* to do its job.

And when I finally realized, through the thick haze of sleepiness, that it hadn't gone off, it was too late. I was already late for work. And when I say *work*, I mean my brand-new job—job of my dreams—as a fashion assistant at *Glamorous Girl* mag. The quintessential magazine for the "fun, fierce, and fabulously stylish South African girl™."

I'd just made a total career change, leaving behind a successful job as a stylist in advertising to pursue a job in the magazine industry. It was early days, so I was still desperately trying to impress by being perfect, polite, and oh so obliging. Whether it was the request for the latte to be served at 97.7 degrees with no sugar, soy milk froth, and a sprinkling of organic cocoa powder flown in directly from the foothills of the Andes. Or whether it was for the jasmine-and-lavender-scented candles to be burned in the office for exactly ten minutes before my boss arrived—*that was me*.

Little Miss Annie Obliging.

Because let's face it, the word *assistant* is just a glammed-up euphemism for *slave*. But I was ambitious and determined, so when I realized I wouldn't be able to attend to the scented candles, or fetch the latte, I panicked. So much so, that I left the house without the said *troublemaking, life-ruining, world-annihilating* shoes.

Let's take a moment to talk about the shoes. They weren't ordinary shoes, *oh no*, they were none other than the just-off-the-Paris-catwalk-and-not-for-sale-to-mere-mortals-yet Christian Louboutins. They also happened to be the centerpieces for that day's shoot.

The same rushed panic that had caused me to forget the shoes in the first place had also left me with barely enough time to scrape my hair back into a casual bun and slip on a creased T-shirt and pair of jeans from my floor.

The latter is a bigger sin than you think. Because where I work, wearing anything other than the most fashionable apparel is sacrilege. People practically throw holy water at you and start wailing in Latin for fear that you've been possessed by the demon of bad fashion. *In fact*, a real demon possession, complete with a backward-rolling head and the ability to speak in tongues, would be preferable to the demon of last season's handbag and Crocs sandals.

So when I finally got to work, underdressed, out of breath, without the shoes, and over an hour late, I was in serious trouble.

My boss was throwing a hissy fit, due to lack of flowery scents in her office, and her personal assistant Cedric was in the throes of an overly dramatic caffeine withdrawal, due to lack of latte.

And it kept getting worse.

Two hours later the panicky fashion director summoned the Louboutins. Those shoes had been troublemakers from the start. It had been an absolute trauma getting them in the first place. They'd been flown into South Africa late the previous night, and I'd been tasked with collecting them. Everyone was holding their collective breath for the grand arrival. So when I was forced to confess to their absence…*well*, you can only imagine.

When lunch finally arrived, I jumped into my car and sped home. I had exactly one hour to get in and out before the photo shoot, more than enough time.

I pulled into my driveway at breakneck speed, ran for the front door, slipped my house keys into the lock, and turned—

But…

Something made me stop.

Something told me *not* to go inside.

Something was *very* wrong.

I looked around nervously. Everything seemed normal. Peter across the road was blasting his TV as usual, the ratbag Chihuahua from number 45 was running up and down the garden perimeter yapping at an unseen force, and Mildred, my neighbor, was outside watering her hydrangeas.

So why was I hesitating?

I took a deep breath and inched the door open.

Nothing looked out of place.

Everything was exactly the way I'd left it.

Yet *everything* felt wrong.

I slunk down the hallway toward the kitchen, where I knew I'd find the shoes perched next to the coffeepot. But once inside, I was hit by a terribly eerie sensation…*someone was in the house*. A shiver licked the length of my spine when my suspicions were confirmed.

Creeeeaaakkk…A noise was coming from my bedroom directly above me.

Shit, shit, shit, there was an intruder in the house!

I launched myself at the cutlery drawer, grabbing the largest knife I could find while simultaneously dialing the police and still managing to hold on to the shoes for dear life.

"Police! Help, there's an intruder in my house. Forty-Seven Mendelssohn Road, Oaklands. Quick."

Now what? I'd never been in a situation like this before. What was the correct protocol? Should I hide, evacuate the house, attack the intruder, scream loudly? Or perhaps a combination of the above?

I thought for a second before deciding to get the *fuck* out of there! But just as I had one foot safely installed outside the front door, I heard another noise. This time it was different. It was…

It sounded like…

My blood ran cold.

But it couldn't be. Trevv was at work. Trevv had a *very* important day in court, he told me. His client's final hearing was today. Right now, in fact. I'd called him from my office about an hour ago and he'd told me he was in court.

He was in court, dammit!

I started climbing the stairs.

More noises.

Two voices?

But that was impossible...wasn't it?

The noises grew louder and louder the farther up the stairs I went. I'm not really sure at what point I knew what the noises were or knew what I was going to see when I opened the door. But I just knew.

It's one thing walking in on your boyfriend having sex with another woman, but it's another thing entirely walking in on him the second the other woman is coming. She was facing the door but was bouncing up and down so vigorously that her face was a blur. And then suddenly her body stiffened, she threw her head back, opened her mouth, and let out a high-pitched wail. As if that wasn't self-explanatory enough, she decided to toss in a few words for good measure.

"Yes, Trevvy, yes. Oh my God, oh my God, oh Trevvy. Harder! Ah, ah, ah." *Pant, pant, pant* "I'm coming!" *Long high-pitched scream*

Now...there were several things wrong with this picture, aside from the obvious. *Firstly*, who the hell screams like that in bed? No one does! Sex is not *so* good that you have to break the sound barrier with your squealing dolphin sounds. *Secondly*, what the hell was she wearing? She was clad in some kind of leathery studded number that looked like it had been worn by one of the Village People. And to make matters worse, Trevv was blindfolded with the tie that I had bought him two Christmases ago and...*OH MY GOD*...were those, were those...*nipple clamps*?

I felt sick to my stomach.

And thirdly, who was this mystery woman without an ounce of cellulite, without the slightest smidge of fat, and with boobs that seemed to defy all known natural laws of gravity and motion? Which woman can be that damn perfect…

…and then her features came into focus and the answer dawned on me.

Tess.

Tess Blackman.

My boyfriend's work "coworker." The woman I'd invited into my home on several occasions for dinner. The woman that I always phoned when I couldn't get hold of Trevv, because I knew they were probably together working on a case, tired and exhausted and burning the midnight oil when they'd rather be at home with their significant others. She had a fiancé after all.

Poor overworked Trevv and Tess.

God, I was naive.

But the show didn't end there. Tess's eyes were still closed when Trevv started making some delightful grunting-moaning-squeaking sounds. *He'd never made sounds like that with me before.* His sweaty hands reached up and grabbed at her hungrily.

Faster.

Harder.

Loud, long moan.

I was frozen. It's hard to know what to do when you watch your partner of two years with his penis somewhere you wouldn't even like to imagine, let alone witness in full blinding daylight.

Once all their postcoital panting had tapered off, Tess opened her eyes and saw me standing in the doorway. The look on her face was indescribable. Shock and horror and fear all at the same time. And then she opened her mouth and screamed.

Trevv then turned his head toward the door and whipped off his blindfold. Our eyes locked and then he did something truly bizarre. Unexpected. He grabbed Tess by the hand and dragged her to the other side of the bed.

"Anne, please…you don't want to do this." Trevv threw his hands in the air defensively. He looked terrified. She was bleating hysterically by this stage.

What was going on? Wasn't *I* the jilted one? Wasn't *I* the one that was supposed to be upset? I started walking toward them, which seemed to only make matters worse.

"Anne, please. Please." He seemed to be begging now. "Think about what you're doing. I know this is bad, but this isn't the way to handle it. Please don't do this."

Things happened pretty quickly after that. Suddenly, the room was filled with armed police officers. I was about to tell them they could all go home, when Trevv cut me off.

"She has a knife. She's going to kill us!" he shouted, pointing at me.

What knife? I glanced at my hands, and that's when I realized I was still holding the large knife, and it was pointed in their direction.

I quickly turned to explain. "I wasn't going to—"

"Ma'am…" One of the police officers cut me off and started creeping toward me as if I was a feral pit bull that hadn't eaten in a week. "Put down your weapon."

"I swear, this isn't what you think, I was just trying to—"

BAM! Face on floor, handcuffs around wrists.

Three really painful things happened at that point: One, the knife slipped and cut the entire length of my palm. Two, some of my newly acquired, gorgeous nails broke off. And three, the crystal-encrusted, six-inch heel of the priceless Louboutin snapped off, rolled across the floor lifelessly, and disappeared under the bed. As I was being dragged out, I glanced up and saw that Trevv was clutching Tess in his arms. He gently planted a kiss on her forehead.

"It's going to be okay, baby, it's going to be okay."

CHAPTER ONE

A broken Louboutin is not a pretty sight.

A naked woman on top of your boyfriend is not a pretty sight.

Your boyfriend wearing nipple clamps is definitely not a pretty sight.

But, do you want to know what's worse?

Try the inside of a holding cell.

I was trembling from the shock. My heart was thumping from the surging adrenaline. I felt physically sick, and strange, and utterly confused…My brain felt like a little hamster sprinting at full speed on his little wheel.

What had just happened? Had he really? With her? Like *that?* Surely it wasn't possible. It had to be some kind of misunderstanding, because last time I checked, Trevv was not *just* my boyfriend. Trevv was my soon-to-be fiancé. Not that he'd asked me yet, but I knew it was very imminent. *There were signs…*

One, we were scheduled to have dinner at my favorite restaurant tonight (clear sign). *Two*, I'd found a receipt in the trash can for the purchase of a very expensive piece of jewelry (red, flashing sign). *Three*, he didn't know this but I'd seen a massive bouquet of red roses on the backseat of his car this morning. (How much bigger does the sign need to be, for heaven's sake?)

Trevv was going to ask me to marry him. Tonight! And I was going to say yes because even though we'd been going through a little slump lately, I loved him and this engagement was exactly what we needed to get the romance back. I was *so* ready to marry him.

My friends had confirmed my suspicions, too. As had my waxologist (who works miracles down there), my hairdresser, the woman that plucked my brows, and my manicurist who'd done my nails yesterday so that I could Instagram the perfect pic of my new ring later today. Everyone agreed—he was definitely going to ask me to marry him. So why, *why oh why oh fucking why*, was he having sex with someone else?

I slapped my hand down on the bench and winced in pain. The bandage did little to protect me from the intense stinging now emanating from where the blade had sliced into me.

But it wasn't just my hand that hurt; my head was throbbing from being smashed into the floor by a couple of heavier-than-they-should-be police officers. To make matters worse, I was sandwiched between what appeared to be a crack addict on a bad comedown, an old leather-skinned woman who was babbling about "the invasion" (whatever that was), and what was clearly a working girl (either that or Halloween had come early this year).

I was desperate for a moment alone, but there was no privacy. The toilet was completely open and reeked of urine and sour vomit. A chipped concrete basin, solitary dripping tap, and a makeshift toilet roll holder completed the minimalist decor.

"What ya in for, babe?" a raspy voice suddenly piped up.

I turned and came face-to-face with a barely covered boob.

"Um…"

"I'm Angel, by the way." She extended her hand, and not wanting to offend—I wasn't au fait with the finer points of criminal etiquette—I shook it.

"I'm not really sure actually."

She scoffed loudly. "I know what ya mean, babe. Sometimes I think they harass me for the sake of it. This is the third time this month I've been here."

"Me too," said the older woman. "And all I'm trying to do is warn people about the impending invasion."

Angel looked at me and rolled her eyes. "Yes, yes, Margie, we know. The flying saucers and little green men—"

"They're not green, they're gray!" Margie cut her off angrily.

"Pink, purple, blue, whatever." The sarcasm in Angel's voice was undeniable.

And then without warning, Margie jumped up, rather nimbly for a woman who looked like she was on the wrong side of a hundred. "This is what I'm talking about. You mock me now, but wait until they're here with their probes and their mind control devices. Wait until they assimilate our DNA and turn us into drones and—"

Margie barely had a chance to finish her sentence when, *BANG*, Angel pushed her. Alien Lady wasted no time in pushing her back, and soon I was watching a live episode of *Jerry Springer*—and way too close for my liking. Margie was screaming something about the pyramids being transporter beacons and Tom Cruise being involved in the global conspiracy, while Angel taunted her by flashing her boobs. Even the crack addict joined in, making a strange throaty cackling sound that I assume was meant to resemble laughter and egging them on.

I'd *never* seen anything like it before, and I crept backward, trying to retreat into a corner. I was frightened. I mean, I know what goes on in prisons. I watch *Orange Is the New Black*.

I didn't belong here.

I really, *really* didn't belong here.

"Miss Anderson." One of the guards came up to the cell and started unlocking the gate. "You're free to go."

"Oh, thank God." The relief was instant, and I practically threw myself out of the cell, without daring to look back at my fellow inmates—who were now on the floor wrestling. I walked into the waiting area of the police station, and that's when I saw *him*. My stomach lurched.

He looked every bit the lawyer wearing that crisp, suave black suit and clicking his expensive Montblanc pen impatiently. He looked up and saw me.

"I've come to spring you, as they say." He smiled at me like a Cheshire cat, and then looked at the officer behind the desk. "I'm usually the one putting them behind bars, not setting them free." He gave a small chuckle. "Lawyer…if anyone ever needs one." He took a card out of his pocket and slid it across the reception desk, before winking at the woman. He never missed a PR opportunity. Even now.

"Anne…" He oozed silver-tongued charm as he sauntered up to me and then reached out and took me by the hands. "Tess and I have agreed to drop the charges. We realize that it was a bit of an emotional moment for all of us, and maybe you just lost your head a bit. But no harm done."

No harm done? "What?"

I was stunned. I was downright offended. This was *not* the reaction I was expecting. Where the hell was my apology? Where the hell was the deep shame and the guilt and the relentless begging on bended knees?

"Tess and I?" I asked with an edge of desperation in my voice. "Since when is there a 'Tess and I'?" My voice went slightly quivery and my knees seemed to follow suit. Suddenly I didn't feel very well. Especially when I saw how he was looking at me.

"Listen, Anne. Let's be honest here." He cocked his head to the side. "It hasn't been working for a while now with us. Let's be adult enough to acknowledge that. *Mmmm?*" Another head cock. I hated that condescending tone in his voice.

"But…but…," I stammered, and shook my head in absolute disbelief. This was all wrong. Trevv had obviously been handed the wrong script. He was on the wrong page, too, and this was *definitely* the wrong scene.

"But what about dinner at Piccolo Primi tonight?" I asked.

"I was going to talk about us. I was going to tell you about Tess and—"

I cut him off. "Yes…You were going to tell me that this is all just a terrible, horrible mistake. That it meant nothing and then you were going to propose to me. You were going to ask me to marry you and I was going to say yes because we've been together for two years and we love each other and we're going to be so happy together." The words were flying out of my mouth like uncontrollable bullets. "Look, I know we've been going through a rough patch lately, but all couples go through this, it's perfectly normal, and getting engaged would fix it."

Trevv looked at me with what seemed to be total confusion. He nodded slowly, as if he was trying to process what I was saying, and then brought his hand up to his chin and rubbed it in a thoughtful manner.

"Why did you think I was going to propose to you?"

"Trevv, I found the receipt for the ring you bought and I saw the red roses in your car."

"Those weren't for you, Anne."

"What?" My mind went blank. That news shocked me almost as much as seeing them in bed together. "But…but…I had my nails done. We're getting married. You're marrying *me*…"

As soon as those words were out of my mouth, I realized just how pathetic and illogical and mad I was being. Why would I want to marry a man that had just cheated on me? Where the fuck was my brain when I needed it? But despite all that, I decided to continue. I decided to do away with any tiny iota of self-respect that I might still have.

"…because she means nothing to you. We love each other and I'm going to be your wife."

Trevv moved closer to me and for the first time since he'd arrived, I got the slightest glimmer of sincerity in him. "I think we should talk about this outside."

I gasped loudly. "She doesn't mean nothing to you?" I looked at Trevv and his expression said it all. "Oh God, she's not a fling. Do you love her? Do you still love me? How could you do this? How long has it been going on?"

"*Ssshhhhh!*" Trevv tried to shush me as my voice got uncontrollably loud and shrill. "Let's take this outside. This is all getting a tad awkward." He tried to put an arm around me, but his supposed sincerity just pissed me off even more, and a wall of rage slammed into me with such force that I thought I might fall over.

"Awkward? *Awkward?*" I screeched like a deranged banshee. "You call walking in on you having sex with your coworker a bit 'awkward'?" I gestured some dramatic air quotes and several cops turned around and stared.

"*Sssshhh,*" he hissed, looking around self-consciously. "Anne, this is all very inappropriate."

"Inappropriate?" I scoffed loudly. "You know what I call inappropriate? Try walking in on you wearing nipple clamps." I had definitely gotten people's attention now. Some of the cops even put down their paperwork and turned to watch.

"Oh, and I'm so very glad you found such a good use for the tie I bought you. Funny, the man that sold it to me never mentioned that it could also be used as a kinky-sex blindfold."

Trevv looked angry now. "Outside, Anne!" he demanded curtly. *How dare he make demands at a time like this!*

"No! I don't want to." I stomped my foot like a petulant toddler having a tantrum. "I want to talk about this here. Surely you're not embarrassed? Not embarrassed that you had sex with another woman in our bed and got caught out? *Nooo,* I wouldn't be embarrassed if I were you!"

A collective gasp rose up from the room, and one of the female cops clicked her tongue in blatant disapproval.

"Bastard," she said, shooting some death stares in Trevv's direction, which I was ever so grateful for. Another voice pierced the air; it was Angel. "I would have cut it off!" she yelled from across the room.

"Anne." His tone was now annoyingly diplomatic. "I think it's best if you come around tomorrow and remove all your things."

"You want me to—"

"Move out. Yes." Cue head cock to the left.

"But…it's my home."

"Technically it's *my* home. You were just staying there."

"*Just staying there?* Wow, is that all I was doing?" His words stung me, implying I was nothing more than a guest in his house. A house we had shared together for eighteen months.

Cue head cock to the right. "Maybe your sister could take you in? Or one of your millions of friends and cousins?" He said it with such contempt that it made me fume. He'd never liked my friends.

Take me in? Like I was some scaly, flea-bitten, half-breed mutt that needed rescuing from a dirty sewer?

Shitface spoke again. "Of course, Tess and I don't expect you to get all your stuff out immediately, but maybe just the basics. Clothes, toiletries."

"Oh, how very generous of you and *Tess*." I said her name as if it were poison, or a hideous infectious disease. "Aren't you and Tess just so damn thoughtful."

"Good-bye, Anne."

The bastard had the audacity to kiss me on the forehead before turning and walking away. I stood and watched as he got closer and closer to the exit, and just as he was about to open the door and walk out of my life, I was gripped by a kind of irrational panic. I didn't want him to walk away. Despite everything that he'd done, I didn't want him to leave.

"Trevv. Wait." My panicked voice quivered as a lump started forming in my throat. He turned around, looking somewhat irritated by now, although still trying very hard to maintain the thin veil of "professional lawyer" that he had left.

"What?"

I opened my mouth to speak, but there were no words for what I was feeling. It was a nauseating paradox of rage and desperation—all still covered by the haze of confusion that hadn't quite lifted yet.

"Nothing, Trevv. Nothing and everything."

Trevv shook his head slightly before pushing the door open and stepping outside. I watched him as he ambled to his car, as if he was going for a leisurely stroll on the beach. Tess was waiting for him in the passenger seat. *My* passenger seat. And then he drove off, out of my life.

When I was about six, I was doing a twirly thing on the top bar of my jungle gym and lost my grip. I fell so far and so hard, that when I hit the ground the wind was knocked out of me. I must have gasped for several seconds before finally sucking in the oxygen my aching lungs were so desperate for. It was one of the most frightening moments of my life. I thought I was dying.

That's how I felt right as I watched them drive away together.

After that, things just went from bad to worse. The horror of that day, the thirteenth of January to be specific (and it wasn't even a Friday, if you believe in that sort of thing), was not yet over. Not by a long shot. By now I had totally missed the photo shoot, not to mention broken the pièce de résistance.

My boss, Sonja, is fashion personified. What was hot and what was not began and ended with one syllable from her pert little mouth. A severe and impossibly shiny black bob framed sharp pointy features and piercing blue eyes. She was tall and rail thin, so she could wear all the gorgeous things that went wafting through our office. It was rumored that she hadn't eaten solids since 1998, living entirely on a diet of carrot juice and kale. Her skin glowed, her lips sparkled with the latest shade of lip gloss, and she was so effortlessly stylish, she could make a plastic bag look like haute couture.

But she was also renowned for her razor-sharp tongue, her deadly ambition, and a supreme set of balls that made her as competitive and ruthless as any male CEO.

And she had also called me into her office.

"So I believe you were arrested for attempted murder earlier today." She said it with total indifference and a deadpan stare that looked straight through me.

"No, it was a misunderstanding, they had it wrong—" How had she even found out about my arrest?

"Oh no, don't get me wrong, darling. You caught your boyfriend cheating. Perhaps you planned on maiming him a little…I can respect that." She smiled at me as she slid out of her Perspex seat and sashayed over to the window, gazing out over the Johannesburg skyline. "What I can't respect, though, is that you totally fucked up my photo shoot, not to mention the shoes that Christian himself specially shipped here. *Do you know how much those shoes cost?* And the photo shoot? It's not cheap renting camels."

"Camels?"

"Not to mention the Ethiopian refugees," the fashion director, a younger carbon copy of Sonja, piped up. "We were going for that whole third-world-poverty-chic vibe. Can you imagine what a statement starving, dehydrated children wearing Louboutins would have made?" She was furious now. "But you just had to go and fuck it up."

Sonja nodded. "And that's why you're fired."

Even though I knew I was probably—*NO*, definitely—going to lose my job over this, it was still rather shocking to hear the words spoken out loud. The situation was broken beyond repair—like the shoes. No doubt there was a meaningful metaphor lurking in there somewhere, I just wasn't in the mood to find it. There was nothing I could do or say to redeem myself, so I turned and walked out of the office, trying not to burst into tears.

"Oh and Annie," Evil Boss Bitch spoke again, "if you do ever work in the fashion industry again, which is highly doubtful…" She looked at me as if she'd just caught the whiff of rotting fish eggs. "Try not to wear boyfriend jeans. They went out two seasons ago."

Her snide punch line completed, I exited. And that was it. The end of my enviable job at the most glamorous fashion mag in South Africa. And the ugly end to my dreams of becoming a fashion director.

I walked out through the ostentatious, gold-framed front doors and stood on the sidewalk with slumped shoulders. *Now what?* I took a few miserable steps until I realized my legs were no longer capable of working properly. I leaned against the nearest thing I could find, a trash can, and hung my head. *Now fucking what?* I was wallowing in miserable splendor and, quite frankly, didn't care who saw me…

Only I did care. Because when some caring soul placed five dollars in my hand and told me to buy a hot meal, I knew I had to do something. So I did the only thing my muddled brain could think to do and walked to my friend Jane's office. She worked part-time in her father's dental practice as his assistant while finishing up at dental school. Her father wanted her to learn the business ropes since he had grand plans of her taking over his practice soon. I wasn't sure she was thrilled with the idea, but I was grateful the office was just a few blocks away.

The first thing that always strikes me about a dental practice is the smell. That strange medical smell that is totally unique to dental rooms alone. And then there is the drilling. The repetitive whirring sound as it grinds away at some poor person's tooth, followed by that disguising suction sound. Usually those sounds make my skin crawl, but today they felt rather soothing. Perhaps it was because I was imagining chasing after Trevv with a dental drill?

I sat down and waited for her to finish with the patient she was currently helping her father torture. Mind you, right now I would've gladly exchanged places with them. I would much rather be enjoying the sharp pain of an unanesthetized extraction than enduring *this*. I was physically shaking from the adrenaline overload, and my palpitating heart felt like it was being ripped out of my chest while someone punched me in the stomach. Finally, after an hour or so, Jane and her dad emerged.

"Hello, Annie," Dr. Smith said with a smile. I'd known Jane for over ten years now and her dad had been doing my teeth ever since. "Are you flossing like I told you to?"

I forced a nod and the best smile I could muster under the circumstances. "After every meal."

"Excellent. Now if you'll excuse me." I was relieved when he walked off. Not because I didn't like him, but because I was struggling to hold it all together.

"Annie?" Jane rushed over to me. "You look…What's wrong?"

"It's Trevv…" It was all I could manage without breaking down and flooding the room with another gush of tears.

Jane lowered herself next to me. "What happened?"

"Imagine the worst thing that you could ever walk in on your boyfriend doing. And then, multiply that by ten and throw in nipple clamps and a blindfold."

"Oh?" Jane looked at me for a moment or two, "*Ooohhh!* I see." She finally got it. "So you walked in on him doing…?"

"Sex."

"With?"

"Kinky sex things."

"And?"

"Tess."

"That girl from his work?" Jane gasped. "The one with a fiancé? We all had dinner with them a month ago!"

I nodded. "Same one. Apparently he's in love with her."

"But I thought he was going to ask you to—"

"Obviously not!" I cut her off quickly. I didn't want to hear that word out loud again.

"How long has this been going on?"

"I don't know." I wailed so loudly that it drowned out the drilling sound coming from the other room "*Oh*, and he wants me to move out of *his* house today. *Oh*, and he also had me arrested. I've just been in jail."

"What?"

"And I also broke the fucking shooo," I moaned.

"Tess's shoe?"

"No, that would have actually been enjoyable. Because it seems that I broke the world's most important shoe. The most important, special, shiny, expensive bloody shoe that has ever been bloody made, and now I've been fired because of it."

"Okay." Jane snapped into organizational mode. "What do you need me to do?"

"Will you help me move out?"

"Of course." Jane canceled her appointments for the rest of the afternoon and an hour later, boyfriendless, homeless, jobless, and just *less*, I was standing in my soon-to-be-former house ready to pack up my life—well, what had been my life for the last year and a half, anyway. I'd given up a gorgeous downtown loft to move in with Trevv because he'd asked me to. He'd loved me once…or had he? It was all so surreal, and I wasn't sure what I was meant to be feeling: anger, sadness, depression?

Maybe I was just numb. All I knew was that I just had to get through, even if it was on autopilot.

But when I walked into the bedroom and saw the rumpled sheets, the pillows on the floor, and the tie draped across the bed, the numbness quickly evaporated. I scanned the room and all I could see was *her*. I glanced down at the floor and something caught my attention. I bent down and picked up the two broken tips from my newly manicured nails. My cheeks flushed red and my skin stung from the sudden, overwhelming surge of embarrassment that rushed through me. I'd made such a big deal about it. I'd told the entire world we were getting engaged. I'd endured painful eyebrow plucking.

How could I have been so stupid?

Jane marched up to me, took the nails away, and tossed them into the trash can. "The faster we do this, the better," she said, ushering me into the bathroom. I was glad it was Jane with me right now. She was the least outwardly emotional in our group, and I needed someone like her right then, or else I might have crumpled to the floor in a heap.

"Look." I pointed my finger across the bathroom to where the basin was. "*Looooook*," I hissed in a voice I barely recognized. "It's pink."

Trevv and I kept our toothbrushes in a cup next to the sink. Mine is lime green, my favorite color, and Trevv's is blue. But there, squashed between the green and the blue, was a pink one. I moved closer, bending down to stare it right in its bristly little face. It seemed to taunt me with its diagonal bristles for those hard-to-reach places. Both brushes were leaning against the blue one, and the irony of the situation struck me as both laughable and simultaneously disgusting.

Jane and I stared at the cup for a while, and then she turned to me with wide eyes, as if she could sense what I was thinking.

"No, Annie. Don't do it. Be the better, bigger person. Rise above it."

I walked over to the cup and took the pink toothbrush between my fingers.

"No, Annie. Rise. Rise."

I shook my head.

No. I wasn't above it.

No. I wasn't the bigger woman.

And, *no*, I wasn't about turning the other cheek and rising today.

"Oh God, I can't watch." Jane turned away quickly.

I took the brush and ran it over the inside of the toilet bowl, then dunked it into the water for good measure before slipping it back into the cup from whence the evil thing came.

The idea that Tess might come down with a deadly strain of E. coli poisoning did make me feel better. It felt like the only revenge I could get right now. But the thought only made me feel better for a minute.

Six small boxes, two full suitcases, and three hours later, Jane and I were ready to go. I stood in the driveway looking up at the home that I'd shared with my boyfriend. Even though it was officially Trevv's house, I could see signs of myself everywhere. I'd planted a bed of roses by the kitchen window—they were in full bloom. I'd painted our front door red, and that little crack in the window by the lounge—that was made when I haphazardly opened a bottle of champagne to celebrate getting my new job.

And now…I was just walking away?

Closing the door on a chapter of my life.

What the hell was I going to do next?

CHAPTER TWO

 ⟳

I had officially crossed over to the dark side. I was devastated in that gothic-writing, angsty-poetry, threatening-to-self-harm, burning-black-morbid-candles, and not-washing-their-hair kind of way. Which is never a good look for anyone.

I was so depressed that I'd even started listening to a Depeche Mode mix that Damien had once inflicted on me. Right now I was listening to them drone on about pain and suffering and relating to every single word.

My days of sudden unemployment also gave me too much time to think, and I'd spent the first week staring at my phone, waiting for Trevv to call me and tell me the whole thing had been a terrible, *terrible* mistake.

That he was desperately sorry. That he was a bastard. That he deserved to be punished—and I could do it. That he was wrong and had made a mistake and loved me, not her. God, I felt pathetic.

I was rapidly vacillating between wanting Trevv to come running back to me begging, to wanting him to beg for his life before I ran him over with a combine harvester. I was one step away from needing a frontal lobotomy, a straitjacket, and drastic electroshock therapy.

It's bad enough breaking up with someone, but to walk in on them having kinky sex with someone else just adds a whole new layer to the devastation. In retrospect, there'd been some signs that Trevv's bedroom proclivities were a touch on the *twist my nipple until it bleeds* side.

One evening, while innocently cooking a chicken-and-mushroom casserole, he'd taken out the spatula and spanked me on the ass— *hard*. Of course I was horrified, and very concerned that he'd left a greasy mark on my MaxMaras. On another occasion he'd suggested hot wax. When I ascertained that he was not talking about hair removal, I just thought he was joking.

Obviously I'd been mistaken.

But the devastation became even more unbearable when I got a phone call from my hairdresser wanting to know when she should book me in for bridal hair. A message from my manicurist soon followed, asking for a picture of the gorgeous ring. I didn't know what felt worse: the pain of my heart breaking, or the searing embarrassment of having to explain to people why, *no*, we are not getting married.

Even when I slept, I couldn't escape it. My dreams were plagued by images of Tess, and in every single one she was perfect. And the more I saw her, the more imperfections I saw in myself every time I walked past a mirror…no wonder he wanted her and not me. She was gorgeous. And clearly she was able to give him something I couldn't in bed.

Maybe I was just bad in bed? Clearly I bored him.

Was that why he had gone looking elsewhere? Maybe I wasn't pretty enough? Boobs not big enough? Bum not pert enough? Body not bendy enough? With each thought, I ripped another strip of myself away. The ambitious, confident girl I once was, was disappearing until I started to feel like a totally different person, plagued by insecurity, fueled by anger, and stung by the injustice of it all.

But by the tenth day, when Trevv still hadn't rung, *I lost it*.

It was eight p.m., I was pacing the lounge, and overwhelmed by this insatiable, almost physically painful need to see him. And because Jane was working late, there was unfortunately no one there to stop me.

I needed to see Trevv. And, more importantly, I needed to see what his life looked like. I hoped it was falling apart like mine. I hoped he was sitting miserably in a chair contemplating what a bastard he'd been. Wallowing and choking on his own guilt and realizing what a terrible mistake he'd made…

Driving there felt so natural, and everything looked exactly as I'd left it. Nothing had changed since I'd been gone, and it pissed me off. In moments like this, when everything is falling apart, you expect the rest of the world to be going through the same thing and it's almost offensive when you discover they're not. While your entire life has come to a grinding stop, everyone else's just seems to be carrying on as normal.

I parked the car a few houses away, turned off the lights, and climbed out. I was wearing cargo pants and a black hoodie and knew that I probably looked like someone who belonged on the sex offender's registry. But I was so drunk on insanity and adrenaline that I didn't care. I crept up to the house and peered through the window.

All the lights were on, and through the net curtains I could just make out a silhouette in the kitchen. Trevv?

I got as close as I could, carefully navigating my way through the thorny rosebushes. For a split second the thought did flash through my mind…

Annie. What the flipping, fucking fuck are you doing?

But as quickly as the thought had come, it was gone and I was peering through the kitchen window like a Peeping Tom.

I could hear talking but couldn't make it out. I could see movement but nothing definitive. The window was slightly open…Should I stick my hand though it and pull the curtain aside, just for a quick peep?

No, Annie, no! a voice from above seemed to yell at me.

Do it, Annie, do it! an even louder voice wailed. And so I did. I slid my hand through as silently as I could and with my fingertips, grabbed the edge of the curtain, and pulled it aside.

A candlelit dinner for two at the table…red roses in a vase, a heart-shaped note hanging from them…My stomach churned, and bile rose up my esophagus.

Handholding, eye staring, smiles, and whispers…I wanted to cry.

But at the same time, I couldn't tear my eyes away. It was like looking into a mirror, but the person looking back wasn't me. It should be me, though. It was my kitchen. I had chosen those wine-glasses, that saltshaker, even the table they were sitting at had been my idea. So how had another woman stolen my entire life?

I stayed glued to the window out of morbid fascination, watching as two actors played out the life that had once been mine. But when Trevv leaned in and kissed her like he'd never kissed me before, I let go of the curtain and slumped down. I tried to hold the tears back, but there were just too many. I crumpled to the ground and heard a soft involuntary moan escape my lips.

My shoulders started to shake as I sat in the cold, wet soil silently crying my eyes out. It was the kind of crying that seems to take over your entire body and paralyze you. I must have sat in the flower bed for ages, the rose thorns scratching at my skin. I bit my lip and dug my fingers into the ground to stop myself from screaming and punching something.

I finally managed to climb back into my car at some stage. Covered in mud and blood and aching from top to toe. My bones felt sore, my skin itched, and I wanted to crawl up into a ball and die. How pathetic and embarrassing can you get? Crying in the dirt outside your ex-boyfriend and his new girlfriend's house. I hated myself so much for doing that.

I drove off and vowed I wasn't going to tell anyone about this. Not even my friends. I'd just keep it to myself and use it as yet another thing to drive myself mad with.

And when I wasn't making myself mad, some of my friends were doing it for me, especially my cousin Lilly. A few years ago she'd been dramatically abandoned at the altar in front of five hundred wedding guests. At the time she'd been devastated, but it had all worked out for the best, because she'd met Damien. But now she was tossing around deep, philosophical advice like ice cream sprinkles. Stuffing an endless stream of clichés down my throat until I was practically choking on them.

"Everything happens for a reason…"

"…meant to be…"

"…blessing in bloody disguise…"

But I just wasn't ready to see the Dr. Phil side of life. My only friend that wasn't plying me with platitudes, besides Jane, was Stormy-Rain. As soon as I'd told her what had happened, she hadn't rushed to soothe me; rather, she simply said, "I knew it would happen eventually. It was in the cards."

She had been very vocal when I'd gotten together with Trevv. She had thrown around words like *arrogant* and *capitalist money-suckering tick* (she wasn't known for subtlety). But I was blinded, as one is in those early intoxicating days. Through the misty haze of dopamine and lots of sex-induced endorphins, I couldn't see any of the things she was saying.

With Trevv it had been that love-at-first-sight thing, although he seemed to be everything I never knew I wanted in a guy. Prior to him I'd dated a string of complete losers. In fact, it seemed that in my early dating days I'd gone out of my way to pick men that were fundamentally wrong for me. At the time I was very much into the fashion-y types. Those cool, elusive kinds who were *sooo* weird that they had to be creative geniuses headed for greatness. You know the type, those quiet, intense types that looked like they needed a vitamin-infused IV, a razor blade, and a tan.

Being in the creative industry meant that there were plenty to choose from, too. My personal preference always lay with the tortured, struggling artists, with their knitted cardigans, scruffy paint-stained jeans, worn sneakers, and hair that looked like it needed a good brushing. But after a few years of dating guys like that, the novelty just wore off. I was no longer into dating guys that seemed more sensitive and emotional than me and had thighs half the size of mine. A strange longing for a *real* man—whatever that meant—took hold of me.

So, one night when I was out drinking with my friends at some fancy place we could ill afford—I saw him. We were all sipping the same drink we'd ordered over an hour before, in an attempt to make it last longer. I did well as a stylist working in advertising (a job I hated, by the way), but not well enough that twenty dollars for a cocktail seemed even vaguely reasonable. But then Trevv went striding past. I smelled him before I saw him. I'll never forget; he smelled of sandalwood and tropical rain—a strangely intoxicating combination that made me swoon. And in that moment he must have seen me looking at him (gawking perhaps), because a few minutes later he was at our table.

"Can I offer you ladies a drink?" He was so gentlemanly, something I was completely unaccustomed to. I was also unaccustomed to a man who wielded a shiny credit card with the power to buy cocktails for everyone—usually my dates would be scrounging for coins in their jean pockets and cursing because they had forgotten that this pair had the holes.

"Sure. Since none of us can afford to buy a glass of water here," I said, which made him laugh. And by that I mean he *really* laughed, as if I was some kind of stand-up comedian. So several drinks—and three hours of conversation—later, I made the decision that he was exactly what I needed. There I was, longing for change, and just like that a man like him came falling into my lap! And he was into me; perhaps it was because I was some kind of an exotic creature to him, a departure from the corporate pinstriped pantsuits he usually dated. Although, that's what he went back to in the end.

And I liked the fact that he was a bit cocky and sure of himself. Confident and even slightly arrogant. It was very appealing. All the qualities that Stormy had pointed out to me as possible shortcomings were actually the qualities that I found most appealing.

And he was terribly good-looking, in that total model-slash-actor way. Universally good-looking, the kind of good-looking that your ninety-year-old grandmother would find attractive. Perhaps I should have known he was *too* good-looking, especially for someone like me.

After Nipple-Gate, as my friends and I affectionately called it, dear Jane took me in rent-free, since I currently found myself with a very rapidly diminishing savings account. It was great for the first month or two—we fell into a pleasant, predictable routine; I wallowed on the couch in self-pity all day while she went to work, and in the evenings we watched the documentary channel.

I'd always wondered where Jane's abundance of facts and figures came from, and now I knew. I also knew that you replace every particle in your body every seven years, vending machines kill four times as many people as sharks, and when male bees climax, their testicles explode and then they die. This put the slightest smile on my face as I started imaging this happening to humans and that Trevv's balls were currently bouncing off the bedroom walls.

For the first two months, Jane's apartment felt like a peaceful sanctuary, a safe house from the madness of the world outside. Until I realized just how often her mother made impromptu visits. One morning I awoke to her instructing a team of people to rip up the carpets and replace them with wooden floors. She'd done this without consulting Jane, just as she'd done when she'd removed all carbohydrates from the pantry and reupholstered several of the living room chairs.

Jane's mother is something *very* special. We always thought Jane was exaggerating the stories about her, but I can say with confidence that she is not. If anything, she is downplaying them. Mrs.

Smith, as I still call her, has absolutely no concept of personal boundaries and space. She is also obsessed with trying to find Jane a boyfriend, and as soon as she discovered I was single, too, well, she doubled her efforts. She even asked for personal pictures so she could set up an online dating profile for me. She'd secretly set one up for Jane, who only discovered this by accident when a man recognized her on the street.

"Try to give me a variety," she'd said one day after walking into my room unannounced. "Men like women who can be versatile. And make sure you give me a bikini one; those are always the most popular. But not a bikini that say's you're easy. The bikini needs to say, 'I'm modern, classy, and confident but don't have sex on the first date even though I still expect you to pay for dinner and open the car door for me.'"

I wasn't even aware that bikinis spoke.

Given her mother's constant presence in our lives, Jane wasn't offended when I told her I needed to find a place of my own, not to mention a job. I'd been lounging around aimlessly for ages and I knew it was time to stop. I had this vision that moving into my own place would be a good thing, a positive step in the right direction, and that things would get better after that. Only they didn't. They got worse.

The months ahead were pretty much all downhill. A steep, winding downhill where you could easily lose your footing or sprain an ankle, especially if you were wearing heels.

Luckily I wasn't wearing heels, nor was I anywhere near a heel, for that matter. Sonja had been right; I couldn't find another job at a fashion mag. Apparently no one wanted to employ a ruiner of very expensive photo shoots, not to mention an attempted murderer. *Yes,* the incident had been completely blown out of all rational proportions. The gossipmongers had had a field day with it. Stretching, elaborating, exaggerating, and milking it for all it was worth.

Of course the fact that no charges were ever brought against me was of no consequence to anyone. Why let facts ruin a perfectly good story, hey?

Several versions were in circulation. In one, I'd suffered a psychotic break and voices had told me to pick up a knife. And in another, I had been planning on committing a Lorena Bobbitt.

For those of you who don't remember the story, Lorena—not unprovoked, mind you—chopped off her husband's willy, took it for a little drive, and tossed it out of the window into a field. Some hailed her as mad, while others called her a hero. The penis was eventually reattached, and her ex-husband enjoyed a brief career as a porn star. *True story!*

But at some stage I knew they would grow tired of me; the fashion industry is fickle that way, especially if a famous model admitted to having bulimia, a substance abuse problem, or showed up on shoot with cellulite.

I had no desire to go back to the highly stressful world of being a stylist. I wouldn't have been able to cope with that in my current state. I had also been so vocal about getting out of that industry and moving on to greater things that I felt too embarrassed to admit defeat and failure. Especially since everything else in my life was a failure, too. Besides, dressing people in corporate yet down-to-earth relatable clothes so that they can sell life insurance policies on TV isn't really my thing.

So I opted for a far more relaxed job (it was the only one I could get). I got work at Patel and Son's Dressmakers, a family-run business that did everything from shortening pants and sewing on buttons to creating colorful saris for weddings and other special occasions. It was a small, cramped shop inside the very unglamorous Oriental Plaza, located in a rougher part of Johannesburg. It was tucked between a store that sold every plastic item imaginable and a spice store. Sometimes the smell was so pungent and overwhelming that it would give me an instant headache. But it was also loud and colorful and full of life there, too, and on certain days going to work felt like walking onto a Bollywood film set. I was always waiting for someone to break into unprovoked song or bust a dramatic choreographed move.

But some days the only thing that kept me going while spending hours hemming was imagining sewing Trevv's nut-sack to the wall. And then there were those other times, while listening to the whirr of the machine and watching the repetitive high-speed motion of the needle piercing the fabric, I wondered if Trevv wouldn't actually enjoy that.

A spot of pain. A poke with a sharp needle. A spank with a paddle. What else was he into? The world was filled with bizarre fetishes, after all. God only knew what else he and Tess did behind closed doors. The thought always made me feel violently ill, especially when my imagination conjured up images of a nipple-clamped Trevv handcuffed to the bedpost while Tess poked him with a cattle prod, or some such appalling device.

But the best thing about my new job was the Patels themselves. They became like a surrogate family to me, especially Granny Padma. She often brought me leftover curry, or a batch of samosas (I never had the heart to tell her that Indian food gives me heartburn).

The pay wasn't great, though. It was barely enough to live on.

I'd managed to find myself a tiny garden cottage in the student/hippie suburb of Melville. It's amazing what happens to your priorities when you're broke. Because, suddenly, living in the right area and wearing the right labels didn't seem that important in the face of feeding myself. In fact, the poorer I got, the more I let go of all of it.

My landlords were typical Melvillians, as we call them. Gunter ran a small business at home selling biofuel made from discarded vegetable oil that he collected from restaurants—a very messy affair—and Helena ran a small website selling eco-friendly oral hygiene products, like bamboo toothbrushes and recyclable dental floss.

It was a totally different world. For starters I was forced to recycle absolutely everything. On one occasion they'd found a Coke can in my dustbin and acted like I'd committed the ultimate crime. I was instructed to recycle it immediately and given a book to read called *Tears of Blood: Mother Nature Is Dying a Slow and Painful Death*.

My social life became nonexistent. At first I obliged my friends, who had insisted on getting me out of the house and back on the horse. I went out with them a few times, and even went on a blind date. Let's just say it didn't go well. It had ended with some loud wailing cries, humiliating public displays of intense emotion, and lots of runny mascara. He'd been very polite, though…

"I'll call you."

Only he didn't call. Needless to say, I finally realized that I was not well enough for polite society and started seeing less and less of my friends—and certainly no men—in favor of my couch and Facebook stalking Trevv and Tess.

I was basically having a cyber-relationship with them; they just didn't know it. I even went away with them on that romantic getaway to Paris—talk about masochistic.

What was wrong with me? This must be what addiction feels like. Hating something so much, but needing and wanting it at the same time because it's all you know. And maybe you think it's all you deserve, too.

But one night, after canceling on my friends yet again, they all blasted into my house and forced me to cyber–break up with Trevv and Tess.

We all sat down together and I took one last masochistic look at the photo of them cuddling by the roaring wood fire and pressed block. It was like the final little death, the last nail in the coffin. Jane held my hand and I cried. Val cracked open the wine—I suspected she needed it more than I did. Lilly provided the snacks, and Stormy put a crystal outside my front door to trap the negative energy before it came in.

And so began my months of stay-at-home TV binge watching, and self-help books for company. But after a month of reading about journaling, gratitude, and the need for a personal mission statement, whatever that was, I started feeling the need to do something else. I wasn't sure what exactly, which was typical in my current state. I'd gone from someone who was sure about everything, someone who knew what she wanted and made bold decisions like changing careers, to someone who questioned everything. I hated this new uncertain Annie.

The idea had come to me by accident. I'd been climbing out of the car when the strap of my handbag caught in the seat belt. I'd heard a ripping sound, followed by the clank of a million things falling onto the ground.

"Shit."

My lipstick had rolled under the car, and I was forced to lie on the dirty ground and stretch my arm into unimaginable lengths and shapes to retrieve it. Some of my other things had rolled right under the car and out the other side only to be crushed by the tire of a passing car.

The whole experience had left me highly pissed off, not to mention covered in black grime. I got home that night, and since money was a problem, decided to fix the strap of my bag. But after ten minutes of looking through still-packed boxes and bags of crap, I realized that my sewing machine was at Trevv's house.

I suppose it was inevitable. The moment when I had to face Trevv again was finally here. It took me about ten minutes to compose a message to him. I read and reread it so many times that the words were no longer making any sense to me. They were a jumble of meaningless letters.

I felt as if I couldn't even trust myself to write a message to him. I questioned every word and analyzed the tone: too desperate, too angry, too friendly? Before sending it I decided to consult Stormy-Rain; she's an actress after all, she reads lines all the time. Maybe she could tell me if I'd infused my message with a meaning I definitely didn't intend.

She confirmed the message's neutrality, but left me with a warning; "Do not let the enemy see the weakness in your eyes. Dogs can smell fear."

And she was right. I had to remain cool and calm and completely unaffected when I saw him. I could not give him the satisfaction of knowing what a mess I was. I finally messaged him after another ten minutes of staring at the now-blurry words.

Hi. It's Anne. I left my sewing machine in the spare room. Can I come over and fetch it?

He'd messaged me right back. I wasn't surprised. He basically had his phone surgically attached to his hand, or that's how it had seemed anyway for the last few months of our…

Suddenly it clicked. How the hell had I been so blind and stupid? It was only in retrospect that I could see all the signs. I imagined all the hushed, whispered, sexy conversations he'd had with her while I'd been downstairs or in the bath.

The pain of knowing that I'd been deceived for so long, and the embarrassment and anger I felt for being so ignorant was overwhelming but I needed to get this done.

When I finally arrived at his house, it was so surreal walking in after all that time. All the traces of me were gone, as if he'd taken a giant eraser and rubbed me out. Tess was everywhere, though.

The expensive lawyer-y coat that hung by the front door, the vase of fresh lilies in the entrance hall, and then there was that pair of high-heeled shoes propped up neatly on the floor. I stepped in.

"Sorry, if you don't mind…" Trevv looked down at my feet. "We take our shoes off now before walking in the house."

"Oh. Okay." I was taken aback by this but slipped my pumps off and reluctantly put them next to Tess's.

"It's better for feng shui," Trevv muttered from above me.

Feng fucking shui. Since when was Trevv into anything like that? He was far too obsessed with money and status to care whether the positive vibes were flowing freely though his house.

"Is Tess…I mean…?" I stuttered, despite the fact that I'd sworn not to show any signs of weakness.

"No, she's at Pil-oga." Trevv flashed me a smile and I swear his teeth seemed even whiter. "Cross between yoga and Pilates, very good for your core, you know."

"Mmmmm," I muttered as I followed Trevv through the house and into the spare room, which had clearly been turned into a gym in my absence. I felt a slight pang of guilt at the sight of the tread-mill and sucked my stomach in. I hadn't seen the inside of a gym in months. I found my sewing machine neatly packed up and ready for me to take. I was just about to grab it when Trevv's hand shot out.

"Allow me," he said, sounding so thoughtful and kind, as if car-rying my not-that-heavy sewing machine to my car would somehow exonerate him. What a shithead. I waited for him to move, but he didn't.

"So…" He looked at me intently. "How are you, Anne?"

The question completely threw me, and I felt my stomach twist into knots. The last thing I wanted to do was talk to him. But…*Show no weakness.*

"Great! Good." I nodded vigorously. Too vigorously.

"Glad to hear it." He sounded sincere, but I knew him. This line of questioning had nothing to do with genuine concern for my well-being, but rather everything to do with his morbid curiosity. He was probably going to tell Tess tonight what a loser I was. How terri-ble I looked, despite the fact that I'd spent hours doing my hair and makeup before coming. *"Never let the enemy see you looking weak."*

"So, where are you staying?" he persisted, and my stomach con-tinued to twist.

"I was staying with Jane for a while, but I've found myself a nice garden cottage now."

"Lovely. How quaint." I could hear the subtle mocking quality to his voice and I wanted to lash out and slap him, or something worse. He was getting to me. Creeping and crawling under my skin.

"Yes, it's lovely." I tried to sound the right mix of upbeat, yet aloof—if that's even a thing.

"And are you seeing anyone?" As the question was out, all the cool aloofness I was trying so desperately to put on vanished. I flicked my eyes up, and for a second, they locked with Trevv's. I knew exactly what he wanted to hear.

No, I wasn't seeing anyone and my life was terrible without him. I was lonely and insecure and my life no longer had any meaning. (Sadly, it was all kind of true.)

I nodded again. *God, what the hell was I doing?* "Yes. As a matter of a fact I am."

For a second he looked surprised, but quickly corrected. "That's good, Anne."

"Yes, he's great. Really great."

"Would I know him?" Trevv asked, looking genuinely curious. He was probably hoping it was some wildly unsuccessful loser that he could boast about being better than. Everything with Trevv was always a competition.

"No," I said quickly, and then, without thinking, I started digging my own grave. "He's from out of town."

"Really? Where?"

"He's from, from…uh." And then it happened. I scanned my brain for any other place but here. Any South African city would have done, any. But my mind drew a blank. I scanned the room hoping for a clue, and before I could apply any rational thinking to it, I saw it, OUTBACK TREADMILL AND FITNESS EQUIPMENT, and the word came flying out of my mouth.

"Australia."

"Australia?"

Fuck! "Sydney, actually," I said confidently.

"How exotic." Trevv was mocking me. "What's his name?"

"His name?" I repeated.

"Yes. His name?"

"Right, his name." Blank. Totally, utterly, stupidly blank.

Of all the millions and millions of men's names out there, my mind struggled to find one. I scanned the room again. A shopping bag in the corner caught my attention. SISSY BOY.

"Boyyy-den. His name is Boyden."

Trevv nodded suspiciously. I couldn't blame him. Was that even a name?

"Boyden from Sydney, Australia?" he asked.

"That's right, and come to think of it"—I raised my watch to my eye (I was such a bad, bad actress)—"look at the time. Running late for my date with Boyden and you know what they say about Australians…" I paused. *What did they say about Australians? Why had I said that? What was wrong with me?* A look of panic must have flashed across my face as I desperately grasped for something to say.

"Always on time!" I declared triumphantly. "Australians are never late. Punctual people."

And now I wanted to burst into tears. The hole was getting deeper by the second and I might as well have buried myself in it right there and then. Without saying another word (I couldn't afford to), I grabbed the sewing machine out of Trevv's hand and ran toward the front door.

"Anne," Trevv called after me. I stopped dead in my tracks.

"Yes?"

"There's no need to make up boyfriends and dates. I would completely understand it if you—"

"Boyden is very real!" I swung around so violently I almost dropped the sewing machine. "He is so, so real!"

"Sorry, I didn't mean to offend you." He smiled smugly and suddenly I wanted to rub my imaginary relationship in his face.

"And guess what?" I snapped viciously.

"What?" He still looked vaguely amused and I wanted to cut him down to size.

"He is amazing, and kind, and good to animals and children and very, *very* successful, and he is also better than you in *bed*!" I screamed that last word and instantly regretted it.

I was coming across as the mad, scorned woman. *Maybe I was mad!* I needed to go. I turned and ran out the door, climbed into my car, and pulled away as quickly as I could. As soon as I was out of sight, I stopped my car on the side of the road.

"Boyden from Sydney fucking Australia!" I put my hands over my face. How embarrassing. I wanted to crawl under a rock; no doubt he and Tess would laugh about this later over their organic, feng shui'd dinners.

"Poor, sad, pathetic Annie, making up imaginary boyfriends from Down Under."

I felt a strange sensation on my feet and looked down. I was barefoot. I'd left my shoes at Trevv's. I sighed and drove off. They could stay there. I never wanted to see him again and I certainly couldn't afford to bump into him, either, what with Boyden from Down Under not being on my arm.

That night I got home feeling extra sorry for myself and started mending the bag. There was something so satisfying about putting it back together. I couldn't fix my life, but I could fix this bag, and I could make it even better, too. And I did. I'd transformed the bag from functional to fun and funky, and that's when it hit me. This. This was something I could do in the quiet evenings. Something to busy my hands and take my mind away from all the many things I didn't want to—and still wasn't ready to—think about.

Nothing on the cutting edge of fashion or anything. Nothing that would appear on the arm of the fashionable elite, or grace the cat-walks of the world, but bags I liked. Large, colorful totes and beach bags. In fact, the more colorful and bedazzled they were, the more therapeutic I found it.

I imagined Sonja's face when she saw them. *"Kitsch and nasty"* is what she would say. So with every colorful ribbon, shiny swath of fabric, and big bright button, I defied her and everything she stood for. The more over-the-top the bag, the more I felt like I was driving a stake through the beating heart of the fashion industry I once loved and so desperately wanted to be a part of.

"Take that, Sonja!" *Clicks the Bedazzler*

"Die, bitch, die!" *Glues on another kitsch sequin and slaps on another colored fucking feather for good effing measure*

I guess it makes sense that I would find solace in bags. They were the reason I went into fashion after all. You see, when I was about ten, I had a life-changing moment. I walked past a store and saw, all perfectly poised and elegant in the window, a Louis V.

Big, lush, plump, and sophisticated. It was so luxurious. I wanted one.

But trying to convince your parents that Santa should bring you a genuine Louis Vuitton for Christmas when you're just ten years old is not an easy task. So when I got Malibu Barbie instead, I vowed that one day I would own that handbag.

And I did. And now it was listed on eBay. But my rent was

two months late, and you can't live in a handbag, as much as I'd like to!

And so I sat in a kind of torturous limbo that seemed to drag on forever. It was painful. Which is why Lilly's suggestion of a tropical girls-only holiday literally made me cry with excitement!

"Why don't we all go to Mauritius? We can lie in the sun, sip cocktails, and sleep in late." she'd said one night.

"Sounds a bit expensive," I said faintly.

"Don't worry, I'll pay"—she gave me a wink—"and when I mean *I,* I mean Damien."

Her boyfriend, Damien, was the most unusual trust fund baby around. He drove a totally unassuming car, wore sneakers that should have been thrown away in the 90s, owned clothes with authentically acquired holes in them, and worked as a physics lecturer at a community college. But when it came to spending money on friends and family, Damien's trust fund came blissfully blazing to life.

"And if you feel bad for one second, you're wasting your time. Trust me, Damien would love to do this. You know what's he's like."

"Okay," I said before letting out a loud shriek.

"Let's phone everyone and see if they can come." Lilly was practically jumping up and down. "We're going to have such a blast. We can get outrageously tipsy on coconut cocktails and dance to cheesy ABBA at the local disco and maybe we'll find you a holiday fling."

I grimaced. "A holiday fling?"

"Yes, you need to find somone to practice on. Someone nonthreatening. Someone to help you get over this slump."

"Someone to practice on. Uh…I think that's the last thing I need."

CHAPTER THREE

The phone calls came respectively at 5:23 a.m. and then again at 6:27 a.m.

I was fast asleep, dreaming happily about the vacation I was about to go on with my friends in a few hours, when it assaulted my eardrums. A few months ago I'd changed my ringtone to a very angry Linkin Park song, which seemed like a good idea at the time, but now, barely at the crack of dawn, it just gave me a blinding headache.

"BURRNN IT DOWWNNN, AAAHHHHHH!!!" I scrambled quickly for the phone to shut off that offensive screaming.

"Hello!"

"Hey…" It was Lilly and she sounded horrific. "I feel like I'm dying."

"What's wrong?"

"I think I have food poisoning."

"How?" I sat up in bed.

"Um, well you know how Stormy invited us around last night?"

"Yes." Of course I did. I had politely declined.

"She cooked."

"No! You didn't," I gasped.

"I did. I think it was that strange organic, vegan, yellow-browny gelatinous-looking thing."

I shook my head to myself. Everyone knows *not* to eat anything Stormy prepares. Experimental veganism, she calls it.

"I'm at the ER and the doctor says I'll be okay in a few days, but there's no way I can travel with you today," she was practically wailing.

"What? You're not coming?"

"No, I'm coming, I just have to move my flight out by a few days. I'm not getting on a plane like this."

"I can't believe it." I couldn't hide the disappointment in my voice, which made me feel terribly selfish. "Sorry. I didn't mean to make this about me. Just get better. Jane and I will brave it alone for a few days. "

"You guys will have fun! Maybe you'll find a scuba instructor to practice on."

"Doubtful."

"Oh my God, I think I'm going to get siiickkk." She hung up.

But then, just as I was thinking about her, Jane phoned with the exact same story; sick, practically on her deathbed, clinging to a bucket…not pretty. I had sudden visions of myself alone on vacation while all those loved-up honeymooners and groups of happy tourists had fun in the sun. I would stick out like a sore, lonely, pathetic, single thumb. I was self-conscious enough as it was without people pointing and staring at me like the last lonely rhino in the zoo. Besides, who would put sunscreen on my back?

It was in that moment that I wished my other two friends weren't so damn complicated. Stormy-Rain and Val had both declined Lilly's invitation, for very different, but equally ridiculous, reasons.

Stormy-Rain because she believed that humans weren't meant to fly and that airplanes were unnatural, and Val because Mark (the neighbor she'd been secretly in love with for years) had invited her to a family wedding. She was convinced—*yet again*—that he was going to realize he was in love with her, and her limbo of torturous, unrequited love would finally be over. I wasn't going to hold my breath for that; this traumatic saga had been dragging on for years, like a story line from a bad soap opera that went round and round in repetitive circles.

I'd been so excited about this trip, but the idea of going alone terrified me, even if it was only for a few days. For a moment I contemplated pushing my flight out, too, but then I looked out the window and saw the sight I dreaded most.

Perhaps I should have mentioned earlier that Gunter, my landlord-slash-neighbor, is very "open" with his body. Maybe it's a German thing, maybe it's because he'd been a nudist in the seventies?

But whatever the reason, *in my humble opinion*, no sixty-five-year-old man should clean his pool, bending over often, I might add, in a tiny red Speedo. He's also a hairy man, and I'm not just talking about his chest. Let's just say it always looks like he's smuggling a poodle in his speedo.

"Hi, Annie." He waved at me, exposing the Santa beard he had tucked under his armpit.

"Hi, Gunter." I smiled politely and waved back, deciding that I definitely *should* go to Mauritius that morning. It was summer after all, and the pool would need regular cleaning, not to mention regular bending.

I grabbed my ticket and ran just as Gunter started leaning over to clean the leaves out of the filter.

***

The flight to Mauritius was only three hours and I spent the entire time entertaining myself with a series of happy thoughts. Happy thoughts that helped me get rid of images of that red Speedo.

The turquoise sea. I could almost hear it.

The warm sun. I could almost *feel* it.

White sandy beaches.

Lush palm trees swaying in a warm tropical breeze.

Cocktails, margaritas, mojitos, cosmos, and sex on the beaches (and I mean that in the purely alcoholic sense). There would be no sex on the beach for me, or anywhere else for that matter. I'd come to terms with a kind of self-imposed vow of celibacy. It was obvious that I needed a lot more practice in bed first, before jumping into one. I was continuously plagued by thoughts of total sexual inadequacy, which I'd never had before. I'd once considered myself to be a girl who knew her way around a bedroom. When I'd mentioned this to my friends, Stormy had come up with a very Stormy suggestion.

"If you're looking for sex tips, you should watch a porno," she'd suggested enthusiastically.

"A porno?" The last time I'd watched a porno was with my college roommate; we'd laughed the whole way through it.

"Just think about it. Those people are paid to have sex. *Paid*!" she'd said while sipping on a glass of muddy, green-colored sludge. "That makes them professionals. If anyone knows how to do it, they do."

At first I'd dismissed her suggestion. But a few weeks later I watched a TV program on infidelity—one of those true-life things where the wife hires a private investigator to track down her miserable cheating man-whore—and I changed my mind. When confronted, the man-whore showed no remorse, instead citing his wife's lackluster bedroom performance as one of the main reasons for "straying."

Maybe Stormy was right after all. What the hell? What did I have to lose? So with that in mind, I Googled the nearest adult store. I'd initially decided on online porn, but Stormy had insisted we have a real-life experience, not a virtual one. I'd never been to an adult store before, so the prospect was rather daunting. And cruelly, most seemed to be located on rather busy main roads, forcing you to engage in some kind of public walk of shame, thus increasing your chances of getting spotted. And I could *not* risk being seen. Half the fashion world already thought I was a willy-chopping weirdo.

I contemplated going in some sort of a disguise. But after I'd experimented with a trench coat, a cap, and oversized glasses, I realized that I looked like a deranged stripper and was at risk of being arrested...again.

The news of my sexual expedition spread, and one Saturday morning Stormy, Jane, Val, Lilly, and I found ourselves sitting in my car together across the road from the sex shop.

"I can't believe we're actually doing this," Jane said. If anyone needed this, though, it was probably Jane. She hadn't had sex in years, not since her bad experience with the man that had a secret wife on the side.

"It's so exciting," Lilly said. Once the biggest sexual prude around, she now enjoyed wild and very frequent sex with Damien. "Maybe I'll get one to watch with Damien later."

And then there was Stormy, who had turned this into a whole production. She had arrived in a disguise. Wig, strange vaguely Victorian-looking clothes, and a terrible accent that seemed to be a mixture of Australian and Transylvanian. She was the least prudish of the group, but she had seen this an opportunity to flex her acting muscles. Val was also there looking tear stained. Word on the street was that neighbor-boy had started seeing someone.

We all gazed out of the car. ADULT EXTRAVAGANZA. The shop certainly made no attempt to blend in or be discreet in any way, shape, or form. In fact, it was just the opposite. It screamed and waved its arms wildly. It boasted a large, flashing red *X* that could no doubt be seen by intelligent life forms living in another galaxy.

And there was nothing subtle about the interior, either. It was so dimly lit by a seedy red light that it took a few seconds for my eyes to adjust. And once they had, I reviewed my surroundings. I felt like I'd taken a tumble through the rabbit hole and walked straight into Alice's Wonderland for adults. Half of the shop was dedicated to toys and accessories and the other half to DVDs. Currently we were surrounded by…mmmm, what euphemism can I use here…*female pleasure appliances*?

"Look at ull zee giant dildos," Stormy said in her loudest possible voice. We didn't need her to point them out, though. Because we were all already staring at them. Some were pretty ordinary-looking things, while others looked like something you might buy from the gift shop at SeaWorld. One giant luminous yellow-looking thing caught my eye. I pointed at it for everyone to look when—

"Nice choice." A voice startled us and we all jumped. Jane, who is far too tall for her center of gravity, stumbled backward, and *boom*.

Disaster struck.

The shelf wobbled.

It tilted.

It swayed.

And then it fell, taking its contents with it.

Suddenly the floor around us was a sea of sex toys. A purple vibrator unexpectedly sprung to life, vibrating and shaking so hard that it actually started crawling across the floor like a large snake.

We all bent down trying to pick up the wobbly, shaky, battery-operated creatures. I glanced up briefly and ascertained that the voice in question belonged to a pale geeky-looking guy wearing a Star Wars T-shirt and a pair of army boots.

"Don't worry about it," he said, bending down and standing up again, holding something that looked like the love child of a Christmas decoration and an automatic pool cleaner.

"I'm so sorry, you startled us and—" Jane started to splutter.

"No worries, it happens all the time."

"Vat? Zat people knock over ze shelf?" Stormy asked, trying to find the off switch to a distinctly tropical-looking thing that also seemed to be belting out reggae music.

"No. That I startle people." He said it with a deadpan delivery and somewhat vacant desert-wasteland eyes. It was a little creepy. I could see why he might startle people.

A few minutes later we had finally managed to get all the battery-operated toys shut down and back onto the shelves.

"So, is there something I can help you ladies with?" He spoke again.

"Yes, we're looking for a movie," Lilly said confidently.

"You've come to the right place. So, what you girls into?"

"Um…" We all looked at each other.

"Woman on woman, man on man and woman, S and M, BDSM, CFNM, BBW, M and M, hard-core, soft-core, somewhere-in-the-middle-core, bisexual, transsexual, trisexual, or latex?"

"Normal stuff, I guess," I said.

"Aaah." He nodded as if I'd just answered a really deep and meaningful question. "Vanilla. I've got just the stuff for you."

We followed him around the corner past a rail of outfits. Out of the corner of my eye I thought I recognized one. Leathery. Studded. Chain-y. I shuddered, wondering if Trevv and Tess had been in here.

"This is where you'll find your softer stuff. I can recommend some, if you like?"

"No, no thanks. I think we'll be okay." I smiled at him and he took this as his cue to leave, going back to the counter from whence he came.

We looked around: *Lord of the G-Strings*, *Driving into Miss Daisy*, *Spankenstein*, *Free My Willy*, *American Booty*, and *Ocean's 11 Inches*. Without any discussion we picked *11 Inches* up and inched our way up to the counter. I slid the DVD across the table.

"That'll be ten dollars." And then he winked at us. At least I thought it was a wink; it was hard to tell behind those thick, dusty glasses he was wearing. "You ladies are going to love it."

We smiled politely, paid, slipped our newly acquired purchase into a handbag, and scuttled off.

Once home and safely installed on the couch, I pressed play on *Ocean's 11 Inches*.

Let's just say we didn't learn a great deal about the intricacies of sex.

All we learned was…

"Guys…" My eyes felt like they were going to pop out of my head.

"I know! I know!" Val leaned forward, examining the TV screen carefully.

Lilly, Stormy, and Jane crept across the floor to get a closer look.

"It's…," I whispered in shock.

"I know. I know!" Stormy said.

"It's…," I tried again, but the words failed me.

"It can't be," Jane said. "Press pause. We need to find a tape measure."

"No. It definitely is," Lilly said emphatically.

We were all silent. We stared at the close-up shot that was filling the entire screen.

"It's halfway down to his knee!" Val screeched.

"It's the size of an elephant's trunk!" Stormy tapped on the TV screen.

"I know. I know," we all echoed.

"It has to be a prosthetic," Jane finally said.

We all stopped for a moment. "That actually makes sense," I said, "because I've seen some amazing prosthetics on set. You should see what they can do these days."

"Exactly!" Lilly exclaimed. "Didn't they put a prosthetic nose on Nicole Kidman for that movie?"

"Totally," I quickly verified.

"Um, guys…" Stormy had pressed play again. "But if it was prosthetic, would he be able to do *that* with it?"

CHAPTER FOUR

*M*auritius is beautiful. Exquisite even. The interior of the island is comprised mainly of huge—as far as the eye can see—fields of bright green sugar cane. In places, the sugar cane stretches for miles and miles, and the only things breaking the flat, monotonous green horizon are the large jagged mountains that rise up straight out of the earth.

Wide-open spaces are punctuated by small roadside towns, an eclectic mix of old and new. Street markets selling pineapples and coconuts are located next to a McDonald's, an interesting blend of old architecture next to modern buildings.

And then there's the sea. Brilliant, turquoise, and more inviting than a sale at your favorite shop. The beaches looked as white as snow and as soft as cotton wool, and I couldn't wait to stretch out across one. In some parts the water was so clear it was transparent, and the small boat sailing past looked like it was floating, suspended on nothing but air. I opened the car window and the humid, salty smell of the sea rushed in.

This place was magical. Perfect. And for the first time in forever, I felt at peace. Nothing was going to ruin this vacation for me.

I finally arrived at my resort—Le Trou aux Biches—around midday. I won't even go about trying to pronounce that name out loud; my French is very rusty and the first time I attempted it, it came out as *Le Troo axe Bitches*. I'm pretty sure that is not the intended pronunciation, considering the way the customs officer glared at me after I'd told him that's where I was headed.

But the question of how to say it really doesn't matter once you are inside this thing of tropical beauty. The lobby is grand. Triple-volume ceilings rise up, giving the feeling of ultimate space and freedom. The floor is made entirely of white beach sand with actual palms planted in it.

From there I had to cross a small moat of water to get to the rest of the hotel, and once across the bridge, I found myself in a dense tropical garden.

Several paths cut their way through the thick flora, dotted with signs that read POOL, SPA, SALON, SHOP, TENNIS COURT. (*As if!*) I followed the bellhop through the beautiful tropical gardens, past the bright pink flowers, the large lush leaves, and huge palm trees that were heavy with coconuts.

I finally reached my room, a small stand-alone bungalow on Jasmine Lane. There were about ten other small bungalows, and I assumed the ones next door were reserved for Lilly and Jane. The best thing about the rooms was their location, only thirty feet from the beach. I stood there for a moment, as the bellhop fiddled with the key card, and took it all in.

The sea was dead calm, as still as bathwater and probably the same color and temperature. The water looked shallow, and I imagined that you could probably walk all the way to the distant reef where the sea became a dark sapphire color. The beach was scattered with deliciously inviting-looking loungers positioned under umbrellas made of dried palm leaves. People were lying like lizards in the sun, while others bobbed up and down idly in the water. It was picture perfect. A postcard depicting the very best of lazy, hot holiday relaxation.

It felt like two hundred degrees Fahrenheit outside, and I grabbed a cold Coke from the bar fridge and climbed into a hammock, which was swinging invitingly on the patio. Nestled comfortably in its folds, I experienced this amazing sensation of weightlessness, as if I was suspended in midair, floating on the wind itself.

Instant relaxation. Immediate bliss.

I lay there sipping my Coke happily—although I did think I would be choosing a G&T next—while looking out over the quiet sea. With each cool sip, each gentle sway, and the feeling of the cool sea breeze on my face, I started to feel more calm and serene than I'd felt in ages. The feeling was like catching up with an old dear friend who I hadn't seen in years.

And then a thought.

Why the hell sit and look at the beach, when I could be on it?

I jumped out of the hammock and quickly changed into my bathing suit.

Sunglasses. *Check.*

Sunscreen. *Check.*

Towel. *Check.*

Hat and book. *Check.*

Upbeat vacation attitude. *Double check.*

I shoved everything into my beach bag, one of my own creations, and headed out as fast as I could. I was halfway to the lounge chairs—

When I froze, right there on the snow-white sand. Something was very wrong.

It took a few seconds for my brain to realize that I'd forgotten my flip-flops as the hot sand scalded my feet. I ran screeching for the nearest lounger and jumped onto it, eagerly rubbing my fiery feet.

When the stinging had finally worn off to a mild glow, I stretched out and got to focus on my most important job—relaxing. Well, just as soon as I covered my pale body in SPF 50+ (at least). My quest to find the perfect sunscreen, one that doesn't wash off and doesn't smell like a banana and a coconut had a child, is very ongoing. But I think I've finally found it. This one didn't wash off; in fact, it was so permanent it would probably survive the total nuclear destruction of the planet. Once the billowing mushroom clouds and ash had settled, all that would be left were cockroaches wearing this sunscreen.

And I needed to wear sunscreen like that because I don't tan, I burn. Being blessed with strawberry blond hair and a freckly complexion means I never really change color—to anything other than bright red, that is. If I'd had the money, I might have considered a spray tan so that when I pulled off my dress and exposed my body, I didn't look like I glowed in the dark.

"Bonjour, madame," a little singsong voice said behind me. I turned. "Would you like a drink?" the waiter asked in a thick French accent, which always makes things sound so much more appealing.

Now that is the life. Lying on the beach while waiters bring you fabulous drinks. I scanned the menu until I found my poison.

"This one," I said, pointing at the picture of a coconut shell oozing with umbrellas and pieces of pineapple.

"Of course, madame." He turned and disappeared.

I gazed around the beach again. A few people looked like they'd been lying in the sun for days, dark and bronzed to the point of being shiny. A couple of children were splashing in the shallow waters and attempting to build sandcastles, but the sand was so soft and flyaway that they were failing dismally. Some energetic souls were canoeing while others were playing Frisbee. In the distance I could even make out the small silhouette of someone fishing on the sandbar. Personally, I've never really seen the point of physical exertion on holiday.

Soon my waiter was back and handing me the most tropical drink I'd ever seen. Navigating your lips to the rim was a challenge in itself; one had to first part the sea of umbrellas and twirly straws, and then push through the sea of floating fruit.

But when I sipped it…

Cool.

Strong.

Delicious.

I placed it on the little table that was attached to the lounger and opened my book, but as I started raising it, something caught my attention. *Someone.*

To my left, about three loungers down, sat a man. The person of interest stuck out like a sore thumb, and I couldn't believe I hadn't noticed him sooner. For starters, he was the only person *not* wearing a bathing suit. Instead, he was dressed in a shirt and shorts. He didn't look relaxed, either. Far, *far* from it.

He sat bolt upright in his chair, had a laptop perched on his crossed knees and an iPad and cell phone on the table next to him. Technology overload, especially for the beach.

Stranger than the menagerie of gadgets, though, was the fact that his hands were hovering just above the keys.

Not moving. Not typing.

I must have watched him for about five minutes, and in that time he did nothing more than stare at the computer screen. He was so still that I wondered if he hadn't fallen asleep, or in some bizarre twist of fate, had maybe died in that position and rigor mortis had set in. I studied him a bit more.

Scruffy thing.

Messy, dark blond hair highlighted with flecks of gray. Not that he was old, he was obviously just one of those guys who acquired the Clooney-style salt-and-pepper look early on. If I had to guess his age, I would say midthirties. Big, dark sunglasses, not the cool kind, either. *Well*, nothing I recognized anyway. He also had more than the start of a beard—definitely a week or two more than a five-o'clock shadow. Perhaps he was a hipster? Perhaps he was contemplating obscure ukulele bands, wondering whether vinyl was too mainstream, if it was time to switch back to cassette tapes, or what filter to put on his next Instagram pic?

But whatever he was, he was not my thing. *At all*. He might have been my type several years ago, but all that had changed since clean-cut Trevv…I sighed. I would probably never date such a good-looking guy again. That's shallow, I know. But it did feel good having someone so good-looking on my arm.

My eyes moved from his hairy, unkempt face to his shirt. He was wearing a short-sleeve button-down shirt, off-whitish in color.

But when I studied it closer, I realized that it had definitely once been white. Poor thing had probably ended up in the colored load of washing, giving it a strange sort of bilious greeny-creamy, beige hue. The top few buttons of his shirt were undone, and you could definitely see a fair splattering of chest hair. Again, not really my thing.

His shorts were another story altogether. They were a strange length, neither here nor there. Sort of knee length, sort of not. They were made from a hot, heavy-looking black fabric—who wears that to the beach? He looked tall. Not freakishly so, but definitely taller than average. Large, broad, and well built. Not a gym bunny, though. In fact, he looked like the kind of guy that had never set foot in a gym—not his thing.

Creative type, I imagined. Advertising maybe? Advertising types often have that intense vibe about them—trust me, I know. They always look like they're ready to pounce and sell you something "new and improved" with a "money-back guarantee"…*but wait there's more*.

And then, just as I was convinced he was indeed dead and rigor mortis had set in and perhaps I should investigate further, he opened his mouth and started mumbling something.

He was talking to himself!

What on earth was he saying? The mumbling soon escalated until it looked like he was having a full-blown conversation with himself. His hands even joined in at times, gesticulating and flapping. In fact, if I watched closely enough, I could almost distinguish two different personalities having a conversation with each other.

It was quite comical, really. I was still staring at him and coming up with scenarios in my head that could explain his behavior—most ended with him being some kind of crazy person, like the guy that stands on the highway preaching at the passing cars. I was just starting to wonder if he, too, believed in the "invasion" when I was jolted back to reality by a sudden movement and loud noise. He had, very suddenly—and very violently—slammed his computer shut and was now looking straight into my prying gaze. It was as if he'd sensed I was staring at him. Mortified, I quickly averted my eyes and buried my face in my book, hoping that I hadn't caused any offense.

CHAPTER FIVE

ص

*I*t was suddenly very quiet around me—the shrill, excited shrieks of children and the splashing of water had all disappeared. I guess I must have fallen asleep because suddenly…

"Hey." Someone shook my arm rather hard. "I think you need to get out of the sun. You've been asleep for a while."

I jumped. Shocked by the voice that was suddenly very real and right next to me—an American voice. I rubbed my eyes and looked up, coming face-to-face with a pair of Bradley Cooper–blue eyes.

I must still be asleep. Dreaming.

"Thought I would wake you, you're getting really burned." Blue-Eyed Cooper spoke again in a husky, sexy-sounding voice.

How truly peculiar. If dreams had hidden meanings, what the hell did this mean? Or if Dr. Freud was right and everyone in your dreams actually represents a part of yourself; what did a male version of me as Bradley Cooper standing on the beach mean? Curious.

The blue eyes looked at me oddly. "Um…are you okay? I think maybe you've had too much sun or something?"

Suddenly I started getting a strange feeling. Very strange. This was starting to feel less and less like a dream. I squinted my eyes in an attempt to block out the glare that was partially silhouetting him. And as the blinding light lessened and the rest of his facial features came into proper focus, I noticed the beard, the scruffy dark blond hair, and those grayish streaks...

It was Laptop Guy.

"I think you need to get out of the sun," he repeated.

My confusion must have shown on my face, because he leaned in close, looking at me with the kind of concern you might have if you saw someone mixing paisley and pinstripes.

He spoke again. This time his words were slow and deliberate.

"The...sun...HOT...too...long...in...it."

Why was he speaking like Yoda?

I looked around. The sun had shifted its position in the sky, and then I became aware of an intense stinging sensation coating my entire body.

"How long have I been here?"

"Long enough," he said.

I tried to move, but winced. "Ouch." I glanced down at my various appendages and could see they had turned a lobster-esque color.

"Shit."

"Yep. Like I said. Too much sun."

"I didn't realize I'd fallen asleep."

He stuck out an accusing finger and pointed straight ahead at my empty coconut cocktail. "Those things are deadly. I had one yesterday and walked around in a daze. Bit liberal with the rum, if you ask me."

I nodded and when I did, noticed that my head felt heavy. Laptop Guy continued to stand there casting a much-needed shadow across me as I set about gathering my things and shoving them into my bag. But as I swung my feet over the side of the lounger and onto the sand…

"Crap, that's hot."

I immediately recoiled. Like touching a frying pan that had been left on the stove overnight.

"Don't you have sandals?"

I shook my head, "I forgot to bring them."

"Well," he said quite seriously, "I could throw you over my shoulder?"

"Huh?" I looked up at Laptop Guy and scrutinized his face for the telltale signs of jest—there were none. So I waited a moment or two for the…*"Just joking!"* to come, but it didn't.

"You're not being serious?"

"Well, what other options do you have?"

"No! I'm not letting you fling me over your shoulder. That's just…weird."

"Fine," he said, looking totally unfazed before shrugging his shoulders and walking away. "Good luck!" I heard him say as he disappeared out of sight.

Was that supposed to be sarcastic? It was hard to tell by the tone of his voice. Because *"Good luck!"* is usually the kind of thing you say to someone who's about to take an exam or their driver's license test. Not someone who's about to burn the soles of their feet to a cinder. That's just sarcastic.

Oh, I'm about to stick my hand in a blender…*"Good luck!"*

Oh, I'm about to fall face-first off a very high cliff…*"Good luck!"*

Oh, I'm about to have my toes burned off by a wayward fireball… *"Good luck!"*

Now I didn't care if he had the eyes of Bradley Cooper and the face of Ian Somerhalder—he was just a big sarcastic prick with a beard and weird shorts. This sudden surge of irritation gave me the boost of adrenaline I needed to counteract my slightly woozy, wobbly feeling. My room was only a few yards away, but the sand felt like it had been baking on the surface of Mercury. I was going to have to muster up the courage to make a quick dash and hope that I reached the other side without scalding blisters and boils.

And so I ran.

You know what it's like…you're at the gym, you're on the treadmill, or the stepper, and you're watching the countdown clock. You swore blind that you'd do twenty minutes of exercise, but as the timer reaches the last minute, the last thirty seconds, it feels *impossible* to carry on. Each step becomes painful, as if your entire body is weighted down by a hundred pounds of concrete. That's how it felt. The closer I got to my room, the worse it got. And the last few steps were completely unbearable.

Finally I reached my room, flung open the door, and ran for the bathtub. The cool water couldn't have come soon enough and I felt instant relief.

But not so relieved when I looked in the mirror and an apparition stared back at me.

Red is not my color. I avoid it at all costs and in all forms: lipstick, dresses, accessories, and sometimes I even avoid standing next to people dressed in red, or stop signs. It really doesn't jell with my red hair and freckles. So when I looked in the mirror and realized I was red from head to toe, *well*, I was very unhappy.

Worst of all were the big white stripes down the sides of my face and large white circles around my eyes where my sunglasses had been.

I looked positively freakish. *Hey*, just throw me into one of those shows next to the bearded woman and the fire-eating dragon man; I would have fit right in. I *tsk*ed loudly at my stupidity and realized that my lips also felt burned. There goes the possibility of making out with a scuba instructor, or any kind of instructor—or any member of the male species for that matter. Not that I was expecting any such holiday dalliance.

Luckily I'd brought a bottle of moisturizing after-sun cream. I couldn't believe I had let this happen. I started applying the soothing cream as liberally as I could, but my skin was so hot and dry that it seemed to suck the cream up like a thirsty camel. About ten layers later, the stinging started to dissipate, and my thoughts went back to Laptop Guy.

Only one thought, really:

Why were men such a-holes? I'd definitely developed a general mistrust of men. I now suspected most—*if not all*—of cheating, and most—*if not all*—of being monstrous, evil pigs. I had become sensitive, cautious, and suspicious. Rightfully so.

If a guy held the door open for me, I was sure he was just trying to sneak a peek at my ass as I walked in front of him.

If a man let me go in front of him in a line—the same thing applied.

If a man said he was running late—out drinking with the guys and flirting with chicks.

Going out to buy milk—banging his secretary.

Playing golf with his friends—definitely clubbing baby seals.

I'd often thought back to all of Trevv's late nights, conferences away, out-of-town fund-raisers, and other such things that I never went to because, *"Shame, you'd be bored to death, babe. Not your cup of tea."*

We had been leading such separate lives for the last six months of our relationship. The signs were all there, staring me straight in the face, but I'd missed them, or maybe ignored them.

I thought about one evening in particular. It had been another one of those "not my cup of tea" functions, according to Trevv anyway. In retrospect he'd been saying that a lot, and now I could see it had nothing to do with his gentlemanly consideration of my feelings, and everything to do with wanting to spend alone time with Tess. Clearly I was a terrible inconvenience.

I'd gone in the end, but it had been one of the most painful evenings of my life. From the moment I arrived, it felt as though everyone in the room was whispering and staring. At the time I'd written it off to jealousy; I was carrying the latest—not yet in the shops—Chloé bag and was wearing a rather fabulous dress by a new up-and-coming South African designer that was *so* cutting edge. But looking back now, they were staring because they knew.

"Shame, there she is. I wonder if she knows about Trevv and Tess?"

"Oh my God, I can't believe he brought her. With Tess right there?"

Tess had been so nice to me, too, that evening. God, I'd been so blind.

I couldn't help wondering how many of our mutual friends had known, too, or at least suspected and not bothered to tell me. How mortifying. I thought back to all those dinners we attended, that time I went shopping with his best friend to buy him a thirtieth birthday present. The idea that everyone knew, except me, left me feeling sick to my stomach. Had I been a laughingstock? Had he been high-fiving his friends while telling them he was fucking the hottest girl in the world and his stupid girlfriend didn't even know?

God! I was driving myself mad again. So I pushed the thoughts out of my mind and forced myself to get dressed and ready for dinner. I poured half a bottle of thick foundation on my red face, which just made me look like I was wearing a mask. I then tried to hide the cracked red landscape of my lips with an excessive dollop of lip gloss—this just made me look like I could charge by the hour. *Oh well*, it's not like I was trying to impress anyone, and I could probably do with the extra cash anyway.

I walked down to the bar feeling like I was radiating UV heat onto all of the people around me—and of course in my mind they were staring. But I kept a brave—if somewhat scary-looking—face and walked as fast as I could without chafing my sensitive skin.

The whole place looked mystical at night. The lights from the buildings shined onto the white sand and sea, giving them an iridescent quality, as if someone had tipped a can of gold paint into the water.

I walked down a long path through the lush gardens, which were made even more lush and tropical-looking under the green lights that were shining on them. And when I got there, the bar was amazing. It was actually an island built right in the middle of the pool with a little bridge that leads you there—a bridge that I would hate to walk across after a few drinks.

On the one side of the bar you could swim all the way up to the counter and sit in seats that rose up out of the water, giving you the opportunity to sip drinks while half-submerged. Definitely something to put on the to-do list.

Something that was definitely *not* on the to-do list, though, was bumping into Laptop Guy again. But there he was. Sitting front and center at the bar. Still with his fingers hovering over the computer keys. Still not typing. I turned and tried to slink away unseen into the shadows but...

"Hey!" I heard him call out. I froze. Was he calling for me?

"Hey, sunshine."

Great. He clearly hadn't left his sarcasm back on the beach.

CHAPTER SIX

I figured a few things could happen at this stage:

1. I could wait patiently for my invisibility superpower to kick in and vanish into thin air.
2. I could play possum, and pretend to be dead so he'd leave me alone.
3. I could pretend I didn't hear him and start walking away as fast as possible and hope he didn't call out to me again.
4. I could jump into the pool and swim away—although that might come across as slightly suspicious.
5. Or I could just turn around, smile, and pretend I was really happy to see him (even though I wasn't).

"Heeyyyaaa there, stranger." I mentally slapped myself the second the words were out of my mouth. Way, *way* too enthusiastic.

He looked at me with a blank expression; at least I thought it was blank. It was difficult to tell through the beard that obscured the bottom half of his face and the shadow that obscured the top half.

"Hey." His greeting was far less enthusiastic and much more appropriate.

"*Heeeyyyaaa*," I answered again with excessive cool, calm, and collected indifference, hoping it might counteract my overly enthused opening line. "So, nice night…or whatever." I ended the sentence with a shrug that felt painful. It was all such a terrible and unconvincing display of casualness. What had happened to me? I used to be so fricking cool, always the coolest girl in my group. Where the hell had that girl gone?

He smiled at me. "Yeah, it's a nice night…or whatever, I guess. Can I get you a drink? Or not…whatever."

No, you can't, you sarcastic prick. "Sure. Thanks. That would be nice."

"Nothing with rum in it, I'm guessing?"

"God no! Something with no alcohol would be great."

He slammed his laptop shut again and ordered two Cokes.

"I'm Chris, by the way," he said, extending his hand for the obligatory shaking. I shook it.

"Anne, or Annie, some people call me Annie." Truthfully only Trevv had called me Anne. Stormy always maintained it was a very bad sign that he didn't have a pet name for me. She was a huge believer in pet names; she even made up names for inanimate objects.

"Nice to meet you, Annie Anne."

The bartender placed the glasses on the bar, and the sound of the clinking ice as it knocked against the glass and the pop-fizz of the bubbles was very inviting. I made my way to the bar and pulled out a stool, but as I was lowering myself onto it I winced in red-hot sun-burned pain.

"Looks like you *really* got too much sun today," Chris said, eyeing me up and down.

"That's an understatement."

"Yeah." He shrugged. "I thought about waking you up earlier, but I didn't want to come across as pervy or anything," he said, sipping his drink.

"Why pervy?"

"Well, I didn't want you to think I was staring at you...or staring back at you." I think I detected a smirk underneath all that beardy fuzz.

I felt my cheeks go hot—hotter than they already were. Thank God I was bright red from the sunburn, because otherwise my cheeks would have flushed a neon crimson color. Oh, embarrass-ment, my constant companion.

"Sorry about that. I was just wondering what you were doing. It sort of looked like you were talking to yourself."

He smiled, and I have to admit that despite the Sasquatch-style fa-cial hair, his smile was nice. Dazzling even. It had a quality to it that was contagious, and without thinking about it, I felt a small smile twitching on my lips.

"Occupational hazard," he replied casually.

"Oh really?" I wondered what occupation led to talking to your-self in public.

"I'm a screenwriter. It's always best to write dialogue when you're saying it out loud. It's more natural that way. So I find I talk to myself a lot."

A mental light bulb switched on and I wondered why I hadn't

guessed it earlier. Of course he was a writer. That explained it all. The unkempt hairy face and unintentional hobo-chic vibe he had going on. He probably smoked way too many cigarettes and drank copious amounts of coffee, too.

"So what are you working on at the moment?" I must admit I was intrigued; it's not every day you meet a screenwriter.

"Now that's the million-dollar question, isn't it?" His tone had changed suddenly. "Let's just say, I've got a bit of writer's block. Which is a big problem, since my script is due in two weeks."

"How much have you written?"

He opened his computer again and the screen lit up. "Exactly two words. 'Scene One.'" He slammed it shut once more and I wondered how the poor thing survived that constant battery. He swigged his Coke down as if it was hard liquor and he was hoping it would calm his clearly jittery nerves.

"I kind of noticed you weren't really typing. So what can you do to get over the block? How do you get inspired again?"

"You're looking at it." He said, leaning back in his bar stool and indicating his surroundings with open arms. "That's why I came here. I'm supposed to be writing a romantic comedy about a couple who meet at a tropical resort—*yeah, yeah*, I know it sounds clichéd. *Forgetting Sarah Marshall* meets *Just Go with It*, but it's what people want."

"Those are great movies. I love Jennifer Aniston."

Chris did a weird little swivel on his chair and looked at me mockingly. "Don't tell me you're into the whole 'a girl is left at the altar and goes on her honeymoon alone where she unexpectedly falls in love—'"

"That actually happened to my cousin."

"You're kidding!" He sounded amused.

"Nope. She met the guy on the plane, they've been together for a year already."

"Okay, what about 'a guy is in a plane crash, gets amnesia, and forgets he has a pregnant wife but ends up falling in love with her all over again because they are meant to be together.'"

"That hasn't happened to anyone I know...*yet*." I found myself smiling at the thought, because if that was going to ever happen, it would probably happen to one of my friends. "But I love that, it sounds great."

Chris held his face in his hands dramatically. "So you like the whole 'a girl falls in love with a guy just by reading his blog, and she goes in search of him but it turns out it was her best friend all along, and then she realizes she's been in love with him for years,' too?"

"Love it," I said happily.

He shook his head even harder. "You're too far gone, aren't you? A hopeless case."

I wasn't sure whether he was joking, or whether I should be offended by his statement. It was hard to tell if he was being rude or sarcastic or funny. "What do you mean 'hopeless'?"

"I bet you've bought into the Valentine's Day conspiracy, too. You probably buy chocolate hearts and sentimental cards without realizing that it's all just a moneymaking scam. And I bet you fall in love without realizing that it's all just an illusion, just the neurons in your brain firing in a specific way that gives you that warm fuzzy feeling. Chemistry, not love."

I blinked for a few moments, trying to take in the full implications of his words. "So you write romantic comedies? But don't believe in love?"

"Bingo!" Chris said, clicking his fingers for the waiter to bring him another drink. "You don't have to believe in something to write about it."

"No wonder you've got writer's block!"

Chris looked at me for a while as if he was really processing my words. "Or maybe I've just finally run out of soppy, clichéd 'boy meet-cutes girl and has funny happy ending' ideas. Maybe I'm just a cynical bastard." He gave a small chuckle. "Anyway, I doubt I'll get inspired here. I hate the beach."

"No one hates the beach!" I laughed a little.

"I do."

"But look." I swept my arms around. "Warm, tropical, beautiful, relaxing."

"It's that whole water part I don't like. I haven't swum since I was six."

"Really? Why?"

"Let's just say"—Chris forced a small smile—"that the water and I had a bit of a disagreement and it nearly won."

It took me a moment to get what he was saying. "God, you nearly drowned?"

He shrugged casually, as if it wasn't a big deal. "Our relationship's never been the same since. But enough about me. I feel like I've just told a total stranger my entire life story. Your turn."

"What do you want to know?" I suddenly felt a little disappointed. I was enjoying this conversation; it was a welcome distraction to think about someone and something else for a change.

"Okay. What does Annie Anne do?" He looked at me with genuine interest as he ran his fingers through that salt-and-pepper hair.

I wondered what he looked like under that beard. Probably really good-looking.

"I'm a…well, no. I *was* a stylist for TV ads and such. Then I gave that up to work at a fashion magazine. But that didn't really work out." I must have given something away in my tone and body language, because he was leaning in curiously.

"Mmm, I can sense a story there." He leaned in further.

I rolled my eyes dramatically and gave a sigh. "You have no idea!"

Chris eyed me for a moment or two. "Okay, Annie, you got me. I'm officially intrigued. Bring it on."

"Mmmm." I was thoughtful for a moment. I wasn't sure if I should tell him, but there is something nice about talking to a total stranger. Someone completely removed from the situation. And he had such nice eyes, too.

"Okay. Why not?" And then I opened my mouth, and it all just fell out.

The nipple clamps and live sex show with leather straps. The arrest and attempted murder misunderstanding, the broken (priceless— worth more than my annual salary) shoe. The camels (and starving, dehydrated orphans) that had been rented for the photo shoot. Getting fired, getting my heart broken, and getting an unglamorous job. Living on a diet of self-help books. And finally, my nudist landlord and his obsession with recycling.

And the more I talked, the more Chris laughed. As if my recent life story was the funniest thing he'd ever heard. By the time I got to the part about the vibrators crawling across the floor, I swear he had actual tears in his eyes. Up until that point I'd never seen any of those incidents as vaguely humorous.

But as I was telling the story—with enough distance, emotionally as well as physically—I started seeing the absurd comedy of it all. It happened slowly at first; a small chuckle, a little smile, and then as if I'd opened the floodgates, I started laughing. And by the time I told him about Trevv spanking me with the greasy spatula, I, too, was in full-blown fits of crying laughter. I could feel the tears rolling down my cheeks, and at some stage I think I actually heard myself snort. But I didn't care.

"Their names are actually Trevv and Tess?" he asked in between grunts and snorts of laughter. "How cheesy can you get? You couldn't make that shit up. Trevv and Tess. Wow!"

"Yes, and he spells Trevv with a double *v*. He says it stands out on a business card. It's pretty lame." I guffawed loudly, which only seemed to egg him on further. But as our laughter tapered off, our eyes met and a little flicker of something jetted up my spine.

What was it? Attraction? It couldn't be. I hadn't been attracted to anyone in ages; did I even know what that still felt like? Maybe I was confusing the feeling with the hot tingling sensation of my sun-burned skin and residual rum hangover.

Chris then raised his glass in a toast. "To Trevv and Tess. May they enjoy many happy years of nipple clamping, spanking, and introducing themselves to people with the most sickening couple name on the planet."

"They could turn it into one of those celebrity couple names, *Tress*," I suggested, holding my glass up. This made Chris smile even more.

"To Tress then."

"And if we were a couple, we could call ourselves Crannie," Chris quickly said, which caused me to laugh.

"Annis," I suddenly added, laughing at the sound of it.

"Touché, Annie Anne." Chris clinked my glass and smiled at me.

"I was going to go to dinner, would you like to join me?" Chris suddenly asked.

"Uh…" I hesitated. Images of the last time I had dinner with a man went flying through my head…crying so much he'd offered up his napkin mid-entrée. I wasn't sure I was fit enough to eat food with members of the opposite sex. Like a horse that hadn't been broken in yet, I was not to be trusted.

But then I remembered what Lilly had said about finding a man to practice on, and Chris seemed like a good option. Nonthreatening, not my type, no chance of messy feelings.

Why not?

"Fine." I climbed off the bar stool, still feeling slightly uncertain.

Chris shot me a playful smile. "Don't worry, Annie Anne. It's just dinner. It's not like I'm expecting to get lucky at the end of it."

CHAPTER SEVEN

~

*I*nside the restaurant, we were ushered to a small table that was right on the edge of the pool. It was illuminated only by candlelight and, dare I say it, was a little awkwardly romantic. We sat and I immediately began studying the menu, to give me something to do. After a moment or two I put the menu down and looked across at Chris. He peered over his menu at me with a quizzical eye.

"What's wrong?" Chris suddenly asked.

I shook my head. "It's just so weird to be having dinner with a complete stranger. In a strange place."

He put down his menu and smiled softly. "Sure beats eating alone, though, doesn't it?"

"I guess."

We both lifted our menus simultaneously, and after a few more seconds of reading through the delicious dishes, he added, "Besides, I don't think we qualify as strangers anymore." He said it with a knowing look. "So feel free to order the prawns without being worried about me judging you for using your hands. Hey, take it one step further if you want and get crab and a pair of pliers."

I laughed, let out a huge, dramatic sigh, and immediately felt more comfortable. "Oh, you say that now. But you haven't seen me eat prawns. It gets messy."

"Is that a challenge? Bring it." He called the waiter over and ordered a massive plate of prawns to share, asking him to bring a few extra napkins.

And Chris was so right; this was definitely better than eating alone.

Two hours later, a large pile of prawn remains, and five hundred and seventy-five jokes, puns, and jibes about Trevv and Tess behind us, Chris and I found ourselves finishing dessert. But as the last bite was had, the whole mood suddenly changed and Chris looked serious. Oh God, had I done something wrong…again? Was he thinking of an excuse to get away from me? I waited anxiously for him to say something.

"I'm sorry, though," he finally said, looking up at me.

"Sorry about what?"

"About what happened to you, Trevv cheating."

I shrugged. "What can you do, hey?"

"I could beat him up for you."

I laughed. "You?"

"Why not? I work out." He flexed his fairly unimpressive bicep. "Besides, you'd probably be doing me a favor."

"Why?" I was curious now. Very.

Chris took a slow sip of his drink and put the glass down. He played with the water droplets that were running down the side of it for a while, then he looked up at me again and smiled. His mood changed so quickly, it was jarring. "My dad cheated on my mom."

"Wow, I'm sorry."

"It's fine. It was a long time ago. We're all okay, except my mom's never really been the same since."

"I can relate," I said slowly as I felt the emotion sweeping over me. Something in me had died the day I'd found Trevv with Tess, and all that was left was this insecure, unsure shadow of the person I once was.

"She always said that the lying was the worst part. If he had just told her—"

"Exactly! If Trevv had just told me instead of running round behind my back lying constantly."

Chris went back to fiddling with his glass, and I could tell there was still more to this story.

Chris perked up again. I could see he was trying to shake off the dark cloud hanging over him. He seemed to do that a lot. "Anyway, beating Trevv up might help me work through some of my daddy issues. It would be therapeutic."

I laughed. "And a lot cheaper than seeing a shrink."

"Exactly. Now you have to let me do it."

"As much as I would love to see Trevv beaten to a pulp by a big, strong man like you, it just wouldn't be enough. Besides, he'd probably enjoy it."

Chris started nodding vigorously. "The classic Medea story. That's what you need."

"Medea?"

"It's a Greek tragedy about a wife who takes revenge on her unfaithful husband. In fact, the scorned woman seeking revenge is a very popular movie plot."

"And did Medea get her revenge in the end?"

"She killed all their children."

"Oh."

"But in your case I wouldn't go full *Fatal Attraction*. I'd go from some light revenge comedy, like *First Wives Club*, or *The Women*."

I burst out laughing. "I loved those movies."

"Everyone loves to see the scorned girl get her revenge."

"I wish. I'm still waiting for mine."

"You'll get your revenge one day, Annie Anne. In the meantime, do you want to go for a walk on the beach? Get rid of some of these calories?" Chris patted his stomach and stuck it out for added effect. He was the kind of guy that just seemed so natural and relaxed. There was something sexy about a man that was just himself. Not some Ken doll version of a human, which was Trevv.

Maybe Trevv hadn't been so good-looking after all.

"Sounds nice," I replied.

I always think the beach looks better at night. It has a mystical quality to it. When the sounds of people have vanished and all you can hear are the soft, gentle movements of the water as it crashes lightly against the rocks and crawls up the sand. The sky looked like a child had thrown silver glitter across it, and the sand still felt warm from the day.

We walked in silence for a while before I decided to broach the subject again with a question that had been troubling me throughout dinner. "Do you really not believe in love?"

"Nope." His answer came out fast, and sounded so matter-of-fact.

"Do you think it was because of your parents?"

"Oh please, now you just sound like my school counselor."

"Well, maybe she was right?"

"*He* was a total quack. He actually suggested that I write a letter to my six-year-old self and forgive him."

"Forgive him for what?" As I asked, the smile on Chris's face faltered again. But only for a second. He quickly recovered from whatever feeling he was having.

He shrugged playfully. "Like I said, the guy was a total weirdo. Never listen to someone that wears handmade leather sandals."

"Why?"

"Come on, Annie. Don't you know anything? Only organic-vegan nudists and people who think they're the second coming wear sandals like that."

I burst out laughing. Chris was funny, no doubt about it. But in the short time I'd known him, I also realized he had an uncanny ability to steer the conversation away from anything vaguely serious by using humor. Not that I minded, God knows I needed the laughs. But it just made me aware that there was so much more to Chris than met the eye, and so much more to this story of his. But I left it alone and played along; I hadn't had this much fun in ages.

"My cousin Lilly went to a therapist once who kept repeating her name…" I cleared my throat and put on my best therapist voice. "Lilly, what is your first memory? And how did that make you feel, Lilly?"

"See! Besides, we men aren't meant to talk about our feelings. We're meant to grow beards and chop wood and wrestle animals to the ground. Feelings are for you womenfolk."

"While we're cooking your dinner barefoot and polishing your shoes?"

"Exactly," he said.

"Okay, Chris." I stopped walking. "I just want to get this straight…so you *don't* believe in real love and are *never* going to get married?"

"Exactly. And even if I wanted to tie the knot, I probably never would, because I've never been in love and I'm pretty sure I'm incapable of those feelings."

"What?" I was taken aback by his statement. "How's that even possible? How old are you?"

"Why, how old are you?"

"Twenty-seven. You?"

"Thirty-three."

"Okay, okay…" I was trying to gather my thoughts. This was possibly one of the most bizarre things I'd heard in a while. Who's never been in love? "So you've never dated before?"

"I've dated. I've had a few serious girlfriends, but it was never love. They all ended badly, as you can imagine. They all thought they would be the girl that would change me. Make me believe in love, melt my cold heart or something…" He tapered off.

I thought about those poor women, desperately in love and waiting for reciprocation that never came. It all seemed kind of cruel to me. I mean, why even get into a relationship if you didn't see it going anywhere?

"I never led any of them on, if that's what you're thinking. I told them all up front that I don't believe in love," he added quite quickly and defensively, as if he had guessed what I'd been thinking.

My feelings of pity then switched allegiances; it was Chris that I now felt sorry for. I wondered what else could have happened in his life to make him feel like this. Even if he was working very hard at denying it, everyone wanted to be loved.

"Look what happened to you. All in the name of love. Don't you wish you'd never fallen in love with Trevv in the first place?"

I thought hard about his question, and while it was true that I'd been devastated, and it had affected almost every aspect of my life, I still believed in love and ultimately wanted it one day, despite my current self-imposed dry spell.

"Nah, I like Valentine's hearts and soppy sentimental cards." I smiled and Chris smiled back. "If you don't believe in love, I'm pretty sure I can change your mind. All you have to do is hang out with my cousin Lilly and her new BF Damien. Trust me, they are *sooo* in love it's almost obscene."

"But that's only an illusion. They *think* they're in love. But trust me, when the chemicals stop flowing it will wilt and die like a dead flower."

"Whoa! Cynical much?"

He smiled at me again. "Realistic."

"So all relationships are doomed to become dead flora?"

"Look at yours."

"But not all relationships are like that," I defended.

"Name one famous person that hasn't been divorced."

I started thinking about it and he was right. Every single celebrity I could think of had gotten divorced, many more than twice. Even my parents had gotten divorced, and Lilly's mother was better than Joan Collins at getting divorced. She'd basically turned it into an Olympic sport.

"But that's terrible proof. Everyone knows celebrities aren't real people anyway," I said.

"I'm not so sure about that. I dated a semifamous actress once, and that pasta strainer she threw across the kitchen felt very real to me."

"And why was she tossing kitchen utensils at you?"

"It probably had something to do with my previously mentioned philosophy on love. Or perhaps she just hated the pasta strainer."

I laughed again. We'd been talking so much that I hadn't noticed how far we'd walked until I turned around and saw that the lights from the resort looked like glowing pinpricks. It dawned on me how completely alone we were.

Behind us stood what looked like a large, deserted beach house. You could see that it had been abandoned for quite some time. Vines and palm trees were growing through empty windowpanes and doorways. It was nothing more than a mere skeleton, and paint was peeling off its dry bones in thick chunks. But it was eerily beautiful, in a sad way. The floor of the patio was completely covered in white sand from the years of wind blowing through the empty rooms.

"Come, let's go check it out," Chris said, striding across the beach and beckoning for me to follow. The house was designed in that typical Mauritian style. Deep wraparound verandas with overhanging roofs propped up by imposing columns. I could only imagine what it must have looked like in its heyday.

There's always something creepy about an abandoned house, and as you well know, they are the common start to many a horror film. Teens find an abandoned cabin in the woods, and three scenes later someone is chopping off their arms with a chainsaw.

And the inside was even creepier. Bits of broken furniture lay scattered across the floor like old dry bones, and the walls were decorated with graffiti. We moved through the rooms, old leaves and God only knows what else crunching under our feet, until we reached a steep staircase.

"Watch your step," Chris said suddenly, taking me by the hand

and helping me up the dark staircase. We walked up to the top and peered around the corner.

"Ooohh." Chris's eyes lit up with devilishness. "What do we have here?"

And there, seated on the floor, were about six teenagers, not older than fourteen, playing spin the bottle. We both watched for a moment or two as a pimply-looking boy with braces spun the bottle. It came to rest pointing at a pretty young brunette with a Cindy Crawford mole. They exchanged awkward, spastic looks before their friends started cheering them on. I cringed as they leaned in and engaged in what was probably the worst kiss I'd ever seen. Clearly these were first—or very near first—kisses.

Chris and I struggled to hold back a laugh.

"Watch this," Chris whispered in my ear before jumping out from the stairwell.

"And what's going on here?" he boomed in an authoritative voice. The reaction was immediate; the kids went scrambling in all directions. One of the girls started shouting like a stuck record, "Please don't tell our parents. Please don't tell our parents. Please don't tell our parents."

I couldn't help my loud laughter.

"Just joking," Chris said. "You guys carry on as you were. We were just leaving."

"So you're not going to tell our parents?" the wide-eyed, frightened girl asked with a kind of desperation in her voice.

"I don't even know who your parents are." This seemed to allay their fears. Chris and I then turned, ran down the stairs, and bolted for the beach. We were barely able to contain our laughter, and the second we got outside, it erupted.

"Did you see their little faces," he said, falling to the sand. "It looked like they'd just seen a ghost."

"That was so cruel, by the way. You're a sick sadist. Imagine how you would have felt at that age if an adult did that to you!" We were still laughing as we both settled comfortably onto the sand.

"God, I remember my first kiss as if it were yesterday. It was a total disaster. Also during a game of spin the bottle." Chris's laughter had tapered off as he spoke. "The girl actually told me I was a bad kisser. I don't really blame her, though. I'm sure I sucked—literally, too. Do you know how many years it took me to pluck up the courage to kiss another girl again?"

Chris looked at me and smiled. It made me shift in the sand. All this talk of kissing was giving me a strange feeling. This was one of those conversations that could easily lead to loaded innuendo and flirtation, if you wanted it to. Lilly's words ran through my head again, *a guy to practice on*.

I gazed at Chris; he definitely fit the bill. He didn't believe in love and since I'd sworn off relationships, there was no way I was going to fall in love with him, either. He was the perfect candidate for an innocent practice flirt.

Okay, here goes nothing, Annie.

"And now?" I tried to make my voice sound whispery and sexy. "Has your kissing improved much?" I let the implication hang in the air.

Chris turned and looked at me intensely. "Are you trying to flirt with me, Annie?" His voice was equally whispery and I was wondering what the hell I'd just started here. Maybe this hadn't been such a great idea.

"Uh, sort of." This was suddenly very embarrassing. "I was just seeing if I still had it. You know, practicing. It's been so long."

"It's been a while for me, too, actually."

"Really?"

Chris nodded and gave me this smile that lit up his eyes. I knew his eyes were blue, but I hadn't truly noticed how damn blue they really were. The light blue color jumped out against large jet-black pupils.

"You were pretty good, by the way. You've still got it. I would have definitely gone for it."

"Good to know," I reciprocated with a smile and started to wonder what would have happened if he'd taken the bait and said something like, *"Why don't you be the judge of that yourself"* and leaned in for a kiss. That beard! I'd never kissed a guy with so much facial hair, and all I could think about was the possible prickliness of it all.

We sat in silence for a while. Something strange was happening. The innocent flirting had definitely changed the mood between us. Thankfully Chris finally broke it.

"So, have you dated since Nipple-Gate?"

"Oh my God! I also call it Nipple-Gate!" I shrieked.

"What can I say? Great minds." We shared a tiny look of recognition.

"One. But it was a disaster."

"What happened?"

"I'm pretty sure I scared him shitless. So I've officially removed myself from the market until I'm sane enough to date again."

"That must be hard. You probably get asked out a lot."

I felt a slight fluttering at that comment, even though it was totally untrue.

"Truth is…you know how it took you courage to kiss someone again, because you thought you weren't good at it? Well, that's kind of how I feel."

"That you're not good at kissing?" he asked.

"No, not good at…*you know*…Since Trevv needed to get it somewhere else…and like *that*." I couldn't believe how honest I'd just been with a total stranger, but somehow he seemed to inspire a comfort that I hadn't felt with anyone before.

Chris turned and looked at me, as I focused all my attention and energy on a tiny purple shell that was lying in the sand. I felt way too vulnerable right now to make eye contact. And I was regretting this conversation and hoped he would deflect with humor, as opposed to going into a lengthy discussion about my sexual ability. *Why had I even told him that?*

"Well, we could do it right here if you want and I could rate you out of ten."

We both burst out laughing again. I hadn't laughed like this in months.

"Have you seen Trevv since the incident?"

I hung my head at the mere thought. "Yes. Twice."

"And?"

"It was *sooo* bad. I made a complete idiot of myself."

"I feel your pain. I'm no stranger to embarrassment, either."

I was about to ask him what had happened, when he jumped in again quickly. Avoidance alert.

"So tell me of your embarrassing woes."

"My woes are great indeed," I said.

"I can handle them."

I looked at Chris; there was something so nonthreatening about him. He seemed like the kind of person you could tell anything to. Besides, the memory had been bubbling away for far too long, and it was dying to come out.

"I haven't told anyone this before. It's so totally pathetic."

Chris leaned in.

"I went to his house in the middle of the night and just stared at him and Tess through the kitchen window, for ages. Watching them have a romantic, candlelit dinner, watching them holding hands and kissing. And then I collapsed in the rosebushes and cried like a baby in the mud. How much more pathetic could I get?"

"That's not pathetic, Annie. That's just what heartbreak does to you. You should have seen what it did to my mom. Just another reason I avoid it at all costs."

I nodded. "And the next time I saw Trevv, I ended up telling him I was seeing someone, when I wasn't. I made the guy up on the spot, some imaginary boyfriend called Boyden. And it gets worse, apparently Boyden is from Australia. And is *very* good in bed."

Chris laughed next to me.

"Hey, it's not funny." I nudged him playfully. "If I ever bump into Trevv, I'm going to have to somehow magically conjure myself a man from Down Under, or face even more horrific embarrassment. And I think I've endured enough to last me ten lifetimes."

"Boyden? Is that even a name?"

"Apparently. I looked it up after the fiasco. It's Anglo-Saxon. It means 'messenger.'"

This caused another laugh. "I can just see you Googling it the second you had a chance."

"I phoned my friend Stormy-Rain—"

"Wait, that's a real name?"

"Apparently her mother gave it to her on the day she was born on a green hill, inside a nudist colony during a storm."

"You have interesting friends."

"I do, maybe you'll meet them. Two of them should be here soon. Anyway, Stormy believes that the meaning of names is as important as where you're born and the star sign you're born under. You can tell *everything* about a person with those three things." I rolled my eyes playfully. "She's really weird and we all love her to death for it."

"I wonder what she'd say about Gemini Sven Christophersen of German descent?"

"Who's thaa…Oh, you?" I laughed. I couldn't help it.

"You can see why I chose Chris instead?" He quickly looked down at his watch and tapped it in my direction, and I was surprised to see it was already after twelve.

"It's getting late. I need my beauty sleep." He stood and helped me up.

We walked back to the resort in absolute silence. Strangely it wasn't one of those awkward silences that has you constantly thinking about what to say to break it. It was comfortable. So comfortable that I hadn't really noticed we were back until Chris pointed it out.

"Well this is me"—his words brought me back to reality—"my room."

I looked at it. "Holy shit! You got the big one."

"That's how I roll, baby. Deluxe presidential suite. There're only two." He was deliberately hamming it up for my benefit.

I eyed him up and down—not the kind of guy I would have pegged for a presidential suite.

"What does it look like inside?" But I didn't wait for him to reply or offer. I'd never been in a presidential suite before and was already halfway through the door.

Chris clapped his hands together loudly and rubbed them triumphantly. "Score! And I didn't even have to ply you with alcohol to get you to come back to my room."

"Ha-ha. You wish!" I said, winking at him. We'd sort of naturally fallen into this witty repartee, which I was finding really enjoyable. The kind you might have with a platonic friend you've known for years. Trevv and I had never laughed this much. Maybe in the beginning, but over the two years that laughter had been replaced by a certain silent formality. Especially toward the end. Clear warning sign, I'd just chosen to ignore it.

I'd ignored and overlooked a lot about Trevv actually. *Why?* His image, his outward success, and good looks had gone a long way in making me feel better about myself. If I had a man like that on my arm…That seemed so shallow now. But I guess that was how I'd rolled.

Chris's room was quite frankly ridiculous. Over-the-top. Plush, lush, delish. I didn't know quite where to look first. A massive four-poster bed was pushed up against one of the walls, and a huge open-plan living room came sprawling off it. On the other side of the bed, a palm-filled atrium with massive open shower and Jacuzzi bath seemed to call my name.

"What's up there?" I pointed to the curved staircase that wound its way through the middle of the living space.

"I haven't really been up there properly."

"What!" I started walking up the staircase and emerged into absolute paradise.

I found myself standing on a large wooden deck with a brilliant blue plunge pool in the center. Tall palm trees grew next to the villa, their huge leaves stretching out over the deck, giving you the illusion that you might actually be in the middle of the jungle.

"This is amazing." I walked up to the edge and looked over. Another villa stood next to this one, but you could barely see it tucked behind all the green foliage. "Is that another room?" I pointed across the deck. "How many rooms does this place have?"

"Just the two." Chris was smiling at me.

"This suite is enormous. It's bigger than where I live." I bent down and felt the water; it was so warm. I wouldn't be able to afford a room like this if I saved up my entire salary for the next year. "I'm officially impressed, you must be a very good writer."

"I try," he said, before adding, "although I may not be able to afford this again when I'm an out-of-work screenwriter in two weeks' time."

"I'm sure something will inspire you. How could you not be inspired by this?"

"I hope so." I could hear the worry in his voice. He glanced down at the pool suspiciously, like it was a snake hiding in the grass that could strike at any second. He really did hate water. No wonder he hadn't been up here.

"Well, it's time for me to go back to my little hovel. Think of me while I'm slumming it." I slipped back down the stairs and Chris followed.

"Do you think you'll survive the night, Annie Anne?"

"I'm not sure. It will be very touch-and-go." I walked out of his room onto the wraparound veranda and stopped. I turned around.

Chris was leaning against the doorway and smiled at me. Slowly.

And then it happened again, only this time I knew *exactly* what it was. It was not the sunburn or the residual rum overload. It was totally unexpected, but completely familiar.

My stomach flipped. A rush of warmth started in my face and crept all the way down to my toes. Something inside me glowed and flickered. My lips sprung into a smile that I couldn't help and my thoughts went all fuzzy.

"You know what…I like you, Annie."

Damn, double fuzzy, extra flickery, and flippy.

"What?" I tried not to gush.

"You're not like the girls I usually meet."

"You're not like the guys I usually meet, either." I tried to hold back the massive smile that was threatening to rip my face wide open.

"I had fun tonight." His voice had gone a little whispery again. Had someone suddenly turned up the thermostat?

"We should hang out again tomorrow. If you want?" he asked.

"Yes." That sounded way too eager. *Reel it in, Annie.* "I mean…that would be cool."

And then without thinking, as if I was guided by something instinctual, I walked up to him and planted a kiss on his cheek. He smelled good. His hand came up momentarily and touched my arm and then dropped back to his side.

"Night, Annie Anne." He started closing the door and I was about to walk away, but didn't.

"Why am I not like the girls you usually meet?" I asked tentatively.

Chris raised a brow as if my question had caught him off guard, and I was gripped by a sudden rush of crampy-panic. I shouldn't have asked that; maybe he'd just said it to be nice. Like Disaster Date Guy's *"I'll call you sometime."*

"Never mind. It was a dumb question." I started making my escape again.

"Because you're funny, without trying to be." He said it so loudly that I stopped. "You're a little bit weird, too, in a good way."

"I'm not weird." I swung around and faced him again.

"Of course, sorry, I made a mistake, or not, or whatever, or something or nothing, et cetera." He was trying, but he couldn't keep a smile from forming.

I rolled my eyes. "Fine. Point taken."

"In movies there are different types of heroines, archetypes, and you're the best kind."

"What kind is that?"

"The Plucky Girl, the Girl Next Door."

"Plucky? That doesn't sound great." It sounded somewhat chicken-y.

"No. It is." Chris took a big step toward me. "Trust me. That's the best kind. It's the kind I like to write. The kind the hero always falls for in the end."

I shook my head. "No. That's where you're *very* wrong."

"It's true. You just haven't found the right hero yet. Because when you do, the Annie character will beat all the others hands down."

"Why?"

"Because Annie is the interesting one. The one that lights up the screen with her smile. The one that everyone in the room gravitates toward. The one that wins your heart. She's the forever girl."

"Okay. Wow. Okay. I see." Words fell out of my mouth like water through a sieve. A mad rush of emotion overwhelmed me.

My breath caught in my throat and I realized I was actually close to tears, I could feel them stinging my eyes. "For a nonromantic guy, you really know what to say to a girl. Thank you."

Something inside me was telling me to run up and hug him, but my legs were having none of it and they forced me to turn and walk away without looking back.

That was the nicest thing anyone had ever said to me. *Ever.*

CHAPTER EIGHT

⌣

I woke up bright and early that morning, despite the late night, and found my mind drifting to thoughts of Chris almost immediately. I couldn't stop replaying the things he'd said about me, and I'd been on a kind of buzzy cloud nine ever since. They awakened something inside me that I hadn't felt in ages, not since Trevv anyway.

Confidence. Slight, but there. I was the plucky girl after all. The *forever* girl.

I made myself a cup of coffee and took it outside to the patio. I had a few messages on my phone from Lilly and Jane confirming that they were starting to feel better. I answered the messages and then put the phone away. The world around me hadn't woken up yet. The sea was still and smooth as a piece of polished marble. There was no breeze and everything looked like it had been frozen in time, as if in some kind of suspended animation. The sun was already warm and the air already thick and humid. I took a deep breath, breathing in the calm and tranquility of my surroundings. I felt happy. For the first time in ages.

In fact, I was more than happy. I was full of the sunny, tropical joys of the day; nothing was going to spoil my mood, that is, until I caught a glimpse of myself in the mirror.

How was it possible that I was even redder than yesterday? The skin on my shoulders was already starting to peel, making me look like a scaly amphibian. I moaned loudly and mentally scolded myself for yesterday's stupidity. Today there would be absolutely no activities that involved the sun! So with that in mind, I marched to the reception desk to see what UV-free activities I could book…Hopefully Chris would join me.

But as I walked up to the counter and was just about to ring the bell for service—

I suddenly I felt it.

An intense burning sensation.

As if someone had harnessed the sun's rays with a magnifying glass and was attempting to burn a hole through my already burned back.

And just like the time I'd slipped my keys into my front door and instinctively known something was wrong…I knew now that something was very, *very* wrong.

I froze, refusing to turn around. Instead I focused all my attention and energy onto the piece of carved wooden art hanging on the wall in front of me.

But the burning only intensified until it was almost unbearable.

"Yo, gurlfriend." I looked up and saw Chris coming toward me, and I'd never been so happy to see someone in my entire life.

"Sssshhhhh." I slapped my finger over my lips. "Quick, come here."

Chris slid up to me with a curious look. "Why are we being

conspiratorial? Are you planning on stealing that piece of art you've been staring at? Personally it's not really my taste. Maybe a big tropical painting of a parrot or something."

"Shh. This is serious. I need to ask you something—"

"No we didn't have sex last night."

"What?"

"Although you did flirt outrageously. But I was a real gentleman and controlled myself."

"Now is not the time to be funny! I need you to look behind me and tell me if you see a couple. He has dark hair and she has the perfect body with legs that seem to—"

At the mention of that, Chris looked. "Damn, you weren't kidding. Amazing legs. That has got to be one of the hottest chicks I've ever seen."

Oh hello, painful pang of jealousy! "Thanks for that. Rub it in, why don't you."

"Sorry," Chris said sort of flippantly before adding, "she does look a lot like Megan Fox, though, doesn't she?"

"Jesus—can you stop already!" I gave him a smack on the arm. "So they're there?"

"Well, if you're referring to the good-looking couple who look like they need to get a room then yes, they're here."

Panic.

"Shit, shit, fuck, shitballs from hell."

Chris laughed, "That's original."

"It's *them*." I gave Chris a meaningful, knowing look, and his eyes instantly widened in absolute shock.

"No! You're kidding…it's Tress in the flesh? The chances of that are like, one hundred and twenty to one."

"That's specific."

"That's how many hotels there are on this island."

"Are you sure it's them?" I asked in a whisper.

"No, I'm not. I don't know what they look like. Why don't you just turn around and look for yourself?"

My skin crawled at the thought. "No. I can't. But I need to be sure it's them."

"Okay, I'll take a photo of them."

Chris broke away and walked across the room, whistling some nondescript tune, his way of looking casual I guess...*Not working*. Out of the far corner of my eye I could see that he was taking photos of an arbitrary palm tree, with an occasional "Mmmm" thrown in for good measure. And then when he had it, he dashed back to me.

"Here, is this them?" he asked, holding out his phone.

My heart climbed up my esophagus and lodged itself in my throat. I wanted to throw up.

"Yes."

And then Chris burst out laughing. Way, way too loudly.

I slapped him on the arm. "I'm glad you're finding this so flippin' funny," I hissed at him, trying to keep my voice down so as not to draw any more unnecessary attention to us.

"Sorry, I don't mean to laugh, but think about it. Out of all the hotels on the whole island, all the possible dates on the calendar. This has got to be the craziest coincidence in the history of humankind. You couldn't make this shit up. Now this, *this*, is a great story line for a movie—" A strange look washed over Chris's face.

"Excuse me, but my life is not some movie for your entertainment. This is real. And it's a real fucking problem," I protested and slapped him on the arm again.

Chris put his hand up. "You're right. Sorry."

"What am I going to do?" Panic had officially gripped me and was twisting me into knots.

"Why don't you just turn around, say a quick 'hi,' and get it over with? Otherwise you're going to be dodging them for the next seven days."

"I can't." I put my head in my hands. It felt like it was going to explode. *And this day started out so well!*

"I'm here for you. And afterward, I'll take you for a strong drink." I felt a reassuring hand on my back. But it wasn't helping.

"Do you know how pathetic I look right now?" I looked up at Chris. "On holiday on my own. No Boyden in sight, I might add. Just lonely old spinster me and my sunburn to keep me company. I would hate him to get satisfaction out of this." I hung my head in what was becoming such a familiar feeling of embarrassment. My brain raced, trying to figure a way out of this. "Unless I tell him that he couldn't come—why would my boyfriend not be able to come on vacation? Or, I could tell him that we broke up—he'd still get satisfaction out of that." Smarmy, smuggy, egotistical, white-toothy satisfaction. I hated him!

"I'm getting out of here." I started half moonwalking, half crab walking my way out of the room. Past the reception desk, past the sofa, I was almost at the door when…

"Anne?" It was Trevv's voice and it was too late.

"Anne, is that you?" He genuinely sounded happy to see me. Lawyers are such good actors. They should have an Academy Awards ceremony just for them. *"My client is innocent of this crime, Your Honor."*

Deep breath in, and in three, two, one…

"Trevv, Tess!" I turned around to face them. My enemies. "What a surprise!" (I'd almost called them Tress.) I gushed nervously and it definitely sounded fake. I was no lawyer, and certainly no actress.

"It is you. Are you staying here?" Trevv asked with that familiar sickly sweetness. I glanced over at Tess. She looked gorgeous, as usual. Suddenly the image of her thrashing about wildly as she screamed her way through an orgasm flashed through my mind.

"Mmmm. Yes." I think I threw up in my mouth a bit.

"What a coincidence." Tess piped up now. "You look great. Really *greeeaaaatt.*"

What a bitch. She knew I didn't look great. I had a bright sunglasses tan across my face and my once-pale legs were the color of blood. Anyone could see I was anything but great.

"Thanks, you too." Now I really threw up in my mouth. Why had I said that?

"So, are you here with your boyfriend, what was his name again?" Trevv asked with a pleased tone. I'm pretty sure he knew I wasn't dating anyone. He was just trying to rub salt in the wound. As if it wasn't already seasoned enough.

"Uh…," I stammered, "well actually, we…that is to say that I'm here…um…" I'd lost it. I was tanking. I was in free fall. *Mayday! Mayday!* I was going down. I was about to crash and burn and there was no one there to save me. But then…

"She's with me. G'day, mate!"

I stared in shock as Chris suddenly muscled in and started shaking Trevv's hand. "I'm Boyden, nice to meet you, mate. The blokes call me Boyd, though." I didn't know whether to burst out laughing, or cringe at the Australian accent he was putting on.

And then he slid his arm around my waist and pulled me closer to him.

The look on Trevv's face was priceless. I know him, and the idea that he had one up on me—because I was still single and had lied about having a boyfriend—was something he enjoyed. It was the ultimate ego boost…*"Poor Anne, she still hasn't moved on. Must be hard getting over me. So hard she had to conjure up fantasy boyfriends."*

And then that slimy lawyer look washed over his face again.

"Boyd?" Trevv said with that smarmy inflection of his. "I'm Trevv. Double 'v.' Nice to meet you."

"Likewise," Chris said. "And that's Boyden with a silent 'h' by the way."

I bit my bottom lip to stop myself from laughing while Trevv-Double-*V* stared at Chris with a confused expression.

"Interesting accent. Where you from again?" he challenged Chris.

"Born and bred in the outback of Ozzie, mate!"

"Well then, 'throw another shrimp on the barbie' as they say there." Trevv and Tess burst out laughing at his ridiculous joke. *Had he always been this cheesy?*

"So what do you do, mate?" Trevv mocked.

Wow! No pleasantries. No *"How are you?"* or anything like that. Just straight into the dick-swinging contest.

"Check out how big my manly member is. It's about as large as my bank account—hahahaha! I am so handsome and successful and rich and hung like a donkey on steroids."

"I'm a writer," Chris said with confidence.

"Aaaah"—that sounded very patronizing—"unpredictable work, isn't it? Not very regular? Don't really know where your next paycheck is coming from, hey?"

"Um...I guess you could say that in a way." Chris seemed genuinely confused by his question.

Trevv nodded. "I shouldn't imagine there's much stability in that game."

I hate it when people use the word *game* in reference to work. I could see Chris getting genuinely peeved, so I decided to jump in. "Boyd writes movies."

"Oh yeah?" A competitive streak flashed in Trevv's eyes as if I'd just challenged him to a duel. Or Chris had revealed his secret extra inch and a half. "Didn't know they made movies Down Under." Trevv gave a wicked-sounding chuckle. "What kind of movies?"

"Mainly romantic comedies." Chris was acting very nonchalant now, as if he was the coolest person on the planet. In my eyes, he was.

"Really?" Trevv looked amused. "I thought only women wrote those types of things with those soppy romance-y endings." He nudged Tess in the ribs, making no attempt to hide his mirth.

Chris's expression changed, too. Suddenly he looked pissed. "There are some female writers but—"

Trevv cut him off again. "Just pulling your leg, buddy. But seriously, Tess and I don't watch many rom-coms. Not really our thing, hey, babe?"

Tess smiled and nodded. "Not our thing," she repeated like she was a robot programmed to repeat everything Trevv said. A drop-dead-gorgeous robot.

"We usually watch more serious stuff. You know, movies with depth, don't we, baby?"

She nodded again. "And a lot of legal dramas, too," Tess added with a flutter of her long eyelashes. I wanted to rip them from her eye sockets.

"But each to his own I guess." Trevv forced a laugh and Tess joined in. God, they were disgusting.

I could feel Chris squirming next to me. But there was no reprieve; Trevv continued like a bulldozer demolishing an entire city block.

"So do you scuba, Boyd?"

"Scuba? No, not really."

"Tennis?"

"Never been good at ball sports."

"Aaahhh." Extra patronizing. "That's a pity. So no golf then?"

"Nope, like I said, not good at ball sports. Or just sports in general for that matter. Don't really like them. I preferred going walkabout and playing the didgeridoo."

My blood froze. What the hell was Chris doing? Trevv was *sooo* going to see through this. I nudged him in the ribs, hard, and he winced next to me.

Trevv looked at us curiously and cocked his head to the left. (God, that was familiar.) "That's strange, I thought all you Aussies loved sports."

"Nope. Exception to the rule." Chris's tone had a bite to it, and I wondered if he was having the same allergic reaction to Trevv that I was.

Trevv nodded his head sincerely. "Couldn't have been easy growing up, not being good at sports. I was first team rugby *and* cricket." He then did something that made my skin crawl. He mimed catching a rugby ball and then finished it off with a little *pow*.

Chris's eyes widened in what must have been shock as Trevv playfully punched his arm. "That's a shame, buddy, I was going to suggest we have a round together." He clicked his fingers at Chris. "On me. Obviously!" And then he flashed a smile that was so white it could blind people.

I blinked; this was officially the weirdest conversation I'd ever been privy to.

And then after exhausting Chris, he turned his attention to me. "So how's work, Anne? Didn't I hear you were working at a tailor's?" The conceit in his voice was undeniable. "At the Oriental Plaza? I didn't even know that place was still going."

He was going for the jugular now.

"Mmm. Yes. I've been doing some of that…you know?"

"That must be *quite* a change from the glamorous life of a fashion magazine." He was clearly going for the carotid artery, too.

I managed another "Mmmm" through my very clenched teeth.

"Well, we've had a great year so far. Tess and I." And then he turned to Chris again. "We just won that Harrison case, you may have heard of it. It was on the news?"

Next to me Chris folded his arms and I could tell that he was genuinely wound up. Who could blame him, really?

"No, I don't watch the news," he snapped back.

"Oh yes." Trevv nodded. "I suppose you don't, being a *creative* type and all."

Trevv said the words *creative type* with such poisonous venom that it actually made the hairs on my arms stand to attention.

"We got so much publicity from that trial that we decided to go out and start our own firm. Didn't we, baby?"

Tess nodded. "And it's been going great. So totally great. In fact, so great that we're moving to London at the end of the month, big, BIG international client."

"London. So great. Big clients," he echoed, just in case we hadn't gotten the fact that work was going so GREAT for them. Oh, sorry, did I mention that it was going *great* for them?

"And great in our personal life, too. In fact, we're also getting married. Right here. Beach wedding. Yay." Tess's eyes sparkled as she held out her hand to show me her ring.

"Isn't it beautiful?" she cooed through her pouty lips.

These two had to be mental! Either that, or they were the most self-obsessed narcissists that had ever lived and breathed. Perhaps ever, in the history of the human species. They were acting as if nothing had happened between us. How could they not remember having me arrested, and blinding me with their kinky, nipple-clamping ways? Had they forgotten that they were both cheating whore-people? Clearly they had.

"Four carats," Trevv said as he puffed out his chest. "Cost a pretty penny, but what can I say. When it feels right, it feels right."

"Aaaah." Tess's voice was dreamy now. "The wedding is going to be so beautiful. It's going to be at sunset. We're going to have candles on the beach, and flowers. I planned the whole thing from SA, what a mission, but so worth it when I see my Trevvy at the top of the aisle...well, at the top of the beach." She giggled, and I just wanted to slap her. An image popped into my head...Trevv and Tess swimming innocently in the sea. A shark appears and bites her beautiful legs off and the blood starts spraying everywhere. And then flesh-eating plankton feed on her fingers.

Chris suddenly jumped up and clapped his hands. "Congrats! Crickey, that's a real whopper."

"A whopper?" Trevv repeated in disbelief.

I knew very little about Australia, other than it had kanga-bloody-roos and Kylie Minogue. But clearly Trevv knew a little more than I did, because he was not buying this. I could see it and it was making me feel sick with panic.

"We're very happy together," Trevv added as he pulled Tess into a hug.

"Well, when you find the right sheila, you gotta hang on to her." Chris reciprocated by pulling me into a big bear hug. My ribs! My ribs were about to crack. "Isn't that right, baby angel." He squeezed even harder. I couldn't breathe.

You could have cut the competitive tension in the air with a blunt, plastic knife. Trevv glared at Chris with such self-satisfaction as he pulled Tess toward him and kissed her passionately. Trevv smiled again. "So nice to see you, Anne. So glad you're doing so well. Tess and I were worried about you at one point."

"No need to worry about this one," Chris said loudly while smacking me playfully on the bum. "She's a fighter."

"Oooh!" I jumped in fright and Chris turned to me. "Isn't that right, baby doll?"

"Mmm." I nodded. *Baby doll?*

"Well, nice meeting you, Boyd. And we must do dinner sometime. Cheerio!" Trevv said before walking off.

I turned and looked at Chris. He looked like he had just bitten into a sour lemon.

"Cheerio? Who says 'cheerio'? Seriously! And can that guy be any more of a prick?" Chris put his hands on his hips and I saw the competitive streak flash in his eyes.

"Who the hell says 'crickey' and 'whopper' and 'sheila' and 'mate'?"

"An Australian," Chris answered.

I grabbed my head in absolute disbelief. "I can't believe that just happened. I can't believe you pretended to be my Australian boyfriend, for heaven's sake." Not that I hadn't been massively relieved when he'd come to my rescue. But now what?

"I had to! Did you see how self-righteous they were getting about their perfect little beach wedding, not to mention her perfect four-carat diamond and their great, *great* life? Did I mention they have a great life?"

"They're going to see right through this. Your Australian accent is terrible."

"What do you mean, mate?"

"Stop saying 'mate'!" I squealed. "You're being so obvious. You might as well sing 'Waltzing bloody Matilda.'"

Chris started to open his mouth and I shot a finger out at him. "Don't you dare. This isn't funny, Chris. This is serious. This isn't some plot in one of your movies."

"But don't you see, Annie. This is your revenge story line. This is the moment you have been waiting for, to get Trevv back for all he's done."

I stopped for a second. He was right. This was my Medea moment, without the murder.

"Come on, let's go get your bags." Chris started pulling me out the lobby.

"Why?"

"Because you're moving in with me. Remember?"

"What?"

"We're a couple now, we have to act like one."

I heaved a massive sigh. "This is crazy. How the hell are we going to pull this off?"

He grabbed my hands and held them to his chest. "Baby doll," he said with sickly sweetness, "don't you remember telling me how much you loved me?"

I pulled my hands away angrily. "Chris! This is not one of your romantic comedy movies. It's my life. And I *don't* think it's funny." My tone of voice shot up, and by the last word, I felt on the verge of tears.

"Shit. Okay. I'm sorry. You're right." He put his hands on his hips and shook his head. "It's just. Dammit, Annie. That guy got to me. I mean, what a complete asshole. You can't let him win."

Suddenly Chris took my hands again and looked at me earnestly. "We can do this. We can show them. I took some acting lessons a hundred years ago, maybe I can give you some pointers. And I'll brush up on my accent tonight. We'll listen to 'The Locomotion.'" He flashed me another playful, brilliant Chris smile. *Damn*, there was something so persuasive about that grin.

But there was more to this than just putting on a smile and pretending. There were real practicalities attached to this, to making it work.

"I really don't think you understand what this means. We would have to walk around for the next seven days pretending to be together. God, there might actually have to be some hand-holding. Breakfast, lunch, supper together every day. You are going to get totally sick of me at some point—"

"Never," Chris said. "Let's just think of it as two friends hanging out and having fun…with the occasional hand hold and possible hectic making out and groping."

"Hey." I held my hand up. "I draw the line at kissing and certainly at groping."

"Can't blame a guy for trying."

I sighed in resignation, still in disbelief. *What the hell had I just agreed to?*

CHAPTER NINE

*W*hen I was twelve, I was cast as a tree in my school play. Not because I was particularly willowy in stature, or because I was tree-like in any way, shape, or form. I was cast as a tree because I couldn't act. A little bug-eyed boy called Charles, who was about as delinquent as they come, and *moi* stood at the back of the stage, covered in green cardboard cutouts of leaves, and waved our arms from side to side as the only two trees in a play set in Antarctica. On my report card my teacher had commented on my participation in the school play, *Annie tried really hard in the play.*

And now I was cast in the role of fake girlfriend and had no idea how I was going to pull it off. Especially in front of Trevv, who seemed to have this uncanny ability to sniff out bullshitters, liars, and cheats. (Takes one to know one I guess.) The prospect of playing "couple in love" for the next seven days was terrifying. And I could only imagine what my friends were going to say when they arrived, especially Dr. Jane.

"Okay, so maybe I took it a bit far with all my Australian-ness.

I'll try and tone that down," Chris said as he helped me throw my clothes and cosmetics into my suitcases. It was as if the activity of moving my stuff was making it a bit clearer to him how severe our situation really was. *Men.* They just always do things and worry about the consequences later.

"But those two were just driving me mad with their perfect, great—*sooo great*—little life. I couldn't help myself!"

"A *bit* too far?"

"No!" He held his hand up. "No time for negativity and second-guessing ourselves. We are going to do this! Boyd can handle the challenge." Chris zipped up the last of my bags and pulled them out the door. "What do you think about me giving the character of Boyd a limp, or maybe making him colorblind?"

"What?" I spun around and glared at Chris.

"Just kidding, babe. Come on…" He pulled me into a brief squeeze. "It's not like we'll be bumping into them every five seconds. It's a big resort."

Famous last words—Because as we closed the door behind us and started walking down the path…

"Anne. Boyd." That smug little nasal voice again. Was his voice always like that, or had I just gotten used to it? Perhaps that had been one of the irritating things that I'd also chosen to ignore, too.

"What are you guys doing with bags?" I could hear the conniving suspicion in his voice. He was dying to catch us out. I could tell from the second that Chris had introduced himself as my significant other, he hadn't believed us.

"Um…" I looked at Chris, hoping he had some clever story; he was the writer after all.

"We're upgrading rooms. The presidential suite." Chris really enunciated those last two words and Trevv shuddered in response. "The presidential suite was only available from tonight, so we're just doing the old room switcheroo." Chris shot him a dazzling smile.

"Reel it in," I hissed under my breath.

"Presidential suite, hey? I didn't know they had them here."

"Honestly, it's not as good as some of the others we've stayed in, but it'll do."

It was hard not to burst out laughing. Chris was milking the moment for all it was worth and despite the insane situation I now found myself in, I was thrilled to finally be getting the opportunity to kick Trevv where it would hurt most—*in his ego*. I might be able to go along with this after all. I just needed to keep reminding myself of the reward—getting back at Trevv for what he had done to me.

I looked over at Trevv. He looked pissed off, but was trying to conceal it under his usual grin.

"Well, enjoy," Trevv said through a slightly clenched jaw. It was said with such blatant insincerity that I could almost hear what he really wanted to say: *"I hope the roof caves in on you two and a giant tsunami rushes in and washes you both out to the deep sea where you are swallowed by a ferocious killer whale."*

But he smiled and waved and trotted off down the path, dragging Tess and her long legs behind him.

We arrived at the room, and Chris opened the door and put my bags down. Even though I had already seen this room, it still boggled me. And I wondered just how much something like this might cost a night. I could probably fit my whole cottage in this place at least twice.

"Why don't you take the room downstairs and I'll take the one upstairs," Chris said.

"No, it's fine. I'll take upstairs."

"Downstairs is nicer, though." Chris switched the air-conditioning on and a glorious blast of cool air rushed in.

"It's okay. Besides, I like the view from upstairs." The truth was that I felt weird sleeping in his bed. It felt way too intimate. He was practically a stranger.

"So," Chris said with a weird inflection in his voice, "have you noticed anything new?"

"About what?" I automatically started scanning the room.

"About me." Chris said.

I looked at him and couldn't believe I hadn't noticed earlier. The Trevv and Tess debacle had obviously blinded me to the glaring change.

"You've trimmed the beard."

"Bingo." He looked pleased within himself and ran his hand over his now-smoother face.

"It looks good." In fact, he looked amazing. He looked absolutely...*wow*, the familiar feeling was back. My body temperature rose as if the air-conditioning had just been switched off.

I could finally see the face that had been hiding beneath the hair. The beard wasn't completely gone, but in its place was a dark five-o'clock shadow. The most striking thing about the change was that I could finally see his full smile. I'd only had a taste of it last night. But like this, it was big, wide, friendly, and totally contagious—it lit up his entire face.

It had a certain mischievous quality to it and caused the lines at the side of his eyes to crinkle, which I really liked. Trevv's smile had always felt rehearsed, not to mention that his face never crinkled; he used more facial product than I did. His perfect smile seemed identical in every photo, as if he'd practiced it in front of the mirror, which he probably had.

In looks, Chris was the antithesis of Trevv. And then there was his personality, chalk and cheese. Chris was natural and laid-back, whereas everything with Trevv had always seemed like a carefully constructed performance. A performance that I'd only been too happy to go along with. But who the hell had we been performing to?

"You look good," I said again, a little softer and more breathily than I would have liked. The smile, coupled with those light watery blue eyes, coupled with that sexy laid-back quality...

I wouldn't mind practicing a few more things on him actually.

"Okay, I'm going upstairs now to unpack." I grabbed my bag and started making a move for the stairs to avoid shamelessly throwing myself at him.

"Cool. What do you want to do later?" Chris asked.

His question momentarily caught me off guard. Of course we were going to be doing things later. We were a couple now. Couples did things. They hung out. They held hands. They held other things, too—which, in our case, would *not* be happening. "I can't afford to spend any more time in the sun."

"What about a massage at the spa?" he suggested.

"That sounds ah-mazing. Since bumping into Tress I think I've developed a pain in my neck."

"Ha-ha, Annie. Cheesy, but good."

"Thanks. Besides, we're also less likely to bump into them there. Knowing them they're probably on the beach flaunting their model physiques."

But unfortunately when we finally did walk into the spa, there they were (surprise, surprise), sitting in the waiting area. Tess looked like she might be modeling in a photo shoot for Guess swimwear. She'd changed into a bikini and had barely covered her bottom half with a see-through sarong. I glanced down at my clothes, and felt a sudden pang of embarrassment.

I was wearing a less-than-fashionable shirt and, *Oh God*, please will the deity of fashion forgive me, a cheesecloth skirt straight out of an episode of *Friends*. I'd found it in the back of my closet and been forced to bring it; the loose fit hid the little stomach I was developing from all those chocolate binges. *Why had I put this on today? Why did I eat so much chocolate, why hadn't I gone to the gym instead?*

I made a mental note to go and buy something that made me look like I was part of this decade.

"Well, well, we meet again." Trevv was the first to speak. Naturally. "We just keep bumping into each other, don't we?" He stood up and gave Chris a manly pat on the back. "Are you guys following us?" He finished this sentence with another fake laugh.

"Busted!" Chris was full Australian again and reciprocated by slapping Trevv back; it was perhaps a little hard. "You guys are just so interesting that we can't help following you around," Chris added in insincere mock jest, topping it off with his best fake laugh.

And then something awful happened: the room erupted into a cacophony of fake, forced laughter. We sounded more like a pack of hyenas than a happy group of friends. And you just knew that under the *hahahahahaha*s were deep feelings of hatred and annoyance. But no one was going to show them, so we all just pretended to find everything very amusing and interesting.

"Your rooms are ready." Thankfully the petite masseuse interrupted the artificial merriment.

"*Rooms?*" Trevv's keen lawyer senses had kicked in. "Didn't you guys get a couple's room like we did?" He was testing us again, I could see it in the way he ran his eyes up and down, as if trying to read us like a column of words.

"There were none available when we booked." The answer just flew out of my mouth but was quickly rebutted when the masseuse informed us that there was indeed a couple's room available.

"Great. Well that's good news!" I quickly piped up, trying to look genuinely happy as the therapist indicated for Chris and me to follow her.

But it wasn't good news. It was the worst news ever. *Chris and I were going to share a massage room.* Half-naked I might add.

CHAPTER TEN

I looked at Chris.

And he looked at me.

I cleared my throat.

Chris cleared his.

I scratched my head—it wasn't itchy.

Chris ran his fingers through his hair—I doubt it was necessary.

I pretended to smell a flower.

Chris pretended to look out the window.

"So…" I finally mustered the courage to speak.

"So…," Chris echoed back to me.

"So…" Words had officially escaped my brain. "Um…"

Then silence.

A silence that was so loaded and loud that it was deafening.

And then thankfully he spoke.

"Okay, let me be the first to say that this is awkward."

The relief that came from acknowledging the situation for what it was, was instant.

"*So* awkward."

"So what are we going to do?" Chris said, peering around the door to check whether the therapists were coming yet.

"We could *not* have the massage and just sit here for an hour pretending we were?" This was the only thing I could think of at the time.

Chris shook his head. "I think that ex of yours is starting to get suspicious."

"So you're saying…that we should…together…in the same room…*almost naked*?"

I looked around—there was nowhere to get dressed or undressed, and there was hardly any room between the beds, either. Everything was open, and very, very *romantic*. Clearly the couple's room was laid out for maximum relaxation and optimum romance; magnolia flowers lay scattered across the floor, and bright pink bougainvillea graced the pillows of the beds.

"Well it's not like we'll be sharing the same massage bed."

"But we'll be half-naked. In the same room."

Chris shot me one of his mischievous smiles. "Not as weird as if we were both totally naked!"

"This is no time for jokes, Chris."

Knock, knock.

We both turned and looked at the door, as if some kind of dreadful creature was lurking behind it, ready to rush inside and pounce.

"Are you ready yet?" the little French voice asked softly through the door.

"Give us another minute, please." Chris was quick with his reply and then walked over to me. He squared off and looked me straight in the eyes.

"It won't be that bad. I'll turn around and you can undress. I won't peep, I promise."

I looked at Chris for a moment, scrutinizing him, trying to weigh up his character—a character that, quite frankly, I knew absolutely nothing about. And my conclusion was this: *This boyfriend farce was the stupidest thing I'd ever been a part of.*

It was a mess from which I didn't know how to untangle myself. It was out of control and it had gone way, *way* too far. I could no longer perpetuate it. This was not me. So I decided right there and then that I would put an immediate end to it. No matter how embarrassing. No matter how much smug satisfaction Trevv and Tess would get out of it. But just as I was about to throw in the towel—literally, I was holding one—I heard the sarcastic bleating of Trevv as he walked past.

"Enjoy your massage, guys." There was a pause, and I could almost hear his thoughts, *I know we'll enjoy ours.* His last words dripped with a kind of slimy sexiness that was repulsive.

And that was it. All he needed to say. The smug-eyed, self-righteous, self-serving, ego-inflated bastard turd had challenged me...

"Oh we will," I shouted back. "Trust me. We will. It's going to be *sooo* good. Isn't it, baby?"

I shot Chris the kind of look that said, *If you don't act along now, I will beat you over the head with something hard.*

Chris jumped in quickly like a good little student. "So good."

Once Trevv and Tess were out of earshot, I turned to Chris. "Now take your clothes off and get on that bed immediately!"

That boyish smile lit up his face again and I could sense a clever, witty retort coming on. "And don't you dare say something clever and witty now, just get naked and onto that bloody bed."

My finger was out now, waggling and pointing fervently. This seemed to have the opposite effect, though, because instead of imbuing him with a healthy dose of fear and respect, it only seemed to amuse him further.

"Yes, ma'am," he said, giving me a military salute before pulling his shirt off over his head.

My rational, intellectual brain told me to turn away immediately, but curiosity (*bad, bad, naughty curiosity*) prevailed and I watched him undress. He had broad shoulders and a large, solid frame. He was in good shape, but not in that chiseled, defined gym way. It was actually rather refreshing. Trevv spent hours at the gym, and on several occasions I'd caught him in front of the mirror flexing. He worked out until everything was perfect and honed; every muscle was a defined work of art, and every line sat in the right place. But I've since learned that apparent perfection is not all it's cracked up to be.

Chris had a splattering of chest hair; Trevv was as smooth as a baby's bottom.

His shoulders were dotted with wayward freckles; Trevv's complexion was even, to the point of being porcelain.

He had a small scar on his stomach where it looked like he'd had an appendix removed and a small bruise on his shoulder.

He was completely and utterly imperfect, and in that imperfection, totally flippin' hot.

So hot in fact that I felt my breath involuntarily quicken and my mouth go dry. Unable to move, I continued to stare as he pulled his shorts off. I really should have turned around at this point—*I should have turned around*.

"Take a picture. It lasts longer." Chris sounded amused.

"Sorry, I didn't mean to." Mortified, I instinctually smacked my hands over my eyes and swung round.

I heard a soft chuckle behind me. "Your turn. I'll turn around, though."

I peered back tentatively to see if he had indeed turned around, which he had. But taking off my clothes felt like an impossible task. The thought of exposing myself in the same room as a stranger felt beyond bizarre. But it had to be done. I wondered if I couldn't just leave my bra on and the masseuse could work around it. That seemed like a more reasonable idea, and one that I was definitely more comfortable with.

I pulled my dress off slowly and dropped it to the floor. The cool sea breeze felt good against my skin, and I slipped under the towel on the bed.

"Okay, you can turn around now."

Chris climbed onto the bed just as the masseuse came through the door. If I were a fly on the wall right now, an objective observer to this scene, I might have laughed out loud. The pure, unadulterated ludicrousness of my current situation was undeniable. It felt more like surreal insanity than actually reality.

But it was real. And it was happening.

And I had a feeling that this wasn't going to be the last awkward situation we'd find ourselves in. And I was right.

"I'll just push them together," the masseuse said and suddenly started pushing Chris's bed next to mine. I stared in horror as Chris's half-naked body got closer, and closer and—

"You can stop there!" I said quickly. "That won't be necessary." I tried to protest but she wasn't having it.

"Mauritius is for romance." She gave one last push—she was surprisingly strong—and voilà, Chris was lying next to me. The beds were so narrow and close that our shoulders were touching. I squeezed my eyes shut, hoping that when I opened them he wouldn't be so damn close to me. But he was. And I could hear his breathing.

"Hi, neighbor," he whispered.

"Heya." *Trying to be cool, collected, and casual but actually dying inside*

Another masseuse came into the room and I vaguely heard someone mumble something like "No bra."

The words went in one ear and straight out the other because I was way too busy focusing on the electric feeling of Chris's shoulder rubbing against mine. So before I was able to mount any kind of a protest, I felt it. Quick, nimble fingers went to work on my bra strap and within seconds, she'd unclipped it like a pro.

"Wait. Stop." But just like the bed, she wasn't having it, and I felt it being pulled out from under me.

"Wait!" I raised my body off the bed and swung around, trying to pull my bra back. It was an instinctual move, like instantly pulling your skirt down when the wind blows it up. But in my panicked state, I really hadn't thought this through. At all.

There were several things wrong with my hasty, un-thought-out plan.

Firstly, in raising my body off the bed, I flashed my boobs to the entire room—Chris included. And secondly, in collapsing back down to the bed with vigor, given the close proximity, I mushed my boob into Chris's outstretched hand on the bed.

Awesome. Chris and I had basically just gone to second base.

CHAPTER ELEVEN

I should have floated out of the room feeling relaxed. Feeling as light as a feather, as soft as silk, and as warm and content as a baby wrapped in its mother's arms.

But I didn't.

I walked out feeling very unrelaxed. I had been feeling tense since the unfortunate boob incident. And what made it even worse was the way Chris had responded.

He hadn't looked away in embarrassment, or apologized or laughed at the silly mistake. *No*, he'd held my gaze. Held it with such intensity that it had frozen me in place. Our eyes locked; it probably only lasted for a second, but it felt like forever. I couldn't disengage from the stare no matter how hard I willed my eyes to look away.

His eyes changed, his pupils dilated, and something darker washed through them. And when I finally managed to pry my eyes away, I stuck my head through the hole in the bed as fast as I possibly could and kept it there.

All I could then feel, the whole way through the massage, was the warmth of his skin against my breast. And even when the masseuse painfully dug her elbows into my back, it was still all I could feel. So instead of relaxing while very expert hands worked away my tensions, I spent the next ninety minutes counting down the seconds until I could escape.

The moment the masseuses clapped their hands to signal the end of our torture, I hopped off the table and scrambled for my clothes.

"Hey, wait," Chris called after me as I dashed out of the room.

"Mmmm?" I mumbled, not turning around to look at him.

"Why are you in such a rush?"

"I'm not in a rush." I tried to be casual.

"Oh please, you practically threw yourself out of the room."

"Did I?" I tried to sound innocent.

"Are you trying to get away from me, Annie?"

"What? Why would you say that?"

"Did it have something to do with…" Chris moved closer to me and I tightened my arms across my chest. "With what happened?"

"What happened?" I feigned ignorance, badly. I tried to contort my face into all kinds of nonchalant looks, but I just started to feel like my face was having a seizure. I was such a terrible actress.

"You know, with your…"

"My breast," I blurted out. "You saw my…it touched you…your hand and I didn't mean to. I apologize." I was curt.

Chris smiled. "I didn't mind."

I swayed from side to side. This conversation was making me feel so awkward and…*I was turned on*. So turned on, and all my breast wanted to do was fly right back into his hand.

I decided to remove my misbehaving mammary from the situation. "I need to buy a decent dress, or something." I could probably only afford a sarong, but hey, anything was better than what I was currently wearing.

Chris nodded. "There's a shop by the lobby that sells beachwear. I'll have a drink at the bar and wait for you?"

"Okay." I ran off to the shop, glad to be away from him.

The shop was tropical themed. *Tropical* might be an understatement. Because in case you hadn't already worked out that you were staying on a very tropical island, the shop was here to remind you. Every corner was decorated with tropical sarongs, palm fronds, and magnolias, and there were clumps of large shells on the floor, which was made of sand.

"Can I help you?" a woman said, coming forward.

"I'm looking for some beachwear, dresses, maybe a sarong." I was stating the obvious. You couldn't buy anything else from this shop.

"Mmmm"—the woman looked me up and down—"maybe something, *not* so, how you say in English, *red*?"

She had a very strong French accent, but there was no way she didn't know what the word *red* was in English. She was just one of those bitchy shop attendants, making me feel like Julia Roberts in *Pretty Woman*, except I didn't have some rich, handsome man waiting for me in a hotel room. *Well, I did*, but not a real one. She grabbed me by the arm and started heading toward the dress section, shouting, "Come, come!"

After holding up a few dresses in front of me, she finally nodded and handed me a flowy, white midlength dress with pretty straps and a crisscross effect on the back. It was beautiful. And the white actually downplayed the redness of my skin, making it look more tanned than burned.

She marched me toward the dressing room, pushed me in, and

then turned and disappeared into the jungle. I hung the dress up against the wall and started undressing in front of the mirror. I hate dressing room mirrors. They have obviously been wickedly designed to accentuate everything that is wrong with your body. They possess some microscopic, magic ability to accentuate even the smallest lump of cellulite. So I turned my back on the evil thing and started trying on the dress.

In retrospect, I should have taken a few minutes to figure out how the dress worked. After five minutes of struggling, I was clutching a mess of straps, and bits of fabric that I couldn't get into a position that looked like it would fit over my body.

But I persisted. I pushed my head and arms through the dress and tried to wiggle it over my rib cage. But moments later my arms got stuck, my shoulder became tangled, and I think I might have forced my head through what was meant to be the sleeve.

You would think that with a degree in fashion, something like this wouldn't have confounded me. But it had. And now I was officially stuck. And the more I tried to dislodge myself, the more tangled I got and the tighter the dress became. It bunched around my shoulders and neck and forced my arms to stretch out in front of me. I looked like a zombie with its dead arms extended in front of it.

From my neck down, I was only wearing my underwear. I couldn't move. And then I didn't want to move, as I heard the door to the changing room next to mine open and the shop assistant saying "Oh *oui, oui*. Very nice. You look like ze movie star. I'll find ze right shoes. In red perhaps?"

Red, I scoffed. *Bitch*.

There was silence for a few moments before a violent knock on my door nearly made me fall over.

"Mademoiselle. You are ready?"

"Uh. Just a minute." I tried vigorously to untangle myself again, or at least to free my left arm so I could pull the dress down a bit so it covered my bra. But it was as if I had gotten myself into a straitjacket that pulled tighter the more I struggled.

"Actually…" I managed to bend my body over in a forty-five-degree angle in order to reach the lock on the door and open it. "Can you please help me?" I said as I stepped out.

But instead of seeing the shop assistant, I saw Tess. She swiveled and looked at me with a mixture of shock and confusion.

"Annie, is that you?"

I felt like replying with something snarky, witty, and clever, like Chris might have done. But with the strap around my neck cutting off the blood supply to my brain, nothing came. Instead all I said was, "Help."

Within seconds the shop assistant was there, clucking her tongue in blatant disapproval. As if I'd done this on purpose.

"Oh no, no. Maybe zis dress is not ze right one for you, no." Her French accent was now laced with condescension.

She started pulling and pushing on all my body parts and pulling and pushing on the dress…but it didn't budge.

"I need help," I heard her say, and suddenly Tess joined in. *Oh God!* How much more mortifying could you get? Four hands went to work on the stubborn dress, and I felt like a marionette puppet as I was pulled and manipulated and then…

Rrrrriiiiipppp.

The sound of the tear was the loudest thing I'd ever heard. And although utterly impossible, the noise echoed and reverberated through the now-silent room. Everyone turned and watched as the dress fell to the floor, as if in slow motion. And that's when I realized I was in my underwear, in front of Tess. My body ached and I had red lines carved into my neck and back where the straps had dug into me.

"You must pay for zis," the French B said while picking the dress up like it was now nothing more than a discarded dirty diaper.

Tess rushed forward with a kind of faux concern that was almost believable. *Almost.* "Annie, my God, are you okay?"

Let's review. *Was I okay?* Standing in my (nonmatching) underwear in front of the woman who had kinky sex with my boyfriend, in our bed. Who broke up my relationship and destroyed my self-esteem and any confidence I once had about my "boudoir" performance. Who was perfect, and hot, and made me look short and fat and plain.

"I'm fine, thanks, Tess, thanks for asking," I managed before walking into the dressing room. I closed the door behind me and collapsed on the floor.

"It really was a lovely dress, though," Tess said through the door. "If I were you I would take another one. I'm sure Boyson can help you get into it."

"Boyden."

"What?"

"His name's Boyden."

"Oh, right. Of course. Isn't that what I said? Oopsie."

How was this woman even a lawyer? She came across as someone who had an IQ of a sea urchin. I pulled my old dress on, grabbed my bag, and walked out of the dressing room trying to salvage the little dignity I had left. Tess was still standing there admiring herself in the full-length mirror.

"So Boyd seems nice." She smiled happily at me.

How was it that she didn't feel awkward in front of me? If I had done what she had, I would be so wracked with guilt that I wouldn't be able to look the woman in the eye. But she was a different breed, it seemed. Different species perhaps?

"So tell me, how did you and Boyd meet? I must know. I love romantic stories."

Oh shit! Chris and I hadn't really discussed the logistics of our "relationship." What was I supposed to say? I was still wracking my brain to come up with the right answer when the assistant returned with a light blue boob tube dress—no straps involved.

"Try zis. More suited to you, I think." Her tone made me want to smack her over the head with a baguette.

I grabbed the dress and ducked into the changing room. I was actually able to get this one on so I opened the door and came out.

"Mmmm." The shop attendant looked at me and tilted her head a few times. "It is better, yes. But maybe it's a bit…" She looked at Tess, who was also tilting her head from side to side, examining me like a creature in the zoo.

"Maybe a *tiny* bit too small." Tess emphasized the word *tiny*, I guess to try to cushion the blow of being told I was basically fat.

Oh God! As if this couldn't get any worse. Tess then looked down at my stomach and I instinctively pulled it in as much as I could.

"*Oui,* maybe one size bigger." She started looking on the rack for another one when I jumped in.

"NO!" The word came out a little too loudly and the shop assistant spun around. "It's fine. I don't want another one. I just want to pay for the other dress and go. Thanks."

I felt so desperate to get out of this shop, and away from the prying eyes of Tess and her shop assistant sidekick. I dove back into the dressing room and was only too happy to slip into my crappy dress again. God, I was mortified and I felt like I was about to crack.

Okay, so I know I've put on ten pounds this year. And I know nearly every one has found its way to my middle section. But to have it pointed out to me by a bitchy shop assistant and my ex-boyfriend's mistress, *well*, that's just plain rude. Suddenly I was filled with a mad anger.

I glared at Tess. "Actually, Tessssss"—I hissed the *s* out like a snake—"I'm not okay. Okay?"

She looked at me as if I was speaking Greek.

"I am not okay with you and Trevv being here in this hotel on this island. I'm not okay with what you and Trevv did, either." The shop attendant turned and looked at us now. "And I am not okay that you are ten sizes smaller than me and that your hair is so fucking shiny. Okay?"

For the first time ever I saw something soft in Tess's eyes. Was that remorse? Was this woman capable of such an emotion, or was it my imagination? Was I just projecting my feelings onto her, because I was so desperate for her to feel them?

Guilt and shame for what she had done to me. For how she'd destroyed my life and destroyed the person I used to be. She'd done more than just sleep with my boyfriend, she had stolen everything from me: my confidence, my job, all the dreams and ambitions I once had. They had all been ripped out from under me and I was still struggling to get them all back, no matter what I did. The old Annie seemed so far away right now, and I didn't like the new one that had moved in.

Tess opened her mouth and paused, and my eyes dropped to her lips, willing the words out of her.

"We were very upset you had to find out that way. It wasn't meant to happen like that."

I waited, wanting to hear more. I stared at her lips, but they didn't move.

"And?" I urged.

"And what?" She looked genuinely confused.

"Really? Is that all you have to say? Is that it?" I was still holding on to this idea of a grand apology. But, like Trevv, she seemed totally oblivious to the feelings of others. I shook my head. It was like speaking to a wall.

"Whatever," I said as I walked toward the door of the shop.

"Annie," Tess called after me and I turned. "I use a macadamia nut oil conditioner on it."

"On what?"

"My hair." She twirled a strand between her fingers.

I blinked at her a few confused times. What the hell was I meant to do with that little nugget of info? Be grateful and pleased that she had let me in on a beauty secret like a friend might do when they discover the perfect lipstick? Maybe I should tell her about my amazing sun cream and then we can have a slumber party and braid each other's hair and talk about kissing boys?

And then she extended the strangest olive branch ever. "You can borrow it if you like. It will definitely help with the dullness."

And now I had dull hair, too! I turned and walked out of the shop feeling worse than I had in a while. In fact, I felt about as shitty as I had the day my life had exploded. I felt completely deflated and defeated once again. That little spark of confidence that I'd felt this morning was gone. She'd taken it away from me once more. *Why the fuck did I let her have so much power over me?*

The minute Chris saw me heading toward him at the bar, he gave a little whistle and wiggled his eyebrows at me. But it wasn't enough to cheer me up. I sat down next to him and slumped into my chair.

"Can I buy you a drink?" he asked in his best suave, charming Casanova voice. Under normal circumstances, I might have laughed.

"Chris. Do you think I look fat?"

He burst out laughing, and I wasn't sure how to take that. "Wow. Look at the two of us. Just like a real couple."

"I'm not joking. And does my hair lack luster?"

His laughter grew but then suddenly stopped when he must have noticed the distinctly unamused look on my face.

"And since you've seen them, practically fondled them, do my breasts lack perkiness?"

"Annie Anne, you have great breasts."

I slumped over and placed my head on the bar counter and let out the loudest sigh.

"Annie"—I felt a hand on my back—"you look amazing. Seriously."

I regarded him, my face still pressed against the bar.

"Really?"

Chris nodded and then reached down, brushing the hair out of my face. "Aren't redheads meant to have more fun anyway?"

"That's blondes." I sat up straight. "Or in my case, shiny, raven-haired women. Are you still going to buy me that that drink, by the way?"

"Whatever you want, my dear," he said with a smile.

"And don't go easy on the rum this time."

***

Two exotic cocktails later, a slightly tipsier disposition and an hour spent in Chris's company had made me forget all about the incident in the shop. I really did have fun with him. What was not fun, however, was trying to navigate the bridge across the pool in my current state.

"I'm not *sh*ure this is such a good look for me," I said to Chris, very aware of the slightest little slur in that sentence. I was hoping Chris hadn't heard it. But of course he had.

"If I wasn't *sh*uch a nice guy I could totally take advantage of you right now, Annie Anne."

"Get your head out of the gutter and just help me over the bridge." I held my hands out to him, thinking he would just support me across it. Instead he scooped me up in his arms and carried me. Shocked, I let out a shriek of surprise.

"This is so not dignified," I screeched as he walked me over the bridge. I wrapped my hands around his neck so as not to lose my grip and suddenly found myself really liking it. I liked the close proximity to him. I liked the way he was so strong and was carrying me as if I was light as a feather (despite previous references to my weight). I tightened my arms around him and realized I hadn't been this close to a guy in ages.

He carried me all the way to our room, which was totally unnecessary and caught the eye of a few passing people. But hey, I wasn't objecting. After making a quick joke about carrying me over the threshold, he popped me down gently on the couch.

"Thanks for that," I said.

"Hey, what are fake boyfriends for?"

"So, I think I might go for an afternoon nap." I pointed to my room.

"Do you think you can climb the stairs, or should I carry you to your bed?" His eyes flashed with a mischievous wickedness, and I put my hand up in the air to stop him.

"Down, boy!" I gave him one last smile before climbing the stairs.

"Just shout if you need someone to keep you company," he called after me as I threw myself down onto the soft bed.

I lay there looking up at the ceiling as a thought ran screaming through my mind. It ran back and forth until I could no longer ignore it. *Do I want him to keep me company?* I sat up and looked at the door. It seemed to call to me. *"Open me, let Chris in."*

I was a little bit tipsy, a little bit—*no*, a lot—sexually attracted to him, and I was seconds away from walking out that door, down those stairs, and demanding that he did more than just keep me company.

Fuck it.

I threw myself out the door and down the stairs as quickly as I could in case something stopped me.

"Chris!" I said loudly the second my foot flew off the final stair. He turned and looked up at me from his computer.

"Yes?"

"There's something I need to tell you."

CHAPTER TWELVE

Who was I kidding?

The words came out as insecurity and self-doubt came rushing in.

"I'm going to take a nap."

"Okay," he said, looking confused as hell. He went back to his computer and I was left looking at the back of him. I rushed upstairs silently cursing myself. I crawled into bed and closed my eyes.

***

When I woke up, it was dusk. The temperature was cooler and the air was tinged with a mauve that seemed to melt into pale yellow. I must have slept the entire afternoon away.

A frantic *tick, tick, tick, tick*ing was coming from downstairs, and I went to investigate.

Chris was seated at a table, three big empty coffee cups in front of him, wearing a large pair of reading glasses. His laptop was open, his iPad was lit up like a Christmas tree, and he was typing faster than I'd ever seen anyone type before.

I watched in silence; he was chuckling to himself, and every now and then he paused for a moment or two, before whispering a few words out loud. He was so wrapped up in his own world that it felt like a sin to interrupt.

But as my foot reached the bottom stair, it creaked. He turned around immediately and looked up at me with a kind of manic intensity, and then practically slammed his computer closed.

"I see you got inspired?" I said, indicating the now-closed computer.

His face scrunched up into a look that can only be described as sheepish. For a second he looked shy. Coy. He was probably one of these creative types that got bashful about his work.

"Yeah, I got inspired."

"Read some to me." I'd never read a movie script before. It sounded exciting.

"No. I never read to people while I'm still writing." He was firm.

"Can't you make an exception for your wonderful girlfriend?"

He shook his adamantly. "Not even for you."

I let out a sigh, "Oh well…So what do you want to do now… *boyfriend*?" I asked playfully, collapsing into the most absurdly comfortable couch my derrière had ever had the pleasure of sitting on.

Chris came over and joined me. "Personally," he said, "I could quite happily get room service and watch movies all night."

Room service and movies? It just sounded so…*pedestrian*. Like dry toast and bland, milky tea. I could do that any day of the week. Why would I do that on my tropical island paradise vacation? But the more I sat there trying to hype myself up to do something more exciting, I felt the undeniable tug of the couch's gravity—and the further I sank into its unbelievable comfort, the more the idea started appealing to me. So I found a compromise.

"How about, instead, we eat dinner on the roof and look out over the sea."

"We could do that," Chris said, reaching for the room service menu.

The view from the roof was spectacular. By the time we were up there with our food, the sun was already setting. Shafts of warm golden light shot through the sky like those beams you find outside nightclubs. The sea was now a pale violet hue; it was as if the two colors—amber and blue—had mixed to create the shimmery color that was now rippling across the surface of the water. The palms and trees were tinged with a soft orange hue, and one small, faint star was poking its way into the sky. We both sat at the table in silent appreciation.

"That's a pretty crappy view." Funnyman Chris clearly never let an opportunity for sarcasm and razor-sharp wit pass him by. "Disgusting, in fact," he added with a repulsed cringe.

And again I found myself laughing. The way he seemed to find the funny side to everything was refreshing. It was interesting and entertaining and unique, and he was just so, *so*—

I stopped laughing and found myself staring at him as I was thinking about what exactly he was. He, too, had stopped laughing and his eyes came up to meet mine. My stomach instantly constricted. The way we were looking at each other in that moment was something…*else*. There was nothing friendly, casual, or mundane about this look. Nothing *"Yo, yo, buddy, what up?"* No. There was definitely something very *other* about it.

I had enough self-awareness to know that I found him attractive, but I found lots of guys attractive and I didn't get a stiletto-in-the-stomach feeling when they looked at me.

I cleared my throat.

It looked like the moment had gotten uncomfortable for him, too, because his hands were unnecessarily moving through his hair and letting it fall back into his face, which just intensified my desire to keep staring.

"So perhaps we should get to know each other a bit now that we're in a relationship and all," he said, putting his feet up on the chair in front of him. I could see he was trying to act cool and casual again. It was only half working.

"Okay. I suppose we should. Let's play a game of twenty questions, then. I'll go first."

"Oh God, *no*." Chris slapped his hand on the table. "Please, that's so *Cosmopolitan* magazine, 'How to Know Your Boyfriend Better,' 'Is Your Boyfriend a Moron or a Keeper,' 'Is He Willing to Let You Pick Out His Clothes,' and 'Does He Love His Mother More Than You.'"

"You sound like you read *Cosmopolitan* magazine."

Chris flinched a little in his chair.

"Oh my God—you read *Cosmo*!"

"I have to read it for my job, okay? I need to understand the truly un-understandable complexities of the female psyche!"

I burst out laughing. "You read *Cosmo*!"

"Only little bits." Chris smiled with such coyness that I almost felt compelled to jump across the table and hug him.

"Okay, fine…twenty questions it is." He folded his arms in mock defeat.

I sat back in my chair for a moment and contemplated the questions I might ask him. There were a million things I wanted to know about him. I decided to start with the fundamentals...

"Where do you live?"

"LA."

"Where did you grow up?"

"LA. My grandparents moved there from Germany."

"Siblings?"

"One brother, one sister."

"Favorite color?"

"Mmmm, blue."

"Favorite food?"

"Chinese. Definitely Chinese."

"Favorite car?"

"Porsche."

"Do you have one?"

"Yes."

"Are you rich?"

"I do okay." I regarded him quickly. For a guy that drove a Porsche, he was completely down-to-earth. Not like Trevv.

"Hobbies?"

"Watching movies."

"Favorite movie of all time?"

"Too many to choose from."

"Favorite author?" I felt like I was seriously running out of questions now.

"Dr. Seuss."

"The children's book writer?" This answer had surprised me.

"You clearly haven't read *Oh, the Places You'll Go!*"

I shook my head.

"I think you'd like it."

"Favorite vacation spot?"

"Definitely Mauritius now." He flashed me a loaded look and smile. "Even though I hate the water." His smile grew even more and, as if it was somehow connected to mine with an invisible string, my lips followed suit. Suddenly I feel a bit silly, giddy, reduced to some prepubescent version of myself.

I suddenly forgot what we were doing…Oh, questions. Getting to know him. Getting to know Chris, my fake boyfriend.

"Facebook or Twitter?" I asked when the smile finally petered out enough for me to move my lips again.

"Neither. Social media repulses me."

"Um…?" I was running out of questions. "Okay, describe yourself in five words."

He flashed that mischievous grin again. "Funny. Devilishly good-looking. Sexy as hell and—"

"That's more than five words."

We looked at each other for a few amused seconds before laughing again.

"Okay, I have one more, actually two," I said. "How did you become a comedy guy? And why are you so afraid of water?" As soon as I'd asked the question his mood changed. His smile was gone and he looked serious. I hadn't expected that reaction.

"Honestly…?" he asked, leaning forward and looking directly at me.

"Well, aren't the fundamental pillars of any successful relationship honesty?"

"Okay, honestly…when I was at school I was the fat nerdy kid."

"No," I gasped, looking him up and down.

"I'm serious. I was this big, fat, nerdy kid with glasses and braces. The kids used to tease and bully me. They called me…" He paused for the longest time as if the memory still had a physical hold over him. I guess it did. "They called me Svetty, another reason I dropped that name."

"No. That's terrible."

"And the only way I could deal with it, or get people to like me, was to become the funny one. So I became the funny fat guy."

"Wow!" I didn't really know what to say. I felt my heart break a bit, imagining that little kid getting teased on the playground. Jane had been teased a lot at school. She's adopted and looks nothing like the rest of her family. She's also unusually tall, unique-looking and even has two different-colored eyes. Talk about a walking target! So I'd seen firsthand how devastating and life-altering teasing could be. I know she's still dealing with the effects of it, and I could see Chris was, too.

"But now you're good-looking, rich, and successful," I offered enthusiastically.

"Yes, and it's funny how all the girls only like me like this."

Something flickered in my mind, and a little thought started forming. Of course he didn't believe in *real* love, if he'd only experienced it as conditional; more specifically, conditional to how he looked, or how well he was doing.

"And water?" I asked. The mood had definitely changed. It was far more serious, and I wondered when Chris was going to throw in a funny comment to lure me off this line of questioning. Only he didn't.

"Let's just say that the bullies thought it would be funny to push me in the pool and then keep pushing me and pulling me down until I thought I was going to die."

"That's horrible." I reached out and touched his arm.

He shrugged. And here came the casual downplaying. "What can you do, kids can be cruel."

"But that wasn't right. I'm sorry it happened to you."

He shrugged again and I could see was searching for some witty retort. A joke, some humorous subterfuge. This time I wasn't going to let him, though.

"And I'm sorry your parents got divorced. Mine did, too, and it sucks. I know."

Chris started fiddling with a small piece of palm that had fallen on the table. I was starting to realize that he fiddled when he was uncomfortable. "It was my best friend's mom, you know." His voice was soft and he looked completely vulnerable. "He was my only friend really, but after that we didn't speak much."

My hand was still resting on his arm and I tightened my grip.

"In a way, I actually introduced them. My dad to her."

"You don't think it's your fault, do you?"

"Well, if I hadn't been friends with her son—"

"No." I stopped him dead. "It had nothing to do with you, you get that, right?"

"When you're six years old it's all a bit confusing. Especially when your mother climbs into bed one day and doesn't come out for a while."

"I'm sure it is." God, I wanted to hug him. To throw my arms around him and tell him it was all okay, and make him feel better. He didn't deserve to feel this way, and if I thought I was attracted to him before, I liked him even more now. Funny Chris was great, but this Chris…was perfect.

"So that's me, Annie Anne. My wildly traumatic story. Now tell me about you. And make it as traumatic as possible, so I can feel good about myself." He was back to being funny Chris again.

"Okay…my parents also got divorced when I was sixteen. It's nothing dramatic like your story, they just grew apart."

"What else?"

"I hate Wednesdays." I don't know why I said it, it kind of just came out.

"Why?"

"Hump day. You know, right in the middle of the week."

Chris laughed. "What else?"

"Well, I have a sister and a brother-in-law, they're great. I have a gorgeous little niece who has these chubby little cheeks that you just want to eat."

"Yeah. I love kids," Chris said.

"Really?" This statement caught me off guard. He didn't seem like the type who would like kids, not that I knew what that type looked like, exactly.

"My ex has a son, he was three when we got together. He was pretty awesome; in fact, a few years down the line he was actually the only reason I was staying in the relationship…hence the pasta strainer." His voice was softer now and his fun demeanor had faded away.

"You must miss him," I said.

"I do see him from time to time, but it's not really the same."

"So you want to be a dad one day?" I asked.

"Sure. That would be cool."

"But you don't believe in love and marriage?" I asked.

"Maybe I'll just pull an Angelina or Madonna and get myself an orphan. They're very fashionable in Hollywood these days." He was all smiles again, as if he could turn it on and off at the snap of his fingers.

"But enough about me...you still haven't given me any angst, Annie."

"Angst. Oh, you mean, besides the fact I walked in on my future husband cheating and my whole fucking life fell into a large pile of crap."

"Your whole life hasn't fallen apart."

"Oh, trust me. It has. I'm not the person I was before it happened. I have no idea where the hell that Annie went."

"Maybe the new version of Annie is a better one?"

"No, she's terrible. She's lame, she's always making an idiot of herself, she's insecure and—"

"I think she's fucking great." His words stopped my talking. "I think she's perfect, just the way she is." And now they stopped my heart.

"Why are you being so nice to me, saying all these things?"

"Hey, what are fake boyfriends for?"

And then my heart plummeted. Of course, I'd almost forgotten, none of this was real. This was all part of the script we were playing out.

A loud noise made us both jump and we turned to investigate. I looked at the wall of jungle-like palm trees. The noise was definitely coming from there. And then suddenly a hand appeared.

I jumped.

What the hell was a hand doing all the way up there in the palm tree?

And then another hand appeared, and the two hands pushed the palm fronds apart to reveal a face.

It was Trevv.

And he was beaming at us dangerously.

"Busted!" he shouted, waggling a finger in the air.

Oh God, this was it, he'd heard our entire conversation and now this game with Chris was over before it had even begun.

CHAPTER THIRTEEN

⌒

*C*hris and I exchanged nervous looks. I could see he was thinking the exact same thing as I was.

"Busted, what?" I finally managed to stutter. If this was it, Trevv should just get it over with instead of dragging it out.

"Busted having fun."

And then he burst out laughing and both Chris and I joined in. It wasn't a forced laugh, either. It was genuine, the kind that comes from total relief.

"But seriously, howdy, neighbors!" he said, attempting a terribly cheesy Australian accent. It was almost as bad as Chris's.

Why, pray tell, was he doing that? There seemed to be no way of shaking the T-Squared scourge. They were like an irritating rash that wouldn't go away. That itch that was impossible to scratch. That big, painful pimple in the place you couldn't reach to pop, or that unwanted pile. And God, I wished I could pop his little head right now. Trevv had obviously gone to a lot of trouble to get the other presidential suite, just to be next to us.

But why?

To get one up on us again?

Was he really so egotistical that he couldn't bear the idea that our room was bigger and better than his? (Swinging his dick in the wind again.)

"Heya, guys." Then Tess's face appeared, sandwiched between Trevv and a big green palm leaf that looked like it was poking her in the eye.

They looked absurd.

Two little heads completely surrounded by green foliage.

Looking at us.

Blinking and smiling.

I was starting to get the distinct impression that perhaps they were both psychotic, bordering on the edge of lunacy. And then just to prove my point, as if I needed any more convincing, Trevv uttered the unthinkable.

"Do you want to join us for some rooftop drinks?" Bright white dental advert smile again.

Pause.

Let's take a moment to reflect here, please…

They—*cheating, heartbreaking boyfriend, and gorgeous slutty mistress*—were asking us to have drinks with them. As if nothing was wrong. As if nothing had ever transpired between us. Long-lost friends, buddies, pals. I take back that "bordering" part; these two were certifiable. And the sooner they were certified, the bloody better.

The only reason Trevv was asking us for drinks was so he could take center stage in his one-man show entitled *My Wonderful, Super-Awesome Life*. I'm sure all he wanted to do was tell us about his new sports car, his successful new firm, his amazing sex life, and his blessed joys. #happiness #blessed #lifeisgreat #love #mylifeiswayfuckingbetterthanyourlifesobegreenwithenvy

"I don't think so…," I started, but didn't get very far.

"Absolutely!" Chris shouted.

"What?" I shot him sharp dagger eyes. "Absolutely not. We can't. We were just about to…to…" I couldn't think of one thing that sounded like a good enough excuse to get out of drinks and my brain was frantically scrambling for something. "I've stopped drinking." I declared as confidently as I could.

Trevv's eyes drifted down to the table where two glasses of wine sat. *Shit.*

"As of now! I've stopped drinking as of right now." I smiled at him stupidly.

Trevv and Tess nodded and their heads finally disappeared behind the leaves. I swung around and glared at Chris. "Why the hell did you say yes?" I demanded.

He shrugged. "I thought it would be funny. And weird. We would have come back with enough fodder to mock them for the next year!"

"Hey." I stepped forward assertively. "Do I have to remind you again that this is not character research for one of your movies? Or some fun, entertaining story line for your personal amusement. This is my life."

"You're right. I'm sorry, it would have been horrible to put you in such an awkwa—"

"HAHAHAHAH!"

POP!

Raucous laughter pierced the air, followed by the loud pop of a champagne bottle, followed by a thud, as the cork—which had no doubt been intentionally aimed in our direction—flew onto our deck and bounced a few times, before falling into the pool with a tiny splash.

We stared at it. This foreign body, bobbing up and down in our pool. And then…

"HAHAHA!"

CLINK!

"CHEERS!"

It was loud. Too loud. They were doing it deliberately. Trying to smear their merriment in our faces.

"Oh my God, they're not?" Chris walked over to the balcony and peered through a crack in the palms. I joined him to see that Trevv and Tess were toasting and drinking champagne as if they were in one of those glamorous overlit alcohol adverts.

"We cannot let them get away with this," Chris said, running inside and returning with two bottles of champagne. "Okay, on the count of two, I'll pop this one, and on the count of three, you pop the other one." He handed me the bottle and readied himself.

This was ludicrous. "No, I'm not going to do that. I refuse to be pulled into this game." But then…

"Hello, is this room service?" It was Trevv. "Please can you bring me a bottle of Henri Jayer Richebourg Grand Cru, Cotê de Nuits, and your platter of lobster and oysters."

I looked at Chris. "Okay, on one, two…"—Chris popped his bottle—"and three…" I popped mine. The corks flew in different directions and champagne gushed out all over the place.

And then we burst out laughing. Not fake, forced laughter like T-Squared, but genuine laughter that rises up from the pit of your stomach and reverberates throughout your entire body.

"If I had a helicopter right now," Chris said between laughs, "I would take off from this roof and wave down at them as if they were mere peasants, or if I was a big Mafia boss who kept a suitcase of cash in his trunk, I would throw it in the air and let it shower down on them. Then I would set the rest on fire while swimming in my diamond-encrusted pool of Cristal."

We laughed, louder than Trevv and Tess—which I imagine must have really pissed them off. But when the pain in our stomachs and cheeks became too much to bear, we collapsed onto the big comfortable daybed. We were still holding the bottles of champagne and I had no idea what to do with mine, I'd never liked the stuff. Bitter, sour, massive-headache-inducing dreck.

"I hate champagne," Chris said, plonking his bottle down on the floor next to him.

"Me too."

"It's so bitter."

"And sour," I added.

"Like cat pee." Chris inevitably took it a step further.

"Well, I wouldn't go that far."

We were seated about a foot or so away from each other, and I could actually feel the heat coming off his body. It became so intense that at some stage, it was all I could feel. The space between us buzzed and crackled with some kind of electrical charge. It prickled my skin and made my palms sticky.

"Wow!" I sat forward.

"Wow what?"

Oh shit. Did I say that out loud? I had. Hopefully he had no idea what it was in reference to. It could easily be interpreted as *"Wow, amazing weather"* or *"Wow, interesting night."*

But then Chris smiled and said it back. "Wow!" His voice was whispery and strange and I knew that he'd felt it, too. We let the implications of our *wow*s wash over us. Something strange was happening. Something that I couldn't quite explain—

SPLISH. SPLASH. GIGGLE. GIGGLE.

I was immensely grateful when Trevv and Tess's loud water splashing shattered the moment that was starting to make my skin crawl. They were obviously cavorting in their plunge pool and I was about to suggest we get in, too, and splash even louder, when I heard some familiar sounds.

They were not?!?!?

Tess giggled breathily.

Trevv moaned slightly.

I turned and looked at Chris. He raised his eyebrows. "You're kidding."

I shook my head. "I think they are!"

"No, they're not." He sounded adamant. "They can't be?"

"It hasn't stopped them in the past."

"Ooohhh." *Giggle, giggle giggle* "Trevv." *Whisper, whisper, whisper*

I felt positively nauseous.

My stomach turned itself inside out as I imagined the two of them in the pool. I wondered if his nipple clamps were waterproof. This was bringing back a barrage of painful feelings. I felt slightly dizzy and uneasy on my feet as my head swam with the memories and images from that fateful day.

I felt a hand on my shoulder. "Come on, let's go watch a movie."

We walked downstairs and sat on the couch in total silence for a while.

"If it's any consolation, I hate them," Chris said while cracking open a bag of chips and crunching one loudly for added effect.

"But you think Tess is so hot." I couldn't believe I'd actually said that out loud. It sounded so childish and shallow, but the fact that she was so hot definitely hurt. I would be lying if I said it hadn't been a blow to my ego.

"I…I felt like the ugly duckling being kicked out of the nest for the swan." My voice quivered slightly as I spoke, and I couldn't believe I'd just said that out loud.

"Jesus!" The volume and firmness in his voice surprised me and I looked up. "You're crazy."

"You can't deny it, Chris. She's smoking hot. She's basically sex on legs. Any man would let her clamp his nipples, just to be near her!"

"I'll admit that when you first see her, she's pretty hot, but she's also the most irritating person I've ever met." He jumped up off the couch and started doing a Tess impersonation in a high-pitched squeaky voice, *"Oooh, the flowers are like our blooming love, my ring is so shiny and sparkly, giggle giggle, oh, Trevvy, you're the best!"*

He paused to see my reaction. "Trust me. All her hotness fades away the second you spend more than a minute in her company. Besides…" His voice softened slightly. "Besides, you're beautiful."

Wowza.

My body temperature rose by a hundred degrees, but then it dropped again. This wasn't real. None of this was real.

"You can cut out the whole fake boyfriend stuff now, no one is watching."

"It's not fake, Annie." Without warning, Chris slid closer to me.

"It's…it's not?" Tongue tying, legs turning to cooked spaghetti, pulse like a racehorse, dizzying thoughts…it was happening again.

"I mean it, you're really very…" A little pause. A beat. A moment filled with anticipation. And then in one more little movement, he was right next to me. Looking. *What was he doing?*

My eyes drifted to his lips for some reason, and the second they did, he smiled.

"You're one hot bitch, Annie Anne."

CHAPTER FOURTEEN

∽

$\mathcal{I}$'ve been called many things over the years, but "one hot bitch" certainly wasn't one of them. What was I supposed to say to that? And I can't deny I felt somewhat disappointed. I'd been holding out for something like *stunning*. I would even have taken *pretty*, but this? Should I be offended, or amused?

"Okay, you're not one of those feminists who are going to beat me for saying that and then burn your bra in protest, are you?" He put his hands up in front of his face in mock fear.

"I might," I quipped, deciding to go along with the joking tone of this whole thing. I was clearly reading way too much into what was going on, he was just joking. That was his way, this was all pretend.

"Well, in that case I'll get some matches." He gave me a naughty wink. "But seriously, if you're going to punch me, please don't do it in the face. I've been told it's one of my best features."

I smiled at him—I would have to agree.

"That's me fishing for a compliment, by the way," he said, looking at me earnestly.

"Oh…was that what it was? Well in that case, you're very handsome."

"Not hot?"

"Mmmm…maybe at the right angle."

"Ouch." He grabbed his chest dramatically as if he'd been wounded.

"Okay, fine…" I couldn't hide the bashful tone in my voice. "You're pretty hot." I blushed. A proper bright red, warm flush. Without thinking, I touched my cheeks, which only drew attention to them.

"It looks like I'm not the only one who's hot." Of course he would take this opportunity for another witty retort. And then his demeanor changed as his eyes sought mine out.

"I'm being serious, though, Annie Anne."

"About what?"

"You're really great. And you're way hotter than Tess."

At that I burst out laughing. But my laughter was very short lived. It came to a skidding stop when Chris reached over me and put a finger across my lips.

"I'm being serious."

"You're being serious?" I repeated like a drone.

"Why wouldn't I be?" He lowered his finger and for a moment he let it linger on my lips. They were officially on fire.

We sat in silence, both of us, I think, unsure of how to proceed. I, for one, was also confused. I didn't know when he was joking or being serious. When he was saying nice things because he was playing the role of perfect boyfriend, or when he was saying them because he meant them. This suddenly felt strange and awkward. One thing was certain, this game of pretend was really starting to get confusing, for me anyway.

"So, the movie!" I said, trying to steer the conversation in another direction.

"Yes." Chris picked up the remote and started flicking through the channels, but it soon became obvious that all the movies were in French with English subtitles.

"Gives us a chance to brush up on our French," he said, settling into the couch. (Shoulders officially touching now!) The movie started, and I didn't understand any of it. There seemed to be a lot of angst and tension between the two main characters—in black and white. Much intense staring and smoking of Gauloises cigarettes, and then the unthinkable happened.

Before I knew it, *she* (effortlessly chic French woman with petite features and a pixie cut) was naked. *He* (smoldering French man with intense eyes) was aggressively pinning her to the wall. His pants came off, revealing a perfect bum, and he spread her legs and…

They went for it. Like rabid dogs.

It was frantic and sticky and hot and wild and went from the wall to the bed to the floor and back to the bed. It was one of the most hectic sex scenes I'd ever seen in a movie (bar *Ocean's 11 Inches* of course). You actually saw penis! I sat dead still, unable to move. I didn't want to look in Chris's direction. I could feel his muscles tensing and body stiffening. Mine did, too. I was suddenly sitting bolt upright in the chair.

Penis! Penis! *Penis!* It was all I could think about, it was all I could see, even when I flicked my eyes around the room, they were everywhere…can of soda, complimentary pencil, banana in fruit basket and, *oh no*, suddenly I was imagining what Chris's penis looked like and wondering if he knew I was thinking about his penis…

Oh God, stop! I bit down on my lip just in case the word came flying out, too...

"So, Annie, what do you want to do next?"

"Play with your penis!"

No, not a good thing to say, so I folded my arms and kept my lips tightly sealed. And as it turned out, it was also the longest that had ever been shot in the history of cinema (not the penis, the sex scene). And the more it went on, the more turned on I was getting. I tried to fight it, but the combination of sitting next to Chris and watching two gorgeous people engaged in passionate sex was a deadly combination. Just when I thought I was going to die of total embarrassment, they stopped, whipped out cigarettes, and started smoking.

Instant relief. I felt Chris's shoulders relax and heard a loud sigh of relief. I think my sigh was audible, too. *Was Chris feeling it, too?*

The scene was over but the buzz of sex surrounded us like a thick hot blanket. You could feel it in the air, moving between us. Weaving its way in and out and around. The air had been ignited with the promise of something unspoken. There seemed to be only one way out of this situation, and it involved our clothes on the floor.

My mind had never whirled around so fast. It felt like someone had removed all my thoughts and thrown them into a blender and turned it on. I was dizzy from trying to sift through them. There wasn't a single coherent thought I could grab onto, either, just fragments...

Yes, he's hot.

No...don't sleep with strangers, or pretend boyfriends.

But so sexy...

Yes...No!

What if I suck in bed? And not in a good way.

YES, no, YES, no—

SHIT!

It felt like we'd been sitting there for twenty minutes before my thoughts finally settled to a mild simmer. That is to say that there was only *one* thought rushing through my brain now. Flashing in neon red like one of those signs outside Adult Extravaganza.

Sex. Sex. Sex.

But I knew I couldn't. He was basically a stranger after all. And what if I bored him? This moment needed to end, and I needed to be the one to do it.

"Chris." His name came out so loud and fast it was jarring.

"Annie." *Shit*, he was saying my name in a soft, sultry tone.

"Chris!" I said it again, in hopes that he would pick up on the big red line that I was vocally drawing in the sand.

"Annie." His tone was slightly more normal now.

I took a deep breath and started, "I just…" But the words were not coming. "I…I, it's just that—"

"I get it," he said firmly.

"You do?"

"Totally."

He said it all with such authority that I wanted to believe him, but without actual verbal confirmation, we could be speaking about different things.

"What are you talking about?" I asked him.

He looked at me oddly. "Why? What are you talking about?"

We looked at each other blankly.

"Well?" I asked again, "What are *you* talking about?"

"Same thing you're talking about, Annie."

"But I haven't said anything; how do you know what I was going to talk about?"

He shot me an odd look again. "The thing that you were going to say, but then I said not to worry, because I know."

This conversation was going nowhere. We were skating around the subject like absolute idiots. I would have expected Chris to be more straightforward. He said everything else he thought, just not this. If he wasn't going to say it, then I was going to have to be the one to do it.

My mouth opened—

"Sex!"

Chris swallowed hard and his pupils dilated.

"What about sex?" His tone was slightly hushed again. *Screw that hushed tone!*

"We're not having it." I was firm.

"Who said we're having it?"

What? Had I misinterpreted this entire situation? I was mortified.

"I didn't say we *were* having it." I was backtracking and couldn't hide the distinctly defensive tone in my voice.

"No, definitely not," he said again. By now my heart was sinking and the humiliation was rising fast. "We don't have any cigarettes."

"What?"

"Cigarettes. You can't have sex without cigarettes to smoke afterward."

Thank God! He was throwing me a gift—a chance to turn this whole conversation into a joke. To toss it away with humor, which—in my opinion—was the best thing we could do now.

"I agree. And certainly not without subtitles, either."

"Although…" Hang on, what was happening here? His voice was

doing that strange lilting thing again. The soft inflections. The unmistakable huskiness of it. "I did see a vending machine that sells them in the lobby."

"What? Subtitles?" I couldn't resist.

"Of course. And I'm sure I can find a vending machine for cigarettes, too. And we can use the matches that we were going to burn your bra with."

"I've heard that smoking is bad for you," I quipped.

Chris leaned dangerously close to me. "Sometimes, Annie, the best things in life are."

CHAPTER FIFTEEN

❧

$\mathcal{W}$e were face-to-face now. Our eyes locked. I bit my bottom lip and Chris's pupils dilated.

"Like chocolate," I offered.

"Or coconut rum cocktails."

We smiled stupidly at each other. His eyes were brighter than I'd ever seen. His boyish charm was shining through, and a part of me wished that he would just take the reins and steer us in the direction that the not-so-subtle subtext was taking us.

"Annie, can I kiss you? Only for rehearsal purposes of course."

"Rehearsal?"

"Well, if we're playing boyfriend/girlfriend, we should have at least kissed once."

"Just to practice," I said, "I mean, it's not like I find you attractive or anything like that. And this certainly isn't just a ploy to manipulate you into kissing me."

"Of course not."

My eyes were moving down to his lips and noting that they were slightly parted.

"Maybe just a peck on the lips?" Chris said. "I'm not suggesting we go full tongue. Unless you want to?"

"No! Full tongue not necessary," I said.

"Agreed." Chris held his hand out for me to shake. I did. But instead of letting go once the handshake was over, I clung onto it.

"Okay, let's do this." I started leaning in. I tilted my head to the side ever so slightly and closed my eyes. I was really doing this. I moved closer until I could feel the warmth of his breath on my face.

"No! Wait." I pulled away. "You should know, I haven't done this in a while."

"That's okay." Chris smiled as if I was amusing him terribly.

"Okay. Let's do it then." I started leaning in again but then pulled away. "So I could be rusty."

"Okay." Chris nodded again and this time he started leaning in. I closed my eyes and felt his breath again and then—

"So please don't judge me on this kiss or anything, because it probably won't be that good, or maybe it will be okay, but—"

"*Annie*!" He said my name so loudly that I did a double take. "Shut up, I want to kiss you."

Chris took my face between his hands and pulled it all the way up to his. Our lips were so close I could almost feel them. He looked me in the eye one last time before shutting his and bringing his lips to mine.

They touched and for a second we hung in a state of suspended animation. No one moved, no one breathed. I wondered if our hearts were still beating. The moment was wonderfully exquisite and downright painful.

And then his lips started moving. They were warm, and tasted of salt-and-vinegar chips and beer. It felt so good to be kissed again, and I moved closer to him until our bodies were touching; the effect was instant. My entire body felt like it was being kissed at once. And then after a few more blissful seconds, he stopped kissing me and let his lips linger on mine as if he was waiting for something. *An invitation from me to go further?*

"Annie?" he asked, whispering against my mouth.

But instead of going any further, I pulled away gently. The intensity of the kiss had left me feeling uneasy. It hadn't been what I'd expected. I'd expected silly and awkward. Instead it was beautiful. And dangerous. A kiss like that can make a girl start thinking all kinds of things. "It's getting late," I said.

Chris nodded. "I suppose it is."

"I should really go to bed."

"Good plan."

"Okay." I stood up quickly.

"Are you sure you don't want to sleep downstairs?"

I shook my head. "No. Like I said, I like the view."

I started walking away, but before I left the room I felt compelled to look back at him. And when I did, he was looking in my direction.

"Thanks for a nice night, Annie Anne…"

"Pleasure." I walked up the stairs and left Chris in the room. A part of me regretted it, but another part of me—perhaps the bigger part—felt relieved. What had started as something seemingly innocent was changing. Chris was no longer the benign person I could practice on, because I was starting to like him. And Chris was the last person in the world a girl like me should start liking. He lived in LA and he didn't believe in love. It would be a terrible idea to sleep with him because at this point my feelings had moved beyond pretend.

Just as I was opening the door to my room, I heard that familiar rustle of palms. I'd almost forgotten about our unpleasant, sexually rabid neighbors. I turned and Trevv was looking at me suspiciously. He had actually stooped to full-blown spying now.

"Have a disagreement, did you?"

"What?"

"Sleeping upstairs, are you?"

He was firing questions at me in typical lawyer style, waiting for me to make a mistake. I needed to think quickly before our cover was blown.

"No. No. Um…we've run out of dry towels downstairs. We were going to bathe, *together*, and I remember there were some up here." I smiled at him. I hoped he was buying this.

But I could see him eyeing me suspiciously, searching for evidence to prove Chris and I weren't together. Why was it so important to Trevv anyway? Did he really want me to spend the rest of my life miserable and alone?

I ran into the room quickly. *God, I hoped there were towels here!* I looked around frantically, pulling open drawers, throwing blankets off the bed, and looking in the bathroom.

Nada.

Not a towel in sight. The hotel had probably not put towels in the spare room since we were just a "couple" and had no kids staying in the other room.

I walked out of the room and threw my hands in the air. "Well, what do you know? No towels." I shrugged, hoping this little act of mine was working.

"Here." Suddenly Trevv's head disappeared for a moment, and then his hand popped through the foliage, holding two towels. "You can borrow ours."

"No thanks," I said as quickly as possible. The last thing I wanted was *anything* from Trevv, unless of course it was going to be that massive apology I was still waiting on. I would probably still be waiting on it after the world went postapocalyptic and ants colonized the earth.

Trevv shook his head. "I insist, Anne. It's the least we can do."

The least he can do? As if towels were meant to be some kind of consolation prize. Was *this* the apology I had been waiting for?

Sorry I cheated on you and had kinky sex in our bed with a coworker and you went to jail...here, have a lovely towel. It's cotton, you know.

And without any invitation, he tossed them over. They landed at my feet with a sickening *splat*. Trevv was glaring at me and I had no choice but to pick them up.

"Thanks."

"Don't mention it." He flashed me his snow-white smile, which seemed even whiter in the pale moonlight. "What are neighbors for, hey?" He winked.

I tried to muster some kind of smile—at this stage a grimace would have sufficed. But internally I felt sick. The towels reminded me of the toothbrushes squashed into the same cup. Sure, the towels hadn't been used yet, but all I could think about while holding them was their naked bodies rubbing up against the fabric.

"If you need sugar, just let me know." And with that, he was gone. The palms smacked together as his face disappeared. I knew I had no choice but to take the offensive towels and sleep downstairs, for fear that Trevv might investigate later.

But going back down was the last thing I wanted to do. I inched my way down the stairs, trying to psych myself up for seeing Chris again. I was vaguely aware of the sound of running water, but by that stage was so wrapped up in my own thoughts that I didn't quite register—

Chris was in the shower. Stark naked.

He was washing his hair with his back to me, and against all my better judgment—I stared. His back was broad and manly and the bum attached to it was, *well*, perfect. I was overcome by an urge to squeeze it. I could almost feel my nails digging into it. As he washed his hair and shifted his weight from one leg to another it would flex, accentuating those dimples on the sides. *Mmmm...*was I salivating?

And then he turned. And because my eyes were focused on his bum, something else suddenly came into full view.

It was staring me straight in the face.

I couldn't tear my eyes away, I was so shocked and fascinated at the same time. I'd almost forgotten that there was a whole body attached to it. It was all I could see. I've never really been a fan of the way *they* look. They're not exactly the most pleasant-looking things. But his was...perfect.

The shape, the size...*perfect*.

I heard a little gasp. It came from me and it was totally involuntary.

"Annie?"

Suddenly I remembered that there was a head, mouth, eyes, and brain attached to the appendage down south. I jumped backward away from the object of my fascination and banged straight into the hard wall behind me.

"Ouch!" I screamed loudly. Why is hitting your elbow so damn painful? I grabbed it and rubbed hard, trying to quell the sharp pain shooting up my arm now. "Ooooowwee," I moaned loudly again.

"Are you okay, Annie?" Two hands grabbed me under my arms and ushered me to the living room. I came face-to-face with a wet, soapy Chris.

"Sit." His hand came around to the small of my back as he guided me onto the couch.

But as I sat, I came face-to-face with *it* again.

I slapped my hands over my eyes at the same time that Chris slapped his hands over his…

"There's a towel on the floor." My eyes were tightly closed as I pointed in the general vicinity that the towels had fallen. Chris shuffled around, and I heard the soft sound of the fabric as he wrapped the towel around himself.

"It's safe to open your eyes now."

"I'm so sorry, I didn't mean to…but Trevv saw me going into the other bedroom and…"

Chris laughed loudly and collapsed into the other couch. "That was quite a reaction."

"I guess I got a fright."

"Wow. I'm not sure whether that's a compliment, or the biggest insult I've ever gotten in my entire life."

I felt my cheeks go red and hot again. "Good fright," I managed to whisper.

"Glad you approve." Chris sounded rather pleased with himself.

"Sorry," I said again, trying not to look in his direction for fear that my eyes would automatically make a beeline for his crotch.

"It's okay. I guess we're kind of even, considering that breast you thrust in my hand earlier today."

"What!" My eyes flicked up and met his. "I did no such thing. I would never deliberately thrust my breast, or thrust any other part of my body onto you for that matter."

A loud hearty laugh escaped Chris's mouth. "Joking, Annie."

"Okay. Good. Because I wouldn't want you to get the wrong impression about me, you know."

"What impression is that?" His voice was so damn playful and sexy right now and it was messing with my head.

"That I'm a…a…" *What was I trying to say?*

"A thruster?" he offered with a laugh in his voice.

"There's no such word," I said quickly, trying to shake images of all the thrusting I was suddenly imagining.

"As much as I want to continue this conversation, I need to get back into the shower and rinse off."

"Sure, I won't look this time. Promise," I said.

"Why not? It's not like you haven't seen it before."

Chris got up and walked back to the shower. I heard the towel drop to the floor and knew that he was completely naked again.

My blood started doing that hot, rapid-rushing swooshing thing again. My body seemed to react to Chris in such a primal way. A way that was totally out of my conscious control.

God, I wanted him so badly.

I wanted nothing more than to take my clothes off and climb into the shower with him…

CHAPTER SIXTEEN

⟿

*B*ut I didn't. And when the shower finally came to an end, I found myself feeling extremely relieved.

"So, I'll take the couch tonight and you can take the bed?" I heard Chris start brushing his teeth, and I was struck by how intimate this all was.

The bedtime routine. Washing, brushing, and then climbing into your pajamas. This is something you're meant to do with your partner, not a stranger.

"I can take the couch, it's very comfortable," I said.

"I wouldn't be a gentleman if I let you sleep on the couch, Annie. Take the bed."

The point was that I didn't want to sleep in the bed. *His* bed, with *his* scent lingering on the pillows. But I really didn't want to explain all that to him, either, so I accepted graciously.

I climbed into the bed cautiously, soon discovering that it *was* in fact the biggest, softest bed I'd ever been in, *and yes*, the smell of Chris lingered. The earthy sandalwood of his cologne combining with the smell of sweet shampoo, and soap.

Chris climbed onto the couch and turned the lights off. We lay in darkness for a while, and I was acutely aware of him breathing, shuffling, and moving his pillows around.

"Are you comfortable on the couch?" I asked.

"Yes. Very."

There was a pause.

"If I'd said no would you have offered me the other side of the bed?" I could hear the twinkle in his voice and I smiled. *Here we go again—sexual innuendos and loaded witty banter.* How was I supposed to sleep if we carried on like that?

"Maybe," I teased him.

"Shit! I should have said I was uncomfortable!"

"Oh well, your loss." I was smiling like an idiot and was glad for the cover of darkness.

Chris chuckled, "Maybe it's actually your loss!"

"And how do you figure that?"

"I've been told my spooning abilities are pretty good."

"Good night, Chris."

"Night night, Annie Anne."

I closed my eyes and started drifting off to sleep when a sudden, and very loud knock on the door ripped me back to reality. I looked over at Chris as he jolted up.

"Hey, neighbors, thought I would bring you some more towels just in case."

It was Trevv! Chris and I looked at each other in total shock. But that quickly turned to absolute panic when the door handle started to move.

"Can I come in?" Trevv asked in a suspicious-sounding voice. This was not a friendly towel run; he was trying to bust us.

"Um…just give us a moment, we're kind of in the middle of something…," Chris shouted without a hint of an accent in his voice.

"Your accent," I hissed at him.

"My what?" For a second or two he looked at me blankly, and then I saw the realization dawn on him. "Just give us a wee mo there, mate!" He slapped the accent on thick and proper before jumping up, grabbing his sleeping stuff off the couch, and tossing it over to the bed. I quickly arranged it so it looked like he'd been sleeping there.

"We're just…you know, mate. You know."

"Of course!" Trevv said.

Then Chris pulled his shirt off and tossed it across the floor. He ruffled his hair and jumped onto the bed. He turned and looked at me briefly before ruffling my hair so hard it felt like it was standing up straight. Then he started tugging at my shirt.

"Take it off," he hissed in my ear.

"No!"

"Just take it off." And with that, Chris grabbed my top, pulled it over my head, and tossed it up in the air.

"Hey. What are you doing?" I tried to cover myself.

"It needs to look real. You can come in now," he called out to Trevv while pulling me into the crook of his arm.

My first thought was how downright embarrassing this was, but then I saw the look on Trevv's face. I was now very glad that Chris had gone to all the effort, because Trevv walked in with a look of utter suspicion plastered across his face. It was clear he had come to gather evidence.

"You can put them on the couch," Chris pointed and Trevv moved toward it.

I looked over at the couch and gasped when I saw it. *Shit!* Chris had left a pillow there and it had *not* gone unnoticed. Trevv looked down at the pillow curiously, and then he slowly raised his eyes and smiled at us like a serial killer might.

"Well, good night, you two." He flashed us another grin and exited. "Sleep well."

"Shit!" Chris climbed out of bed and rushed over to the pillow. "He's onto us."

I nodded in agreement.

"Shit. Shit. Shit. He's going to have a field day with this! He's going to tell all our so-called mutual friends and everyone we know and then…"

I wasn't even able to finish the sentence, because suddenly Chris was on top of me. How had he managed to get across the room so quickly?

"What are you *oooohhh*…"

He forcefully grabbed my legs, wrapped them around his waist, and then, *and then*, he kissed me. I was in such shock that it took a moment or two to register, reciprocate, or even breathe. But the second I felt the tip of his tongue against my lips, I grabbed him and kissed him back.

Some kind of wild, raw, unadulterated lust gripped me and I heard myself moaning. I felt myself grabbing at his shoulder and writhing under him. I ran my hands through his hair as the kiss got more frantic.

"Oh God," I gasped as Chris raised my hips up off the bed and fell deeper between my legs. What the hell were we doing? The loud sound of the door bursting open caught my attention. I looked across the room just as Trevv walked back in.

"Trevv! Oh my God, what you doing here?" I was out of breath from the kiss.

"Jeez, Trevv, do you mind...we're kind of in the middle of something here," Chris said, equally breathy and looking a little red in the cheeks.

Trevv stared at us in disbelief. "Just came back to suggest you lock your doors tonight. You never know who's wandering around out there. Watching you through the window from the flower beds," he said before slithering out the door again.

His words cut me to the quick. How did he know? Had he seen me? Mortifying! And worse, he was rubbing it in my face.

"That was fucking close," Chris said, raising his head and looking directly into my eyes. Our faces were mere inches apart, and I could feel the warmth of his breath as he spoke. "I heard him coming back so..."

"So you thought you would attack me?"

He smiled. It was so sexy I forgot all about Trevv. Oh God, Chris was hot. And oh God, he was on top of me. "You enjoyed it. Admit it. You've been secretly hoping I would attack you for ages now."

"No!" I said indignantly.

"Yes you have, you naughty girl." Chris was still on top of me even though it was totally unnecessary.

"You know you can get off me, right?" I said, not really wanting him to, though.

"I know."

"So are you?"

"No. Not right now. I'm pretty comfortable like this, aren't you?"

Comfortable wasn't exactly the word I would use to describe the feeling of lying underneath him with his previously naked man-part dangerously close to mine.

"You're a really good kisser, Annie Anne."

"I was just acting," I said quickly.

"Really? You were very convincing. I think I have scratch marks on my shoulders to prove it."

"What?" I looked at his shoulders and *yes*, there they were. I had clawed at him like some crazed woman, drunk on hormones and horniness. I flushed red with embarrassment.

"I'm sorry, I didn't mean to."

"Don't worry, it'll be nice to have something to show off on the beach tomorrow." Chris smiled down at me with a naughty expression. "Do you want something, too?"

"Like what?"

"Hickey perhaps?"

"No thanks." He was still on top of me and showing no signs of moving.

"Do you mind if I do something? I just need to figure something out quickly." Chris asked but didn't wait for my reply. He leaned in for another kiss. This time I reciprocated immediately. But the kiss was totally different. It was slow and deep, and the kind of kiss you could totally get lost in. I tightened my leg grip and wrapped my arms around him. God, I shouldn't have.

He stopped and whispered against my lips, "I thought so."

"Thought so what?"

"Strawberries. *Strawberries* and mint. I was trying to figure out what you tasted like."

He lifted himself onto his elbows once more and looked down at me again before finally rolling off. "So I better go and sleep on the…" He left the sentence open-ended as if he expected me to complete it.

"The couch," I said.

"Yes, the couch." He started to get up and then stopped. "Unless you think that might be dangerous, what with Trevv lurking around?"

"It might be," I agreed with nervous excitement.

"We wouldn't want him to come back in and see me on the couch, would we?"

"No. We wouldn't." My heart rate quickened at the mere suggestion of sharing a bed with him. "We could just lock the door, though."

"But what if he's the kind of guy that knows how to pick locks?" Chris offered. "You just never know what Trevv is capable of."

"So true," I agreed, although the idea that Trevv might sneak back in the middle of the night and pick our lock was totally preposterous.

Chris smiled. "So should I climb in?"

I gave a small nod as the inside of my mouth dried up like the plains of the savanna. God, I was nervous. I hadn't shared a bed with a man since Trevv.

Chris pulled the duvet down and slipped in. I followed his example, and as if someone was conducting us, our heads touched the pillows and our eyes locked at precisely the same time. We stared again. I felt like a kid playing one of those blinking games, *first one to blink loses*. But what would the winner get?

No one blinked. We stared until my eyes started to water and sting. "So good night then," I said, blinking them repeatedly.

"Good night," Chris replied, and then he leaned in and planted a soft kiss on my cheek. "Sleep well."

***

I'm not sure how long I'd been asleep when I was woken up by the sounds of typing. I opened my sleepy eyes and looked up to find Chris sitting on the couch, slouched over his computer. The usual menagerie surrounded him, his iPad, a few coffee cups, a Coke, and a chocolate.

"Hey." My voice still had that deep sleepy husk to it.

Chris turned around fast, as if he'd received the fright of his life and slammed the computer shut.

"Sorry, I didn't mean to wake you." He got up immediately and slipped the computer into his laptop bag.

"It's okay." I smiled at him. "I'm glad it's going well."

"What is?"

"Your movie—it looks like it's going well."

A halfhearted smile tugged at the corners of his lips. "Thanks."

"So you finally found your inspiration?" I had to admit a small part of me wondered if our kiss had inspired him. But that was a foolish thought. Wasn't it?

Chris's eyes momentarily met mine and then seemed to drift away, as if he was looking at something behind me.

"Go back to sleep, Annie."

***

The sound of a message on my phone woke me the next morning. It was from Lilly; she and Jane were feeling much better and would be arriving tomorrow morning. I shuddered to think what they were going to say to all this—playing a fake couple with Chris with

T-Squared right next door. Jane would definitely not be down for this, and would probably make a list of all the things that could go wrong with this plan, of which there were many. I wasn't completely blind here; I was very aware of the consequences. They were basically screaming at me and I was deliberately choosing not to listen. I was dangerously close to feeling something very real for Chris that would probably never be reciprocated. But I also hadn't felt so alive, so much like myself in ages. And I didn't want the feeling to end.

"Coffee, honey." The rich smell of coffee wafted past me and made my mouth water.

I looked up and smiled at my thoughtful, handsome, sexy fake boyfriend. Sometimes the world is such a cruel place. It dangles the proverbial carrot, and then whips it away.

"Thanks, love," I said, playing along, although truthfully it felt good saying that.

"So what do you want to do today?"

I sipped the dark, warm liquid, and the caffeine instantly went to work on my sleepy brain and body.

"Actually, I wouldn't mind escaping this resort. Getting away from our neighbors."

"Sounds perfect." And it did.

***

Half an hour later, we were in the comfortable seats of our own private speedboat—one that thankfully came with a canopy for shade, because the temperature outside at ten in the morning was already scorching. I looked over at Chris and gave an excited smile as the engines fired to life—and then the boat lurched forward and I nearly fell out of my seat. Chris suddenly grabbed the edge of the boat like his life depended on it, and I'd fucking forgotten. He hated water.

"Are you okay?" I shouted over the roar of the engines and the violent sound of water whipping against the side of the boat.

"Sort of." Chris forced a smile and I moved over onto his side and sat next to him.

"I'm so sorry, I should never have suggested this. You could have said no!" Why hadn't he said no?

"It's okay." He was trying to sound brave and upbeat.

"Here, hold on to me." I took his arm and wrapped it through mine.

He gave a little laugh and indicated for me to grab onto the railing, which I promptly did—and clutched on for dear life as we started flying across the calm water, leaving a white, frothy frenzy in our wake. Very quickly the beach and the resort (along with those on it, thank God) were becoming distant memories. The sea beneath us started getting darker and darker, and we were quite a long way away from the land when the engines finally cut out.

"This is where the dolphins pass." The driver turned to us and pointed across the still water.

A few other boats had also started gathering, equally eager to see the dolphins. We all sat in silence; the only sounds were those of the waves lapping against the sides of the various boats, until someone from another boat shouted, "Over there!"

Silver fins that glinted as they caught the light appeared from all sides, rising and falling back into the water. They surrounded us, and the sea suddenly looked alive. Every now and then a dolphin would jump out of the water in all its sleek, silver-gray glory. They were the most elegant creatures I'd ever seen. Ballerinas of the sea.

They were also curious; some ventured right up to the side of the boat, so close at times that if I'd reached out, I would have touched them. The boat started up again and we sped off. The dolphins seemed to take this as a challenge and started racing the boats, jumping and soaring out of the water. They were so agile and effortlessly graceful, the way they maneuvered in and out of the boats.

"Do you know that dolphins give each other names?" Chris asked, shouting over the sound of the high-speed engines.

"Really?"

"Yes, they develop their own individual whistles that effectively act as their own names. True story!"

"Wow, I didn't know that."

"So if you were a dolphin I might call you—"

And then he did it.

The silliest dolphin impression I've ever heard—well, *to be honest*, I'd never really heard a dolphin impression before so I had absolutely no benchmark from which to measure it. This was a first, and thus definitely the silliest. He opened his mouth and a high-pitched squeaking noise came out. I burst out laughing and tried to outdo him with another equally ridiculous and maybe even higher-pitched noise. And so the great dolphin whistle-off began, until we realized that the boat had stopped and the driver was looking back at us with a concerned expression, as if he hadn't been informed that he was taking the residents of a mental asylum out for an excursion. When Chris and I finally noticed the terrified squint he was giving us, we couldn't contain the eruption of laughter that followed. We guffawed until it hurt.

I felt like I could be completely silly with Chris. Totally free, without fear of judgment or ridicule. He was the first person who'd made me laugh like this…

Crap!

There was no denying it any longer—my feelings for Chris were growing by the second and then something he'd said rang in my ears. *All the women he'd dated thought that they would finally be the one to change him. Melt his heart and make him believe in love.*

I needed to snap out of this. And fast. It was potentially very detrimental to my health—as in my heart could get ripped out of my chest and thrown to sea urchins to feast on. The man in the boat spoke.

"This is where you will snorkel," he said, bringing two sets of flippers and snorkeling goggles to us.

"Oh, no thanks." I waved an arm at him politely. I wasn't going to leave Chris here on the boat by himself while I swam.

"It's okay, go." I could see he was forcing a smile.

"I don't want to leave you here alone."

"I'll be fine," he said, and I didn't believe him.

"I have an idea." I moved closer to him. "Why don't you come with me?"

He shook his head quickly. "No thanks."

"You can swim, right?" I asked.

"Yes, but—"

"So come with me. We'll do it slowly."

"I don't know." He sounded so reluctant.

"Trust me, Chris."

I reached out and took his hand in mine and inched him toward the edge of the boat. I grabbed one of the life jackets and held it out in front of him.

"Take your shirt off," I said, and this time Chris didn't come back with a witty retort like, *"I'll take mine off if you take off yours."*

He started peeling his shirt off, and my eyes locked onto his hands and followed them. Pulling the hem up, lifting the fabric over his stomach, his chest, his head, and finally off. Chris dropped his shirt on the floor of the boat and looked at me.

There was a new emotion bubbling between us this time. And if this were a real relationship, this would be that moment when unconditional trust is formed. When a couple learns that they can rely on each other and face anything together. But this was not a real relationship.

I started putting his life jacket on and fastened the clips in the front. I pulled the strings hard, making sure they were totally secure, and then I led him to the edge of the boat.

"Maybe just one more."

Chris grabbed another life jacket and wrapped it around himself. I watched as he did up the straps. His fingers were shaking slightly but I could see he was trying to hide it. If this had been a comedy I would have laughed; the jackets made him look like the Michelin Man, but there was nothing funny about this moment.

The water wasn't very far below us at all. It was tiny jump, but I knew that for Chris it would probably feel like leaping out of a plane. I looked over at him. He was staring at the water in absolute horror.

"You're not that kid anymore, Chris."

He lifted his head and his eyes met mine. "No?"

"No. You're successful and brilliant and funny and hot and you saved me from total humiliation when you didn't even know me."

He smiled faintly. "Thanks, Annie."

"In fact, you are probably one of the nicest people I've ever met."

His smile grew, mine did not. Because the cruel, painful irony of that statement didn't escape me.

"It's ironic, but my fake relationship with you has probably been the best relationship I've ever been in. You're the best boyfriend I've ever had and you aren't even real."

Sadness gnawed at me. I was twenty-seven years old. I'd spent most of my youth dating losers and assholes, and then when I thought I'd found the right guy, he turned out to be an asshole, too. And now I was on the wrong side of twenty-five, skidding toward thirty, and I still hadn't found the right guy.

"What?" Chris asked. "What're you thinking?"

I looked at him and wished he was mine. But he wasn't. And none of this was really real.

"Nothing, it's fine." I perked up and squeezed his hand. "So are you ready to do this?"

Chris gave me a tiny nod.

"In three, two—"

"Wait." Chris sounded panicked.

"Think of something else," I quickly said.

"Like what?"

"Think happy things. Happy thoughts. Nice, distracting thoughts. What would make you feel better right now? What would make you forget all the bad memories and block it all out?"

Chris gave me that sexy smile I was going to miss. And then he kissed me.

CHAPTER SEVENTEEN

*I*t wasn't a kiss like before. There was nothing small and soft and restrained about it. It wasn't breathy lips that lingered, it was hungry and fiery and it consumed.

I felt my body being pulled off the ground as Chris wrapped his arms around me. I let out a surprised gasp as his lips came down on mine. Hard. It was real and raw and so fucking hot.

I opened my mouth and let Chris in. Our tongues and lips crashed and collided with no finesse whatsoever. It was frantic and uninhibited and desperate, as if I was drowning and he was the last drop of oxygen left in the world.

His arms moved down my body and I shuddered against him. They traveled lower and then he completely lifted me off the ground. I wrapped my legs and arms around him and held on for dear life. The kiss deepened and was almost suffocating. And then I felt us fall. And for a moment or two, we floated through the air as one, nothing stopping us or holding us back. I dug my nails into his back and clung on for dear life until…

Splash. We hit the water. For a moment our heads went under but the life jackets soon pulled us back up to the surface. Our kissing didn't stop but I now wanted more from this moment. I wondered what would happen if I trailed my hand down his stomach and slipped it into his bathing suit. How far were we going to take this acting? *And how far was too far?*

The kissing finally slowed down. He ran the tip of his tongue over my lips and I drew it into my mouth, sucking on it gently. We were so in tune, as if we'd been kissing each other for years.

Chris finally pulled away. "Annie, I have to tell you something." His face had drained of color.

Shit. And there it was. He was going to remind me that it had just been pretend. Make a wise-guy crack about being a good actor, downplay the whole thing, and laugh it off in a way that would break my heart a little.

"You don't have to," I said quickly and broke away from him. I couldn't bear hearing it, and I dove into the water and swam down where I knew he wouldn't follow me.

Now, I've seen some beautiful things in my life. But nothing prepared me for the reef.

The coral came in every shape and color imaginable. The pink and orange bits that swayed like miniature palm trees in the water were by far the most spectacular. Large green bulbous-looking things drew the attention of a school of bright yellow fish. Small and feisty, they nibbled on the coral and darted around it at lightning speed. They were particularly small, but the reef was teeming with some substantially larger sea creatures of all shapes, colors, and sizes.

Blue and yellow fish with bright red lips swam up to my goggles and eyed me curiously. A luminous green fish with a pink-painted face also came to investigate, while the rest busied themselves with eating and swimming. Out of the corner of my eye I saw a large movement and turned to see a giant sea turtle gliding through the water. And by *giant* turtle, I mean that it was at least four feet long, making it more or less the size of a small child.

I looked up and Chris was still bobbing up and down. I finally resurfaced.

"What's it like down there?" he asked.

"Why don't you take your life jackets off and see for yourself."

Chris smiled at me. "Thanks."

"For what?"

"I'm in the water. And I'm not scared. And now I'm going to take the life jackets off."

We spent a good hour down there, popping up for oxygen and going back down. The world below felt mystical, magical, and so full of life and color that I didn't want to leave. But finally the sheer exhaustion of treading water and swimming up and down the reef got to be too much and we both climbed back on the boat.

I collapsed on the bench, took my flippers and goggles off, and looked across at Chris. He was flipping through an underwater camera. I'd been so wrapped up in my own magical world down there that I'd hardly noticed he was taking pictures.

"Where did you get that from?"

"Bought it at the shop this morning while you were getting ready. I figured you might want to take some pics. I didn't think I would be the one taking them, though." He smiled happily to himself and my heart swelled with pride for him. He'd conquered something huge today, and I had helped him. I suppose it was the least I owed him, since he was helping me with Trevv.

I got up and sat next to him. He'd taken some amazing pics: a shy black-and-yellow eel peeping out from underneath a rock, a large blue fish feeding in the swaying arms of an orange anemone, and…

"*Hey!* That's my bum." I grabbed the camera away from him and started looking for the delete button.

"I was trying to take a picture of a fish."

I scrutinized the photo. There was absolutely no evidence of any aquatic life form in the shot. "Oh…and where is this so-called fish?"

"There." Chris pointed to the edge of the frame where I could just make out a tiny (practically invisible) yellow tail disappearing.

I turned and eyeballed him suspiciously. "Mmmm, I think you were just taking a photo of my bum."

"And, so what if I was?" he asked with that dashing grin that lit up his ridiculously blue eyes.

Internal sighing

I zoomed in on the photo. "Well, it's not exactly very flattering. It's not a good angle."

"I think it's a great angle." He snatched the camera away from me and held it up.

"I think you should delete it."

"Why, are you scared I might put it on Facebook and tag you?"

"Who knows what evil plans you have for it." I pulled the camera away again and located the delete button. The picture disappeared and Chris feigned a loud sigh of devastating disappointment. I tried to put on my best bossy face and glared at him.

"But seriously," he said again, his tone more sober this time, "I really was just trying to get the fish. The fact that your bum was in the way was just a bonus." Cue boyish grin that melts my heart again. Trying to resist Chris and fight off the feelings I was having for him seemed to be a useless exercise. Resistance was officially futile.

"I'm having a really good day, Chris."

He smiled. "Me too. And if I believed in love, you might actually be the girl I'd finally fall for."

CHAPTER EIGHTEEN

~

*W*hat? Come again? What the fuck did that even mean?

How was that even a statement? It was just a string of words that all contradicted one another. There was no logic to it at all. Chris was up and speaking to the driver of the boat and I was left sitting there gaping in absolute shock. But Chris seemed as casual as could be. If he was any more laid-back right now, he would be dead.

"He's taking us to another small island now," he said.

"Oh."

"It's uninhabited." Suddenly that sparkle in his eye was back and hope rushed in. Maybe he wanted to talk about things on the island and pick up where we'd left off earlier.

Only this time, it wouldn't just be a kiss.

***

We finally reached our destination twenty minutes later: a small island with the whitest beaches I had ever seen. The beach seemed to slope up into thick, dense forest; there were a few paths that seemed to wind their way into it. After a fresh—plucked from the ocean in front of our eyes—seafood barbeque, we went exploring the small island.

At one point we simply walked in absolute silence, side by side, down the beach, picking up purple cowrie shells and small bits of dried coral that had broken off and washed to shore.

When our intrepid exploration was over, we collapsed down on the beach and sat together looking out over the sea. It was a beautiful day and we were in one of the most magical places on earth. The sea was a pale turquoise color and completely calm. The sand was as white as snow and soft to the touch. I could stay here forever. With Chris. In this perfect fantasy bubble that we'd created.

"So, Annie, what are your plans for the future?" Chris suddenly asked out of the blue.

My heart fluttered at the line of questioning. "That's a bit broad."

"Oh you know, marriage, babies, the suburbs, PTA meetings?"

"PTA meetings?"

"Yeah, you'd look good as one of those soccer moms running your redheaded sons around. You'd definitely be the hottest, and coolest mom at school. The local MILF for sure."

"The things that come out of your mouth sometimes! If I didn't know you by now, I could probably sue for sexual harassment."

"I'm just saying. If I was a senior in high school and you were one of my friends' moms, I'd totally be fantasizing—"

I put my hand over his mouth. "Okay. Stop. I think what you're suggesting is illegal in a million different states."

"And you're a great kisser, by the way." Chris slowly pulled my hand away from his face and held on to it. He laced his fingers though mine and then laid our hands on the warm sand between us. I tried to remain as calm as possible, and not betray the crazy feelings and slightly mad internal monologue that was raging through my mind right then. It was such a small, simple gesture but it felt so incredibly intimate. It felt big.

"So?" he asked again.

"So what?" I was so focused on the feeling of his hand in mine that I'd totally forgotten what we were talking about.

"PTA meetings? Carpooling?"

"Oh. That. Yes," I managed. "Well, to be honest…" I paused. It was still hard to think about this specific detail of that day, let alone talk about it. "I kind of thought that Trevv and I would get married. In fact, that day I walked in on them, I actually thought he was going to be proposing to me that night."

"Seriously?" Chris sounded surprised.

"Stupid, I know. But I found this receipt from a jewelry store and we were having dinner at our favorite restaurant that night and he'd bought red roses. It was so fucking embarrassing, I even asked him about it in the police station."

"And what did he say?" Chris leaned in, looking totally intrigued by this conversation.

"Hey, I hope you're not enjoying this," I said quickly. "I know it's all a bit like a morbid car crash, but seriously, that was probably one of the most embarrassing moments of my life, especially when I got pathetic and said, 'But you're supposed to be marrying me. Why aren't you marrying me? Marry me. Marry me.'"

"Ouch. Sorry." Chris looked less intrigued now and more concerned.

"Tell me about it. I basically begged him to take me back and marry me, even after what he'd just done."

"And now? You don't still have any feelings for him, do you?" He flicked his eyes away from mine. "Romantic feelings?" Chris looked almost shy now, and my heart rate quickened slightly. Excited butterflies pushed their way into my stomach.

"Would it make you jealous if I did?"

"Well, you are my pretend girlfriend, in case you'd forgotten." Chris stopped the eye acrobatics and brought them up to rest on mine again.

"And you're my pretend boyfriend," I repeated, feeling deflated about where this conversation had landed again. Clearly, he truly was incapable of feeling anything real.

* * *

We finally got back to the resort at around five p.m. The evenings always look so beautiful; the light appears tinged with an incandescent pink, making the green of the plants pop even more and turning the water into a subtle rose color. In the delicate pink glow, Chris's eyes looked even bluer. A little darker, deeper, and dreamier.

"Do you want to go for a swim in the pool, now that the sun's not too bad?" Chris asked.

"A swim?" I eyed him.

"Yeah, I wouldn't mind making up for lost time."

"Sure." My skin felt sticky and salty from the sea and slimy from the sunscreen—I could definitely do with a rinse in the pool.

"Sounds good."

We made our way to the pool, picking up cool drinks from the bar as we went. The hotel pool was impressive—although by now I wouldn't have expected anything less from this place. It was a rather large infinity pool that looked out over the beach, surrounded by tables, chairs, and comfortable loungers. We spotted two free ones and headed over.

I sat for a while, taking in the beauty of my surroundings and reflecting on the day I'd had with Chris, when suddenly…Tess was emerging from the pool.

Bloody hell.

I pulled my glasses down and eyed Tess over the top of them. She looked like she was climbing out in slow motion and moving to the imaginary beats of a sultry exotic song with a saxophone. Her tanned, toned body was squeezed into a white bikini, and her long wet black hair clung to her. She lowered her head and flicked it back. Her black locks flew through the air, again, in slow motion. She shook her head and her boobs bounced and wobbled in the tiny bikini top. She reached up and ran her fingers through her hair.

It was like a scene from a shampoo commercial, where the woman casually flicks her long, luscious locks over her shoulder, sending little water drops shooting in all directions. Slow-motion droplets that shimmer and shine when caught in the sun's rays.

I looked at the reactions of the other pool-goers. Her no doubt very deliberate and calculated display was having the predicted effect. Men were scraping their jaws off the ground. Wives looked seriously pissed off, and even the birds on the grass looked like they'd stopped eating and turned to watch. Trevv was glowing with pride and smirking with ownership. The kind you might have if you drove around in a new, shiny red Lamborghini.

Tess waved at him, blew him a kiss, and then winked seductively. I swear every man in a five-mile radius got an involuntary hard-on. She picked up a towel. The little tart then bent over to dry her legs, causing her boobs to squish together and her bum to protrude. (Make that a ten-mile radius.)

I looked back at Chris and I could see he was thinking the exact same thing I was.

"Have you ever?" he said.

"I know!"

"She's such a cock-tease, that one. If Trevv thinks she's going to be Little Miss Doting Wife, he's got another thing coming…"

"Really?" The thought of Tess cheating on Trevv made me giddy with happiness. Hopefully she would do it publicly. Hopefully someone would take a photo of it and post it on social media only for it to go viral for all Trevv's friends and family and colleagues to see. He would be so humiliated. "Tell me more." I was excited and Chris was only too willing to indulge me.

"Yup. I've seen her type before. I understand them. She's the kind of woman that uses her sexuality to get what she wants, but if you had to strip it all away, she's probably deeply insecure and actually thinks that her looks are all that people respond to. Her biggest fear is losing her looks—because then she would just have to be herself. She would be ordinary."

"Jeez, Mr. Psychologist. Where the hell did that come from?"

Chris shrugged nonchalantly. "I'm a writer, it's my job to know people. Know what makes them tick. Otherwise I wouldn't be able to write about them."

"Really? But you don't need to know and understand love in order to write about it? You are contradicting yourself, mister." I pointed a finger in his direction and waggled it. "In fact, you're constantly contradicting yourself. Why?"

Chris shook his head. "Annie Anne, this is all far too deep for casual poolside banter."

I eyed him suspiciously. "You just don't want to answer because I caught you out, didn't I?"

"Caught me out at what?"

"The biggest lie you tell yourself."

At this Chris whipped his head around and looked at me. "And what's that?"

"I don't think you really don't believe in love. I think it's all just a defense." I launched into it. "You believe in love, you just don't allow yourself to feel it."

"Now who's the psychologist?"

"Chris, seriously, it doesn't take a person with a degree to see it. When you were younger and you were—" It felt hurtful saying the words.

"Fat. Chubby. Chunky." Chris said it nonchalantly, but I could tell there was real pain in his voice.

"Yes. Girls didn't like you for who you were. They only started getting interested when you were someone else, successful and good-looking—so of course you don't believe in love. In your experience, love is conditional. So how can it be real?"

Chris nodded. "Interesting observation."

"And then your parents got divorced, you thought it was your fault, and then you saw what a broken heart did to your mom and you just switched it off. I may not be great at relationships and choosing the right guys—in fact, I've started to realize that I had terrible taste in men—but at least I've loved, even if I lost."

"You really believe that? It's worth all that inevitable pain."

"The pain is not inevitable. When two people are right for each other, maybe they *can* live happily ever after."

"Unlikely," he said dismissively, but I wasn't going to let this go until I was satisfied with the answer.

"You don't *not* believe in love. You just choose not to let yourself fall in love, because you think you'll just get hurt. You wear all your humor and witty retorts like some protective padding. You're terrified that if you allow yourself to fall for someone, they'll abandon you like your dad did or you'll be abandoned for being the 'fat kid.'"

Chris was silent for a while. I could tell he was thinking about what I'd said. "Ordinarily I might agree with you, hell, a first-year psych student would agree with you, but…" Chris looked up at me, and every muscle in my body tensed. For a moment I felt like I couldn't breathe; there was something in his look that had rendered me useless. "I'm starting to think that maybe I just haven't met the right girl yet. And maybe when I do, I will eat my words and have to admit that I was wrong all along. Maybe I'm just a lame, thirty-three-year-old bachelor-cynic character who hasn't met his perfect heroine yet."

His gaze intensified and my heart forgot to beat. What was he trying to say?

"Annie…" Chris spoke softly and it gave me a queasy feeling in my stomach.

"Yes…"

"Since we're being all deep and making observations about each other, do you mind if I reciprocate?"

"Sure." But I wasn't so sure actually. I wasn't so sure I wanted to hear it at all.

"Do you have any idea how much you put yourself down?"

"What?" I asked, feeling truly baffled.

"If I had a dollar for every time I've heard you call yourself lame, or pathetic, or told me how much you dislike this new Annie, I'd be able to retire."

I felt my throat close.

"Trevv cheating had nothing to do with you being inadequate in any way. In fact, there is nothing even vaguely inadequate about you, Annie. Because the truth is that you have nothing to feel insecure about. You're smart, funny, gorgeous, and you're obviously a very talented designer."

"How do you know that?"

"That's a pretty interesting, unique piece if you ask me," he said as he pointed at my bag. "And judging by the way you kiss, I'm also pretty sure that you'd be a pretty good lay."

"What?" I burst out laughing. "Did you just say 'lay'?"

If it were anyone else saying it, I would have been highly offended. But for some reason, Chris could get away with saying things like that. "And how would you know that?" I asked.

"Because you're a very sexy woman."

"Not like her, though." I pointed at the poolside hussy who was still entertaining the masses by wiping the water droplets from her breasts.

"Being sexy is also about maintaining a bit of mystery. That..." Chris pointed at Tess, who was bending down again. "There's no mystery there. Her swimsuit is borderline transparent. She might as well be participating in a wet bikini contest."

I looked over at Tess and her bikini bottom had slipped a little, exposing a large chunk of her pert bum.

"I would choose you over her any day of the week."

My heart missed about ten beats. Adrenaline combined with surging hormones, and I felt physically uncomfortable. I was uncomfortable, frustrated, and confused. So confused. One minute he was saying the nicest things in the world to me, and kissing me, and then he was joking and I was losing it, trying to figure out how much of this was real.

Chris reached out and grabbed me by the arm. "Seriously, Annie Anne. It's time to get your confidence back!"

But before I could reply, T-Squared were right beside us.

Fuck! They were really starting to piss me off, especially now that they were interrupting a pivotal moment here. They were like poisonous shadows, always two steps behind us or two heads behind a palm.

"Hey." Trevv's voice was nauseating.

"Hey." I hoped my reply was demonstrating adequately the nonenthusiasm I had for them right now.

"Have a good day?" he asked as if he actually cared.

"Very. Thanks." I wanted to scream, *"Fuck off, Chris and I are in the middle of a very important conversation, you slimy toad of a man."*

"So glad. So glad." Trevv nodded with sincere insincerity. And then he knelt and looked me straight in the eye.

"I'm happy that you're happy," he said. I wanted to throw up right there and then. "I know how happy Tess and I were when we got engaged. Oh, that reminds me, you never did tell us how you met?" His smile melted away for a brief moment, revealing the arrogant douche bag behind it and the real reason for the question. He was still trying to catch us out.

"I would love to hear that story, too," Tess piped in, and then they actually pulled up a lounger and sat, as if they'd been invited. As if we were all friends.

"Well"—Chris put his arm on my leg—"that is a very interesting story."

"It is, is it?" Trevv leaned in.

"Oh yes, definitely." Chris sounded very confident and I was glad. He was the storyteller after all, not me.

"It was about five months ago, hey, baby?"

"Really." Trevv's eyes lit up. "But didn't you come round to my house and tell me about Boyden over six months ago?"

"Did I say five months, I meant six. Definitely six," Chris corrected like a pro. "I had just arrived in South Africa, we were looking at locations for a movie, and I bumped into Annie in the airport. Literally. Isn't that right, honey?"

"Yes, sweetie." I faked an awful-sounding laugh.

"And what were you doing at the airport, Anne?" Trevv asked as if this was a cross-examination.

"Um, I was…I was…" Fuck. What was I doing?

"She was picking up Stormy-Rain. Weren't you?" Chris quickly saved me by cleverly throwing in one of my friend's names.

"But I thought Stormy didn't fly. Doesn't she not believe in air travel or something stupid like that?" Trevv rolled his eyes. He and Stormy hadn't ever clicked.

"Exactly!" Chris clicked his fingers. "She thought she was going to fly, but chickened out at the last minute and phoned Annie to pick her up."

Trevv scrutinized my face, and I tried to hold the knowing nod and smile that I was currently attempting.

"I saw her before she saw me. I mean, you of all people should know how she stands out from the crowd." Out of the corner of my eye I saw Chris look at me and felt his hand tighten its grip on my thigh. "She was the most beautiful woman I'd ever seen and, I'm not afraid to admit, I was staring."

My body stiffened next to him as he began to shift closer to me.

"And cute. She looked so cute. All her hair was piled up on her head except for those adorable little strands that are shorter than the rest." His voice had taken on a different quality now, and I instinctively brushed one of those strands away from my face. I couldn't believe he'd actually noticed such a small detail about me.

"I was trying to get the courage to talk to her, but couldn't. And just when I was mentally kicking myself for being such a coward, I walked into her outside the airport. We collided and both fell onto the floor."

"How romantic," Tess said.

"It was, especially because she was lying on top of me."

"That's so sweet, don't you think, Trevv?" Tess poked Trevv in the ribs with an elbow and he grunted.

"It was fate, because then something very strange happened between us. Our eyes met and it felt like we were looking into each other's souls. It was electric and I just knew."

"Knew what?" I turned to look at Chris.

His eyes met mine and it *did* feel like he was trying to look into my soul. "I knew that she was the woman I wanted to be with…so I just kissed her."

"You kissed a total stranger at an airport on the floor?" Trevv sounded very unconvinced.

"Yes. We didn't need to say a word to each other, either, because in that moment I could see she knew, too. It was perfect. I couldn't have written a better scene into a script if I'd tried." Chris moved even closer. "It was the kind of kiss you get lost in, you know?"

A strange, giddy, electric feeling rushed through me again as he continued his approach. "The kind of kiss that says so much in total silence...the kind of kiss that makes you forget the world even exists."

Oh God, he was going to kiss me...again! His eyes moved down to my lips and I readied myself.

"A kiss just like this..." In my stupor I thought I heard his Australian accent falter, and then totally disappear. He leaned in and as soon as his lips touched mine, I melted.

"It's the kind of kiss that makes you finally believe in love."

CHAPTER NINETEEN

∽

The second Trevv and Tess got up to leave, Chris pulled away and gave me a truly million-dollar smile.

"That was amazing," he said.

"I know." I was still in a half-dreamy state.

"We totally fooled them there. I couldn't have written more perfect dialogue if I'd fucking tried."

"What?"

"Annie and Boyden just scored!" He held his hand up in the air for me to high-five. I didn't. Instead I got up, grabbed my bag, and started walking back to the room. I needed to get a grip on my emotions. One minute I was on cloud nine, succumbing to the bliss of the best kiss I'd ever had, and the next minute the cloud was being ripped out from under me and I was plummeting to the ground.

"What's wrong?" Chris shot up and started following me.

I kept walking. I was furious with him right now, even though I knew it was completely misplaced. He was just doing was what expected of him, and he was playing the role perfectly.

"Why are you getting so upset, Annie?"

I stopped walking and turned around. I stared at him and wanted to say something, but I couldn't. How could I tell him that I was falling for all his perfect dialogue? I was falling for each and every one of his perfectly created scenes in this giant movie he was so expertly writing and directing.

"Nothing. I'm just tired, I want to get back to the room."

After that he didn't press me anymore, and we walked back to the room together in total silence. As soon as we walked through the door, I made a beeline for the stairs but Chris blocked me.

"Are you going to tell me what's wrong?" he asked.

I shook my head. "Nothing is wrong."

"Oh please, 'nothing' is women speak for *everything* is wrong."

I paused and took a deep breath in. "I'm just confused. That's all. This…" I gestured between us. "Is confusing."

"What about it is confusing?"

"Why did you kiss me on the boat?"

"Because you told me I needed a distraction."

"Exactly," I said. My point had been proven once again. This whole thing really was in my head, and I'd been projecting my own fantasy onto it the entire time.

"And because I wanted to," he quickly added.

"You wanted to?" I shook my head. "But what does that mean, Chris? I don't get it. What are we doing here? Why are we kissing each other and why are you saying all these nice things to me and…" I stopped when I realized how I sounded. Vaguely desperate and pathetic.

"I'm confused, too," Chris said, moving toward me.

"About what exactly?"

"This, us, what's happening. I like spending time with you and I really, really like kissing you but…" He stopped talking.

"But what? You think you don't believe in love because it's cheesy and you're all cynical and writer-y and hate romance and sweet stories about old people who are in love and people with amnesia?"

"Let's have dinner," he said suddenly, totaling derailing my line of questioning.

"Huh? I thought that was the plan. We've got to eat."

"No, I mean, have dinner with *me*." He stressed the word *me* like I'd forgotten that we were doing everything together at the moment anyway.

"I was going to include you." I was irritated now.

Chris stepped forward and placed his hands on my shoulders. "I mean a date. Go on a date with me, Annie."

"A date?"

"Yes, it's a very normal form of courtship for most couples." He smiled at me playfully, but I couldn't reciprocate.

"To what end, Chris?" I asked him. "We live in different countries, I'm leaving in a few days. I'm going to go back to my crap life and you're going back to your glamorous one in LA. So what's the point of going on a date?"

Chris shrugged. "All I know is that I want to be able to hold your hand tonight and look at you across the table without pretending that I'm not."

I went silent for a while. This wasn't making me as happy as I thought it would. Perhaps it was the reminder that this was finite and had a very definite end.

"Please don't make me beg," Chris whispered. His hands left my shoulder and traveled down my arms. His fingertips grazed them gently as they went, and my skin screamed.

"The way I see it"—Chris's hands continued all the way down until they found mine—"we have a few days together, let's just make the most of them."

"Make the most of them," I repeated. Those words made me feel so sad.

"What do you say, our first date?"

"And possibly our last," I mumbled.

"Let's not think about that right now, let's just enjoy ourselves tonight."

My heart and head were screaming very different things. One wanted to say yes, but the other wasn't so sure this was a great idea. But in the end one voice came out on top. "Okay, let's give it a try."

Moments later I was upstairs, rummaging through my suitcase looking for something vaguely date-ish. It hadn't occurred to me to bring anything other than simple beach attire, and since my previous shopping spree had proven so unsuccessful and yielded no results, I currently found myself seriously fashionably challenged. There was only one slightly promising item, a simple white sleeveless shift dress that had a bit of lace detailing around the neckline. I slipped it on and noticed it was slightly tighter in a few places. Damn, why the hell didn't I love kale and quinoa more?

I fastened my hair into a loose, messy bun. Some wavy, rebellious tendrils fell down into my face and I tucked them behind my ears. I coated my lashes with some mascara, splashed a little highlighter onto my cheeks, and smeared on a good dollop of translucent pink lip gloss. This was as good as it got under the circumstances, I'm afraid. Shit, suddenly I was feeling nervous. It was crazy how a little four-letter word changed absolutely everything about this evening…

D-a-t-e.

I gave myself one last mirror check and was ready to go. I walked out onto the deck and took a deep breath. The evening smelled sweet and tropical, and the night was perfect. Warm, with the slightest hint of a breeze to take the edge off the heat. All in all, it was the perfect weather for a romantic date. I started walking downstairs and saw Chris standing at the bottom with his back to me. My sandal made a noise on the stair and he swung around.

"Wow." His mouth fell open and his eyes widened. I couldn't help the fluttery feeling that filled my stomach.

"You look incredible." Chris took a step closer and I could see that he'd also gotten dressed up for the occasion. He'd actually "styled" his hair; that is to say it looked like he'd dragged a brush through it. He was also wearing a nonstained shirt and a pair of smartish-looking jeans. Halfway down the stairs I could smell him. The warm, rich, welcoming scent of musky sandalwood.

"Thanks. You look pretty handsome yourself." I tried to give him a vaguely normal-looking smile, not a doe-eyed, eyelash-batting one.

"The white dress really complements your sunburn."

"Oh thanks." I felt a little deflated. "Give me a compliment and then take it away, why don't you."

It was obvious Chris could see what I was feeling, because he quickly added, "Annie Anne, surely by now you've noticed that I deflect with humor. It's my defense mechanism. You know…if something feels too real, I make a joke. If something feels too awkward…I make a joke."

"Is this awkward? We don't have to make this a date, you know." My heart sank at the thought that he might take me up on it and back out.

A coy look played on his face. "Well, I always feel awkward in the presence of a really hot chick."

I rolled my eyes. "You must be surrounded by hot Hollywood starlets all the time! I bet they all fawn over you, hoping you'll write them a starring role in your next movie, or—"

He shrugged. "That still doesn't mean you're not one hot chick." He flashed me the kind of smile that might make me trip over something.

"Thanks."

"Oh, Annie, Annie, Annie, what am I going to do with you?" He shook his head and looked at me, and suddenly I was on a roller coaster going through a million stomach-churning loops.

He stepped forward. "Shall we?" He had a dangerous glint in his eye and I couldn't help but notice how his gaze flicked up and down my body as I got closer and took his arm. I felt naked under his intense gaze, and I liked it. *What would it feel like to really be naked with him?*

I laced my arm through his. "Lead the way."

"Oh, I will." He winked at me playfully and a chill ran up my spine.

We walked arm in arm without saying another word. Our legs moved together in unison, we swayed as one, and it felt like our bodies were totally in tune with each other. I couldn't help but wonder in what other ways our bodies would be in tune.

"Where're we going?" I asked as we walked past the restaurant that we'd eaten in the other night.

"You didn't think I'd take you to that old place on our first date, did you?"

"So where then?"

"No idea. I asked the hotel to recommend the best first date place and call a taxi for us."

We walked through the lobby and out to where the car was parked. The idea of getting out of the resort was very appealing. As big as it was, there was something very claustrophobic about being there with Trevv and Tess. Especially since they'd rudely moved in next door.

The car started moving, and I sat back and watched as the scenery around us changed. We drove inland, away from the coast toward the green fields of the sugar cane plantations. Soon we climbed higher and higher up a narrow winding road. Finally, we drove through huge wrought iron gates and up a long driveway. I gasped when I saw what was in front of us.

"It's amazing." I was in awe of the huge mansion sprawled at the end of the drive.

A long driveway took us all the way up to the front of the house, a massive plantation home that must have been nearly two hundred years old. An imposing fountain stood in the middle of the driveway, and when I opened the door and stepped out, tiny droplets of water flicked up and landed on my skin. Inside, everything was formal and romantic, oh so romantic. Candlelight, flowers, soft music in the background—the hotel was right; this was a perfect first date place. We were ushered to a table by the window and sat. A live jazz band was playing, which only added to the overall romance of the place. And when you looked out the window, you could see all the way down to the coast, which was now far in the distance.

"Wine?" Chris asked, opening the menu.

"Actually"—I pointed at the colorful, tropical thing that wafted past me on the waiter's tray—"I'll have one of those."

"Are you trying to get drunk, Annie Anne?"

"Maybe." I smiled playfully.

"Because you know…" He leaned across the table and our eyes met. His voice had changed; it was like liquid sex. *What was he doing?* "The other night when you got a little tipsy, I was a total gentleman, but now that we're dating, I might not be."

How was it possible to feel the sound waves of his voice travel along my spine?

"I thought you hadn't been on a date in a while."

"I haven't." He was still holding my gaze and wielding that sexy voice that had the power to turn me into a puddle. "Why do you ask?"

"It's just, you seem rather good at it. Well practiced."

Chris shook his head. "I'm just good at this with you, Annie Anne."

How had he delivered that line so perfectly? How was it that I felt drunk on his words? I wasn't sure I even needed that cocktail now; Chris had intoxicated me. I wasn't hungry anymore, either. My stomach was too full of nerves.

"I don't have sex on the first date, anyway," I whispered so no passersby would hear. It was true, too; I didn't. It was more of a fourth, fifth date kind of thing.

"I didn't think you did."

"Well as long as we get that straight. I wouldn't want you to think I'm the kind of girl you can take advantage of, even though we've already been kissing up a storm."

"I would never take advantage of you, Annie. In fact…" The sexy tone in his voice was gone now and he sounded serious.

"What?"

"I have to ask you something. I've been wanting to ask you this for a while, and before this goes any further, I need to know something."

"Oh God, what? This sounds serious."

"Trevv? What did you ever see in him? I just cannot imagine the two of you together, no matter how hard I try."

"Oh, that." I hung my head and then took a deep breath. "I've been thinking about that a lot actually."

"And? Please tell me you've arrived at a reason that makes some kind of sense. Because how could someone like you, someone smart, funny, down-to-earth, adorable, be with a total fucking douche bag like him?"

"I wasn't that down-to-earth before. My recent poverty has changed that somewhat, I think."

"I can't really imagine that," Chris said.

"It's true. I think I used to be a bit shallow before. Looks, status, what was cool…those things were important to me. I think Trevv fit into that."

"Well, I'm nothing like him, and if that is what you like—"

"*No!* No, I don't like that anymore. In fact, I think I like something *completely* different now. *A lot*." I managed to raise my eyes up to meet his, even though I felt so naked and vulnerable by the blatant confession of feelings I'd just made. Chris smiled.

"I'm glad, Annie. My tastes seem to have changed rather drastically, too."

The waiter walked up to our table and disturbed our perfect

moment. "Two glasses of champagne for you." He placed the flutes on the table.

"We didn't order this." Chris started giving the glass back.

"It's from that gentleman sitting over there."

Gentleman? He didn't warrant the name. It was Trevv, sitting about seven tables over from us. Tess waved at us and then Trevv gave us an upbeat thumbs-up.

"It's the Krug Clos du Mesnil Blanc de Blancs," the waiter said in a tone that sounded like he was trying to elicit awe.

"What the hell is the Krug de Clog de Blank de Blank whatever?" Chris asked.

The waiter blinked at Chris. "Sir, it's the most expensive champagne we have on the menu here."

"Really?" Chris looked wildly unimpressed. "Is everything with this guy always a competition?" he asked me.

"I guess so." It was true. Trevv was always trying to prove he was better than everyone else, even when we were dating. It hadn't really gotten to me back then; in fact, I'd thought there was something sexy in his self-assured confidence. Now all I saw was arrogance.

"What are the cheapest, nastiest drinks you have on the menu?" Chris asked the waiter.

The man did a slight double take. "I beg your pardon?"

"You heard me."

"We don't have"—he cleared his throat as if he was trying to dislodge something that was stopping him from saying the words—"cheap, nasty things on the menu. But we do have a cocktail and shooter menu on the back of the wine page."

"Chris, just leave it. Can't we just ignore them tonight?"

"No, we can't, Annie. I am so sick and tired of this guy trying to make you feel bad about yourself. He's always trying to prove how much better he is than you and how much better his life is than yours. I've had enough of him putting you down like this. Someone needs to fight back for you. And that someone is going to be me."

I smiled and blushed and went gooey all at once. No one had ever stood up for me like this; in fact, since I'd met Chris, that's all he'd done. Jumping in to rescue me when I needed him. Playing Boyden—albeit badly at times—and for no other reason than just to be nice to me.

A filthy four-letter word started beating around in my brain. The filthiest, and most dangerous of all…

L-o-v-e…I was falling. Hard. I just hoped there was something at the bottom to cushion the blow.

I watched as Chris flipped through the menu. His eyes moved from left to right as he scanned the various options. Then they stopped. They widened and a smile broke out across his face. He slowly lowered the menu.

"Please, with our compliments of course, would you send them two 'slippery nipples'?"

Loud, giddy laugher fell from my lips. "No! You're not." I clapped my hands over my mouth in a mixture of shock and sheer delight.

"Watch me." Chris slapped the menu down triumphantly and turned to Tress. He shot them a friendly smile, a wave, and then two thumbs-up. We turned back to each other and waited. I wanted to squeal with excitement, and it was obvious that Chris felt the same way. I felt like a naughty schoolchild that had just done something bad and was waiting for the consequences.

"Ha. Ha. Very funny!" Trevv's voice cut through the chatter and clink of knives and forks. A few patrons looked up curiously.

"Just having a bit of a ripper with you, mate," Chris said in his broadest Australian accent. He shot them an even bigger smile. "All in good spirits, right?"

Suddenly I burst out laughing. It was the kind of laughter that came with rolling tears and shaking shoulders. Chris joined in, and soon we were both choking on our hysteria. The patrons that had looked up before were now staring, and we were definitely destroying the romantic ambiance that this place obviously worked so hard to preserve.

Our waiter came sliding up to us again, and I half expected him to ask us to keep quiet, only he didn't. He placed two red drinks in front of us.

"From the other table." The man's voice was low and whispery, and he leaned toward a still-laughing Chris. And then, in a split second, everything changed. I didn't hear what the waiter said to Chris, but suddenly he wasn't laughing.

"That's it. Someone needs to teach this asshole his place," he roared. And then in one swift movement he was out of his chair and striding across the room toward Trevv.

CHAPTER TWENTY

$\mathcal{I}$ watched in horror as Trevv jumped out of his chair like a jack-in-the-box.

"Oh yeah? Want to try me, *mate?*" Trevv sneered the word and then threw his napkin down on the table, knocking the two shooters onto the floor.

The sounds of shattering glass filled the room. Followed by the sounds of gasps, of knives and forks being put down, and chatter. I jumped out of my seat and started making my way through the tables toward the eye of the storm.

Trevv stepped forward and dramatically shot a hand out and pointed a finger at Chris. He looked ridiculous, like some Spanish matador trying to pull a Michael Jackson dance move.

And Chris looked equally ridiculous. He'd stopped in front of the table and thrown his hands onto his hips. it was all very "*Vogue / Strike a pose.*"

"*Well,* maybe I will do something about it. Okay!" Chris boomed, holding his fashionably fierce pose and stamping a foot down.

"Oh yeah?" Trevv boomed.

"Yeah," Chris echoed loudly.

Trevv made a loud, sarcastic tutting noise and rolled his eyes dramatically. "I don't think so." He cocked his head to the side with a fast snap.

They looked absolutely absurd, and if I had been an impartial bystander, I might have laughed. The one was jutting a hip out like he was on a catwalk, and the other was swaying his head back and forth like Beyoncé, and I still had no idea what was going on. I could see that Tess was just as confused as I was.

"Trevvy baby, what's happening?" she cooed and pouted with concern. You know those massive industrial staplers? Her pursed duck lips were almost begging me to drive one through them. *Snap!*

Trevv threw out a protective arm, and in some pseudo warrior voice, as if he'd just walked off the battlefields of Winterfell after chopping some heads and arms off, said, "Get back, baby. This doesn't concern you. This is between him and me."

What was between them? What the fuck was going on?

"Chris, what's going on?" I asked, coming up behind him. He almost knocked me off my feet when his arm also came flying out.

"You too, Annie…baby. This has nothing to do with you ladies."

"Us *ladies*?" Why was he talking like he was trapped in an old Western right now?

And then, as if that wasn't ridiculous enough already, an uptight, short man in a tuxedo stepped between them.

"Zis is enough, jentelmen." His French accent was so thick it was hard to understand. And then more were added to the fray, as a madlooking chef with a big white hat holding a duck leg in his hand barreled out of the kitchen.

"*Que se passe-t-il?*" he shouted, shaking the piece of poultry.

"I'm hendling it," the short man in the tuxedo shouted back. "Jes make ze duck à l'orange."

"I cannit cook with zis noise. How em I zupose to cook like zis," the man cried out, waving the meat about.

All eyes were definitely on us now. The jazz band had stopped playing, everyone had stopped eating, and Trevv and Chris were squaring off as if all hell was about to break loose.

"Chris, just please tell me what's happening?" I begged.

"What's happening is that Trevv is going to be apologizing to you, right here, right now. For every awful thing he ever did."

Trevv burst out laughing at the mere suggestion. The laugh was more of an evil, rasping cackle, as if the gates to hell had just been cracked open and Satan himself had just stepped out. "I don't apologize for anything. Ever. Apologizing is for the weak."

"Well, you're going to be apologizing today."

"Really?"

"Yes fucking really," Chris spat.

More gasps rose up and the Man in the Tuxedo started shouting. "Stop. Stop." He was so short that he was now jumping up and down trying to make aggressive eye contact with Trevv and Chris—as if that was somehow intimidating.

"If you do not stop, I vill call for security."

More heinous laughter rose up from Trevv. "That shouldn't be a problem for Annie, she's used to getting arrested."

"That's it!" Chris launched himself at Trevv, pushing the manager out of the way. Was he going to hit him? Neither of these men looked like they knew how to throw a punch, or had ever successfully thrown one in their entire lives. Trevv had muscles, for sure, but those were all for show. They were more window dressing than actual elbow grease. And as for Chris, let's just say you can't throw a punch when it appears that your hands are still awkwardly superglued to your hips.

But no one hit anyone. Instead, Chris stopped right in front of Trevv's face and leaned in.

"One day you're going to realize what an idiot you were for letting Annie go."

Chris's remark clearly pissed Tess off, who moved toward her precious Trevvy and hooked an arm around him.

"I doubt that," she hissed at Chris through a clenched jaw. I was still the only one not in on the action, but I couldn't move. I stood there watching this whole thing unfold before my eyes. I was vaguely impressed and officially flattered. I'd never had a fight break out over me before—albeit a lame one.

"Zat's it, I'm phoning security." The man gave up on his jumping and rushed off to the other end of the room. As soon as the man left, Chris took the opportunity to get right up into Trevv's perfect little face.

"You never deserved Annie anyway. She's too good for you," he said.

"Oh please, she never deserved me!"

"How dare you!" And then he did it and I didn't know whether to laugh, or cheer.

Chris slapped Trevv across the face. A big open-handed girl slap. Trevv looked like he had seen a ghost; I don't think anyone had ever laid a hand on his pretty face. He looked shocked for a moment, then horrified. Then pure evil flashed in his eyes.

And then he struck back. Chris tried to block him with a swish of his arm, and then the two were in full-blown slap wars. A miracle occurred at that point, too; the once-dead duck took flight and hurtled through the air, hitting not Trevv, not Chris, but Tess. She screamed as the duck leg momentarily clung to her hair. She wildly beat at her hair as if a bat was tangled in it.

I jumped in this time and grabbed Chris around the waist, trying to pull him back. A couple of diners had gotten involved, too, and a man was ushering a now-crying Tess to a seat. (I doubt he had any concern for her well-being, he was just enjoying the fact that he was able to wrap his arm around her disgustingly sexy body as he guided her.) His wife shot him several death stares.

"*Well!*" Trevv screamed the word so loudly that everyone in the room stopped what they were doing and looked. "Well…we can definitely scratch them off the guest list, isn't that right, Tessy." His tone was deeply sarcastic.

"What guest list?" I stepped forward now. Intrigued.

"We were—out of the goodness of our hearts and in the spirit of reconciliation—"

"Re-con-cil-iation!" Chris hooted.

"Yes! Tess and I were going to invite you to our wedding." He turned to his captive audience now, as if he assumed people were watching him and hanging on his every word because they liked him. "We're having a beach wedding at dusk the day after tomorrow."

Chris laughed. "That's a joke, right?"

Trevv shook his head. "It's going to be perfect. Tess will be the center of attention and everyone's eyes will be on her and her alone."

"Why on fucking earth would you think we would ever want to go to your wedding?" Chris snapped back, his Australian accent slipping once more.

I was horrified. Nauseated that Trevv was trying to rub his relationship in my face once more. His happiness and his so-called perfect life. And in that moment, I think I hated Trevv more than I had hated any human being before.

I hated the fact he spelled his name with two pretentious *v*'s! I hated the fact that his hair and teeth were so perfect and his shirts were always ironed so fucking anally. He was the worst kind of person: sleazy, manipulative, cunning, hurtful, boastful, egotistical, patronizing…the list could go on forever but I didn't want to waste any more brain cells on him.

I was officially done.

"I just thought it might be informative for the two of you," Trevv said. He was puffing his chest up once more and the look in his eyes was undeniable…*a challenge*.

He was building up to something, I could feel it. Then he smiled. The smuggest smile I had ever seen in my entire life. It was disturbing. It was bordering on evil. The kind of smile a demon-zombie might give you before it ripped your head off.

"I thought it might give you two the opportunity to see what a *real* couple looks like, a *real* couple in love."

He was putting way too much emphasis on the word *real* and it was starting to worry me.

"Isn't that right…*Boyyyden from Australia, mate*!"

My blood ran cold as Trevv removed his eyes from Chris and planted them firmly onto me. He knew. *He knew*. He rolled his eyes. I wanted to pull them from their sockets—maybe use the industrial stapler on them, too. And then he graced me with the same serpentine smile. "Pathetic, Annie, really pathetic. Did you think you would get away with it?"

I inhaled sharply as tears started burning the back of my throat and eyes, and I bit my lip hard. I didn't want to cry, not now, not in front of him. I didn't want to give Trevv anything more to be smug and satisfied about.

Trevv shook his head. "I mean, *Boyden*. From *Australia*?" He left out a wild, shrill laugh that would easily compete with a pack of hyenas.

I was gutted. In that moment it felt like my world came crumbling down once more. Chris turned to me, and through my now-blurry eyes, I thought I saw him mouth something. I couldn't make it out.

"Thanks so much for the invite, Trevv!" Chris shouted, looking smug himself now. "But we wouldn't have been able to come to your wedding anyway. Annie and I will be a little busy ourselves."

"Oh?" Trevv raised a quizzical eyebrow.

"Annie!" Chris swung around and started walking toward me. "I was going to do this later, but I guess now is as good a time as any." Chris continued his approach and suddenly nerves gripped me. There was something strange about the way he was looking at me. *Very* strange.

"Annie." He was right in front of me now and took my hands in his. "Since the moment I met you, at the airport that day, I knew in my heart that you, gorgeous beautiful Annie, were the woman, the only woman in the world, that I wanted to spend the rest of my life with. Forever. Until my dying day."

"Sorry…what?" I interrupted him and Chris shot me a look as if to say *play along*. Play along with what? I was so confused right now. I still didn't even know why this whole thing had broken out in the first place.

And then Chris started lowering his body. Lower, lower, lower still until he was on the floor. On one knee. *In front of me!*

A few *aaahhh*s and *sweet*s rose up from the crowd, but I don't quite think I had fully grasped what was going on yet. It was all just so surreal; one moment Chris and I were on our first date, enjoying each other's company, and now he was kneeling in front of me, in front of Tress and an entire room of people, including a jazz band that had stopped playing, a manager who was busy making frantic calls, and a chef who looked homicidal.

Chris continued. "I wanted it to be a surprise. I know how much you like surprises. I organized the whole thing. A small romantic beach wedding, just like you always wanted. Just like we talked about all those nights while lying in bed together in each other's arms."

"Oh please!" I heard Trevv snort from the sidelines.

"Your friends helped, of course, you can't stop Lilly and Jane from getting involved, you know. They're even flying out here tomorrow for the special day."

"Chris…I…what, are you…?" I said under my breath.

"Annie. Annie, Anne. Love of my life. Woman of my dreams. You complete me. You make me whole, you make me a better man, you make me believe in love. Will you make me the happiest man alive and accept my hand in marriage?"

"Your what?" I whispered in total shock.

"Marry me, Annie."

CHAPTER TWENTY-ONE

*M*y mouth fell open. My jaw slackened, and if it loosened any more, I would probably be scooping it up off the floor in a few moments. I felt a crushing sensation in my hands and realized that Chris was squeezing them.

"Oh please!" Trevv snorted again. "This is the most ridiculous thing I've ever seen."

"Annie?" Chris smiled up at me from the floor. This was certainly not the proposal I had dreamed of. And it was certainly not with the person I imagined. But despite all that, there was something so perfect about it.

Chris was perfect. The way he was smiling at me now, his eyes crinkling and his entire face lighting up. I felt myself getting swept away, swept up in the moment, caught up in the romance of it all.

This is not real, Annie. This is not real.

But no matter how many times I said it to myself, the way my body was reacting to this moment made me believe otherwise.

"Is anyone actually buying this charade?" Trevv laughed loudly again. I'd forgotten he was there. "You would never go for a guy like him, he's a loser, and you, Anne—"

"Love him. I love him and I am going to marry him!" I screamed across the room. The whole romantic moment I had just been caught up in was over, Trevv had burst it, and now this was all about getting even with him.

"*Yes!*" I shouted down at Chris. "I'll marry you."

Without waiting for a response from Chris, I threw myself into his arms and kissed him. We stumbled and fell onto the ground, and I continued my mad lip assault. The kiss was completely over-the-top, so fierce and melodramatic. It was the kind of kiss you see in daytime soap operas. When the long-lost lover, who you thought had been dead for years from that freak meteor shower, returns as his better-looking twin and kisses his lover for the first time again. It had that same sense of delicious overblown drama.

Chris wrapped his arms around me and laughed against my mouth. I soon joined in.

"Oh, Annie fucking Anne," he said. We were half laughing, half kissing on the floor and must have looked like total lunatics.

"There they are," the man in the tux shouted. I looked up from the kiss to see security guards burst through the door of the restaurant. Chris reacted instantly, and quickly pulled us both off the floor.

"Come." He grabbed me by the hand and started dragging me through the restaurant. "Bye, guys," he shouted over his shoulder as we ran past the angry manager, past the jazz band and the chef, and out the back door.

Adrenaline sloshed through my veins and was manifesting itself in wild, crazy laughter. We burst through the door and ran outside straight into the pouring rain. I hadn't noticed it had started raining. Chris picked up his pace and I was struggling to keep up.

Running through the rain was exhilarating, and I hadn't felt so alive in years. We ran across the large lawn and down the long driveway. I was so out of breath now and my lungs were stinging, but it felt amazing. We ran out through the wrought iron gates, and it was only when we were back on the main road that we finally stopped.

"I can't believe that just happened," Chris said through sharp, jagged breaths.

"Oh my God, you proposed to me." I laughed even harder until my ribs started to ache. "You were on one knee." Suddenly the image was the funniest thing in the world. "Your kneeeeeeeee…," I wailed, and it hurt.

"And now we have a wedding to plan!" Chris was borderline hysterical with laughter and I was not far behind. "What the fuck!"

"The duck!" I screeched. "Did you see the duck leg?"

"Her face." Chris was holding his sides now. "I thought she was going to have a seizure."

"And you slapped him." I squealed between the laughter. "I can't believe you slapped him!" The rain was coming down hard, which was making it even more difficult to talk and catch our breath.

"God, it felt so good!" Chris mimed the slap in midair and made a sound to go along with it. "The look on his face was priceless."

"You're my hero!" I screamed through the loud rain.

"But you know what felt better than slapping him?" Chris quickly added.

"What?"

"This."

Chris walked me backward until I was pressed into the wall. He grabbed my hands and pushed them above my head. He had me pinned to the wall now, and I had never been more turned on in my entire life as Chris bought his lips down on mine. But we couldn't kiss. We were still too out of breath. We smiled at each other and locked eyes as we both panted frantically against each other's mouth, waiting for the oxygen to adequately fill our lungs.

The rain was still coming down and I could taste it and feel it all over my body. My dress was soaked and my hair was hanging in my face. Our breathing finally tapered off and as it did, just as I was able to take the long deep breath I needed, Chris kissed me. It was hard and deep and possessive. It was filled with desire and need, pure necessity. We needed to kiss each other right then like we needed air to live. His hands left mine and they trailed down my arms and my sides. They worked their way down the sides of my body and came to rest on my hips.

"Yes," I whispered as I pushed my hips into him. He responded with a moan and ground into me. I parted my legs and let him slip between them. His body crushed me into the wall even harder.

"Annie." His hand traveled lower. My dress was wet and clung to my body like a second skin, but his fingers started tugging at it, peeling it off my leg. I almost screamed at the feel of his palm moving up my thigh. I threw my head back and he brought his lips down onto my neck. His hand traveled higher and his lips moved lower until I felt them in the gap between my breasts. His hand climbed higher still, and his fingers grazed my panties.

"Fuck." I bit down on my lip and rocked my hips forward. It felt so good. Amazing.

Chris slipped a finger underneath the fabric of my underwear, and I instantly raised my leg and wrapped it around him. I wanted him so badly. I'd never wanted anything more in my entire life. His mouth traveled back up, and his hungry lips found mine again.

I could barely kiss properly, especially when his finger slipped inside me. My entire body shuddered and my mind went blank. I ground my hips into him even more and started rocking against him. He moved perfectly with my rhythm. The rocking soon turned to an almost frantic thrashing as I panted harder and harder. The sensations ripping through my body now threatened to overwhelm every one of my senses. I was so close now and Chris could feel it.

"You're so fucking sexy, Annie."

I moaned and he slipped another finger inside. I grabbed him by the shoulders, digging my fingers into them. The rain was still washing over us and the moment was so intense. I was drunk on adrenaline and giddy from the running and laughing. I was overjoyed, I was exhilarated, and I was feeling sexier than I had ever felt with anyone.

My body stiffened and I took one last gulp of oxygen before it all exploded. Shattered. I let out a moan that was so primal and guttural that it sounded like an animal. The rain drowned out my cry and flooded my now-open mouth. I felt the last of the waves rushing through me, and my body started going limp. God, that was not enough. I needed more of him, more. I wanted all of him. My hands traveled down between us and I started tugging at his zipper.

"Annie." I loved the sound of my name on his lips; it was driving me wild. I pushed my hand inside his pants and suddenly remembered what he looked like. I wrapped my hand around him; he was so hard and I wanted it. Chris started fiddling with the button on his jeans as I pushed my hand under the material of his boxers.

"Fuck," he gasped. I was so engrossed in the moment that it took me a second to react to the sound of the honking car horn.

Like a pin being pushed into a balloon, the moment popped. It popped so loudly that I jumped. For a second, time stood still and reality came flooding back in.

CHAPTER TWENTY-TWO

My hands went up to Chris's chest and I pushed him back. I frantically grabbed at my wet, clinging dress and tried to pull it back down. Out of the corner of my eye, I could see Chris struggling to zip his jeans up and pull his shirt back down.

I tasted iron in my mouth and ran my hand over it. Blood. A tiny bit of blood from the bite on my lip. The bite that I had inflicted on myself because the pleasure had been so intense.

I was shocked. It shocked me to my very core, twisted my guts, and made my heart feel like it was thumping in my chest. My cheeks stung hot in the cool rain and I threw my hands over them. I'd totally lost it in the moment, and God knows what I would have let Chris do to me against that wall. *Well*, I did know. If that car hadn't stopped us...

I looked up at him and he was staring at me with wide eyes. I couldn't bear to hold his gaze, and my eyes flicked down to his mouth, the mouth that had been on my breast.

My eyes moved down his arms to his hands, his hands that had been all over my body. My eyes looked at his fingers. They had just been inside me, taking me to the edge of total abandon.

I moaned as if I was only realizing it now. And in a way I was. Some other Annie had been lost in that moment; some other mad, intoxicated woman had ground and rocked and thrashed on him.

My eyes moved to his pants. He was still straining against his jeans, and I felt my hand burn with the memory of holding him tightly in my grip. What had I done? Was I out of my mind?

"Annie, I…" Chris started coming toward me, and I held a hand out to stop him.

"Stop! Just, stop."

"I never meant for that to…I wouldn't have, it was…"

"Stop."

The ground was spinning as shock merged with deep, deep embarrassment. *How had I let it get that far?* And against a wall on the side of a road?

"We were caught up in a moment, Annie."

"Stop!" My voice came out loud and firm now.

Chris stopped. The rain started slowing down. And just as fast as it had started, it vanished. We stood there looking at each other for a while. You could have cut the awkward tension with a blunt, cardboard knife.

"I want to go back to the hotel," I said.

My small handbag lay on the ground and I picked it up. I reached inside and thankfully the water hadn't killed my phone. I opened my Uber app and located one nearby.

"Uber will be here in seven minutes."

It was the longest seven minutes of my life. Chris and I sat on the pavement next to each other, wet, cold, shivering, and in total silence. I was trying to make sense of what had just happened. And I couldn't quite put my finger on what I felt.

A part of me was angry. It was hard to explain, other than for some reason I felt like I had been cheapened by the moment we'd just shared. Would he really have fucked me up against a wall on a street? Was he that kind of guy? *Was I that kind of girl?*

A part of me was also just embarrassed. I'd just had a loud, thrashing, screaming orgasm against a wall on the side of a public road, after causing a massive scene in a restaurant and getting dramatically engaged and possibly nearly arrested once more. I felt my cheeks go hot again. I'd behaved like a woman possessed. Suddenly I wondered what Chris thought of me. Was he now also wondering if I was the kind of girl that would fuck a guy on the side of the road?

"Jesus." I hadn't meant to say it out loud.

Chris turned. "I know. I'm sorry."

"Sssshhhh," I hushed him again. "I don't want to talk about it."

"Well, I do." He turned his whole body in my direction now and I cringed. "I should never have let it go that far. Please don't feel like I just took advantage of you or something. It was all my fault and I'm sorry and I hope you don't feel like I was using you or would have actually—"

"Oh please. You wouldn't have stopped." I cut him off.

"Would you?" he asked.

I turned and looked at him. "We both let it go too far. This whole night just snowballed. I mean, you fucking proposed to me in a room full of people, in front of Trevv, and now supposedly we're getting married. We crossed some weird line tonight, Chris. I'm sorry. I don't really know what got into me, either."

We didn't say another word to each other for the rest of the way back to the hotel. I was too busy trying to figure out how to get out of this mess.

Chapter Twenty-Three

$\mathcal{I}$ lay in the bath staring up at the ceiling. The warm water was soothing and had been very welcome when we'd finally gotten back to the room and my teeth actually stopped chattering.

Chris was downstairs, I could hear him typing away on his computer. He'd been typing for ages already. I'd thought a lot since the incident against the wall, and my thoughts were definitely a little more coherent now.

The whole thing had just shocked and terrified me. The total loss of inhibition and control had frightened me. I didn't really recognize it and wasn't even sure of where it had come from in the first place. Since meeting Chris I had done things that I would never normally do; it was clear he wielded some kind of power over me. God, I even thought I…

I…

I sat up in the bath, refusing to let that little thought enter my head again. I got out and wrapped a towel around me.

That I…

Persistent little fucker. I grabbed a toothbrush and started frantically brushing, but it was no use. That thought was going to surface whether I liked it or not.

I was falling in love with him.

I held on to the bathroom sink and shook my head. Everything about Chris and me was spiraling out of control. Everything about the way I felt about him, the kinds of things I wanted to do with him and nearly did…all out of control.

But I had finally settled on a way out of this mess. I just needed to tell Chris. I got dressed in a pair of pajamas and walked downstairs, where I found him hunched over his computer.

"Hi," I called out and he turned immediately.

"Hey." He reached a hand back and closed his computer.

"Still don't want me to see it?" I said, forcing a faint smile.

He shook his head. "No."

I walked over to the sofa and sat. "I wanted to tell you what I've decided to do."

"Okay." Chris walked over and was just about to sit next to me, when he moved away and sat on the other sofa.

"I'm going to tell Trevv tomorrow that the whole thing was a lie."

"What? You can't."

"I have to. It's all just too crazy and has been blown so far out of proportion. And I…I also can't keep pretending like this anymore."

"But don't you care what he'll think?"

"Oh, I do care, I care that he's going to be right about me, that I'm pathetic."

"You're not pathetic, Annie."

"I am. Anyone that pretends to have a boyfriend, and gets fake engaged just to prove to someone else that they're not lonely and sad and miserable, is lame and pathetic."

"Annie…"

"No. It's okay. I can deal with it. What I can't deal with any longer is this, though. It's just getting…it's…"

"We took it too far tonight." Chris nodded.

"Yup. I mean, it reads like some ridiculous story line from one of those revenge comedy movies we spoke about."

Chris suddenly looked uncomfortable. "I suppose." His voice was soft and slightly quivery.

"So I'm going to tell him tomorrow and face whatever smug laughter comes my way."

"I'll come with you."

"No. It's fine. This is something I have to do by myself."

Chris was nodding, but I could see he didn't quite agree.

"And then in the morning, I'm going to be moving back into my old room because my friends are coming."

"Are you breaking up with me, Annie Anne?" Chris looked up and gave a faint smile.

"Yup!" I smiled back.

"Will I still see you?"

"Sure. We can still hang out…as friends."

"But we're not, are we? We were on a date last night and, correct me if I'm wrong, it was going pretty well."

I smiled. I'd forgotten about that. In all the madness of the night I had almost forgotten those moments that we'd shared together before Tress had ruined it all.

"I'm not sure I'd call a first date that ended in a first fight, a proposal, and an almost arrest one that went well. Hey, you never did tell me why you decided to fight Trevv in the first place."

"Never mind," Chris said dismissively.

"Tell me."

"The drinks he sent us. Let's just say they weren't very flattering."

"No. You can't say stuff like that and not tell me."

Chris eyed me for a few moments, "They were called redheaded... rhymes with *nuts*..."

"Redheaded *sluts*? He sent over redheaded *sluts*?" I stood up, suddenly feeling enraged all over again. "The fucking bastard. If anyone is a slut it's him. And her. Filthy man-whore and his roaming bloody penis! And her and her macadamia-nut-oil hair and her bouncy breasts. I can't believe it!"

Chris stood up looking like he was about to get worked up again, too. "So you see why I had to defend your honor."

"Now I wish I'd hit him myself."

"You should have!"

"I think I would have aimed a little more south, though. And it wouldn't have been a slap, it might have been a knee, or a chair."

"You can still do it."

"I wish!"

"You can, Annie. Hit him where it really hurts. Let's go through with our fake wedding. Come on, you can't let him fucking win!"

For a second I got carried away in the idea of it all again, but shook it off. "No. I think it's time to call this whole thing quits."

"It's your call." Chris sat back down in the couch again.

"I'm going to pack my bags and then I'm going to bed. Night, Chris." I started walking away from him.

"About the wall," he called after me.

"Okay." I took a deep breath. "What exactly about the wall?"

"You were right, I probably wouldn't have been able to stop."

Something shot up my spine, and I instinctively folded my arms across my chest.

"But if it had happened, like that, I would have really regretted it."

"Oh?"

Chris climbed out the chair and started walking toward me, and my traitorous body reacted by sending shivers along my spine.

"I wouldn't have wanted it to happen like that. There. And in that way."

"Mmmmm…" My arms loosened and the words were on the tip of my tongue: *"How would you have wanted it to happen? Show me, Chris. Show me."* But I didn't say it. This was exactly what I meant. The line. There was a line and the two of us kept stepping over it. This was one of those times, despite contradictory messages being screamed at me by my body, to stay on the right side of it. It was getting too real and too painful to keep stepping over it like this.

"You don't believe in love, correct?" I blurted out. That was not what I'd wanted to say.

"I…I…," Chris stuttered, clearly thrown by the question. God, *I* was thrown by the question.

"You don't believe in love and you live on the other side of the world. I believe in love and roses and Valentine's cards, and even if it's hard and it hurts and sometimes I hate it, I still believe in it. And you just want to have fun for a few days, make the most of our time together and kiss me and be the perfect pretend boyfriend and I…I don't, I can't do it anymore."

I waited for him to say something. For him to open his mouth and tell me he was wrong about it all, that he did now believe in love and that it was because of me.

But he didn't.

I sighed. Stupid Annie, now I was that girl that thought she could change his mind and melt his cold heart.

"Good night, Chris."

CHAPTER TWENTY-FOUR

⌒

I snuck out early before the sun was up to avoid Chris's detection. When I got downstairs he was slumped over his computer fast asleep. He must have written all night. He looked like he'd made himself a little nest again: coffee cups, empty bags of chips, and a pair of terribly ugly and unfashionable reading glasses that I'd never seen before.

He was so perfectly imperfect.

I crept out, closing the door behind me, and returned to my little hovel. As soon as I got there I dropped my bag on the floor and climbed on top of the blanket and closed my eyes again. I'd barely gotten any sleep last night thinking about how Chris was just downstairs. Besides, it was way too early to be awake.

"Annie! Annie!" I woke up to loud banging and calling. I knew exactly who it was. Lilly.

"Hang on a second." I climbed off the bed and walked over to the door. As soon as it was open, an overly enthusiastic Lilly burst in and hugged me. Jane followed, looking a little less enthusiastic; she hated traveling, her height made it a truly uncomfortable, cramped experience.

"We're finally here! I thought we'd never get here." Lilly flounced into the room like she always did. "I swear I thought I was going to die at one stage. I'm totally better now, though, thank God, and I am so ready to drink cocktails and lie on the beach and tan and drink more cocktails and dance and…In fact, let's start now."

Lilly made a move for the bar fridge as Jane threw herself down on the bed, stretching out her legs.

"Ooohh, what do we have here?" Lilly pulled out a little dinky bottle of sparkling wine. "Small, but it will do for our first official holiday toast." She bent down and grabbed two wineglasses and a coffee cup. "Not enough glasses."

She was like a hurricane of holiday happiness, and I was feeling very overwhelmed as she swayed this way and that way.

"Here we go." She thrust a glass into my hand—there were probably only two sips in it—and gave the other one to Jane.

"To us." Lilly held her coffee cup in the air. "To having an amazing vacation, even though it's a little short, and to…" She stopped dead in the middle of her sentence and stared at me.

"Annie?" She lowered her glass and walked all the way up to me. Her face scrunched up and she gazed at me suspiciously. "What's going on? You seem…"

Lilly walked around me, and I felt myself crumbling under her penetrative gaze. "Something is definitely up, you seem very…"

"Yes!" Jane piped up. "I can see it. Something is different. And it is not the sunburn."

"What's going on?" Lilly put her cup down. She and Jane moved to stand in front of me. I downed the two sips in my glass, and then did the same to Lilly and Jane's.

"Frankly, I don't even know where to start."

"Hey, Annie," Damien called as he stuck his head through the door. Lilly squirmed a little and looked at me apologetically.

"I know we said girls' holiday, but you know…and it's just Damien, I mean he's practically one of the girls anyway…sort of."

"Hi." I waved at Damien as he walked in and wrapped an arm around Lilly.

"They just can't go for more than a day without having sex," Jane said and dropped into the chair. "You won't believe what they did in the plane."

Lilly giggled as Damien nuzzled into her neck. Jane rolled her eyes and sighed.

"Let's just say it was the longest 'bathroom' break"—Jane wildly gestured air quotes all over the place—"in Mauritius Air's history."

"It could have been longer," Lilly said with a slight giggle. "But there's always later."

"Oh God, you two. Stop! Please, you're making me feel sick again," Jane teased. "Besides, Annie was about to tell us something."

"Okay, I'll leave you guys to your girl talk." Damien turned.

"No. Wait. It might be good to get a male's opinion," I said. "But first, this calls for a lot more alcohol."

"Why?" Lilly asked, looking concerned again.

"Trevv and Tess are here!"

"What?" A chorus of gasps and shocked *what*s rose up, and everyone's eyes widened.

"Jesus, why the hell didn't you call and tell us?" Lilly rushed forward.

"We would have totally booked you into another hotel." Damien came and laid a hand on my shoulder.

"So what have you been doing?" Lilly said. "Hiding in this room the whole time? Have you seen them? What did you say to them? Oh God, what did he say to you, did they apologize, did they—"

"*Stop!*" Jane was now standing in the middle of the room scanning it. "This is not right." She walked up to the dressing table and ran her hands over the surface. She opened the bathroom door and stuck her head in. She walked up to the cupboard and peered inside. She even dropped to her hands and knees and looked under the bed.

"I lived with you for two months, Annie, and in all that time, there was always something lying on the floor. There was always a mess…" Jane rested her intense gaze on me and I felt like I was crumbling under it. She could be so intimidating at times; it was those different-colored eyes.

"Where have you been sleeping, Annie?" She folded her arms.

"Oh my God!" Lilly gasped and jumped back. "You and Trevv are back together. How did it happen? Where is Tess? Did he beg, have you been having sex with him, *noooo*, tell me you haven't used nipple clamps!"

"Annie!" Jane sounded furious. "Just tell me you didn't. Not Trevv. Don't you remember what he did to you?"

"Guys." I tried to stop them but they were off.

"Guys!" I shouted and they stopped. "His name is Chris. Okay. It's not Trevv. It's Chris."

"Who's Chris?" Lilly had finally calmed down.

"He's sort of, well, we've kind of been…"

They all leaned in. "Been *what*?" Jane's eyes were wider than before.

"He's been pretending to be my Boyden for the last few days."

"Boyden from Down Under?" Damien spoke. He'd been watching this whole thing unfold with something that resembled quiet amusement. He was used to Lilly's intensely dramatic moments. She was rather known for them actually, and as much as she would hate to admit it, she had more in common with her theater actress mother than she thought.

"It's a really long and complicated story."

"Well then, you better get started," Jane said.

CHAPTER TWENTY-FIVE

*I*t felt like I'd been talking for hours. We were all seated on my veranda, Damien swaying in the hammock and Lilly and Jane sitting across the table from me.

When it was all finally over, when I had told them about every single tiny detail (apart from the wall), they looked at me and said nothing for the longest time.

"I know." I held my head in my hands. "I know what you guys are all going to say. That it's ridiculous, it's the stupidest thing I've ever done in my life. It's embarrassing and totally mad and it got totally out of control and that's why I've decided I'm just going to tell Trevv the truth so I don't have to run around pretending anymore and so we can all just put this thing behind us. I *know*."

I downed the last sip of the bright green cocktail that Damien had commandeered for us all about halfway through the story, when I think he was starting to get bored.

"So?" I looked at them all, willing them to say something.

"It's fucking genius." Damien was the first to speak, and my mouth fell open.

"What?" I asked, looking straight at him, trying to read his expression.

"What?" Jane swung around. "You can't be serious, Damien."

"It's brilliant. It's the best thing I've heard in ages. Congratulations for pulling something like that off. I salute you!" He held his glass up. "And whoever this Chris is, he deserves an Oscar, I mean…" Damien started to chuckle now. "An Australian accent. For two days straight."

This was not the reaction I had been expecting, at all. But Damien's sudden laughter caused the corners of my mouth to curve into the tiniest smile. "It was such a terrible accent."

Damien laughed a little more. "In fact, I wish we'd come earlier to see this whole thing play out."

"Are you serious?" Jane's voice cut through the building laughter; Lilly had also joined in.

"Did he say 'g'day' and 'mate' and…?" Damian asked, barely able to control another round of choking laughter.

"He called me his sheila once!" I added as my smiles had turned to soft chuckles. This even caused Jane to start laughing. I face-palmed and shook my head in my hands. "And this one time, he told Trevv that he liked to play his didgeridoo while on walkabout."

Well that was it. Chaos broke out as we all started laughing. Damien almost fell out of the hammock and Lilly reached for him as she desperately tried to say something through the laughing.

"Oooh, oohh…what was that Australian guy called, the one that wrestled crocodiles and wore their teeth as a necklace?" Lilly was snapping her fingers in between the laughs.

"Crocodile Dundee!" Jane quickly jumped up. Typical, she

basically knew everything. Every tiny, seemingly insignificant fact was firmly planted inside that supersmart brain of hers.

When the laughter finally stopped, I was feeling so much better. "Fuck, you guys are the best. Seriously, I needed that. These last few days have been so crazy, I'm glad you're all here."

"So am I," Damien said rather seriously, "because I'm not going to let you tell Trevv the truth." He climbed out of the hammock and stood opposite me.

"What do you mean?"

"You can't tell him. Do you know how much he's going to love it? It will basically make his life, Annie."

"What other options do I have? I can't go through with our fake wedding tomorrow."

"Why not?" Damien said. "It's perfect. We're all here. And do you know how much it would ruin Trevv's day not to be in the spotlight? Totally upstaged by his ex Annie and her hulking man from the outback."

"Wait! Especially if your wedding is nicer than his!" Lilly jumped up as if a firecracker had propelled her. "He always had to have the best and latest of everything, imagine how he'd feel if your wedding was nicer. If you looked more gorgeous than Tess and everyone's eyes were on you, not her."

She started walking up and down as if she was imagining the thing playing out in front of her. "Everyone is watching Boyden and Annie and no one gives a shit about Trevv and Tess's lame little seaside excuse for a wedding! Yes!" Lilly was jumping up and down with excitement now. "It's brilliant. It's amazing, it's—"

"The most ridiculous thing I've ever heard!" Jane pulled Lilly back down to the seat. "Annie, a fake wedding? Really?"

"Oh, stop being such a party pooper, Jane," Damien teased. "You hated Trevv just as much as we all did."

"Yeah, but…"

"They've already put in all the legwork, they've been pretending to be a couple for days already. They almost got bloody arrested during their big public proposal." Damien threw me a look. "In our Annie's case, she almost got arrested *again*."

"Ha-ha," I said sarcastically. Damien loved to tease me about my arrest. He always thought I should wear it like a badge of honor; it gave me street cred, he said.

"It would be such a waste not to follow through with the whole thing now."

Logical Jane rolled her eyes. "Those drinks were too strong, because you're not making any sense."

"What's the harm?" Damian asked. "It's not like you two are falling in love or anything. You're just two buddies helping each other out. One friend helping the other through a difficult patch, like the time you gave me extra laughing gas when I came in for that filling."

Jane burst out laughing. "Stupidest analogy I have heard all day. Especially for a supposedly intelligent astrophysicist. Are you going to start quoting Depeche Mode next to support your argument?"

"Sure, it's only 'A Question of Time.'"

"Stop!" Jane held her hands in the air. "Honestly, I don't know how I'm friends with any of you. I'm the only sane one in the group, the rest of you are all mad."

"Oh, Jane, you're madder than all of us combined, you just haven't been pushed to the breaking point yet," Lilly said. We all looked at Jane.

"Hey, why is everyone looking at me like that?"

Lilly shrugged. "You know it's your turn next to lose your marbles. I did, Annie did, Stormy-Rain lost hers the day she was born...you are so next."

"Unlikely." Jane dismissed us all with a flick of the wrist. "Val will be doing that way before me."

There was a pause as everyone considered that.

"True!" Lilly said.

"I agree," I concurred.

"But we're veering off course here, guys," Jane said loudly. "This is about Annie losing her marbles."

"Sssshhh.'" Damien actually waved his hand at Jane to quiet her down. "Annie, just take a moment to imagine how good it would be to see the look on that dickhead's face. Plus you cannot give him the satisfaction of thinking he was right about you this whole time."

Jane opened her mouth to object once more, and Damien raced over and stood in front of her, blocking her from view. "Ignore the sensible one here. Ignore her and all her perfectly sound logic. Because there is nothing logical or rational about this. So just do it. Come on, it'll be fun."

Jane cleared her throat loudly and pushed her head around Damien. "Even if this was a good idea in some parallel universe somewhere, there is no time to pull it off."

"Sure there is. Places like this have weddings all the time; they probably have wedding planners on staff who can do these things with their eyes closed. Besides, Lilly's really good at planning weddings that don't actually result in marriage," Damien said with a playful wink in Lilly's direction.

Lilly gasped and slapped him in the arm playfully. "Bastard."

"Should I?" I suddenly became excited by the thought. Maybe I should just go through with it. Maybe Damien was right. Mind you, I wasn't sure how supportive they would be of the idea if they knew how I was really feeling about Chris. I had planned on telling them as the story had unfolded, but something stopped me. I think I was just embarrassed.

"Do it!" Lilly reached over and grabbed my hands.

"No, fuck!" I stopped dead. "What am I thinking? Even a fake wedding costs money."

"Some rose petals on the sand? Some candles and pretty hanging light things? Tons of champagne for the massive five-hundred-strong wedding party?" Damien said sarcastically. "You can charge it to my room."

I looked at him and knew he was being deadly serious. He was like that when he wanted to do something. Or when he wanted to help a friend out. There were no lengths that Damien wouldn't go to to make sure all the people that were important to him were happy. And in the last year or so, we'd all become very important to him, as he had to us.

"Jane?" I looked over at her and she shrugged.

"Annie, if you want to do it, fine, then go for it. It's still the silliest thing I've ever heard and clearly only something a movie writer could come up with. But if it's going to make you happy?"

"Okay!" I said. "Okay. I'll go back to Chris and tell him the whole thing is back on. Let's do it."

Lilly hugged me. "This is going to be the best fake wedding *ever*!"

CHAPTER TWENTY-SIX

ℐ walked through the garden toward Chris's room, the room I'd shared with him for the past few days. All I could hear was Lilly blathering on next to me. "A band…orchids…fairy lights between the palm trees…a gazebo…floating candles on the sea…Don't worry, Damien won't mind…a champagne fountain…Asian finger foods…"

Maybe since I'd left Chris he'd had some time to think and had actually decided he didn't want to go through with this farce. What would I do then?

We arrived outside the palatial villa and it felt odd to do it, but I knocked. I stood outside and heard some shuffling, some walking, and after what felt like an eternity, the door opened.

"Annie." He smiled at me like he hadn't seen me in years. He had his strange reading glasses on, and suddenly he looked like a nerdy hipster librarian who crocheted his own scarves and read books with really long titles about ironic hamsters and their philosophies.

I smiled, trying to hold back a laugh. "Chris, you look…"

"Oh." He reached for his glasses and pulled them off, looking embarrassed. "They make me look way smarter than I actually am."

"Oh, he looks nothing like Crocodile Dundee," Lilly said in my ear. "Nothing."

"Yeah, I would hope not, mate," Chris said in his broadest Australian accent to date and we all burst out laughing.

"God, you weren't kidding," Jane said, "it's terrible."

"Oh, this is Jane, by the way, and this is Lilly," I quickly said as Chris held the door open for us and we all walked in.

"Oh wow!" Lilly looked around briefly. "It's stunning; anyway, no time for all that." She marched over to the couch and sat down. "We need to start planning this right away if we're going to pull it off and make it look real."

"Pull what off?" Chris looked from Lilly to me, and back again.

"Surprise, the wedding's back on," I said making light of it.

"Really?" Chris looked confused. "But I thought you didn't want to…that you were going to tell—"

"Over our dead bodies," Lilly piped up from the couch. "Right, so let's get to it, there's no time and so much to do."

"If you still want to?" I quickly asked Chris.

"Sure. If you?" He threw the question right back at me.

"She does! Trust me." How was Lilly capable of doing so many things at once?

"Are you sure, Annie Anne?" Chris came closer and said in a lowered voice. His soft whispering brought memories and feelings rushing back in. *Mmmm, did I want to pretend to get married to the man I was falling in love with, knowing that he would never love me back? Let me think…*

I shrugged. "Why not, right?" I tried to sound upbeat and blasé, but I was failing.

"Because if you don't, the offer still stands. I'll come with you to tell Trevv—"

"No one is saying a word to Trevv and Tess," Lilly butted in again. "The only words Trevv and Tess are going to hear are the sound of *I do*s as we drown out their wedding with one of our very own."

I smiled faintly at Chris. "You heard the woman. We're getting married."

Chris walked over to the desk and shut his laptop; the collection of coffee mugs and junk food wrappers had grown since I'd left. I followed him with my eyes and was transported back to the wall. To the way he'd made me feel and the way he'd felt in my hand. As if he knew what I was thinking, he turned and looked at me. Like two pieces of Velcro coming together and clinging to each other, our eyes met and we didn't let go.

"Guys…we have to do this." Lilly's voice did little to break the hold we had over each other in this moment.

"*Guys*!" she said, louder this time, and I looked toward her. But as I did, I caught sight of Jane. Staring at us.

"You heard the woman," Chris said, moving to the living room where Lilly was anxiously pacing.

"What?" I mouthed at Jane.

She walked up to me and looped an arm though mine. "You clearly left out the important bits of your story, didn't you?"

"Like what?" I whispered as we walked to the living room.

"Like that fact that you two are having…" She leaned to my ear. "*Sex*," she whispered.

"We are *not*."

Jane stopped and eyed me. "Well you're having *something,* Annie. That's for sure."

***

The rest of the afternoon went by in some sort of strange, surreal blur. Lilly was having the time of her life, and there was no stopping her. Every few seconds she had added something else to our wedding. Another detail that was going to make it better than Trevv and Tess's. She'd drawn up several to-do lists and was handing them out.

"So we all agree then?" After what felt like hours, she finally sat back in her chair and closed her little notebook just as her phone beeped.

"It's Damien. What room number is this?" she asked Chris.

"It's Bougainvillea Villa three."

"Yes!" Lilly opened her pad again. "I knew I was forgetting something." She took her pen out and read as she wrote, "Bou-gain-villea."

She messaged Damien back and within seconds he was at the door. We all watched as they did their obligatory "hello kiss session" like they hadn't seen each other in years. Like he had been away in Afghanistan and she had been sitting at home waiting for years for him to return.

Damien introduced himself to Chris. "So, I believe congratulations are in order." Damien gave Chris one of those manly pats, which to be honest I hadn't ever seen him do before. "You got a good sheila here," he said in an Australian accent.

"She's a wee keeper," Chris replied.

"Wrong country," Jane corrected. "They say things like 'wee this' and 'wee that' in Britain, not Australia."

"Seriously?" Chris's eyes widened and met mine. "Ooops. I've said 'wee' more in the last two days than I have in my entire life."

We all laughed again. This Australian thing had legs, real comic mileage. Like the time Lilly boarded a plane to Thailand in her pajamas. We'd managed to get a year out of that, at least.

"So, I kind of did something." Damien's tone got serious.

"What?" Lilly swiveled.

"I ran into Trevv and Tess at the pool."

"And?" Lilly asked.

"I sort of said something, a few things really...God, I fucking couldn't help it. They were going on and on about their wedding and then I kept telling them about your wedding and how I got specially ordained online so I could do it."

Jane laughed so loudly at this that we all looked at her. "Sorry, carry on."

"And then Tess was talking about these stupid white doves they were going to be releasing when they kissed for the first time, and I sort of told them that you'd be having peacocks."

"What?"

Lilly and Jane burst out laughing simultaneously. I, however, did not. This was why I'd wanted to back out of the thing in the first place; this one-upmanship was causing everyone to go crazy.

"Where are we going to get peacocks?" I asked.

"They are all over this resort. I've seen about five this morning already," Damien said.

"So, we're going to what? Wrangle peacocks and make them

walk down the aisle like the good-behaving birds they are?" I said sarcastically.

Everyone laughed harder now. Even Jane had gotten into the spirit of things.

"Look, if I can wrangle the crocs back home in the bayous—" Chris started saying.

"Bayous are in America, not Australia," Jane quickly corrected.

He didn't miss a beat. "The ol' crocs in the swamps—"

"Wetlands," Jane quickly corrected.

"The crocs in the water, where it is wet and muddy." Chris looked at Jane and raised a questioning brow.

"That will be adequate," she replied.

"I think this ol' Ozzie can catch himself a few peacocks."

More laughter rose up. Okay, maybe this Australian thing should *not* have legs. Maybe it needed to die, now!

"Oooh, you know what else we should have." Lilly jumped up. "Lipizzaner horses. White, majestic horses that deliver the ring down the aisle."

"Or dinosaurs," Jane added. "We'll just bring them back to life and have you ride off into the sunset on the long neck of a bron-tosaurus."

Even I finally laughed at that. It was funny. What wasn't funny, though, were the feelings I was having inside. I was vacillating be-tween genuine excitement for my fake wedding, excitement to see the looks on Trevv and Tess's faces, and especially to see Chris stand-ing at the top of the aisle. But the other part kept reminding me what a bad idea this was. Playing pretend-relationship with real feelings was a game that was only going to end up hurting me.

"Are you okay?" I felt a soft hand on my back. It was Chris. He leaned in and put his head so close to my ear that I could feel his warm breath. I closed my eyes for a second and let myself enjoy the feeling of it caressing my skin. "You can still back out of this if you don't want to do it."

"Why, do you not want to do it?" I opened my eyes.

"No. I want nothing more than to fake marry you, Annie Anne."

Fake.

"Hey." Lilly came over to us. "You guys better not be getting cold feet. We've rounded up the peacocks and a yacht. You two will be sailing off into the sunset in style!"

CHAPTER TWENTY-SEVEN

$\mathcal{W}$e all stayed at Chris's for the rest of the afternoon and well into the evening. I couldn't believe how he'd just slotted in with my friends. It was as if he'd always been there. Strangely enough, he and Jane were hitting it off, which was rare to see. She was usually so reserved with strangers, to the point of total social awkwardness at times. But she seemed so easy and relaxed with Chris.

Perhaps they could sense their similarities, the two kids that had been cruelly teased on the playground and hadn't had the easiest time growing up. It warmed my heart to see it, but also broke it a bit at the same time. This was probably the last time we would ever all spend together. In a few days, I would probably never see Chris again.

Damien ended up ordering room service at some stage and we all found ourselves upstairs on the deck playing a game of Monopoly that we'd found in a cupboard in the spare room. Drinks had been flowing all day, and truthfully we were all a little tipsy.

Jane and Damien had been engaged in a constant, and rather amusing argument over the rules of the game. It was so entertaining to watch the two arguing so passionately with each other, as if their lives depended on it, that we only noticed Lilly's absence when we heard the scream from downstairs.

"Aaaahhh!" The sound of her taking the steps two at a time made us all turn.

"It's perfect, Chris. I'd forgotten all about getting one! It's amazing. It's so *real*-looking."

She was holding a ring box in her hand, and my heart quickened. Chris had bought me a fake ring, for our fake wedding? Lilly looked mesmerized by it.

She reached into the box and pulled the ring out. She looked positively orgasmic by this stage. She held it in the air in awe. *It was fucking huge*. I mean massive. It was probably the biggest diamond I had ever seen, that's the only way you could tell it was fake.

"It's the most beautiful ring I've ever seen." As if in slow motion, she slipped her finger through it and gazed in astonished wonder at the giant thing that was now glittering from her hand.

"It's so perfect." It looked like she was about to cry and I turned to Chris and smiled, expecting him to be just as amused as I was. But he was staring at the ring in total bewilderment. Fast movements caught my eye and I looked across at Damien.

He was frantically patting his pockets, and he pulled one out and stuck his finger through the giant hole at the bottom. "Fuck," he swore under this breath, and I instantly got it.

"Oh dear." I looked over at Chris, who'd just figured it out, too. Then I looked across at Jane, who was shaking her head and grimacing.

"I want it." Lilly let out a long, loud sigh. She looked like she was about to start making out with it. "Oh, look, it has an engraving on it." She held it up to the light and squinted. "A moon, how…a moon? Why would you put a…?"

"Because it's for you," Damien said, stepping forward.

"What do you mean?" The magic powers of the ring finally released Lilly and she looked over at Damien. He grinned lamely. It looked like it took Lilly a few seconds to figure it out. Her face went from confused and blank, to wide-eyed, dropped-jawed shock.

"It's for *me*?" she asked.

"It's kind of ruined now, so I guess all I can say is—"

"No! Stop." Lilly held her hand out. "No, no, no. This is not how it's supposed to happen." She took the ring off and put it back in the box. "I didn't see it. I never found it." She ran up to Damien and thrust it into his hand.

Damien laughed, "Lilly, you saw it. You wore it, no taking it back now."

"But this is not how you're supposed to propose to me."

Damien burst out laughing again. "When has anything gone the way it was supposed to with us?" He moved closer to Lilly and then dropped to one knee. I'd never pictured him as the one-knee kind of guy. But it worked. It worked because it stole her breath away.

"Lilly, sorry it wasn't meant to go like this. I have ten thousand rose petals in our room and champagne and candles—"

"He left an open flame in his room," I heard Jane whisper from behind me.

"I also had this whole speech planned, but now I can't think of a single word. Anyway, words are pretty meaningless and forgettable."

I cringed at the Depeche Mode reference and looked over at Jane, who was doing the exact same thing. But Lilly didn't seem to mind; her eyes were lit up like firecrackers, her cheeks were flushed a soft pink, and she looked so incredibly beautiful in the moonlight. Happiness and love seemed to radiate from every one of her pores. I looked up at Chris to see what his reaction was to this all. Cynical, Mr. Anti-Love. But he wasn't looking at them, he was looking at me.

CHAPTER TWENTY-EIGHT

⌒

As soon as we left Chris's suite that night, Jane grabbed me by the arm and marched me onto the beach.

"Where are we going?" I asked, breathless. She was moving so fast she was practically dragging me.

"We're going to have a chat. I don't really want to go back to the room, since mine is next to the happy couple's and as much as I love them, I have no desire to listen to them have sex for the next twenty-four hours."

We walked onto the beach and sat down on the soft sand.

"You're in love with him." It was a statement of fact. Not a question. Jane already knew the answer, so there was no use denying it to her.

"Yes."

"And you're pretending to get married tomorrow?"

"Yup!"

"Does he know how you feel?" she asked.

"No. I don't think so. He knows I like him, but not that I, you know."

"Say it. I think you need to hear it out loud."

I looked over at Jane; her eyes were soft and kind. "I love him. I've fallen in love with him."

"Did you tell him you like him?" she asked.

"Yes. And he sort of told me, too. We were actually on a real date last night before Trevv and Tess ruined everything."

"A date? As in romance, open flames, and petals?"

I nodded. "He took me to this really nice restaurant and it was going really well until they showed up."

"Do you think he feels the same way?"

I shook my head. "No. He doesn't. He doesn't really believe in love. I gave him a chance to tell me last night, but he didn't. I'm just a bit of fun for him. A vacation fling."

"No, you're much, *much* more than that." Jane sounded adamant. "I saw the way he was looking at you tonight. He definitely likes you, a lot."

"But it's not going to go anywhere. He lives in another country, and he's not the kind of guy you get into a serious relationship with. He might like you, but he'll never love you. Or he might, but he'll fight it so much that he never feels it or…he's so fucking complicated. I don't think he knows what he wants. One minute he's kissing me and telling me how beautiful I am, and the next minute he's cracking jokes about the whole thing."

"You've kissed him?"

"Yes, and…" My body shuddered at the memory. When I thought about it, I could actually feel his hands on my body.

"So you *are* having sex with him."

"No!" I quickly defended myself. "Not sex exactly."

"*Exactly?* He's either popping his penis into your vagina, or he's not!"

"Jane!" I slapped her on the arm. "Please never say 'penis' and 'vagina' and never use the word 'popping' in the same sentence with them ever again, either."

"But penis and vagina are involved?" She was teasing now.

"They might be," I admitted.

Jane cocked her head at me.

"Okay, they're involved. But there hasn't been any popping, nearly, but no."

Jane was silent for a while.

"You think I'm mad for going through with this? For putting my-self through this because when he thinks it's all fun and games, I'm going to be walking down the aisle and wishing it was real."

"Why didn't you tell us?"

"You guys all thought it was so funny. And it is, in a way. Then the whole thing just snowballed and now we have peacocks, possibly horses, and tomorrow morning it will probably be a cruise ship, not a yacht."

"Why don't you just call the whole thing off?"

I looked up at Jane and wanted to cry at the mere suggestion.

"You hope that when he sees you walking down the aisle he's go-ing to suddenly realize he's in love with you and then this whole fairy tale comes true?" she asked softly.

I winced at the sound of it. "I'm so lame."

"You're not lame. But you are setting yourself up for some serious potential heartbreak."

"I know," I sighed.

"Whatever you do, just don't have sex with him on your fake wedding night." Jane held her hand out.

"What's that for?"

"Pinkie swear."

I laughed. We used to pinkie swear as kids. I used to think it was wildly uncool, since I was a little bit older than all of them, but soon I was also pinkie swearing. I'd probably never have been friends with all of them if Lilly wasn't my cousin. She was the glue that stuck us all together, she always had been. I'd made plenty of other fiends over the years, but I always kept coming back to them—they were family.

"Pinkie swear." Jane didn't wait for my finger; she leapt right in there and wrapped her pinkie around mine.

"I swear."

"It's all fun and games and laughs until someone gets hurt, Annie. And that person is going to be you, especially if you consummate this thing."

"I know."

Jane laid a hand on my shoulder and gave it a squeeze. "Do you think those two have finished?"

"Doubtful," I said.

She yawned. "Well, I can't put it off any longer. I'm going to go and take myself to bed. Big day tomorrow."

Jane got up and walked away. I didn't feel like going back to my room. I didn't feel like sitting on a beach all night, either. I did feel like seeing Chris.

I got up and started walking back to his place. When I got there the door was open and he wasn't downstairs. He wasn't in the shower, either. I walked upstairs and was surprised to find him sitting with his feet in the pool, computer on lap and typing away.

"I thought you hated water."

He looked up at me from the pool. "I think I changed my mind."

"Mmm, and what would have done that?"

"It may have had something to do with this girl, and a kiss."

"Sounds like an interesting story."

"It is."

"Looks like you've gotten inspired again." I motioned to the computer on his lap.

Chris closed his computer and pushed it away. "Want to join me? The water is amazing."

I sat down next to him, leaving a foot or two between us. I slipped my shoes off and stuck my feet into the water. It was amazing.

"So what's it about? Your movie?"

"Well, it's a story about a girl and a guy who meet on an island, like this."

"I gathered that much, but what happens?"

"The usual. There's love and some kissing and intense staring."

"And it's going well?" I asked.

"It's writing itself." His voice grew soft and he splashed his legs in the water a little harder, causing some drops to fly through the air and land on me. I giggled and wiped them off my face.

"So what happens in the end? Do they fall in love and live happily ever after?" My question was so loaded. I wasn't asking about some fictitious characters in a movie anymore, and I'm pretty sure Chris knew that.

"That all depends," he replied.

"On what?"

"I'm not sure yet." I felt his shoulders shrug next to me.

"You know that doesn't make any sense, right?"

"Life doesn't make much sense sometimes, Annie."

CHAPTER TWENTY-NINE

*W*ant to swim?" He stood up and reached out a hand for me to take.

"I don't have a bathing suit."

"Who said you need one?" His eyes glinted and a dirty smile played on the corners of his mouth. I felt a sharp sensation shoot through me, settling between my legs, and I immediately crossed them.

"Sorry. I shouldn't have said that." He looked genuinely sorry. "I didn't mean to take it there, again."

"It's okay."

"Can't blame a guy for trying, though." He smiled weakly at me and I reciprocated.

"This whole wedding tomorrow." He continued the apologetic tone. "Your friends have really, sort of…"

"Run with it. Taken over. Yes, they are like that."

"You don't have to do it, if you don't want to."

I looked at him and wondered if this was his way of trying to let me down gently. He knew that I had feelings for him and he didn't want to be responsible for hurting me.

"Do you want to do it?" I asked.

"Only if you do."

"That's not very helpful," I replied.

"Yes. I want to do it. I don't want us to back out of it now, especially since Damien has promised peacocks. If tomorrow is called off, Trevv would get so much satisfaction out of it. But I don't want to do it if it's going to make things awkward between us."

"You mean more awkward?"

Chris smiled. "Yeah. I guess." I was just about to respond when I heard what sounded like a mariachi band that had crept up behind us and started playing.

"What the hell?" I looked around. The sound was coming from the direction of the beach.

"What the hell is that noise?" Chris walked over to the edge of the balcony and looked over. "Oh, Annie…" He waved me over with his hand. "You will never believe this."

I ran to the edge and peered over. And there, standing at the bottom of the villa, was Trevv. He was flanked by a small troupe of men playing instruments and he was… *singing?*

I followed his gaze and Tess was standing on the balcony looking down adoringly at Trevv, who was now thrusting his hips to the music and serenading her.

Chris widened his eyes. "Is this actually happening? We're not dreaming, right?"

"No. I don't think we are."

I watched in jaw-dropping astonishment as Trevv got louder and louder and his hips shook so violently, he reminded me of a jackhammer drilling into the cement. When the song came to an end (thank God), Tess clapped adoringly and Trevv blew her a kiss. He then very deliberately turned to us, as if he'd known we were watching the whole time.

Of course he had, though. This little performance hadn't been for Tess at all, it was for us.

"Sorry there, did I disturb you?" he asked with sickly faux concern.

"Not at all." I smiled.

"I didn't mean to wake you. I know you have a big day tomorrow, too, what with the *wedding*…" He said *wedding* like he was a spitting camel. "Damien tells me he even got ordained for the big day."

He eyed us. "Anyway, sorry about that. I just wanted to do something special for Tess on the last night of her not being Mrs. Tremblay."

"Sorry, what?" Chris perked up. "Did you say Tremblay? As in Trevv Tremblay and Tess Tremblay?" Chris didn't hold back his laughter.

"What's your problem?" Trevv glared at him.

"Nothing. Good night."

He turned to me. "Annie, how could you forget to tell me that his last name started with a 'T' as well? We could have made at least another hundred puns, jibes, and jokes about that. I feel like you deprived me."

"You know what?" Trevv shouted up to us again and we both went to look over the balcony again. "I'm still not buying it, *Annie*." He had very deliberately just called me Annie for the first time, ever. And I hated the way it sounded on his lips. Suddenly I felt myself being pulled right back into it all over again.

He smirked at me. "If you'll excuse me, I have a gorgeous woman waiting for me" He strutted back inside and vanished into his room.

I turned to Chris. "You better not get cold feet. Because I'm marrying you tomorrow whether you like it or not!"

CHAPTER THIRTY

⌣

$\mathcal{T}$he day passed at such a whirlwind rate. Lilly hadn't stopped for a second (except to admire her ring, which she was now wearing). She'd been coordinating the whole thing with the hotel wedding planner, who was used to whipping events up quickly.

But while the wedding chaos was in full swing, I'd woken up feeling like I'd slept with a tightly wrapped ball of elastic bands in my head and someone had been snapping them all night long. I was plagued with more of the same contradictory feeling about my so-called wedding.

The only thing that vaguely took my mind off it all was going dress shopping. We'd driven into the cosmopolitan town of Grand Baie. The main shopping road, aptly named Sunset Boulevard, was dotted with small boutique shops and restaurants. Massive palms and trees with bright red leaves lined the street, and multicolored Chinese lanterns (which Lilly was currently eyeing for the wedding) hung from the branches and the roofs of the shops. Flower boxes peppered the pavement, and the air smelled sweet with their scent. It was like shopping in paradise.

A small clothing store caught our eye immediately and we all bundled in excitedly. Jane, not so much. She hated shopping. Her height and foot size always made it hard to find things she liked, something she was very sensitive about. I found something I liked immediately, though.

A beautiful, knee-length, vintage-style dress caught my attention right off the bat. It was a gorgeous warm cream color, with capped lace sleeves and a pale blue ribbon that tied at the waist. It wasn't the wedding dress I had always imagined for myself, a famous designer hadn't made it, but it was perfect. And wearing it made everything feel so real.

And before I knew it, the entire day had passed and I was standing at the top of the aisle. Lilly and Damien were running late; they had actually attempted to herd some peacocks in the direction of the wedding, but had arrived back with two tortoises instead. You cannot make this stuff up. Laughing hysterically, they placed the tortoises down on the beach as well as enough bougainvillea to fill an entire Greek village.

The whole wedding thing was exactly as I imaged it would be. Even better.

Romantic setting sun casting a pale pink light across the warm white sands. *Check*.

The sound of tiny waves lapping. *Check*.

An aisle of velvety, pink petals. *Check*.

Warm glow of the candles. *Check*.

Colorful Chinese lanterns swaying from palms trees. Rows of fairy lights stretched out between them, a tortoise eating the flowers scattered on the beach in front of me, arches made of palm leaves and bright pink flowers that stretched out all the way to the edge of the warm sea. *Double check.*

But what I hadn't imagined, not accurately anyway, was the extent of the feelings I would have. I knew there would be some, but I didn't know how utterly overwhelmed I would be.

An unbridled fluttering in my stomach—which could only have been caused by huge, genetically modified butterflies.

Chills—despite the warm, tropical weather.

And a light-headed giddiness—without the effects of a coconut cocktail.

I looked up from my trembling hands, and saw Chris. Waiting for me.

I looked past all the beautiful scenery and my eyes went straight to him, standing there in his crisp white linen suit. God, he looked amazing in a suit. He looked up at me—*beamed* up at me, with the biggest smile on his face I had seen so far. My lips uncontrollably split into a smile, too, as the feelings rose inside me.

Chris was looking at me as if I was the most beautiful woman he'd ever seen. He was looking at me like a groom would look at his bride, his real bride. Hope swelled inside me as I started walking down the aisle.

And our timing was perfect. I glanced over to see Trevv standing on the beach, glaring at us. His jaw was clenched so tightly that it looked like his face would explode from the pressure. He was furious.

His wedding looked quaint. There were a few flowers scattered around him, and a few freestanding lanterns lit the way for the bride. Theirs was a sweet little beach wedding. Ours was an über-deluxe beach wedding. In fact, it was already drawing a lot of attention. A few hotel residents and tourists had gathered. Some were taking photos, and a sweet elderly couple was holding hands lovingly, obviously reminiscing about their wedding day.

And then I heard a gasp. It was Tess. She'd walked onto the beach and into her worst nightmare. She did look stunning, though, in her classic white sweetheart wedding dress, holding one long-stemmed red rose. But she soon turned ugly as an angry scowl contorted her features into something hideous. Our wedding made hers look like amateur child's play, and I could see she was painfully aware of that fact. And everyone's eyes were not on her, they were on *me* for a change.

As if by magic, a string quartet appeared behind me and started playing the wedding march. Tess's mouth literally fell open, and she glared at Trevv. The music swelled and it was my cue to start walking.

I took my first step; the rose petals under my feet felt soft and silky. The warm sand squished between my bare toes, and the flared skirt of my dress swished and swayed as I walked. I looked up and saw that Chris's eyes were glued to me.

I'd never been married before, but I was sure that this, right here, was what a real bride would feel. No doubt about it.

Standing next to Chris was Damien. You couldn't wipe the smile off his face if you tried; it looked like he was relishing his new role as minister. He looked fully in character, too, as he said a few words to Chris and patted him on the shoulder in a brotherly fashion. (He was taking his role very seriously, even though he didn't look the part at all. I doubt there are too many ministers with as many tattoos as Damien has.)

And then I was next to Chris, face-to-face. My eyes were cast down because I was sure that if I looked up at him, he would finally see right through me.

He would look straight into my heart and know exactly what I was feeling. That I was totally in love with him. That he was everything I could ever want, and more. He was what I'd been looking for in all the men I'd dated, but never found. He was my forever guy. My perfect hero in this wildly unbelievable, tragicomedy movie that was my life.

I finally looked up and our eyes met. It was more than I'd imagined. It was electric. It was visceral. And it felt so, *so* real. This was no longer pretend, for me anyway.

Chris took my hands in his and the trembling stopped instantly. I felt like I'd come home. Like I belonged here, with him. I allowed myself one last quick glance over at T-Squared and saw nothing but red-hot fury. Tess even looked like she was going to burst into tears. I smiled at her as if nothing about this double wedding on the beach was odd, giving them a taste of their own medicine.

Ah, revenge, it tasted sweet. As sweet as the elaborate, ridiculously over-tiered wedding cake, decorated with a spray of pink sugar-crystal flowers and orchids that stood next to our über-altar.

The sounds and the sights and smells and colors seemed to disappear. All that was left was Chris. And he was everything.

"Well, do you?" Damien's voiced pulled me back to reality. I'd zoned out so much, I hadn't heard a word of the ceremony.

"What?"

"Do you take this strapping man, Boyden Brown, to be your lawfully wedded husband? In sickness and health, in…" Damien faltered. "In good times and in bad, and until you die, or until the average density of the universe is enough to slow down expansion for it to begin contracting under the force of gravity and collapse in on itself to form a singularity of unimaginable density." I could hear Lilly and Jane trying to smother a giggle, and Damien gave us both the tiniest wink.

My voiced quivered and I couldn't help my smile. "I do."

"And you, Boyden, do you take this beautiful woman to be your lawfully wedded wife until all of the previously mentioned things?"

Chris's voice was hushed and soft. "I do."

He pulled my hand closer and took a ring out of his pocket. It was the most beautiful thing I'd ever seen, despite being costume jewelry. A large heart-shaped pink stone was poised on a platinum-colored band, sparkling in the warm light of the candles. As he slipped it onto my finger I gasped.

It moved up my finger slowly, and it felt like the most intimate and erotic thing I'd ever experienced. I looked up to see if Chris had heard my breathy gasp; he had. The look in his eyes confirmed it.

"Well, I guess there's nothing else to say, other than, *you may kiss the bride*."

I braced myself for the kiss as Chris wrapped his arms around me and pulled me closer.

"Annie Anne," he whispered softly, before leaning in and kissing me.

The kiss was delicate, soft and slow. His lips tickled mine and a shiver ran up my spine. He tasted sweet and felt hot. He let out a tiny, breathy moan before cupping my face in his hands. I arched my body closer to him until we were pressed up against each other as tightly as two people could ever be. I opened my mouth a little more and invited him in for a brief moment our tongues touched and—

"Ahumm." Jane cleared her throat. "We have an audience here."

Our kiss was over, but the moment wasn't. I could taste him in my mouth and on my slightly wet lips. The moment continued to linger as our staring intensified.

I knew exactly what he wanted. He was making no secret of it. And neither was I. I didn't know if he felt the same way about me as I did about him. But if I couldn't have him forever and in all the ways I wanted to, I would be satisfied to have him, and pretend with him, for just one night.

I wanted my honeymoon night with Chris. Screw all the consequences and the promises I had made. One night, I wanted it. The feeling of need was so overwhelming that there was only one thing to do, quench it.

"Annie…" Jane tugged at the back of my dress. "Pinkie promise. Pinkie promise."

I turned to her and shook my head just as Chris yanked me by the arm and started pulling me away.

Have you ever watched a wildlife documentary where a lion hunts a buck? They do the whole chase scene in slow motion, so you can see the lion's singular focus, its blood-hungry determination, every muscle in its body rippling. And then when it pounces, they speed it up to real time again. It gives you this impression of an almighty collision. Aggressive, desperate, hungry, intense, ferocious…

That's what this was like.

Chris dragged me by the hand and we ran across the beach, with a quick, unapologetic wave at my friends. We passed T-Squared, who looked at us with total disdain. Jane buried her face in her hands, probably because of embarrassment—she wasn't into public displays of affection, let alone unadulterated lust. A few bystanders whistled and clapped as we carried on running.

It felt like it took forever to get to the room—like I said, slow motion.

But finally we reached our room and we barreled through the door.

Inside the room, we threw ourselves at each other like wild, starving animals.

It was all so dramatic. We smashed against the wall first, then the floor, then somehow managed to claw our way from the couch—which we had somehow found ourselves on—and then to the bed.

It was so carnal, dangerous, and frantic.

Chris had me pinned to the bed as he continued to kiss me. Soft, tiny tips of tongues were long gone. We devoured each other. The kisses were fast and deep and hard.

"I've imagined you like this since the first moment I saw you." His mouth was at my ear now, and the feel of his hot breath against it was such a turn-on—just in case I wasn't turned on enough already.

"Like what?"

"Pinned to the bed. Me on top."

I laughed and Chris quickly shut me up with another forceful kiss.

He started tugging at my dress, desperately looking for a way in. Thank goodness I wasn't wearing the strappy, crisscrossing creation from the store in the hotel lobby, or we would be there for hours.

"How the fuck…?"

"Zip…" I was so breathy by this stage I was hardly able to speak. "…at side, not back, dress."

And then he flipped me onto my side as if I was a tiny rag doll. Suddenly my face was pressed into the bed and Chris was behind me, his hands ripping at the zip and opening it.

His fingertips gently stroked my back, giving me goose bumps.

Then the kisses…

Warm, wet kisses down my spine, all the way to the small of my back. I felt like I was going to explode if he didn't do something more substantial with me…

…as I was thinking that…

Chris stopped. And without warning he was up, walking across the room. He sat down at the window.

I panicked. "What…what's going on, Chris? Have I done something?"

He cut me off immediately. "No. No. You've done nothing. You're great. It's just…"

He got up and walked over to the other window—a pointless exercise. Clearly he was worked up about something. But what?

"Annie, before we do this, I just want to say that…"

I understood.

I knew where this was going. I can't say my heart didn't break, because I'd stupidly let myself go there. Let myself feel for him and get swept up in the romance of it all knowing full well that he would never feel for me what I was feeling for him.

"I know. No love. This is just some fun we're having. We like each other, we're attracted to each other…I get it, you've told me that—"

He cut me off again. "No. That's not what I was going to say."

The look on his face gave it away immediately, and a lump started forming in my throat. My heart started pounding so hard that it was all I could hear. Chris looked at the floor and shuffled his feet around aimlessly, coyly, as if trying to buy himself time to figure out what to say.

"The thing is, Annie Anne…" He looked up and smiled at me. "I kind of like you. A lot. Like I think I *like you, like you*."

"Huh?" Were we suddenly twelve again?

He ran his hands through his hair, letting it fall back into his face. It was damp from sweat and strands stuck to his forehead, giving him a disheveled look.

"What I'm trying to say—*really badly*—is that…*Shit!*"

And then he was up again, striding across the room to the trash can. He reached into it and pulled out a piece of paper and flattened it against the table. He fiddled in a drawer and pulled out a pen.

"I'm a writer, okay. I'm not good at saying these things."

He started scribbling something down on the paper. When he was finished, he strode over to me and dropped it in my lap. "I'm going to shower. Read this and let me know what you think?"

I watched him as he walked away and started peeling his clothes off one by one before turning on the taps and climbing in.

I opened the note.

Annie Anne,
You make me feel things I've never felt before. I can't stop thinking about you, even when I'm with you. And when I'm not with you, all I want to do is be with you. I even woke up this morning looking

forward to our fake wedding. And then, when I saw you walking toward me on the beach, you were the most beautiful woman I'd ever seen. You took my breath away. Stopped my heart. And I felt like the luckiest man alive.

In this short time that we've known each other, you've made me a better person and you see through all my layers of crap. I've never shown anyone the real me before, until I met you. And I don't want to go back to the guy I was a few days ago without you in my life.

I don't know what love feels like, but if I were a betting man, I would put money on the fact that what I'm feeling right now, for you, might just be it. Maybe I've finally met the right girl. You are the heroine in my story and I want to write you into it forever.

I turned toward the shower and saw that he was standing under the water staring at me, completely naked. But instead of looking like the Chris I'd gotten to know over the last few days: self-assured, humorous, kind of macho in that messy *I don't care* way, he looked completely different.

He looked still.

Quiet. Vulnerable. Breakable even.

His lips twitched into a halfhearted nervous smile and his eyes seemed to question me. I knew what the question was.

I got up from the bed and let my dress go. It fell to the floor with a soft thud. I reached around and undid my bra, pulled down my panties, and walked toward him.

The second I stepped into the shower, everything between us changed. The warm water felt good, and Chris felt even better. He pulled me to him and we hugged each other. It was so tender, so full of meaning and full of a million thoughts and sentences that didn't really need to be said in that moment.

And then he kissed me again—softly. Slowly. The warm water rushed over our faces and bodies and when I opened my eyes and looked at him, he had little water droplets clinging to those long eyelashes framing his ridiculous blue eyes.

"You looked beautiful today, in your wedding dress." His hands moved down my arms and he intertwined his fingers in mine. "Really incredible."

"Thanks. So did you."

"I didn't wear a dress, did I?"

I put my finger over his lips. "No more jokes, Chris!"

He rolled his eyes playfully in response. "Fine. I'll try."

And then he put his arms around me, lifted me up, and pushed me into the wall. I opened my legs and wrapped them around him, inviting him in.

"I meant what I wrote…I…I"—he stumbled on his words—"I think I'm in love with you."

He kissed me gently again. "I've never said that before to anyone but—" His mouth moved down my neck and onto my breasts. "I really think I love you." The feeling of the hot water still running over me, Chris's mouth and tongue…was amazing. I moaned and wriggled and arched my back.

"I love you, too," I finally said. It felt so good to get it out that it opened the floodgates. "I really love you, Chris. I'm totally in love with you. I love you."

Chris looked up and smiled. "I can't tell you how amazing that sounds."

He released me from the wall and let me slide down to the floor. The ground was warm and wet and the tiles were hard.

I don't know if you've ever had sex on the slippery tiles of a shower floor. But it's incredible. With every thrust my body slipped up and down the wet surface. I could use my hands to push myself off the wall, meeting him with such force, as my body slipped and slid. The warm water continued to drench us as our bodies slithered, and glided up and down the floor.

Then, without warning, he picked me up, carried me out of the shower, and threw me on the bed. Our wet bodies thumped together and sent drops of water flying. We both burst out laughing as my wet hair slapped against his face. I lay on my back and Chris moved on top of me, parting my legs with his.

His blue eyes sought mine out and our gaze locked. He kept eye contact with me as he lowered himself down and slipped inside me. Slowly, gently. Our stare created a kind of magical bubble around us as we moved together as one.

He smiled down at me. "You look more beautiful from this angle. I could get used to this view, Annie Anne."

At some point I was on top of him. I ran my hands through the hair on his chest, and it was soft and fun to play with. I smiled down at him and he reciprocated.

I didn't care what kinds of sounds were coming out of my mouth now, or how loud they were. I was whimpering and panting and saying his name over and over again as he pulled my hips into a steady rhythm. And then I threw my head back as the feeling ripped through me and I let out a loud cry. Chris suddenly pulled my head down, bringing me face-to-face with him. He held on to the back of my head, making eye contact before letting out a loud moan.

When his body relaxed, he kissed me again. And in that moment I finally understood it: Yes, sex can be *that* good. Yes, you can break the sound barrier with your screams.

"Fifteen, by the way," he whispered as he nibbled my lip gently.

"Fifteen what?"

"Fifteen out of ten."

It took me a minute to get it. It was a reference to that first night together when he said he would rate my sexual ability out of ten.

I giggled. "Thanks. You're not too bad yourself."

"Not too bad…I'm a sex god, what are you talking about?"

He was being playful and we both burst out laughing.

He wrapped his arms around me and I felt so safe. I put my head on his chest; his hair was soft against my face. I'd never liked chest hair before, until now. In fact, I like everything about Chris. We held on to each other tightly for a while, and it felt so ridiculously right.

"Shit!" Chris suddenly said loudly.

"What?" I got a fright as he said it.

"We don't have cigarettes to smoke."

And with that we were laughing again. "I wish we had that wedding cake, though," I said, feeling a sudden craving for sugar.

"Your wish is my command." Chris got up and walked over to the phone and punched some numbers in.

"Yes, reception…hi, my *wife* and I"—he really emphasized the word *wife* and winked at me—"my *wife* and I left our wedding cake on the beach. Would it be possible to get someone to bring it? Thank you."

He put the phone down, jumped back onto the bed, and wrapped his arms around me in a tight bear hug.

"You meant what you said, right?" he asked. "Being in love?"

God, he was cute when he was insecure and vulnerable. "I meant every word, Chris," I said, running my fingers through his hair.

About ten minutes later there was a knock on the door, and the ridiculous three-tiered red velvet monstrosity was wheeled in. I couldn't help it, but as I saw it, I burst out laughing. It was so over-the-top, it was madness. What were we going to do with it?

"Come here." Chris was standing next to the cake holding the knife. "I believe we're supposed to cut it together."

We held the knife and looked at each other before sliding it through the cake. Everything about this moment felt real again, and it *was* this time.

Chris cut a slice. "Shall we do that corny thing where we feed it to each other and then one of us smooshes it into the other person's face?"

"No thanks." I whipped the slice away and sank into the couch eating it.

Chris joined me. We were both still naked and I felt so comfortable with him. Usually I would have gotten a towel by now, or wrapped myself up in the sheet, for fear that when a guy saw me standing up (it's much more flattering lying down) he may notice that a few things weren't as gravity defiant as they should be.

We sat side by side devouring our wedding cake and holding hands.

The sugar crash was intense, and after too many slices of cake we eventually melted together onto the couch and closed our eyes. Just as I was falling into a happy madly in-love sleep, Chris whispered, "Do you want to stay fake married to me, Annie?"

I opened my eyes and looked at my hand. "We'll have to get each other real rings then."

"That is real."

"What?" I popped my head up and looked at him in shock. "I mean…it's huge. Why?"

He smiled a little smile at me as he ran his finger down my nose. "I took a chance, I guess."

My heart burst at the realization. Chris loved me. He'd fallen for me as much as I had for him…

I was his forever girl, and I had the massive ring to prove it.

CHAPTER THIRTY-ONE

I woke up the next morning and for a second, thought that everything that had transpired yesterday was some strange, bizarre dream.

But then I felt a pain in my cheek and looked down to see that I'd slept on my hand and my ring had pressed into the side of my face. I took a second to admire the ring again, knowing now that it was the real thing. It was incredible. Just so utterly different—and perfect. And beautiful.

I got up and went to the mirror, where I noted that I now had a large red heart-shaped indentation in my face, and laughed to myself.

Chris was gone and had left a little note on the table.

Dear Mrs. Christophersen,
I've just gone to make a phone call and I didn't want to disturb you.
I'll be back soon, and then I think we should have some more wild
sex and cake.

Your husband, Chris

PS—You look really pretty when you sleep.

PPS—I kind of think that maybe perhaps and sort of that I might still be in love with you this morning. Or whatever!

I beamed to myself. Of all the strange and wonderful things that could have happened to me, this was right up there. To find love when I least expected it. To fall in love with the guy I was pretending to love—a guy I would never have imagined falling in love with, if I think back to that scruffy, bearded man on the beach that first day. But most of all, the strangest and most wonderful thing that could have happened to me, was to finally be the girl—the first girl—to make him fall. My mouth was dry and I was dying for a glass of water.

I walked over to the bar fridge and pulled out a bottle of water. There was another veranda attached to the room that I'd never been onto; it led into a little courtyard with an open-air shower and small garden. Oh, the many perks of the presidential suite! I walked outside. It was hot, but there was a slight breeze in the air that cooled me down.

Across the yard was a sheltered area with a table and chairs, which I made a beeline for. Chris's laptop was on the table and I saw the familiar collection of coffee cups around it. He must have been up early writing.

Curiosity took over. We were "married" now, after all. I was sure he wouldn't mind me looking. I opened the laptop and the screen came to life. I scrolled to the top and started reading.

My heart sank.

It plummeted.

It fell to my feet and I dropped my bottle of water.

SCENE 1

INT. BEDROOM—MORNING

We open on AMY—25, redhead, attractive—she is walking up a flight of stairs slowly, holding an expensive-looking shoe and a knife. She looks worried, frightened. We hear noises coming from the top of the stairs. AMY creeps toward the door and opens it slowly. She gasps as she sees her boyfriend TAYLOR and another woman TAMARA—25, gorgeous, Megan Fox look-alike—having sex, the kinky kind. AMY looks nauseous as she notices that he is wearing nipple clamps. The woman looks up from the sweaty sex and screams.

TAMARA: *(Shocked)* Oh my God. Amy.

Her boyfriend TAYLOR looks up—also shocked and frightened.

TAYLOR: *(Frightened)* Amy, please. Think about what you're doing. I know it looks bad, but this isn't the way.

AMY looks at them both, confused. Suddenly POLICE rush in and TAYLOR screams out to them.

TAYLOR: *(Screaming, pointing)* She's got a knife. She's going to kill us.

AMY looks at her hand and realizes she's still holding the knife. She is about to open her mouth when the POLICE tackle her to the floor. The shoe breaks as she is being handcuffed.

With shaking hands, I continued to scroll down the page.

SCENE 3

INT. PRISON WAITING ROOM-DAY

AMY is pleading with TAYLOR now as he stands looking nonchalant.

AMY: But you're supposed to be marrying me.

TAYLOR: *(Confused)* Um...sorry, what?

AMY: I found the receipt for the jewelry store, and we're having dinner at our favorite restaurant tonight. You bought roses! You're going to ask me to marry you.

TAYLOR: Oh, this is embarrassing. That receipt wasn't for something I bought for you, and I was taking you out tonight to tell you about Tamara and me.

> **AMY:** *(Shaking head in disbelief)* No you're not. We're getting engaged tonight.
>
> **TAYLOR:** We're not.
>
> **AMY:** But...but...you're meant to marry me. Why won't you marry me?

My blood ran icy cold. I couldn't believe what I was reading. I had trusted Chris with one of the most embarrassing moments of my life and he'd written it down as if it was nothing. He'd used my painful story for his own gain.

I put the computer down and moved away from it. I couldn't read another word. I knew if I did, the hurt I was feeling now would only get worse. I paced the small courtyard, passing the computer every few seconds. Who was I kidding? Of course I was going to read it.

> INT. SEX SHOP-DAY
>
> AMY is scrambling on the floor trying to pick up the vibrators that she's knocked over. They are a strange-looking, colorful bunch. One has flashing pink lights and another is playing a reggae tune. She chases after one that seems to be crawling across the floor by itself.
>
> EXT. TAYLOR HOUSE-NIGHT
>
> AMY is staring into the kitchen window watching TAYLOR and TAMARA eating dinner together. They

```
are laughing and flirting. Tears start streaming
down AMY'S face and she falls to the ground and
starts crying. She falls straight down into the
rosebushes and
```

I stopped as bile rose up in my mouth. I hadn't told anyone that story before. Not even my friends, and he'd taken one of the worst moments of my life and put it in a script.

```
SCENE 10
INT. HOTEL LOBBY-MORNING
AMY looks around nervously. She looks like she's
trying to disappear into the furniture.

    CHAD: Are you sure it's them?
    AMY: No, I'm not sure. I can't see them.
    CHAD: Okay, wait here, I'll take a photo
    of them.

CHAD walks off and takes photos of his surround-
ings. He whistles as he goes, trying to look
casual. He finally gets it and returns to AMY. He
shows her the picture.

    AMY:    (Horror)  Holy  crapping  hell
    balls—it's them. Oh my God, shit!
```

CHAD looks at AMY, amused. He bursts out laughing.

>   **AMY:** *(Cross)* Hey, this isn't funny.

SCENE 11

INT. MASSAGE ROOM—EVENING

CHAD and AMY stand opposite each other awkwardly. They look around the room trying to avoid eye contact and CHAD clears his throat. AMY walks over to the window and looks out, before picking up a candle and smelling it. She gives a little, "Mmmm."

>   **CHAD:** Well, this is awkward. *(Beat)* Okay, let's both turn around at the same time and take them off. I won't look. Promise.
>
>   **AMY:** Are you crazy? I'm not going to get half-naked with you in the same room.
>
>   **CHAD:** Even if I am ridiculously good-looking?

AMY looks at CHAD and rolls her eyes and then shakes her head.

CHAD: Okay, so what do you suggest then?

AMY looks at him and sighs. There is no other choice; they need to go through with this.

> **AMY:** Fine, but if you look I swear I'm going to—

AMY stops talking; she is searching for the word.

> **CHAD:** Going to do what?
>
> **AMY:** I don't know. But I promise you it will be painful. And hard.

I could feel the sweat starting to form on my forehead and the nausea rushing up. I felt sick. And my head was pounding. I continued to scroll down, reading snippets from the various scenes.

SCENE 13

EXT. STREET WALL—NIGHT

AMY is pressed up into a wall and CHAD is

I stopped reading again and skipped ahead. It was just too painful to see some of the moments of my life written like this.

SCENE 15

EXT. BEACH—EVENING

AMY stands at the top of the aisle, dressed in a beautiful vintage wedding dress. She smiles up at CHAD.

TAYLOR glares at them as a string quartet appears out of nowhere and starts playing the wedding march.

CHAD and AMY exchange amused looks; they look pleased and CHAD winks at AMY.

TAMARA walks out and gasps. Her eyes fixate on AMY. Hatred and jealousy flare in them and she seems to challenge AMY to a wedding march walk-off.

TAMARA starts walking up the aisle glaring at her.

AMY starts walking, too. With each step the women become more and more competitive, until TAMARA is practically running up the aisle. AMY starts running, too.

Caught up in the absurdity of the competition, both women throw themselves at the men and begin to kiss them. Each one trying to outdo the other with a more over-the-top spectacular kiss.

I heard a buzzing in my ears as all my senses sharpened and then became dull as if my internal switch has been flicked off. I could feel the warm, wet tears beginning to stream down my face. I couldn't believe this. He didn't love me, he didn't care. I was just a story to him. He was just using me to write a story.

He'd turned the wedding into a farce. He'd taken something that had meant a lot to me and turned it into a big fat joke.

This scene made me out to be a mad, competitive crazy person. Was that really what he thought of me? I could see there was one more page and I was dreading it. Had he written about the sex, and about us saying we loved each other? My heart was thumping and I knew I shouldn't do it, but I did. I scrolled down, one more page…

SCENE 16

INT. HOTEL ROOM-NIGHT

AMY and CHAD throw themselves at each other like crazy people. They come barreling through the door and knock over a vase as they go. CHAD picks her up and tries to push her against the wall, but she keeps slipping down. Her dress is a slippery satin material.

CHAD: Shit!

CHAD grabs at her dress and tries to open it. Get it off her. But he can't. He tugs on it comically but cannot find his way in.

AMY: *(Breathless)* Zip. Back. Now.

CHAD flips her over and unzips her, they scramble
to the couch, clawing their way up onto it,
clothes are flying.

They are rolling around so much that they tumble
off the couch. CHAD is trying to undo her bra but
is struggling.

Clearly the sex hadn't meant anything, either. He'd turned the
whole thing into a slapstick comedy—he might as well have added
a banana peel to the mix. It was obvious he just didn't care—and it
hurt. It hurt so deeply that I could feel a pain in my rib cage as it
seemed to tighten…

I heard a noise and looked up.

Chris was standing there wide-eyed. He had a look of absolute
shock plastered across his face.

"Annie, I can explain."

CHAPTER THIRTY-TWO

*xplain how?" My voice was shrill and wild and I had no control over it.

Chris looked at me blankly for a moment or two. His eyes were as wide as saucers, and his mouth opened and closed like a fish that had been taken out of water. I was so angry that if I was capable of moving, I would have walked right over to him and smacked him across the face. Better yet, I could go and grab a knife and give him another comical scene to write about. When I finally spoke, I spat the words out at him—which almost had the same effect as slapping him in the face.

"Did you or did you not write this?"

"Yes."

"Did you or did you not steal my story without my permission, take the personal things I told you, and put them in a fucking script. For people to laugh at, I might add?"

Mental slap

"Yes, I did but—"

"Did you or did you not manipulate the situation for your own gain? Did you or did you not play me from the moment we met, just to extract some story out of me? And the fake wedding? Did you only come up with that idea because you thought it would be a good plot for your story?"

Mental backhanded slap

"Yes, but—"

"So what the *fuck* is there to explain, Chris? It all seems pretty straightforward to me."

Knockout

I glared at him for a moment or two before feeling like I couldn't bear to look at his face for a second longer. I felt sick to my stomach at the mere sight of him. "And here I thought Trevv was the bad guy."

"I'm not a bad guy, Annie. I wasn't going to use it. I just phoned my producer and told him that I wasn't going to make the deadline, that I didn't have a story. I swear to you—I wasn't going to use it."

"How the hell do you expect me to believe that? After you've done nothing but lie to me this whole time?"

Chris looked defeated now and ran his hands through his hair before walking in a pointless circle. "I didn't mean to hurt you, Annie."

"You didn't *mean* to hurt me?" The sarcasm in my tone was unmistakable and I repeated again for added emphasis, "You didn't mean to hurt me!" God, that statement made me furious. "So when you wrote this...you didn't think there was any possibility that it would hurt me?"

I opened the laptop angrily again and started randomly scrolling. I was fuming now and started reading out loud.

AMY is sitting at home alone on a Saturday night.
She is clearly feeling bad and mopes around in
her pajamas looking disheveled. She flops on the
couch and reads a self-help book while drinking
cheap wine. She is miserable and lonely.

I carried on scrolling and reading, my hands trembling so much
that it was hard to control the cursor.

AMY is at a restaurant with her friend. It is
clear she has been crying; her mascara is runny
and her hair is a mess.

> **AMY:** I can't help thinking that maybe,
> maybe…

AMY looks like she's about to burst into tears.

> **JENNY:** What, sweetie?
>
> **AMY:** Maybe I'm bad in bed or something.
> Maybe he finds me boring because I
> wouldn't let him hit me with the
> spatula?

MAGGIE looks at AMY conspiratorially.

MAGGIE: Well, if you're looking for some sex tips, you should consider renting a porno.

"Should I go on, Chris? Should I continue reading your romantic revenge comedy featuring the pathetic, sad, insecure Amy with runny mascara and no life who is in crazed competition with Tamara as she tries to beat her down the aisle?"

"Shit!" Chris stopped his circular walk—which was really starting to piss me off.

"The least you could have done was change the first letters of all the names!"

"Shit," he repeated.

"Is that all you have to say? After writing thousands of words about *my* life? Is 'shit' the only thing you can say?"

The rage I was feeling was starting to dissipate, giving way to something else. Pain. Despair. I could feel the tears starting to well up in my eyes again, and no matter how hard I tried to fight it, I couldn't stop them.

"Annie, please don't cry…"

"Why? Isn't my character supposed to be a crier? Aren't we all supposed to laugh at her expense because she's miserable, pathetic, and crying again?"

"Annie…" Chris started moving toward me and I blocked him.

"Don't you dare come any closer." I tried to wipe my tears away. Yes, I was sad. But I wasn't crying simply because I felt sad. My tears were filled with anger, disappointment, and humiliation. I was more humiliated now than I had been when I'd found my boyfriend fucking someone else.

"Was *any* of it real? Or was it all a big joke to you? Just material for your next script?"

I sat down on the chair; I felt dizzy now.

"It *was* real." Chris started to approach again cautiously. "That's why I'm not going to use it." He pulled the other chair out and sat opposite me. "Annie, I'm in love with you. It's true. And when I saw you walking down the aisle toward me, I wished that it was real…"

"Again, how do you expect me to believe anything that comes out of your mouth, Chris?"

"But can't you see how I feel? Didn't you feel it last night when we made love? I love you…" His voice sounded desperate now, and even if he *was* telling the truth, he'd hurt me too deeply.

This was beyond forgivable.

He'd used me. He'd lied to me. He'd betrayed me.

I buried my face in my hands, and I felt his arm come up and touch me on the shoulder. I flinched. His touch felt disgusting now.

"I love you, Annie, please. I'm so sorry, I'm so fucking sorry…" And then he jumped up and opened the computer. "Look, I'm going to delete the whole thing." He pressed some buttons and held the thing up. "See?"

WORD COUNT 0

But it was too late. The mere fact that's he'd written it in the first place was enough. That he'd written it behind my back, while I was asleep. Secretive. Manipulative. Devious.

"You know, when I saw Trevv and Tess in bed together, I didn't think I would ever feel anything as painful for the rest of my life. But this…this is worse."

I got up and started walking toward the door.

"What can I do to make it better, Annie? Tell me. I'll do anything."

I turned and looked at him one last time. He was still gorgeous. Sexy as hell. For a moment I'd been happy with him, happier than I'd ever been. For a moment I'd let myself think of him as my husband. Pictures of a house and kids had even flashed through my mind. We'd made love—it had been amazing. The best ever.

It had all been perfect. Too perfect. Because it hadn't been real. Not for him anyway. It was all a brilliant act.

"Nothing, Chris. You lied to me. This whole time you were going behind my back and lying while you wrote that script. You just did exactly what Trevv did to me, and exactly what your dad did to your mother."

His face went pale.

"Good-bye."

He ran toward me and grabbed me by the arm. "Please don't go. I'm so sorry, I'm so, so sorry." I looked up at him and could see tears starting to form in his eyes. I shook his arm free.

"Good-bye."

And then I walked out the door.

CHAPTER THIRTY-THREE

I must have gone over it with my friends a million times, from a million different angles. They of course were fuming by this stage and had to be physically held back by Damien, for fear they might run to Chris's room and maim him permanently.

Why had he done it?

Did he feel anything for me?

Was it all fake?

Was some of it real?

Was he really not going to use it?

Should I forgive him?

Had I overreacted?

But no matter how many times we discussed it, went over it, dissected it…the result was always the same.

I had never felt more betrayed by a person—ever.

But Damien had a different perspective. "If he's deleted it, and he's not going to use it, it means he knows he made a mistake, and if you really love him, you'll forgive him."

"Keep your mouth closed, Damien!" Lilly snapped. I don't think I had ever heard her speak to him like that. "We don't need man logic at a time like this!"

"I'm just saying that guys make mistakes sometimes. I mean, I let Lilly walk away from me once. That was a huge mistake."

"That is so not the same," Lilly said.

"Fine." Damien started inching toward the other room. "I'll just…I'll just go and do something…do something somewhere far away."

"Do you think he really deleted it?" I managed in between sobs.

Jane shrugged. "Does it matter? The fact that he wrote it is enough."

She was right, of course. But I still wanted to know if it was really gone. That he'd deleted it and that in two years I *wouldn't* be seeing my painful story made into a total joke on the silver screen. Maybe he would even get Megan Fox to play Tess, since he found her so fucking good-looking. But it was hard to think because—

"Annie, please, please let me in…" *Knock, knock.*

Knock, knock. "Annie, come on, let me just talk to you."

"Annie, phone my producer, talk to him. I swear I wasn't going to use it." *Knock, knock.*

"Annie, I love you…"

It went on all afternoon. Damien was getting irritated and fed up with having to go to the door and explain to him that *No*, I was not coming out. *No*, I did not want to talk to him.

"F OFF!" Lilly finally screamed. "Annie never wants to see you again. And neither do we!"

That seemed to stop the knocking.

I think it was at about three that morning, while staring at the ceiling and surrounded by a pile of snotty, tear-drenched tissues, that I finally got my first bolt of brilliant, blazing insight.

You know, the kind of insight that hits you after the fact and in retrospect. In a weird way, it was the image of the Annie that Chris had depicted in his screenplay that pushed me to reach this insight more than anything else. Thinking of that sad, pathetic shadow of a girl still clearly haunted by her heartbreak and driven by crazed jealousy to wreak revenge.

My epiphany went a little something like this: Despite it being nearly a year since Nipple-Gate, I still hadn't moved on. In fact, I was completely stuck in a rut. I had absolutely no life, no job prospects, no anything. I had been wallowing in self-pity, which kept me stuck in the past.

My life was in total limbo. I was still reeling from the shock of it all and still constantly, on a daily basis, feeling the acute sense of betrayal that Trevv had inflicted on me. Especially since I had never gotten an actual apology from him, or anything that vaguely resembled one. That was clear from my desire to get revenge on him. But the only true act of revenge would be for me to get over this once and for all. It wasn't really revenge if it took all of this effort from me to try to prove to them I was happy. Instead, I had to actually get out there and *be* happy.

All my baggage from my relationship with Trevv only amplified everything I was feeling in relation to Chris now. It was like adding fuel to the fire. My feelings of betrayal and hatred for Trevv were mixing in with my feelings for Chris, and what I was left with was a thick, messy pot of boiling, ugly anger.

It was glaringly obvious that I was absolutely not ready for any kind of a relationship at this stage in my life, with anyone. I had not gotten over my last one. It still had a hold over me. Still haunted me, and the damage it had caused was still very much part of my daily life. I would need to shrug that off first before I could think about another relationship.

WOW. Deep shit. Finally those self-help books had come in handy. I was seeing everything so clearly now. I knew what I needed to do—I had to let go of my hatred for Trevv and Tess, get back onto the career horse, stop living in fear and embarrassment, and get a fucking life! And I had to tell Chris all of this.

I needed to tell him that no matter what he did now to try to make up for this, that it would never work between us. I was still too damaged to have a proper, healthy relationship.

Was I in love with him? Yes. Absolutely. I looked down at my hand and suddenly realized that I was still wearing my real fake ring. It was the most beautiful thing I'd ever seen and for a moment there, it had felt real.

But now we needed to get fake divorced.

I wasn't able to sleep at all that night and forced myself to wait until at least five a.m. before walking over to Chris's room. The sun wasn't up yet and the crickets were still chirping. The birds all seemed to be having an early morning conversation, too. A breeze made all the palms rustle and all the sounds combined, creating a unique morning aria of sorts—it was rather soothing.

It probably took me another ten minutes or so of standing outside his door to pluck up the courage to knock on it.

"Annie?" I heard him call from inside, and within seconds the door was wide open and a rather disheveled-looking Chris was standing in the doorway. He hugged me immediately, and I let him. It felt good.

"Annie, you came back?" He pulled away from the hug and looked me in the eyes. I could see he'd been crying. I don't think I've ever made a man cry before. I was about to open my mouth and start talking when he stopped me.

"Wait. Sit down. I have this whole speech prepared for you."

There was no harm in letting him talk, I guess. It was only fair to let him have his say before I unleashed my new insights onto him. So I sat and waited for the speech. He paced up and down a few times before striking the pose of a man who was about to deliver a great sermon.

"I'm a total dick. I totally fucked up. I was stupid and cruel and what I did to you was terrible. I don't really have an excuse for it other than I was in a desperate place, there was this deadline, and nothing was inspiring me. And then you came along. And you were funny, and adorable, and your story was interesting…and I guess I just got carried away. But it's no excuse, I know."

"Chris." I held up my hand.

"Wait. I'm not finished. You know how you asked if I'd only suggested that wedding so I could just get more story?"

I nodded. It was one of the most painful realizations of all—how could I forget?

"Well, it's not true. I thought about it and I actually wanted to get married. That's why I got a real ring, because although it was going to be fake, a part of me really wanted it to be real. I wanted to see you coming down the aisle and imagine what it would be like to be with you."

There was something about his tone and his look—I believed him. My heart did a few summersaults in response. I reeled it in quickly.

"So this is what I propose: We start again. Clear the slate. I know it will take you a long time to trust me again, and maybe you will want to punish me, but that's okay. I can take it. I'll take anything you throw my way, as long as you come back to me, because I am totally in love with you—"

"I'm in love with you too, Chris," I whispered.

I've never seen anyone bolt across the floor so quickly, and at the speed of light, he was by my side hugging me.

"Wait!" I pushed him away. "That doesn't mean I *want* to be with you." It was so painful to say those words out loud.

Chris pulled away and looked panicked.

"Because I've been thinking that, well, I don't think I'm ready for a relationship just yet. I don't think I've gotten over the last one properly. In fact, I was thinking that maybe I needed to go to therapy or something, because my life is a mess. I live in a gross garden cottage that I can't afford, and I'm working in a job that is totally beneath me—even though I love my boss. I barely have a social life anymore. I stay home and sit. I'm stuck. And I need to do something about it, and getting into another relationship, when I'm clearly still too fucked up from the previous one, is not the answer."

I hated the look that came over Chris's face right then. It was devastation. He looked like I had just punched him in the stomach.

"It's actually not really about the movie anymore, Chris. Sure, I'm totally pissed off about it. You betrayed me in the worst way possible—but it's about something so much bigger now."

"Can we not do that together...rebuild your life and get you moved on?" His voice was desperate.

I shook my head. "You read *Cosmo*. You already know the answer to that. This is something that I need to do on my own. You're not going to fix me, only I can."

Chris smiled a weak smile. "Those fucking self-help books, huh?"

I smiled back at him. "Yup, finally came in handy."

"Will you be making gratitude lists and a personal mission statement now?"

"I might. Hell, maybe I'll write my own self-help book…"

We smiled at each other, even though both of our hearts were breaking.

"So there's nothing I can say or do to get you back then?" he asked.

"No." Such a tiny word. And yet it was probably the hardest word I'd ever had to say.

"There's got to be something, Annie. *Something?*" I could see his mind working overtime. "What if I wrote a movie about how evil Trevv and Tess were and used their real names, and cast really ugly actors to play them and then made them die in the end—a really painful death?"

I burst out laughing but shook my head. "No more Trevv and Tess. I need to forget that stuff now. Let go of it."

But his mind continued ticking away. "There's got to be something I can do, and I'm not going to stop until I find it—"

"Please, don't say that, you're just making this harder." It was taking all my self-control now not to just throw myself into his arms and forget everything that I knew was true and right.

"So it's completely over for us? Forever? How can you be so sure our story ends here? Maybe we'll bump into each other in thirty years this time under the Eiffel Tower and realize that we're still in love or—"

"Okay. Fine, I don't know. Maybe one day. But not now. Definitely not now."

"Maybe one day?" he repeated, his eyes lighting up with hope. "I can work with that. At least it's not never!"

"But…," I jumped in quickly. I didn't want him to hang on to some kind of false hope. "I didn't say that we would—"

"I understand. But I'm prepared to wait…just in case." He moved toward me again and took my hand. "I'll wait. I've never been in love before, and now that I am, I'm not going to give up without a fight."

"Chris"—I held his hands tightly—"I can't tell you what to do, but I can't make you any promises, so…"

"So you're telling me to move on then. Forget this ever happened." He looked angry now, and I didn't want us to leave angry at each other. I had enough anger in me to last a lifetime, and I didn't want any more. "Because I'm not going to forget this…*ever*. And I won't forget you, either. Can't we just try again? Please?"

I pulled away from him. I needed him to understand. "No! That's not going to happen."

Chris nodded and looked apologetic. "Sorry, Annie. I actually do understand. It all makes perfect sense and you're right, you do owe it to yourself to get better and heal and all that stuff…It's just really hard for me to accept. That's all."

"I know." There was a long silence between us. "So I guess this is good-bye."

And then a very unexpected wicked smiled flashed across his face. "For now."

"What do you mean?"

"Annie Anne, I'm going to get you back. Maybe it won't be

tomorrow, maybe it won't be in six months even, maybe I'll have to wait until I'm old and ugly and gray and a tourist in Paris...but mark my words. One day, I'll make you my *real* wife." He winked at me, and I felt my heart beat faster. I held my hands together tightly and felt the ring; I started sliding it off my finger.

"No, keep it. You're going to need to wear it one day again anyway. So don't lose it." He seemed to be looking happier now, and I got the impression that he was already formulating some grand reunion plan in his head.

"Chris, Chris, Chris..." I shook my head with a smile. His persistence was making him hard to resist and it was also, somewhere deep inside, keeping that spark of hope alive. "What am I going to do with you?"

He stepped forward. "Right now you're going to kiss me." And without warning he took my face between his hands and kissed me. It was so soft and so full of love and care that there was no doubt in my mind that he really did love me.

"So run along now and do your thing. And I believe in you and support you, and when you least expect it, I'm coming for you again."

I laughed, "You make it sound so sinister."

"Maybe it will be. Maybe I'll have to come and kidnap you one day and hold you hostage forever."

I looked up into his eyes. He was so beautiful. I kissed him one last time and started making my way for the door. He called out to me as I was leaving, "For what it's worth, I really, really am sorry."

I smiled. "Thank you."

"I mean it. I messed up. I'm so, so sorry."

"I know."

"I never wanted to hurt you like Trevv did, and certainly not like my dad did my mom. I'm not sure I'll easily forgive myself for doing that to you."

I smiled at him faintly. Because I could see how deeply sorry he was.

"Now go be great, Annie Anne."

* * *

D-day 2

It dawned on me that this was another D-day of sorts. One of those days that comes every now and again and changes your life completely. Shoves you off the path you're on and flings you onto the unfamiliar, less-traveled one—with no map or GPS to guide you. Like "Nipple-Gate Day" this was its own kind of hell. Chris was gone; he'd left the resort but left a little note behind. Four words, that's all.

I love you. Forever.

He didn't need to say much else. T-Squared were also gone—no note, though. I doubted that I'd ever hear from them again. I still had a few days of my vacation left, and I intended to make the most of them even though my heart was snapping into a million pieces.

Jane, Lilly, and I all drank a lot of tropical cocktails and lamented my sorrows, and my friends were both so patient. Although, Lilly did owe me after I'd endured hours of similar heartbroken laments when she broke up with Damien.

"What's with us going to tropical places, meeting men who break our hearts, and then crying over them? I asked. "Are we cursed? Is this the curse of our group?"

"Mine did end happily," Lilly offered, dangling her ring in front of us again. In the sunlight, waving it around like that, the ring had the potential to blind people.

"That's because he didn't betray you and stab you through the heart with a giant dagger."

"True," Lilly said.

"You're next, Jane." I raised my glass to her. "It's your turn to have a mental breakdown and then fly off to some exotic location and fall in love with a man that breaks your heart into a million little pieces."

We all paused for a moment before bursting into laughter. Hell would freeze over before any of us saw Jane rush off and do something so crazy.

"A man"—Lilly held up her hand—"that sweeps you off those big feet of yours and finally makes you do something spontaneous for a change."

"I am spontaneous," Jane said.

"Name one spontaneous thing you've ever done in your entire life." Lilly pulled her sunglasses down and gave her a challenging look.

"That is so rich coming from you, Lilly," Jane shot back.

"Hey, I'm spontaneous now." Lilly took a long loud slurp of her cocktail. "I have sex in airplane bathrooms, don't you know!"

We all burst out laughing again. It was hard to imagine the Lilly of a few years ago joining the mile-high club. Accidentally locking herself in the bathroom or getting her foot stuck in it, maybe, but bumping and grinding in the bathroom…

"I'll never be able to join the mile-high club." Jane almost sounded disappointed. "I'm too tall. I wouldn't fit."

We laughed some more and people started to look.

"God, we're getting a bit drunk, aren't we." Lilly slurped down the last bit of her cocktail.

"Not drunk enough." I waved down a waiter and ordered another three.

"Not for me." Lilly stood up with a smile. "I have somewhere I need to be."

"You two need pills," Jane shouted after her as she walked away. "Pills that make you stop. It's not natural."

Jane and I found ourselves alone again. It was strange, I'd always felt closer to Lilly than anyone else, but this whole thing had really made me appreciate Jane and her excessive level-headedness. It had been exactly what I'd needed this past year. And it was exactly what I needed now.

"But seriously, are you okay?" she asked calmly.

"No. But I will be…*someday*." That word held so much weight, because I had never felt like this before. It had felt like there was never going to be any end to it all, but now I knew that there would be. There had to be. I couldn't keep living like this. I was not living at all.

Jane leaned over and rested a hand on my arm. "Well, you know I'm here for you."

"I know. Thanks."

"You're welcome to stay with me for a while if you need to."

"Nooo, thanks. Not with your mother around."

Jane rolled her eyes. She always tried to make light of it, but we all knew how much her strained relationship with her adoptive mother hurt her. Jane always felt inadequate; her mother's excessive "helpfulness" was nothing more than criticism in her eyes. And she always felt like she was trying to live up to something she could never attain.

"She packed you a gift, by the way."

"What?"

"It's bad. *Really* bad. She got me one, too."

"What could be worse than the time she cut me out the article 'Kale Is King: How to Lose Ten Pounds in Ten Days'?"

Jane laughed. "I actually made one of those smoothies."

"And?"

She scrunched her face up. "Cut grass meets cardboard."

I cringed. "So what's the gift?"

"I swear, my mother is actually going to cause me to die of embarrassment one day…" Jane dug in her handbag, pulled out a T-shirt, and unfolded it.

KEEP CALM AND BE MY BOYFRIEND

"Subtle. I wonder what she's trying to say?" I said sarcastically.

"You know, the more she tries to force a boyfriend on me, the more I don't want one."

Our cocktails arrived and I held mine up in the air. "To being single."

CHAPTER THIRTY-FOUR

*I*t's strange how when you finally open yourself up to things, they come. Last year I'd shut down, run away, drawn the blinds, and hidden. I'd spent my days sewing hems and dreaming of sewing Trevv's penis to the wall. I'd sat eating ice cream, stalking him and Tess on Facebook, and had been paralyzed with fear, insecurity, and embarrassment.

But the second I opened myself up—the second I decided to try to turn my life around and rebuild, a series of fortuitous events happened. Small at first, insignificant really, and then momentum started to build.

The first event happened only a few hours after leaving Mauritius in the duty-free shopping area of O.R. Tambo International Airport in South Africa. I had felt sick the entire flight, because I knew that with each minute that passed, the gap between Chris and me was getting bigger and bigger. I'd been devastated to leave Mauritius; it felt like I was cutting the final tie I had to Chris.

When we finally arrived in Johannesburg, I immediately started looking for some tax-free chocolate to take the edge off the painful Chris sorrow, when I walked into a clothing shop. I was lured by the shiny things in the window. I sauntered inside and stared enviously at a gorgeous pair of earrings that I could ill afford, when I was tapped on the shoulder.

"Nice bag." I turned and came face-to-face with a stylish woman with a big retro Afro.

"Where did you get it?" she asked.

"Oh, this?" I pointed at my crazy, colorful, bedazzled bag. "It's just something I made." I was trying hard to swallow, but the chocolate contained peanut butter and was sticking to the roof of my mouth.

"Really." She looked it up and down. "I think tourists would love it, it has such a unique African flavor to it. It's like Indian meets Zulu meets Cape Malay…"

I nodded. I certainly wasn't going to admit it out loud, but that wasn't the intention at all. In fact, the only reason it looked like that was because I'd made it out of all the off-cuts and discarded items I could find at Patel's.

"You know, it really does merge cultures so well, and captures our unique diversity as South Africans." She put her hand on her hip, and her fabulous, chunky wooden bangles clanked together.

I decided to play along. *Why not?* "Mmmm, that's what I was going for. I really wanted to give it a 'rainbow nation' feel." *Bullshit!!!*

But the lady nodded. She lapped it up. She smiled with her full lip-glossed lips and asked to look at it. She inspected the thing as if it were something foreign and exotic. "You know, I can really see that. The cultural binaries created in the layout of the fabric."

"Mmmm, I really thought hard about positioning. One needed to accentuate the other." *Bigger bullshit!*

"You know"—she said *You know* a lot—"I'd really like to try and sell a few here. I can't promise anything extraordinary, but maybe we can start with five, see how it goes."

"Seriously?" I asked her, feeling totally shocked. I couldn't quite believe I was hearing those words coming from someone's mouth. Let alone someone as fashionably fabulous as she was. I needed to hear them again, just so I knew it was real. And it wasn't some psychosis brought on by Chris withdrawal. "Really?"

"Absolutely! I would love to." She extended her hand for me to shake. I took it happily.

"I'm Zolani, by the way."

"Annie."

I went home that day feeling just a little bit better. I had the tiniest spring in my step. The tiniest glimmer of happy hope, but then…

I walked into my house. I stopped. I stood. I stared.

It was disgusting. There were still boxes that hadn't been unpacked from almost a year ago. No shelves had been hung, so books and DVDs were piled up in the corners of the room, gathering spiderwebs and dead insects. The shower was unused and currently acting as a storage facility. And it just all looked so damn depressing.

When I was with Trevv, I'd taken great pride in my surroundings; everything was neat and clean and beautifully decorated. It was time to pull my pretties out of their dusty boxes and start turning this place into something vaguely decent. Sure, there was nothing I could do about the half-naked man outside just yet, but at least I could counterbalance the hideous view outside with something pretty on the inside.

But starting was extremely overwhelming. Staring into the face of a year's worth of clutter and disorganization, I didn't know where to start, so I began with the DVDs that were strewn across the floor at my feet.

But then I saw it...Bradley Cooper stared back at me from one of the DVDs. And when I saw those deep, dreamy blue eyes, I started crying. I was wailing, in fact, and threw myself down on the couch, clutching the DVD. The familiar misery spot.

"Fuck. No, Annie!" I suspect I shouted that too loudly, because I heard the next-door neighbor's dog bark in response. I pulled the DVD out of its case and tried to snap it in half dramatically...*Do you know those things are bloody unbreakable?* I threw myself back down on the couch and then shot off it again.

No! No, I had already spent a whole year on that couch crying, and I was not going to repeat it. So I tried to pull myself together—still wailing—and continued to unpack boxes. I cried the whole time: It was almost comical. I wailed as I threw out the old things that I no longer needed. I sobbed as I started pulling out some pictures that I wanted to hang on the walls, and I moaned painfully as I went about trying to put up a shelf.

But at least I was doing something constructive—not wallowing on that couch. I swung around and glared at the thing. It was a beige three-seater. Big, comfortable, and perfect for lying on and crying.

I leapt at it with fury; I was going to get rid of it immediately. Sell it and buy myself a chair, one that I couldn't lie down on. I would sit upright, come hell or high water!

But it proved very challenging pulling the thing out of my living room. It weighed a ton, and by the time I'd managed to drag it onto my tiny patio, I was finished. Drenched in sweat and out of breath.

I stumbled into my bedroom, peeled off my clothes, and climbed into bed. And then I noticed the ring on my finger. I looked at it for a second and allowed myself to think back to the moment when Chris had slipped it on. How real it had all felt and how amazing he'd looked in the setting sun. Our fake wedding had been beautiful, one of the best days of my life.

I took it off slowly and looked at it one last time before I opened my drawer and slipped it in.

Maybe I would keep it safe. Just in case.

CHAPTER THIRTY-FIVE

⁓

$\mathcal{T}$he next day I didn't wake with as much enthusiasm as I'd had the night before.

I guess these things work in waves. I wasn't going to feel better overnight; this would be a process, and it was just beginning. In fact, that morning it felt almost impossible to get out of bed and drag myself to work. My legs felt at least ten times heavier than they really were.

I missed Chris like I'd never missed Trevv, and it physically hurt not being with him. But I got up and showered—and cried a little in the shower, it was incredibly dramatic—and then made myself some breakfast. I cried while eating that, too, equally dramatic, especially when I choked on a flake of cereal.

I got ready for work, *yes*, cried again. I even had to apply my mascara twice. The first time it washed away with tears before it had time to set; the second time, I had to bite my lip in order to stop the tears from coming, while frantically fanning them with a magazine to get it to dry quicker. I tried to lift my spirits by reminding myself about the five bags that I needed to make, and decided to talk to the Patels about them that day.

They were thrilled to see me and wanted to know everything about my vacation. So I told them about swimming with the tropical fish (not about how Chris had taken a photo of my bum and pretended it was a mistake), I told them about seeing dolphins (not about the dolphin squeak-off Chris and I had had), and I told them about how beautiful the beaches looked at night (not about the walk we'd taken on our first night together and how I'd flirted with him). I also told them about the bags. And they were thrilled.

In fact, they said that I could use—within reason—fabrics and other stuff I needed. But that first day back at work was hard; the hours seemed to drag on and on and on, and getting through them felt like pulling teeth from a dead sloth. I sighed a lot. It was all I could do to keep pushing down that lump in my chest that seemed to be forming every time I allowed my mind to wander to Chris.

It took all my energy *not* to think about him. I was exhausted from physically trying to chase the thought from my mind. But five o'clock finally came around and I left with a small bundle of fabrics, buttons, ribbons, and other bits and bobs that I'd been allowed to commandeer. And although funds were still desperately tight, I decided I needed to find something more substantial and healthy to eat, other than the packets of nutrient-deficient noodles I'd been eating for the last year. The equivalent of chewing on cardboard covered in MSG and dust.

So even though I didn't feel like it, I dragged myself to the grocery store and walked out with a bag of veggies and whole-wheat bread. I would make a big pot of vegetable soup—it's all I could afford—and eat that for several dinners to come. At least I would be getting some vitamins and minerals. Who knows, maybe they would contribute to my mental well-being, and perhaps help me lose the few extra pounds that Tess had so happily pointed out.

That night after eating my homemade veggie soup, which was actually pretty tasty, and before sitting down to make some bags, I dragged that stupid exercise stepper out that I'd been conned into buying. The man on the late-night TV show with the very obvious hairpiece and orange fake-tanned face had been pretty convincing. He'd promised me twenty pounds in six weeks and a million inches off my hips (terms and conditions apply).

So I dusted the little sucker off and stepped for about five minutes, vowing I would build up to something that could at least vaguely count as physical activity.

Then I sat down at my sewing machine and started thinking. The other bags I'd made in the heat of hatred for Sonja (evil boss bitch from hell) and I had purposefully made them as over-the-top as possible in a rebellious proclamation of passive-aggressive defiance. This time, I was going to make them in a more considered manner. I knew I could make them better with a little extra thought, care, and planning. They would still maintain that frantic colorful feel, but I could bring a little more skill to them. So I started.

I cut all the bits of colored fabric up into different sizes and shapes, and put them together like a multicolored jigsaw puzzle. It looked like a mad patchwork quilt, in a good way. Then something caught my eye; in the corner of the room was an old canvas shopping bag, the kind you toss away or use to store crap in, as I was currently doing. I took it to my sewing station and started arranging the patchwork material on it. I smiled happily to myself as I watched new life being breathed into something that was once discarded, long forgotten, and considered ugly.

I sewed so late into the night that I fell asleep slumped over my sewing machine; I only realized this when my phone beeped with a message.

I looked down at it: six a.m. on a Wednesday. Who the hell was messaging me at this time? It was from an anonymous number, and it took me a few seconds to figure out what the message even meant.

Hey Annie-Anne! A new day is here, so throw on a dress and get your butt into gear.

"Huh?" I read it again. It sounded vaguely familiar. Was it some automated message from a telemarketing place, or some sales pitch from a travel agent telling me I'd won a cruise? But I didn't think so.

And then I got it. The realization skyrocketed my blood pressure and made my heart pound. They were similar to lines from the Dr. Seuss book, *Oh, the Places You'll Go!* Chris's favorite. I read the words over and over again. Each time my smile grew bigger and a little spark in me felt like it was getting ignited.

Hang on ... Wednesday was my hump day. And Chris had remembered that. As much as I loved that he was thinking about me, I had to be wary of that little spark. It could not ignite. Could not. And so, with a sad smile, I put my phone down and didn't acknowledge Chris's text.

It took me precisely seven days to finish the five bags. For one of them I'd used another discarded shopping bag that I'd found, and I even used an old coffee bag to make one of the others. And they had turned out better that I could have ever imagined. And the morning I was excitedly packing them up to take to Zolani, my phone beeped once again. It was a message from the same anonymous number at the exact same time. I opened it and my heart quickened once more.

You've got talent and brains and sexiness too. And even your bitch ex-boss knows that to be true.

The words of encouragement that Chris was sending me all the way from the other end of the world made me want to scream with joy while simultaneously breaking down crying. They were a strange, bittersweet mix. As long as I was still on this journey of mine, I couldn't be with Chris. Not now…maybe not ever.

***

I was feeling so excited and confident when I dropped the bags off at the shop at O.R. Tambo, although I kept trying to remind myself that I shouldn't jump the gun just yet. Five bags was not a fashion empire. I was not Donatella yet. And they would probably take a long time to sell, but at least it was something. A step in the right direction. A direction that I was choosing.

In those early weeks after returning, I also decided to bite the bullet and find myself a therapist. It proved to be a great idea, and with each session I felt a little lighter and more self-assured than I had in a whole year.

I always pictured therapists as old, boring, gray-haired men that somewhat resembled Einstein and that made you lie down on old leather couches.

But Paula (we were on a first-name basis) was a young, witty blond woman that was really easy to talk to, fashionably dressed, and kept me upright on a comfortable pink chair. And what I liked most about her is that she wasn't scared to call me on my bullshit. She was quick to help me discover my self-destructive behaviors and habits and help me to work through them.

Through therapy, I also came to realize that this past year I'd actually been depressed. Not sad, not a little grumpy or down, but properly antidepressant depressed. And she was right; I had been. Only I hadn't really seen it at the time.

She helped me to set goals for myself, personal and professional. And that's when things started to look just a little bit brighter.

I also looked forward to my Wednesday morning messages, and although we hadn't spoken, I felt like Chris was still there, right next to me, cheerleading me on.

You're strong and awesome and know what you know. And YOU, Annie-Anne, are the star of your show.

And he was right. I was finally deciding what to do with my life.

CHAPTER THIRTY-SIX

$\mathcal{A}$nd then four weeks later, while out walking in the park with Stormy-Rain (our new regular Friday afternoon thing), I got a message from Zolani for ten more bags. I jumped for joy when I realized that people actually liked my silly little creations.

Stormy was just as over-the-moon excited. We'd been hanging out a lot lately; she'd been taking me to strange little thrift stores where I'd made some amazing finds for my bags. Vintage buttons, belt buckles, and even a genuine Chanel bag. For some strange reason the allure of the label held little meaning for me anymore, and I ended up dismantling the thing and incorporating it into an over-sized tote of my own creation. Sacrilege, I know.

And then four weeks later another order came in. And then another, and another, until I could no longer keep up with the demand while working full-time.

I could barely believe it; it was all like some kind of strange multicolored dream. But it soon became a reality the day I saw someone carrying my bag on the street. I wanted to run up to her and point and shout, *I made that.*

"So, *you know*, you need a name for your label, babe. These things are selling like hotcakes and everyone keeps asking me who makes them," Zolani had said one day.

"Um…crap, I have no idea."

"Well it's usually your name, you know. Christian Dior, Louis Vuitton…et cetera."

"I know, but Annie Anderson sounds so pedestrian."

"Well, you better think of something quick and get yourself a logo and sew a label in, because I have a feeling that your bags are going to be big."

"I guess I could call my label Annie Anne." I didn't really think about it. It kind of just came tumbling out of my mouth—and when I heard it said out loud, it hurt.

Zolani stopped and seriously considered it for a moment, "Playful, cheeky, flirty, fun, and not serious. Yes. Annie Anne is perfect." She swooshed her bangle-laden arm in the air and spoke in a posh accent, "Bags by Annie Anne…"

And then she threw herself at me to give me the first of many hugs we would share. "You and me, girl! This is it. It's really happening." We squealed like two kids at Christmas until people around us started to stare.

I went home feeling great, and decided to celebrate by cooking myself some real food and drinking a glass of real red wine (not out of a cheap box). Halfway through my meal the phone rang.

I glanced at the phone and the anonymous number, which had become my happy Wednesday morning companion, flashed at me. I shot out of my chair. He was calling. *He was calling!* I tried to compose myself to something that didn't resemble a blithering idiot of nerves and anxiety and excitement and…apprehension. *Should I even speak to him?* I flapped around a little more in my state of uncertainty and then just, "Fuck it!"

I picked the phone up trying to be casual.

"Hello, Annie speaking."

"Hey."

The delicious twang of the American accent wafted through the phone, and my heart literally fluttered. No, *pounded* would be more apt.

"Hey." Nice and neutral sounding on the outside, dying in the inside.

Pause. A seriously long one.

"So hey, hey?" Chris broke the silence.

"Hey!" *(Less neutral, a lot more dying)*

So far this was not the most successful conversation of my life. But if his heart was racing as much as mine was, if his mouth was as dry as mine and his hands shaking as hard as he held the receiver, I couldn't blame him for the monosyllabic words.

"How are you?" he asked.

"Fine. You?"

"Cool," he said, sounding anything but truly cool.

"Cool."

Pause. Not as long as the first one, but still pretty painful. He broke it again.

"So, how's Joburg?" he asked.

"The same. Hotter. How's LA?"

"Horrible," he said flatly.

"Why?"

"Because you're not here."

Pause.

Was he allowed to say things like that to me?

"Should I not have said that, Annie?"

"I'm not sure."

"Well…," Chris said, "there's no rule that says we can't be friends. Is there? Besides, enough time has passed now, right?"

"Who says?"

"I read it in *Cosmopolitan*. They made it quite clear that four months, one week, two days and…"

There was a pause.

"And twelve hours is enough time to strike up a friendship with your ex. Not that I'm counting the seconds or anything."

"Of course not," I said. I didn't tell him that I knew exactly how long it had been, too.

"So how are you, Annie? Are you riding high and ready for anything under the sky?"

"I love those texts!" I lost all coolness and just gushed. "I love them, thanks. They make my Wednesday mornings."

I heard a small chuckle over the phone. "It's my pleasure."

Another pause. The kind of pause that was so damn loud and loaded.

"So, can we be friends?" Chris finally broke it.

I thought about this for a moment. I would love nothing more than to be friends with him. I'd missed him. I'd missed his stupid sense of humor and that smile, God, I missed that smile. And I especially missed the way he made me feel about myself. But wouldn't being friends just prolong the suffering and hinder any chance of getting over him?

"I'm not sure, I'm just only now getting—" I stopped midsentence and swallowed. *Why did this feel so hard to say?* "Getting over you."

"What! You're—you're over me?" He sounded like someone had just stabbed him in the heart.

I bit my lip, trying to be strong. I didn't want to be pulled into this kind of conversation with Chris right now. Everything logical in my mind was telling me to stop this immediately, but the other side was urging me to continue even though I knew what a dangerous path this could lead us down.

"Well, aren't you?" I asked.

"No," he said quickly as if he didn't even need to think about it, "I'm not over you, Annie. I can't just snap my fingers and be over the most amazing woman I've ever met. The only woman I've ever been in love with."

I thought I could actually hear the loud chorus of voices singing in my heart. But then my brain intervened.

"But that means we can't be friends, if you still…and I still."

"You still?" It sounded like he had a smile in his voice. And with that, we had officially crossed over and were walking down the dangerous path now, despite all the warning lights I could see blinking at me.

"Yes. And that's probably why we can't be friends, Chris," I said, even though it went against everything my heart was busy screeching at me.

"So we have to take some more time to get over each other?"

"I guess." My stomach tightened and I felt such a sense of loss and sadness all over again.

"Okay. Bye, Annie." And just like that, he hung up. A part of me couldn't believe it. I was just about to move away from it when it rang again. Same number.

"Chris?"

"Done. I've taken some time and I'm totally over you now."

"You got over me in a few seconds?"

"Yeah, I really think those extra seconds made all the difference." I laughed.

"So can we be friends now?"

This was the worst idea in the world. This was the worst idea in the world. This was the... "Okay, we'll try. But we can't talk to each other every day."

"Every second day?"

"No!"

"Once a week?"

"Maybe. Maybe once every two weeks. Let's see how this one goes first..."

"Deal, Annie. I'm going to make this the best phone conversation of your entire life. It's going to be so good, you'll never want to hang up. You'll want to have the phone surgically attached to your ear so you can always speak to me."

I laughed. As always, he made me laugh.

"Will you still send me my hump day motivation?" I asked.

"I'll send you whatever you want, Annie. All you have to do is ask." He deliberately said it in the voice that he knew would have an effect on me.

"All righty then...," I said, totally ignoring the fact that my skin was currently on fire. "Bye."

And that's kind of how it started between Chris and me again. The odd phone conversation. Sometimes it was once a week, sometimes less, sometimes more. We never spoke about what happened between us, about T-Squared, or our wedding or the *ah-mazing* sex. We also never spoke about what was going on for us; frankly, I didn't want to know if he was having an awesome time in LA and starting to date again and shagging up a celebrity storm. And he never asked me, either, probably for the same reason. In fact, all we did was get to know each other. And it soon became very obvious that we knew absolutely *nothing* about each other, other than what we'd gleaned from those few days together.

I learned that he had a pug named Chopstick, because he likes Chinese food. That his mother was an opera singer, his dad was a poet, his brother was a professor of philosophy at an Ivy League university, and his sister ran a nonprofit organization for women's rights and had published a book on the role of feminism in the 2000s.

"Very fancy, cultured upbringing and family…in fact, I'm sure I'm adopted. Messy screenwriter living in equally messy bachelor pad with no deep and meaningful art hanging on his walls. I'm the black sheep of the family."

I also learned that he actually *did* play sports and was just lying to Trevv. I learned that he hadn't set out to write romantic comedies, he'd just stumbled into it.

He told me that he'd studied to be a journalist, but when he realized he had absolutely no interest in current affairs, or news of any kind, he came to the realization that he was in the wrong job. And so it went on like that.

At some stage I kind of resigned myself to the fact that even if we weren't going to get back together—*it was physically impossible anyway, we lived on opposite sides of the world*—that I think I'd found a real friend in Chris.

Maybe this whole thing had happened between us for a reason. So we could become friends? Maybe we would be at each other's real weddings one day as best buddies, pals, besties. Maybe he would make a speech at my wedding and tell the weird crazy story of how we became friends with a fake wedding of our own. Maybe he would be my future child's godfather. Maybe we would slap each other on the back and say, *"What up, dude?"*

Or maybe I was just fooling myself.

Because I was pretty sure that the second either of us got into a romantic relationship, these little phone calls would definitely stop.

And that would be the end of it.

No more Chris. It was only a matter of time.

CHAPTER THIRTY-SEVEN

❧

$\mathcal{I}$ was already in the kitchen drinking a cup of coffee and waiting for Chris's message to come through when Jane rang. The other thing about his messages is that they'd turned me into Annie the early bird.

The phone rang and I grabbed it, thinking it might be him. But it wasn't.

"Have you seen the latest issue of *Glamorous Girl* magazine? It's just arrived at our office," Jane said.

"What are you doing at work so early?"

"Avoiding my mother. She's taken up early morning yoga and was threatening to come round this morning and fetch me for it."

"Trying to set you up with the instructor?"

"Apparently he's very spiritually enlightened and apparently yoga makes a man very virile," she said in a mocking tone. "And my mother also added that the pants he wears are tight enough to tell his religion and that he seems blessed in that department, too."

"Eeewww." I sipped my coffee trying to get the image of a yoga instructor's crotch bulge out of my head.

"Right, brace yourself, Annie…" She cleared her throat and put on a refined-sounding voice. "Winter Trends: beat the gloom this winter by getting your hands on the latest trend making a colorful splash. Bags by Annie Anne. They are fun, flirty, and colorful, and Sonja S. gives them the thumbs-up as the must-have item for every fashionista's arm this season."

I almost spat my coffee out. "WHAT? You're kidding!"

"Nope. In black and white, with a photo of one of them."

"Which one?"

"Uhhh…I don't know, it's kind of got pink things hanging from it, with those buttons, and it's patchwork-y."

"Don't worry. I'll go grab one myself." Jane didn't really have an eye for fashion.

"Wait!" Jane shouted just as I was about to hang up. "Well done, babe. This is amazing."

"Oh my God! Thank you for calling me. I'm going out now to get one. I can't believe this!" We squealed some more, I thanked her some more, and then I hung up.

I quickly put a hoodie and slippers on and jumped into my car. As soon as I'd started the engine, I saw my phone light up with Chris's message. I almost didn't read it I was so excited, but something compelled me to. And when I did, my eyes blurred with tears.

Annie-Annie, you'll be famous, as famous as can be.
More famous than the Kardashians on terrible reality TV.

I sat in the car for a moment and let it all sink in. My dreams were actually coming true, right before my eyes. I'd managed to turn my whole life around in a matter of months. I tried to imagine the Annie I was a year ago, and I just couldn't recognize her. Who was that girl?

I wiped a small, happy tear away as it rolled down my cheek, and pulled out of my driveway. Within minutes I was at the gas station and inside the convenience store. I grabbed the magazine and there it was. I had to read it at least ten times before it finally sank in. I wanted to cry. I wanted to scream and shout and…so I hugged the guy behind the counter that I always buy chocolates from. I felt such a sense of pride and achievement that it was almost too much to contain. My phone rang again and I answered.

"Have you seen it?" Zolani squealed in my ear.

"I'm standing in my slippers in a shop right now!"

"Oh my God!"

"I know!"

"And as for your ex–bitch boss Sonja, she is finally going to realize she made the biggest mistake of her life when she fired you. And then she's going to come crawling back and begging and you can throw an expensive shoe at her—which you will be able to afford—because we're going to have your own fashion empire!"

"Wait, Zee. Slow down, it's hardly a fashion empire."

"But it could be," she said.

"I can't afford to leave my job at Patel's and do this full-time. How will I afford to feed myself?"

"An investor, Annie."

"And who is going to invest in me?" I asked.

"Me," she said quickly and confidently.

"No, I can't take money from you."

"Stop it. Just listen, I have such a good feeling about this, Annie. We can do this together, we'll be business partners."

"Wait, I need to think about this," I said.

"But don't you want to see your bags gracing the runways and the glossy pages of magazines?" She certainly was painting a nice picture.

"I doubt they will ever be on runways," I quickly corrected.

"Why not? We won't know unless we try."

"True," I said, still shocked at her proposition.

"Great! Then we will need to ramp up production, and we need to get fully stocked. Then we need to get them into some other shops for you, at some point maybe we can have our own tiny shop, and maybe get a website going so people can buy them online, a Facebook page obviously…"

"Wait, wait, this is all moving a bit fast."

"Annie, babe, you have to move fast, because we both know your bags will be out next season."

She was right. This was my window of opportunity and I needed to grab it.

I sat at my breakfast table reviewing things; and to think the bags had been born out of hatred for Sonja, and now she was praising them. Oh, how this world works in mysterious ways.

I thought about the Patels; they'd been so good to me, and I didn't want to stop working for them, but if I set up a studio in the back room of the shop, and bought materials from them, it would be mutually beneficial.

And of course they loved the idea—they even closed the shop over lunch and we all went out to celebrate. And from that moment onward, it moved so fast. We got into that back room of the shop that evening and cleared it out. We set up a table and a workbench and made the thing livable.

With Zolani's investment, I bought another sewing machine, hired a staff member, and bought some—super-discounted—fabric from the Patels. Zolani worked her magic, and soon my bags were being sold in a few shops. She was this powerhouse one-woman machine and I loved working with her; she was the sassiest woman I'd ever met and we soon became fast friends. And Stormy-Rain loved her, possibly more than she loved me. In fact, Stormy insisted that they had been related in a previous life.

And suddenly my life was so much richer and fuller.

But the best part of it all—the cherry of cherries of big fat tasty cherries on top—boss bitch Sonja wanted to do a designer profile on me in the next edition of *Glamorous Girl*. Oh, the sweetness of this revenge. So far she only knew the label as Annie Anne; she didn't know I was behind it.

So that day Zolani dragged me to her house and dressed me in her most fabulous clothes. She even got a hair and makeup woman to do me up, her gift to me. Later that day I walked into the offices of *Glamorous Girl* magazine with my head held high.

The whispers started immediately. I could hear the hushed tones and feel the suspicious eyes on me. Last time these people saw me I had ruined a very expensive shoe, a very expensive photo shoot, and been arrested for "attempted murder."

Sonja's office still smelled like jasmine and lavender, and I wondered what poor eager soul she had running after her now.

"Anne." Her tone was acidic. "Dahling, what a surprise."

"So good to see you, Sonja." And I really meant it, because it was good to see her. For reasons that were about to become abundantly clear.

"Divine, you look fabulous, but I'm sorry if you're here looking for work. I'm afraid your old position is full. And if you will excuse me, I have a very important meeting now—"

I cut her off. "I know. It's with me."

The shock.

The horror.

I could see her brain was working overtime. "Dahling, of course it's you, I was just teasing. And we couldn't be prouder of you here. Could we?" She turned to another carbon copy of herself, who nodded. "Yes, we've been talking about it in the office all day, it's all we talk about. Anne this, Anne that."

Lying bitch.

But I didn't care. I was going to take this opportunity and make the most of it.

"So. Anne. Tell me your whole fabulous story. Where did the inspiration for these bags come from?" Sonja's voice was sticky sweet and disgusting.

I had to resist the urge to tell her the truth. Oh, but what fun it would have been to see her face when I told her that the clamping of each little diamanté had had the cathartic effect of driving a voodoo pin into her head. Instead, I stuck to the pretty story that Zolani and I had discussed.

So I told her my story. I told her that after "leaving" a magazine job I started making the bags as a kind of rebellious declaration against fashion in general. I told her about ending up in a small fabric shop in the heart of Johannesburg. I told her all about the Patels and how the colorful materials and the weird and wonderfully diverse South Africans that came into the store inspired me.

She had nodded and smiled, like she agreed, but inside I knew she was probably mentally wishing she had never met me, never clapped eyes on my bag, and was running me over with her shiny new Jag.

We parted on civil terms, since I wouldn't have done my future career any favors by pissing off the queen.

In celebration of the day's events, Zolani decided to throw a party at her house that night. She invited everyone that meant something to me. Damien and Lilly were there of course. Stormy arrived with her new "boyfriend"—I throw those air quotes in because she only dates guys for exactly six weeks and then breaks up with them. Jane had recognized him immediately and told me that under no circumstances was I to shake hands with him…*ever.*

I later discovered that he was a rather infamous artist that had made a sculpture out of chicken carcasses outside of the KFC to protest corporate farming. Yes, it doesn't quite make sense.

Val was there with Mark, the friend that she's been in love with for years. How he didn't know was still a mystery to us all. She basically hung on his every word and laughed at everything he said.

Zolani had even invited the Patels, all of them. We all squeezed into her small yet wildly stylish apartment, drinking champagne and laughing the night away. I looked around the room, and thought of what a motley crew we were. A bunch of unlikely people brought together by my bag. I guess what Zolani had said about them in the beginning was true; they were a true mix of colorful South African culture. God, that was deep again.

There was only one thing missing from this moment, and that was Chris.

"So you know we're going to be rich and famous now." Zolani came up behind me and slipped an arm around my waist. "Everyone is going to be talking about Annie Anne and her amazing bags."

"Oh, please!" I *tsk*ed.

"Mark my words," she said, handing me another glass of champagne. "A toast." She held her glass up and I followed her lead. "To us. From wildly successful business partners"—Zolani was not short on confidence, that's for sure—"to best of friends."

"Aaahh. That's so…" I gulped back a tear. God, I was feeling so emotional all of a sudden. "I feel the same way."

"Oh please don't cry on me now, you'll ruin that fabulous makeup." She gave me a hug and walked off. I watched her go and felt so lucky to have met her.

* * *

When Chris phoned that week, I was dying to tell him, even though we'd made that unspoken rule about never talking about the daily things in our lives. I couldn't help it.

"So…remember that bag I had in Mauritius?"

"I know."

"What?"

"You're quite the celebrity designer now."

"Have you been stalking me?"

"No, an actress walked on set the other day with one, raving about how she'd picked it up in South Africa. I recognized it immediately."

I swallowed hard; the celebrity carrying my bag meant nothing…

"You're making a movie?"

"I am."

Pause.

"Don't worry, it's not the one you read."

"What's it about?"

I could almost hear the smile. "Wait and see, Annie Anne, wait and see."

CHAPTER THIRTY-EIGHT

*ome months later a large brown envelope arrived on my doorstep. May I just add that my doorstep was now located in a small, modest apartment with no naked neighbors. I'd upgraded slightly. Zolani and I had branched out and were growing the business. I had started designing skirts and dresses, and she had managed to get them into stores across the country. And people were actually buying them. It was far from a million-dollar business, but I was actually able to make a living doing what I loved—which is a gift that most people cannot say they have.

I picked up the envelope and went inside. I was convinced it was probably a friendly reminder from the bank or from a store, to pay them. So I chucked it to one side and forgot about it entirely until later that evening when I actually stepped on it. And that's when I saw the address on the back. It was from Los Angeles, California, USA.

I ripped the thing open as fast as my fingers could manage. I knew who it was from. I didn't know anyone else who lived in America. And there, right before my eyes were…

A plane ticket to LA. And an invitation to the premiere of an independent short film written and directed by Mr. Chris Christophersen entitled, *The World's Stupidest Man*.

I blinked several times and reread that title at least ten times.

He didn't.

Surely not? Written a story about himself? I turned the invite over and read the small blurb on the back:

The World's Stupidest Man is a dark comedy drama about a once cynical and reclusive man who falls in love with a free-spirited woman, but loses her. It's an ironic tale about a man coming to terms with what it means to be in love for the first time in his life and how to go about getting her back.

Um…

I read it again just to be sure. "*Stupidest Man*…once cynical and reclusive…loses her…how to go about getting her back."

I didn't know what to make of this. Was it a joke or was he being serious? Either it was the sweetest, most romantic, albeit completely weird gesture anyone had ever made to me in my entire life, or it was the craziest thing I'd ever heard of. Had he seriously written and directed a movie just to get me back? The answer was obvious when a small handwritten card fell out of the package.

Dear Annie,
You're going to cool places, you're off and away. LA is waiting, so get on your way!

Love,
Chris

PS—Please bring that thing that I told you to keep safe.

PPS—Wear something that makes you look like a hot bitch.

What thing had he asked me to keep sa... Suddenly it clicked. And I barely believed it the second my brain worked it out. I ran to my bedroom and opened the drawer, and there it was. I actually hadn't looked at it in a few months.

I opened the box and my heart exploded with happiness. The ring looked bigger and more beautiful than I remembered. Was this some kind of grand marriage proposal? Was he being serious? The big thing that he'd been planning this whole time? (Or maybe he just wanted it back to sell it; the thing probably cost more than my apartment.)

I wanted so badly to go, but a little voice in the back of my head was saying no. Now I was confused.

The truth was, even if I had been trying to deny it, Chris and I weren't friends.

The hours we spent on the phone giggling and chatting certainly contradicted that. The extended good-byes with neither of us wanting to hang up, the long silences on the phone that felt so comfortable and right. We were never going to go to each other's weddings, hang out drinking cold beer and watching the game together, nor would we slap each other on the back and give high fives or whatever else pals did with each other.

Because, the truth was, I was still in love with him—and now I knew he was still in love with me, too. But this time at least we had better grounds for it; we'd really gotten to know each other this past year. The way *real* relationships should work: You meet someone, you get to know them, and then you fall in love and get married.

First time round we'd skipped the whole "getting to know each other" part and gone right to the *I do*s. But this time it was different. And yet that still didn't render me any less confused.

So I did the only thing I could: I called the logical one for an emergency meeting. And thanks to Jane, a week later I was standing in LAX airport. She had been instrumental in helping me decide to go. Her insistence that it was the worst idea in the world and that I should unequivocally *not* go, just made me realize that I needed to go.

As a South African you hear a lot about LAX. The Carrie Bradshaws of the movie and television world are always rushing off to LAX—while the real-life Sarah Jessica Parkers are spotted disembarking from their private jets, always looking glamorous in their oversized sunglasses. So to actually be standing there felt totally surreal, and to be going to a movie premiere was even more out of this world.

I walked out of the arrivals terminal and felt overwhelmed. It was definitely ten times the size of any airport we had in SA, and just when I was starting to feel panicky, I saw a man in a black suit holding up a sign.

ANNIE ANNE

I was a bit disappointed that Chris wasn't there, but he was probably busy getting ready for tonight.

My disappointment eased slightly at the sight of a large, sleek black limo waiting for me. I'd never been in a limo before.

The inside was even sleeker than the outside, with ridiculously large, comfortable black leather seats. These portable lounge suites stood on a dark gray, velvety, and ever-so-soft carpet, and were flanked by shiny wooden side tables. All that was missing was the champagne.

"A drink, ma'am?" the driver asked me after putting my bags in the trunk. (I stand corrected.)

"Um…sure."

He opened a sliding drawer to reveal a fully stocked bar. Glasses, drinks, snacks—the whole deal. Suddenly I was J. Lo and Rihanna and starring in a hip-hop video.

Driving through LA felt strangely familiar, probably because I've seen it a million times on TV. We continued to drive for a while, when a sign for Beverly Hills came into view. Even though I knew that this is where some of the world's richest people live, nothing prepared me for actually seeing their houses up close. They were palatial.

And then we stopped outside the Four Seasons Hotel. Clearly, Chris was sparing no expense in what was really a very big attempt at winning me back—and I was beyond flattered.

The inside of my hotel room was stunning—bright and airy. And with the décor combination of gleaming white and cream, punctuated by splashes of bright pink, my room was definitely reminiscent of spring. But the best part of all was the small balcony that gave you a view of the whole city sprawled out in front of me.

I set my watch to local time and realized that I only had three hours before the premiere started. The driver had said he would fetch me, and I needed to get ready.

An hour later, I slipped into one of the dresses from my new line, an African-inspired little number with a very plunging neckline. I put on black heels, grabbed one of my bags, and looked at myself.

This was it. Ready or not.

The drive to the event was physically painful it was so nerve-racking. And by the time I'd gotten there, I'd bitten through at least two of my nails. I'd never been more anxious and more excited to see anyone—*ever*!

As soon as I got to the event, I started scanning the dense crowd for Chris. But there were just too many people—and I was starting to feel a bit like a fish out of water in this foreign environment, surrounded by all these foreign people. I tried to phone him, and started to feel slightly more unnerved when I reached his voice mail. Not even the security guy at the door could tell me where I could find Chris.

And just as I was reaching a panic of epic proportions, feeling so uncomfortable that I could climb out of my skin—I saw him.

CHAPTER THIRTY-NINE

*C*hris was standing on the other side of the large room we'd just been herded into: an old retro cinema foyer with red carpet up the wall.

I could only see the back of his head at first, but recognized it straightaway. Salt and pepper, scruffy, a tad long, possibly in need of a trim. Then he turned and I was almost knocked off my feet by an invisible gust of wind.

He was clean-shaven, not a stray hair in sight; it was the first time I'd ever seen him like that. He was also wearing—be still my mad beating heart—a black double-breasted tuxedo with black satin lapels. He still maintained that signature casual Chris element, though, by wearing a dark gray shirt with a few buttons undone. No tie. A little bit of scruff mixed in with sophistication. Perfect.

In contrast to his now even more perfect-looking face, he was surrounded by a bunch of guys with hipster beards, checked shirts, and very intense-looking expressions. They had an almost constant nod going while Chris was talking. His face, as always, was animated and friendly. I just stood and watched for a while, mesmerized by the confidence he spoke with. How full of life his eyes were and how, every now and then, even these serious-looking guys would burst out laughing—I wished I could hear what he was saying, longing to share a laugh with him in person.

The buzz of an alarm went off to signify that the movie was about to start, and I suddenly felt like I was getting pushed by the crowd, away from Chris. I held my hand up in the air and called out, "Chris!" But nothing.

"Chris!" I shouted louder this time until he looked up and found me. The feeling I got when our eyes met again, for the first time in almost a year, is hard to describe. I'll try…

Have you ever been dared to jump into a pool in the middle of winter? The water is icy and biting. And the shock of it is so overwhelming that you feel like you might have a heart attack. Not only is the feeling physical, every part of your body stinging as the icy water rushes over you, but it's mental, too. Suddenly you are wide-wide-*wide* awake. Your heart is pumping, your brain is switched to overdrive, and all your senses are acutely alive. That's how it felt.

Chris smiled at me, and I smiled back. I smiled so wide that the corners of my mouth hurt like someone was tugging on them.

I started moving toward him but seemed to be getting ushered in the opposite direction. I started climbing the velvet rope separating us when a man rushed up and ushered me away. I saw Chris waving. He was mouthing something and pointing his finger in the direction of the cinema. I didn't need a sign language interpreter to figure that one out.

So I went with the crowd, hoping to see him inside. But by the time I got inside it was pitch black, and an annoyingly helpful usher had attached himself to me. I guess their job is to usher, and normally I would be appreciative of said ushering, but now was NOT the time to be ushered, especially if it was in the opposite direction of Chris.

I finally got to my seat and when my eyes adjusted to the light, I started desperately scanning the room again. I was tempted to take out my cell phone and use the flashlight on it, but I didn't.

I thought about calling out one more time or waving my arms in the air, but then I felt something fly into the back of my head. I turned, and about six rows up I saw Chris, throwing a rolled-up piece of paper at me.

The look and the feeling that passed between us in that moment, I'll remember for the rest of my life. It was joy. And relief. I felt—*once again*—like I'd come home. All the hurt of the past had totally melted away. And now, it was like meeting him all over again. For the first time. The movie started, and Chris waggled a naughty finger at me and pointed for me to turn around, so I did.

But it was hard to concentrate, because I could feel his presence behind me. I couldn't help but turn around from time to time, and each time, I would find him staring at me, smiling.

The movie itself was basically the funniest, strangest thing I'd ever seen. It started on a guy with an enormous beard, living at home with his ten cats. He hasn't been outside in over five years, but works as a travel writer, who just goes online and researches the various places he writes about (sounding vaguely familiar).

He meets a girl online and they start dating. The sex scene had the audience in stitches; suddenly everything is in black and white, and the two characters are talking in French with subtitles. After the sex they smoked cigarettes. But the guy in question—not based on a real person of course—has lots of issues, and ends up losing her. And then he begins an elaborate, over-the-top campaign to win her back. It starts small—flowers, chocolates and some singing minstrels—but soon escalates to him jumping out of a plane and into her back garden with a sign that says, WILL YOU MARRY ME? The movie ends. And then some words fly onto the screen:

WILL SHE TAKE HIM BACK?

I knew, even if no one else did, that those words were meant for me. I turned around to look at him, but a sudden standing ovation was in progress. I heard much chatter around me and people threw around words like *genius*, *postmodern*, *minimalist*, *avant-garde*, *noir*, and *Coen brothers–esque*. I surmised that they must have liked it.

All I wanted was to find Chris.

But I didn't need to, because suddenly he was walking down the stairs toward the stage where a mic waited for him. Everyone clapped and I felt myself swell with pride; that was my guy. *Well*, as soon as I could speak to him, that is.

He took to the stage and talked about the great actors, and the director of photography, his supportive producer who believed in the project from the start, even though the project was totally weird. People seemed to be lapping it up, nodding at each other with knowing looks.

He talked about the freedom of making a small-budget independent short film, the joy of making short films, and about exploring his creativity. He thanked everyone for coming, and hoped everyone would enjoy drinks and hors d'oeuvres. He unfortunately would not be there, as he had an urgent personal matter to attend to. There were some sighs of disappointment, but not from me.

And then he walked back up the aisle looking so confident and accomplished and stopped at my row. All he did was hold out his arm, and gesture for me to come.

I got up—everyone was watching us but I didn't care. We linked arms and walked out together without saying a word. Chris strode out of the cinema and across the street to where a limo sat waiting for us. We climbed in.

He closed the door. The car pulled off.

And then, we were alone.

There was nothing really to do but to stare at each other for a while. Silly, big grins were plastered across our faces. Chris reached out and took me by the hands, and our fingers meshed together. There was more silly staring and then he opened his mouth; he had that look about him that suggested he was about to say something funny to defuse the loaded moment.

"Oh, shut up," I said, and kissed him. I've always known you can tell everything from a kiss. It's like a highly coordinated dance. If someone gets the moves wrong, rushes it, or goes too slowly, the whole thing looks bad and doesn't work. It's the same with a kiss. You either have the right rhythm and are compatible, or not.

We were compatible.

The kiss was intense. Slow. Deliberate. I had started it, but very soon Chris had taken over. His hands reached around my head and tugged at my bun, until my hair fell out and he wrapped his fingers through it. His other hand was cradling my face, telling me which way to go. His lips tasted like spearmint and they made mine tingle. His breath was warm on my face and his hands were slightly cold. He made me feel like we were the only two people on the planet, and that we were somehow melting into each other. The kiss made me dizzy and light-headed, and I swear for a moment or two, I think I may have even forgotten my own name.

"So…," he whispered.

"So what?"

"What's the answer?"

"To what?" It was so hard to think straight when he was speaking while kissing me and gently licking my lips.

"To the question?"

I smiled as I bit his lips playfully in response.

"Yes. *Yes she will take him back*."

"Oh, thank God!" Suddenly everything changed and we were no longer kissing.

"Thank God, what?"

"Well, Annie, do you have any idea how awkward this whole thing would have been for me if you'd said no?"

"What would have been awkward?" My heart sank. Wait, was this some kind of elaborate publicity stunt? Why had the car suddenly stopped? Was I about to step out and realize that Chris had actually staged this reunion and I was just another character in one of his plots? I was freaking out.

"This…" Chris pulled me by the hand, out of the car, and onto the beach.

It took me a moment to understand what was going on.

There were no candles illuminating a path this time. No pink flowers lay scattered on the sand, and no Chinese lanterns cast mystical shadowy light. But it was perfect. Better than before, because it was real.

"That's not an actor, by the way…," Chris said, pointing to a man by the sea. And then he looked at me with a smile, "Okay, here goes.

I am going to do something very, very corny, something that I've written a million times before and every time I did, I laughed a loud, cynical snicker…"

My heart started pounding as Chris got down on one knee. "So Annie Anne, hot bitch, will you not fake marry me this time?" His voice was quivering and I could hear that he was nervous.

"Only if you do it with this," I said, pulling the ring out of my bag. Chris took it and looked up at me seriously, more seriously than I'd ever seen him. Chris the funny guy was suddenly gone—and now, it was just Chris.

"Annie. Will you marry me?"

```
We close on ANNIE and CHRIS as they walk hand in
hand down the beach toward the real PRIEST.
```

* * *

One year later

So you're probably wondering how the whole thing turned out. Trevv and Tess? My impromptu (real) wedding? My growing fashion biz? Chris and I?

Well, I can't wait to tell you, because it's been the best year of my life.

I'm afraid I can't give you major details on the T-Squared situation; all I know is that the morning after we ruined, annihilated, crushed, and destroyed their dream wedding, they were gone.

I'd asked at reception and apparently they'd checked out before sunup. And because we have no mutual friends anymore, what happened to them…is still a mystery. Whether they got married and moved to London and are living happily ever after, with their great, really great, oh-so-great law firm, I wouldn't be able to tell you. In retrospect, a year down the line, I do feel a bit bad. Everyone deserves love. Even Trevv.

Lilly and Damien are in the middle of planning their wedding, which is likely to be happening in Europe somewhere. Val is still desperately in love with her neighbor and secretly pining for him. Stormy is still Stormy and dating a guy that juggles fire and can put swords down his throat, and Jane, *well*, Jane seems to be going through something at the moment that none of us really fully understand. We're all a bit worried about her—she's so tightly wound she's about to snap.

I moved to LA of course, to be with my *husband*. I can't say that enough, *husband*. In fact, I try to slip the word into as many interactions as possible:

Grocery shopping—"Yes, my *husband* loves this cereal."

At the post office—"I'm just picking up this package for my *hubby*."

To a total stranger in a parking lot—"Nice day, isn't it. My *husband* checked the weather forecast and it looks like it's going to be hot and sunny for the next week."

And don't get me started on how much I love signing my name. Annie Christophersen.

And what of Chris's movie? The critical acclaim he received after it was overwhelming, and so he's started writing and directing interesting, obscure films where he gets to be more creative. He's finding it more fulfilling, because he gets to show off his quirky sense of humor—that special thing that makes him Chris.

Living in LA has been a bit of a culture shock and adjustment—and since I've been here I've spotted two Kardashians, and the other day (co-incidentally) I passed Bradley Cooper in the street. Chris (my *husband*) is much better looking than Brad C., by the way. Zolani is handling all our business back in South Africa; we've even employed some seam-stresses to carry out my designs, and I am in the process of setting up a shop here. Americans do love a bit of an African vibe.

But the best part of the year?

It seemed that the Christophersen family would be getting an-other addition. And in true Chris fashion, he chose to announce it to the world by sending out a group email that said,

Hey everyone, just to let you know, I knocked my bitch up! BAM.

So maybe those happy Hollywood endings aren't so far-fetched after all?

Turn the page to read an
excerpt from Jane's story,

FINDING YOU

Available now from Headline Eternal

PROLOGUE

⁓

*T*he day of my mental breakdown was a Wednesday.

And when I say "mental breakdown," I don't mean the kind that celebrities have when they check into a luxury spa for medicated mud wraps and Mojitos. I'm talking about the other kind. The messy kind.

It was a normal Wednesday. An unspectacular, uneventful, run-of-the-mill, *not* Monday, *not* Tuesday, but *Wednesday*. There was nothing special about the day.

So why was I feeling like this? *Like what, exactly?*

Well, that's the million-dollar question, isn't it?

Because I couldn't quite put my finger it. The feeling wasn't fully formed yet, but it had gripped me nonetheless. Embedded itself like an arrow in my back or a virus in my bloodstream—invisible, but *deadly*.

Something was wrong. Very wrong.

A mild pressure in my solar plexus. A slight heaviness in my head and a feeling of total disconnectedness. Everything around me screeched that I did not belong here, and suddenly I felt like an alien in my own home.

I rubbed the sticky sleep from my eyes and glanced around my room. The chair in the corner that Mother had insisted on having re-upholstered in Toasted Granola Sunrise Suede and the walls she had insisted I paint in Mystical Song of the Grey Dove looked odd. (Side note: who the hell is coming up with the names of colors these days, anyway?)

I climbed out of bed apprehensively, stalked over to my bathroom, and looked at myself in the mirror. My features were the same—large and distinct. Olive complexion, long black hair, that "signature" mole on my cheek that I'd always hated, and then there are my eyes—one dark brown, one light hazel.

But somehow everything looked different. I looked less like my-self and more like someone else I didn't know. *If that makes sense?*

But of course it doesn't make sense. Because nothing about this so-called "normal" Wednesday was making any sense at all (hence growing suspicions of imminent mental breakdown).

Perhaps I was still asleep and dreaming. That was surely the only possible explanation for these feelings.

I pinched my cheek. *Nothing.*

Splashed water on my face. *Nope.*

I stood in the strange bathroom, looking at this strange person in the mirror. Her name was Jane. Plain Jane Smith. Dr. Plain Jane Smith.

Well, that's my name *now*; it wasn't the name I was born with. But that had nothing to do with the way I was feeling, *did it?*

A soothing cup of tea was surely the antidote that would rid me of these feelings. I walked into the kitchen, turned on the kettle, and waited. I felt out of place here, too.

Tea—one bag.

Sugar—zero.

No milk in sight.

I stirred the liquid that I was pinning my hopes of normality on and sipped. It tasted bitter. Did it always taste like this?

The so-called soothing tea only seemed to intensify the feelings and gave rise to a humming anxiety, which crept slowly like a growing evening shadow.

What was going on with me? I could phone my friend Lilly. But what would I say? *"Help! I think I might have been transported into the Twilight Zone."* (Wait, would Lilly even be my friend in that dimension?)

What the hell was going on?

But nothing had changed, really. I'd just graduated and had started my new job. But no surprises there. It certainly wouldn't be the thing shaking me to my very core. The job had been planned for, organized, and it was inevitable—I was going to be taking over my father's dental practice.

It would be my birthday in a few days, but birthdays came along every year. Again, nothing out of the ordinary.

Drive!

That always cleared my head. I got dressed and brushed my teeth for precisely two minutes—no excuse for bad dental hygiene, even in the face of a total nervous meltdown.

I climbed into my car and started driving up and down the once familiar suburbs. Then I veered left, away from the little houses and toward the city.

The mall. With shops and people and breakfast. That would surely make me feel normal again.

It was early, so most of the shops were closed and the mall looked like an empty school hall: depressing. Like it was waiting for kids to rush in, and without them was just a sad shell of what it had once been. A washed-up carcass on an empty beach.

The pressure in my solar plexus was back. The feelings intensified, so I got out of my car and walked. I walked as fast as I could.

Past the banks, the hardware store, and the shop where I'd bought the exorbitantly overpriced scented candle that I had absolutely no use for but purchased anyway since the shop attendant had been so nice and I'm a people pleaser and can't say no. I passed a coffee shop that had just opened its doors to a single solitary customer in need of their early morning fix.

And then...*I saw it*.

I stood outside Flight and Travel Center, looking up at the electronic display of all the holiday specials. And there it was. At the very top.

Greece.

A special.

Almost sold out.

Buy now. Complimentary beach bag and sunscreen included. *Terms and Conditions apply.*

And that's when the mists of confusion started to evaporate and the picture finally came into focus.

This *was* about my name. This *was* about my job. And this was definitely, *definitely* about my birthday. This was about the day I was born and the circumstances under which I was born.

I slumped down against the wall and pulled out my credit card. I clutched it tightly and waited for someone to open the shop so I could buy the *only* thing that could furnish me with the answers I'd been seeking my entire life.

Un-Acknowledgments

My high school principal once told me I wouldn't amount to anything. So it's no thanks to her that I wrote this book.

WARNING: Being jilted at the altar in front of 500 wedding guests can lead to irrational behaviour, such as going on your honeymoon to Thailand alone. Recovery will lead to partying the night away at Burning Moon festival – and falling in love with the person you least expect . . .

Don't miss *Burning Moon*, the first book in the Destination Love series.

Available now from

HEADLINE
ETERNAL

FIND YOUR HEART'S DESIRE...

VISIT OUR WEBSITE: www.headlineeternal.com
FIND US ON FACEBOOK: facebook.com/eternalromance
FOLLOW US ON TWITTER: @eternal_books
EMAIL US: eternalromance@headline.co.uk